ROOK & REBEL

KATE CREW

To the book girls—may your hot, tattooed man on a motorcycle show up at your doorstep with cookies, so you don't have to leave your house or your book.

CONTENT WARNINGS

Contains talk of parental illness, terminal illness, discussions on house fires, death, and burn victims. Gun violence, knife violence, torture (some on page scenes), mentions of eyeball torture, stalking, talks of cannibalism, and general violence.

Playlist

My Bloody Valentine - Good Charlotte
Monsters in My Mind - Cloudy June
KNIVES - Neoni, Savage Gas$p
Loser - Neoni
hell of a good time - Haiden Henderson
Shadow - Livingston
MATCH MADE IN HELL - Dutch Melrose, benny Mayne
BODY BAG - Neoni
No Angels - Stellar
Nails - Call Me Karizma
Mutiny - Neoni
UH OH - Neoni
HOOLIGAN - Neoni
Helena - My Chemical Romance
Daydreams - We Three
Daylight - David Kushner

ONE

ROOK

The city lights blurred as I gunned the throttle, the roar of my bike drowning out the chaos in my mind.

I was going to kill them—all of them—for dumping these damn jobs on me tonight. The entire day at the shop had gone to hell, and now I wasn't sure if I had broken my hand when I punched the guy.

I had hit him over, and over, working off every ounce of rage I had in me. It had worked for a few minutes until I got on my bike and reality came crashing down.

There weren't enough hours to get everything done. More jobs seemed to fall onto me, and I could barely think straight. I had everything I wanted: two successful businesses, a decent place to live for me and Evie, no shortage of money. Yet, it wasn't enough for me.

I craved power. I wanted to rule every single one of these guys we still had to work for and ruin their lives. Their sick, twisted lives they led, which seemed to have no repercussions for the things they did. CEOs, government officials, and everything in between. The men you'd pass on the street and wave were the ones who turned out to do disgusting and illegal things at night.

I wanted all of them to start at the bottom, to burn their lives down, and see what they could make from the rubble.

I pulled into our shop, the garage door already open so I could ride right in. I revved the bike once, heads snapping up to watch me, as the entire place filled with the loud echo of the engine.

"Damn, you sound pissed," Aiden said, messing with his ear.

"What the fuck are you all doing?" I yelled, ripping off my helmet. "You mean to tell me I'm out running all over the place while you all sit around on your asses having a good time? Do you know how much work we have to do?"

My leg and the side of my stomach ached as I got off. The burn injury always seemed to hurt the longer I rode and fought. I tried to stretch out my leg already knowing it wouldn't help. The pain would get worse before it got better. Hopefully, I would last the rest of the night until I could finally lie down. Then it would hurt like hell and keep me up half the night.

It was an endless cycle of work, more work, pain, and pretending to sleep, only to do it all over again. But I'd do it again and again. We had money, and we were building power all over the city. Evie seemed happy enough, and she was safe, which I worried about the most.

I glanced over as Aiden rolled his eyes at me. Evie did, too.

"Problem?" I asked. My sister had a tendency to always have a smart-ass answer, and I didn't think now would be any different.

"You're always complaining you have to do all these jobs, but then you're the first one to volunteer. Make up your mind. Either let control go or deal with it," Evie said, smiling at me.

"Hero's and Mason's bikes are down," Aiden added, not letting me snap back at Evie. "They are fixing them. Zack is out with the other new guy, doing a few things for us, but they aren't ready to do what you're doing," Aiden explained. "Zack isn't exactly a master interrogator and Kane threw up last time he had to stab a guy."

"And you?" I snapped.

"I'm babysitting. Want to trade?" he said, nodding toward Evie, who curled up in a chair, frowning at her phone now.

"Yes, please trade," she said. "I'm sick of him."

"Then stop fucking texting me when I am right next to you." He shook his head, turning further in his seat not to look at her.

She gave him a sweet smile. "But then I'd have to look over at your disgusting face when I talk."

"What do you have left?" he asked me. "Whatever it is, I'll take it."

"I have to go find Elliot and hit him a few times until he's ready to pay."

"Done. I'll do it. Sit with your psycho sister instead."

"Aww, poor Aiden is mad. He had to come save me from a bad date, and didn't get laid for it."

"Bad date?" I asked. Evie had turned twenty-one a few months ago, and while I didn't care if she dated, I wished she would be more careful about who she went out with. Plenty of people knew us and would use any excuse to get closer to us.

"The guy's an asshole and left her at the restaurant," he said, looking over at her. "But it's possibly because you pulled a gun out of your bag instead of your lipstick, *psycho*. And no, I didn't think I would be getting laid. Don't even make jokes or Rook will kill me."

She pouted out her bottom lip. "Rook, Aiden said he wouldn't save me from my date unless I slept with him."

I ignored them and headed to my toolbox for my other gun. Their bickering pounded into my skull, and I clenched my jaw to keep the headache at bay. They always seemed to be at each other's throat's lately.

"No, seriously," Aiden said. "I'll do it."

"Not a chance. You can stay here and make sure she doesn't go hunt the guy down. I have to go hunt down a different one, and if we both go, we would be out all night looking for her and hiding a body."

She grinned. "If you don't want me to do it, I can send you his address. You can swing by."

"Did he do anything to you besides run out of the restaurant because you scared the man to death?"

"No," she growled with a curl of her lip. "You two are the worst."

The motorcycle shop we ran in front of the building had closed hours ago, and now we would spend the night dealing with the other side of our business. The less-than-legal side, which made us the majority of our money.

I shoved my helmet on and started up my bike. The beautiful murdered out R1 which, currently, was the love of my life. A perfect midnight black that blended me into the night, which would be helpful tonight. I shot off a text to the guy I paid to keep tabs on Elliot, and he quickly let me know Elliot would be attending an art exhibit for a date.

My lip curled. Elliot's family was as rich as they came, but he thought he could skip out on the fifteen thousand dollar gambling debt he had with us. Yet he's spending his Saturday night at some uptight, highbrow art exhibit trying to get laid.

What an asshole.

I headed towards downtown, but I turned off when I recognized the road, taking a quick detour.

Cameron Fletcher's mansion rose in the night, the lights on it a beacon of wealth and regality. He thought of himself as a king, and he had enough money he could buy the title somewhere. Being so narcissistic, he probably already had.

The vivid image of my childhood home in flames hit me, the smell of burning wires and wood making my stomach churn. I hated to think burning flesh had been mixed in, too. Then the harsh chemical scent as we made it out of the garage, Evie's cries and screams as she tried to cough the smoke from her lungs.

And maybe the worst image of all of them. The one burned in my brain and always seemed to appear at the worst times, my parents trapped in the flames as I stood outside.

Now here he was. The man who did it had locked himself up safely inside his own home.

Karma never came for the man who took everything from me. The horrible things he had done never came to bite him in the ass. They say people in glass houses shouldn't throw stones, so Cameron Fletcher took that advice and built a stone house. He kept everything sealed and impenetrable so karma couldn't get to him, and it had worked.

Until now.

Until I grew up and decided I wouldn't wait for fate to intervene. *I* would be his karma.

And nothing made me happier than planning to burn his life to the ground, exactly like he had done to mine.

TWO
REGAN

I wanted to slouch back on the stiff couch, but it wasn't designed for it. Every piece of furniture in my Dad's office felt like this—stiff, expensive, and antique. It demanded perfect posture, so I sat up straight, enduring the discomfort while my dad outlined my to-do list for the next two weeks.

As he listed each event, I realized how unnecessary I'd be at each one. They were all for him and his business. Sometimes, it felt like I was taking up space, contributing nothing, and it embarrassed me to the point I wanted to hide. But for him, I would always do it. He was my dad, and with my mom gone, it felt important to hold onto the last family member I had left.

My dad ran the largest security company in the city. I had dreamed of taking over one day since the moment he told me how much a family legacy meant to him. That was why I gave up any dream I had of going to art school and went to a top college to get my business degree, hoping he'd give me a chance. But now he seemed more focused on growing his business than preparing me to inherit it. And with his illness, I couldn't demand more.

He told me last year that his illness—amyloidosis—would

eventually shut down his organs. Treatment only prolonged his life. We'd come to terms with it over the past year, but I wanted to make every minute with him count. His success remained unmatched, and I wanted to learn everything, but he hadn't let me start yet. I had taken all the right steps, but he still seemed to think I wasn't ready. Maybe he wanted a perfect legacy left, or he didn't want to face me taking over one day anyway, but I still needed to learn.

The tasks he had given me were usually along the lines of going to parties and smiling for everyone in town he might know. A new way to keep him on their mind without him having to lift a finger, and I had agreed to keep doing it, but I hated going. The crowds, the small talk, the looks expecting me to say something smart and funny only made me freeze with anxiety. I rarely spoke to people because I didn't know anyone, and besides those parties, he didn't love me going out. The one he continued droning on about now was apparently another extremely important dinner party coming up soon that would be filled with clients and partners of his business that I needed to help keep happy.

I tried not to roll my eyes. I felt like I was worth more than just sitting around. I wanted challenges, I wanted adventure, and I wanted a life more than sitting around my house. If only he'd realized I was capable of more. He kept running himself into the ground, and I knew no doctor would approve. I didn't know if his health or the stress caused it, but he didn't seem to want me to leave as much. Still, I listened, hoping to make him see I could help him.

I could do...things. I wasn't exactly sure what he would need me to do, but I still felt confident I could learn.

He continued, explaining that we couldn't miss a single event since he had decided to run for mayor next year. It felt like he tried to pack an entire life into the next few years. I tried to understand

and be there for it all, but sitting there and looking pretty for parties was burning me out.

"Those are all fine with me," I said, knowing my agreeing would at least let me get out of the house tonight. "I have plans tonight with Elliot. There's a new art exhibit we are going to."

"Fine. Fine," he said, shuffling through a few more papers. "I'll see you tomorrow at some point."

He didn't glance up as we spoke. It had become common enough, talking to him while he stared at a phone, but it didn't get easier. Each time, I felt more rejected, wondering if I was really that boring.

I didn't get out much anymore since he always wanted me to stay home to be safe. I didn't have any hobbies besides painting and looking at art. I didn't have a job, and as much as I wanted one from my dad, I wasn't getting one, apparently. And there really was only so much I could do from the confines of this house. I stayed around to help with anything he needed, but he seemed to need less and less from me.

Maybe I had become dull.

"Alright." I jumped up, giving him a quick hug before heading to the door. "I guess I'll see you then."

I needed to get out and stop the spiral of doom I seemed to be headed down.

This meant another weekend basically alone in this giant house, since he would stick to his side. Nothing seemed wrong with our house, except its enormous size, and when you spend days alone inside, you start to get a little paranoid.

So, on the list of things I knew about myself, I could add dull and paranoid. I rolled my eyes as I headed down the sidewalk. I really sounded like a great time.

It's my life, though, and I could have worse problems.

At least for now, I'd get out of the house and, hopefully, not be alone all night.

I always loved going to a new art exhibit.

What I quickly realized I didn't love, though, was going with Elliot.

I turned to the next painting, looking over the dark black splashed against the blue paint. It took me three steps back before I realized the artist had meant it to be an eye. The bright blue of it took my breath away.

"How much longer are we looking at this one?" Elliot asked.

"I just stepped in front of it," I said, attempting a small laugh.

He nearly stomped his feet, so I moved on to the next. Swirls of black, red, and yellow made up one bright night sky on fire. At least when my life didn't give me much to feel about it, art did.

"Come on," he said, nuzzling into my neck. "We can go find so many other things to be doing. Very fun, very entertaining things."

As soon as he said it, I knew it wouldn't stop. Anything I said would be met with some sort of sex-related joke until I gave in. It's not like I didn't like Elliot at all. He was fine, but something about the way he went about initiating sex always turned me off.

We moved around the next aisle of paintings, and he pulled at my arm. "Regan," he said, nodding towards the door.

"You know what? I do have to get home," I said, smiling. "We should go."

Of course, I didn't have to get home. Nothing waited there for me, but there wasn't a chance of me wanting to stay here any longer with him.

Elliot eagerly nodded and headed for our coats. I pulled out my phone to text Harper. My best friend knew me well enough to know I would be texting her during my date at some point. I might as well start early.

REGAN

Busy later?

HARPER

Unfortunately. A by-product of divorce is being fought over. Which honestly should be flattering, but it's getting old.

Aren't you with Elliot tonight?

REGAN

I am, and I'm ready to head home. I want a movie, my bed, and a chocolate chip cookie.

HARPER

You do understand you could get those things and sit in bed with Elliot?

REGAN

You know Elliot, so you know it's not really a thing he will do.

HARPER

I know. What type of weirdo doesn't want to hang around half naked with his girlfriend and eat cookies? Honestly, it's grounds to break up with him.

REGAN

Maybe he'll change his mind tonight.

HARPER

For your sake, I hope.

Text me when you're home, so I know Elliot didn't snap and lock you in his basement.

REGAN

Not funny.

We had been watching endless Dateline episodes, which put both of us on guard now. Harper was convinced Elliot would snap one day, and I was starting to agree with her. Lately, he seemed jumpy with every little thing making him spook, but I couldn't figure out why.

I slid my phone back in my bag and headed to the door, already seeing Elliot waiting with my coat.

I truly wasn't desperate enough to be flattered at how eager he seemed tonight.

This date wouldn't make it past the drive home, and I hoped he would understand enough not to push it.

Elliot could be fun.

Elliot could be endless, careless fun, but that wasn't what I wanted tonight.

His hand slipped into mine as he pulled me out onto the sidewalk and immediately took a right turn.

"What are you doing? The car is the opposite way."

"I know," he said, smiling. "I have a place I want to show you."

"What kind of place?"

"There's a nice little overlook to the river down here, and I think you would like it."

"Is this a romantic overlook or a new place for you to attempt your public sex dreams? And down this way? Really?"

The path leading down to whatever overlook he wanted to go to looked less like a cute romantic walk and more like a horror movie. The lights grew farther and farther apart, and the shops only more run down with each block.

"Yeah, right down here."

It seemed strange, but I still followed him. While sitting in bed eating cookies sounded great, I really wasn't looking forward to another night alone in the giant house.

"Elliot, this doesn't seem like a great idea. Maybe we should turn back. There's plenty of other places we could go."

He wrapped an arm around me. "It's alright, babe. It's not far. I've got you. I won't let anything happen to you."

An engine rumbled behind us, its deep growl cutting through the quiet night. I turned my head, a shiver moving down my spine.

A blacked-out motorcycle idled down the road. The headlights were off, but a thin line of pink-hued lights ran underneath it. The pink glow was oddly cute, given where we were.

The clothes the rider wore were as black as the bike, making them nearly blend into the night. I kept my eye on him as we kept going. The rider slowly sat up, cocking his head in my direction, as if he realized I watched him.

It felt like his eyes were boring into me, even from a distance, but the helmet obscured his face to know for sure.

I grabbed Elliot's hand, squeezing it hard as my heart rate spiked. My gut screamed something was wrong. "Is the motorcycle following us?" I whispered.

Elliot glanced back, his eyes widening before he whipped back around, picking up his pace. "I doubt it. Why would a motorcycle be following us?" he said, trying to sound calm, but the tremor in his voice betrayed him.

We walked faster, but the engine's roar persisted, growing louder and closer. My grip on Elliot's hand tightened, sweat forming on my palm.

Each step felt heavier. The darkness thickened around us, pulling us into its suffocating embrace. The eerie shadows between broken streetlights making my skin crawl.

I glanced back. The motorcycle came closer now, its engine rumbling like a predator stalking its prey.

"Elliot," I whispered. "He's definitely following us."

Elliot didn't respond, but he picked up his pace again. His hand shook in mine, and I realized he felt as scared as I did.

So much for his promise that nothing bad would happen. We barely made it two blocks before realizing we were being hunted.

Every hair on my body stood on end, screaming danger. The

road split, and Elliot pulled me to the left. The city sounds faded, drowned out by the motorcycle's roar.

"We need to get out of here," I said, trembling. "Now."

Elliot nodded, finally matching my urgency. We started jogging, but the motorcycle's engine revved, the sound sending another jolt of fear through me.

It was too close.

Without warning, the motorcycle roared past us, cutting us off near an alley. He skidded to a halt, the tires screeching, blocking our path as my breath hitched.

The rider stayed silent, cocking his head as if amused by our fear. We could try to run, but the motorcycle would easily catch up.

We were trapped, with no clear way out.

THREE
REGAN

I stayed glued to the pavement weighing the pros and cons of running.

The bike idled, its lights underneath clicking off as the rider stood up. Black boots, black jeans, a black jacket, and black helmet. There wasn't one thing on him that stood out, and without the sound of the bike idling, I didn't know if I would notice him standing within five feet of me.

He rolled up his sleeves, revealing tattooed hands and forearms, which flexed as he moved.

The glint of metal caught my eye as he raised a gun, my stomach plummeting. "Give me your wallet," he demanded, nodding toward Elliot.

I froze, clutching my bag, debating if I would give it up or fight him for it. My life was in this bag, but I didn't know how to fight a man with a gun.

As I hesitated, torn between surrendering or fighting back, Elliot made his choice. He dropped my hand and spun on his heel, running back the way we had come.

He ran.

Fast, too.

He *fucking* ran.

He made it down the block before I could even process what happened.

He had run off and left me there alone on an empty street with a violent man and a gun.

So much for not letting anything happen to me.

The rider turned back, his face still obscured by the helmet, but I felt the weight of his gaze on me. His head tilted slightly, scrutinizing me with an almost predatory curiosity. Slowly, the gun lowered, as he lifted his shirt, revealing the edge of a dark tattoo snaking across his skin. The gun disappeared into his waistband, and when he reached up, I instinctively flinched, expecting the worst. Instead, he only pulled off his helmet.

"Okay, what the fuck?" he asked. "Weren't you two on a date?"

"Um, yeah, we were. We've been dating for six months now," I said, my words spilling out in a daze.

Had Elliot really ran off without so much as a yell for me to follow or glance back to see if I stayed behind him? Had he left me here so he'd have more time to get away?

"Well, that's sure as fuck long enough not to leave you alone with the man trying to rob him. I have a gun pointed at you guys, and he ran? If your choices are to get shot or spend a night walking around an art gallery, I would think it would be an easy choice of getting shot at, but still, he should have at least tried to help you."

I stood there, stunned, as my would-be mugger talked to me like we were friends, like *he* was surprised at Elliot's behavior.

"I'm sorry. Do *you* feel sorry for *me*?" I asked, finally snapping out of it.

"I mean, more outraged for you, but yeah, he's a pretty

pathetic boyfriend. He should be here with his fucking fists raised."

I stepped back towards the building, leaning against the cool brick, using the feel of it under my fingers to bring me back to reality. "Wow. Oh, wow. I'm so pathetic, the man who needs to rob me at gunpoint feels sorry for me?"

"Hold on. Let's get this straight. I was robbing him. I wasn't coming for you."

"No? You had a gun pointed at me!"

"Mainly, I had a gun pointed at *him*. I only turned it to you for a second. For the shock factor. Your boyfriend owes me money, and I had been the one volunteered to come get it." He shook his head. "Or at least scare him enough to try and get it."

I glanced back at the spot Elliot had been standing. "Well, you managed to scare him, so you accomplished half."

"Yeah, but he doesn't know who I am, so it failed a little. I honestly wasn't expecting him to run away *that* fast. I didn't even get to do my speech. I couldn't even compare him to running away like a girl. I think one of them would have even stayed longer. Shit, one of them did stay longer."

I laughed, regretting it immediately. I couldn't find my would-be robber funny. I stared up at him. The mask covered the bottom half of his face, and his dark hair was wild from the helmet, and his eyes locked onto me. Unfortunately, my next thought after finding him funny went to how hot he looked.

"Alright, come on," he said, reaching out with his helmet in hand as though I should take it.

"Come on, what?"

"Come on, I'm driving you home. Unlike your boyfriend, I'm not leaving you here on a deserted street, at night, all alone. And I have more stuff to do tonight, so come on, get your ass moving."

"Really? You plan more than one mugging a night? Surprising.

And maybe he knows I am a grown, capable woman," I said, straightening my shoulders. Maybe Elliot had only thought I would know how to handle myself and expect me to run with him.

"Considering you didn't even flinch when I pulled up with a gun, I don't doubt it. I thought you were the one who would fight me."

"So, then, what makes you think I can't get home myself?"

He stepped closer, and I noticed the blue in his eyes now. The black of his clothes mixed with blue made me think of the painting. The deep, black hues with bright icy blue. It was as beautiful of a picture as the one I had been looking at. He laughed, the deep sound catching my attention again.

"Do you know where you're at? Because if you think you're going to walk home alone from here and not be bothered, you're wrong. And I don't think any Uber is going to be coming down here for you. Either get on my bike or risk coming across someone else."

"What if they are nicer than you?"

"I'm not currently robbing you, touching you, or planning to do either, so what if they are not?"

The deserted street and creepy path were enough to make my skin crawl, but this man had just pointed a gun at me.

"I think you should know I do know how to defend myself, so if you do try to touch me or rob me, I can fight back."

"You have me shaking in fear. Now get on the bike," he said, the bored tone making me chew on my bottom lip. Technically, if I got on, he could take me anywhere.

But if I didn't, I would be left here.

"I don't really get into cars with strangers, or get on the back of motorcycles...well, ever."

"Then congratulations, you're about to be a rebel for what I can only imagine is the first time in your life."

A man yelled something from down the block, and when I glanced back, I could see him coming our way.

"Get on the fucking bike before I have to either force you on it, leave you with the guy walking towards us, or kill him and make you cry. Which, I would then leave you here anyway, but you would be with a dead body and I couldn't imagine you're good with that."

I grabbed the helmet, pushing my hair back and pulling it on. I could see his smile crack again as he swung his leg over and sat back.

"Good choice, Rebel. You seem to have a brain. What the fuck have you been doing with Elliot?"

"You actually know him?" I asked, lifting the visor slightly. It felt loose, but I was glad he'd at least offered it.

"Oh, yeah. He's well known in our group, and not for the good reasons. Not even the fun, bad reasons," he said with a smirk. "If tonight wasn't enough of an indication, I suggest dropping him. He's also deep in debt, so good for you for keeping an eye on your purse. But I'm not the one who wants it."

He sat back on the bike, and I stood there staring.

"Is this supposed to be my seat?" I asked. The tiny little spot of padding wasn't even going to hold half my ass.

"Yeah, it is. If I have to tell you to get on the fucking bike one more time, we are going to knock down those options I gave you to only one."

"Which one?" I asked, already shaking my head. "No, don't even answer that. You're kind of an asshole, aren't you?"

He cocked his head, his eyes narrowing. "We met with a gun in your face. Do I look like a sweet, innocent boy to you?"

"No. Unfortunately, I don't."

Which meant he firmly didn't fit the type of person I usually hung out with, or so I thought. Apparently, Elliot was far from a sweet, innocent boy, too.

I glanced back at the guy coming down the street. Would it be better to go with an insane man on the motorcycle, who kind of looked like he could kill me, but was offering a ride out of this place? Or risk it with the weird one coming down the deserted street?

I had wanted to do more interesting things in my life. Wouldn't getting on the back of a stranger's motorcycle be one of those things?

"How do I get on?"

He pointed to the pegs, watching over his shoulder as I put one foot on it and tried to get up. I fell back immediately, landing on my feet, at least.

"You hold on to my shoulders to balance when you get on, not fall backwards like a fucking baby deer," he yelled.

"Well, I didn't know if I could touch you!" I yelled back. I glanced down the road. The guy down the block came closer now.

"Fucking hell. Get on, *now*. You're about to touch me a hell of a lot more, so yeah, I assumed there would be some hands on me."

I planted my hands on his shoulders, lifting myself up onto the peg and swinging my leg over. "Oh. It's like getting on a horse," I said, trying to sit back on the small seat.

His head dropped forward, and I could feel him shaking now.

"Are you laughing at me?" I asked.

"I've just never had a girl say that as she got on top of me before."

"I'm not on top of you," I said, straightening up on my small seat. He turned the bike on, the loud rumble vibrating through me. He hit something, making the bike jump forward a few inches, and forced a scream from me as I fell forward, grabbing onto him.

"Yes," he said over the bike. "You are on top of me. An arm around my waist or on the tank. You can hold on to me unless we stop or shift, then use the tank to hold yourself up. Don't squeeze the fucking life out of me or I might leave you to walk. If you have a problem, tap me and I'll stop. Don't make me stop because you're scared. Keep it to yourself. If you grab anything lower than my belt, that's your own damn problem because I haven't had a girl on the back of my bike in months and I guarantee you will be feeling something."

"Wow, there are a lot of rules, and I was kind of right about the being an asshole thing."

He turned to look at me. "You absolutely were. Safety first, *Rebel*," he said, slamming my visor down. "Now hold on."

FOUR

ROOK

I didn't actually know where I was taking her, but I assumed
she would tell me soon enough. I headed back towards
town, making a right towards the rich-side rather than a left
to go towards our place.

There wasn't a chance in hell she came from my side of town.
Not only did she not look or act like it, but there was no way
Elliot would date anyone who wasn't rich as hell. I'm sure he
already had to be digging through her purse and she wouldn't
even know it.

It wasn't long before she tapped my shoulder, and I didn't
hide my groan. Not that she would hear it. I pulled off one of the
most deserted side streets I could find before shutting off the bike.

"Is this where you want to be dropped off?"

She pulled off the helmet, dark hair cascading down over her
shoulders. Her lips were dark red, the lipstick smeared the smallest
amount, and I wondered if Elliot had already been making a move
for the night. It still didn't explain why he would bring her down
the dangerous street, though. There was nothing down there to

see, and no reason to bring a beautiful woman down there to risk her life.

"No, but I figured since we were already passing it, you wouldn't mind if we stopped off at this small bakery right around the corner. They are open late and I want cookies."

"You told me to...stop and get you a cookie?"

"No, I want you to stop so I can get *myself* a cookie."

"Do you think I'm a chauffeur for you? An errand boy? Do you always ask the guys who hold a gun at you to take you out for a snack?"

"The guys I usually ask to take me out for snacks are happy to take me without question."

"I'm sure the guys you ask are willing to do a lot of things to you without question. There's a long list of things *I* would do to you without question, but stopping for a fucking cookie isn't one of them."

She furrowed her eyebrows as she got off the bike. "Well, guess what, *Rook*? We are already here, so I'm going to walk around the corner, and get a cookie. You can either sit there and wait like a good little mugger, leave me here, or come with me, but I've had a really shitty night and I want a fucking cookie," she said, nearly in tears.

The outburst probably should have been expected, but she had been so scared before. I really wasn't planning for it now. She already stomped around the corner of the brick building when I realized what she said.

"Hey!" I yelled, catching up to her. She didn't slow down, so I grabbed her arm, pulling her to a stop. "How the fuck do you know my name?"

She shrugged, trying to look relaxed, but it wasn't working. Half of my life had been spent learning body language. It made intimidating people and getting out of trouble easier when you knew what they were thinking.

And I knew she was currently still terrified.

"Your friend called, and I picked up with the helmet."

"Aiden?"

"Yes."

"I'm going to kill him."

"Why? Don't want the people you were trying to rob to know your name?"

I smirked. "Not particularly, no. What else did he say?"

"That you're in a mood tonight and to keep you out as long as I can because he doesn't want to deal with you."

"So you thought a cookie was a good idea?"

"I wanted one before you robbed me, so it made the most sense."

She spun, pulling open the door to the bakery and heading inside. I hated that I followed her in, but I needed to know what else Aiden said, so I knew how much I'd have to beat the shit out of him for telling a stranger anything about me.

She made it to the counter to order, and I stepped up behind her. I still had my mask on, and the girl behind the counter quickly looked back at her to avoid me.

"Double whatever she's getting."

Rebel girl stepped to the side, looking up at me with her shoulders pulled back.

"What? Now you think I'm paying, too?" I asked.

"You tried to rob me at gunpoint! The least you could do is buy me a cookie."

Behind the counter, the girl's eyes went wide and mouth fell open.

"I didn't actually try to rob her," I said, pulling out more than enough cash to cover the cost and handing it all over. "I tried to rob her boyfriend. You can keep all the extra cash if you don't call the police."

Between the story and the way I looked, the girl seemed scared enough and nodded in agreement.

"No problem," she squeaked. "Let me get your stuff."

"Thanks!" the rebel girl yelled, pushing me away. "Don't be rude."

"I'm not the one running around screaming about the crimes I commit."

"Does this mean you've committed more than one crime?"

My eyebrows furrowed. "Today? Yeah. That part wasn't obvious? And if you start telling people my business, I won't be nearly as kind."

"Is that a threat? And this is you being *nice*?"

I grabbed the box of cookies, handing it to her as we headed back out.

"Of course it's a threat. And you're not left on the side of the road, so yeah, this is me being nice."

"Threaten me again and I'll go right to the cops to talk about you."

"And I'll break into your house and kidnap you so you never see your family, or the cops, ever again," I said, pulling down my mask enough to take a bite of the first cookie. She hadn't been lying. These were amazing.

I didn't realize she had stopped walking until I turned the corner to the alley where I parked my bike. I stepped back, finding her frozen on the sidewalk.

"Problem?"

"Yes, problem. You threatened to kidnap me!"

"Only if you try to turn me in. Otherwise, I never plan to see you again."

"But you would do it?"

"Of course I would do it," I said. "Are you going to eat your cookies or am I stealing them all?"

She grabbed the box, ripping it out of my hands and pressing it to her chest. "I'm eating mine at home. Which, from here, I can get myself there on my own."

I leaned back on my bike, watching her as I ate the last of the one cookie she apparently planned on giving me.

"Running away?"

"From the guy who has now held me at gunpoint and threatened to kidnap me? Yes, I am."

Her phone rang for what felt like the twentieth time since we had gotten off the bike, and like the other times, she clicked to silence it.

"Problems?"

"Elliot keeps calling."

"Give me the phone."

"You think I'm going to hand you my phone now? Are you going to ride off with it?"

"Yeah, I'm short on pink cell phones. Come on," I said, reaching my hand out. I grabbed it, leaning back on the bike as I clicked the speakerphone on.

It rang once before Elliot picked up.

"Babe? Oh my god, babe, are you okay?"

"You think the girl you left with someone you owe money to is okay?" I asked, dropping my voice low and threatening.

She looked up, her tongue darting out to lick her lips.

"You took her?" he asked, the panic in his voice not nearly convincing enough. He was probably more concerned with a police investigation and less with her safety.

"Of course I fucking took her. You left a hot woman on a dangerous road with a guy who hates your guts and has a gun."

I stayed quiet as Elliot yelled an endless string of empty threats.

"Your fault, asshole. Don't leave prized possessions with people you owe money. Bring the cash to the shop and I'll get her home safe."

As if Elliot wanted me to push his buttons, he yelled something about touching her.

"Worried she'll be disappointed with your performance if I do?"

"Rook!" she yelled, a weak attempt at scolding me.

"Damn. I have to go. She's already screaming my name. The money, Elliot. Don't fucking forget it." I clicked the call off and handed it back to her. "Don't pick up for a while. He deserves to think you're getting the best sex of your life with me after what he did to you."

She didn't move, and it gave me time to really look at her. Full red lips, long dark hair, the arrogance of a rich girl who thought I was worthless, she was beautiful.

There really wasn't anything more satisfying than hooking up with a girl who thought I was the monster, getting her off and having her beg for more, only for her to wake up the next day disgusted with herself for how badly she wanted to do it again.

The pure corruption of making someone like her want me, or anyone like me, felt unmatched.

This month marked six months of not sleeping with anyone, which could be clouding my head with these ideas.

"Come here," I said, and unsurprisingly, she didn't move.

I pushed off the bike, stalking over until she stared up at me, mouth open and eyes wide.

"What are you doing?" she asked, still clutching the box against her chest.

I leaned down until my lips were a breath away from hers. "Seeing if you would kiss me or not if I closed the distance."

She didn't move, didn't breathe, but her eyes met mine.

"I won't."

My hand trailed down her side, over her hip, and to the hem of her skirt. "And why not?"

"Because I think you might kill people, and I don't kiss murderers."

"Of course you don't," I said, my fingers moving along her hip until I was brushing down her thigh. "Do you do anything else with killers?"

"No. I don't think so." Her voice hiccuped at the word, and I continued back up her hip.

"Would you like to keep playing rebel and start?" I leaned down, wrapping an arm around her waist to pull her back towards the bike.

"Considering I have to get back on if I want a ride home, I think I've played rebel enough for one night."

"Are you sure? It's so much fun to push limits. I could push you to a few of yours."

My hand gripped her thigh, and I dropped my head, my lips hovering over her neck but never touching her. Her breath hitched, and I could feel her heartbeat quicken under my lips.

"Just say the word, Rebel, and I'll give you something Elliot would never be able to."

FIVE
REGAN

S tupid.

That's me wrapped up in one word. Stupid.

But it wasn't enough to make me not find the man threatening my ex while eating a cookie attractive.

And it wasn't enough to stop me from considering if I should push my new rebellious ways and ask for a few more things than only a ride on a motorcycle. He leaned down, his hand gripping my hip harder.

It wasn't like I would have a boyfriend anymore. Elliot would get one text, and then his number would be blocked.

Rook's lips brushed up my neck, and for one second, I thought about giving in. About being laid out on his bike and finding out exactly what he thought he would give me that Elliot couldn't.

"I thought you said you weren't going to touch me?"

"I lied."

"Well, then, so did I," I said, grabbing a cookie. I brought it up, shoving it in his mouth. "I don't want to be a rebel."

I held my breath as he took in what I had done. For one beat of my racing heart, I remembered we were alone in a dark alley and I was physically rejecting him. I stayed frozen, waiting for whatever type of retaliation would come.

He stood up straight, pulling the cookie from his mouth, laughing. "I wondered if you were going to share more," he said, taking another bite. "You were holding on to them like they were your prized possessions."

"You're...not mad?"

"For this?" he asked, holding up the cookie. "Not at all. It's cute you think you don't want to be a rebel, though. I think I could change your mind really fast."

"I think you should take me home."

He shook his head, swinging onto the bike and waiting for me.

"You really aren't mad? And still taking me home? *Alive*?"

"Strangely enough, I don't feel the need to kill people for not fucking me in alleys. Is this something Elliot does? I mean, I knew the man's morals were low, but this one is surprising," he said with a laugh.

I rolled my eyes. "Forget I even asked," I said, but still hesitated to get on.

My mind raced with doubts and more questions. But the thrill of something new and exciting seemed too strong to resist. I took another deep breath before I grabbed the helmet, shoving it on as I got on behind him. Luckily, I didn't stumble off this time, which was great since my legs were currently useless from him being so close. His fingers trailing up my sides had set me on fire, and as much as I knew I wouldn't be doing anything with him, part of me wanted to.

I was a good, non-rebellious girl. Rook definitely wasn't my type, so why did I feel so excited to wrap my arms around him?

He revved the bike, and I grabbed onto him, trying to keep my hands firmly on his stomach, but each jump of the bike had me going further down until I felt his belt, and then a little lower. He hadn't been lying when he said I would feel something if I went lower than the belt. My hand grazed his jeans, feeling the hard length once before I pulled away. There were only so many places I could touch, though. I moved higher again, running over his hard stomach.

Maybe I didn't have to completely stop being a rebel. My fingers trailed back down again, and I grew more brave. I pulled up the hoodie and shirt underneath, splaying my fingers against bare skin. Heat pooled, my body suddenly aching as I leaned on him for more.

When I realized we were close, I pulled my hands away and pointed down the next road. It wasn't the road to my house, but it would be one annoyingly long walk through two backyards and I was home.

And letting Rook know where I lived seemed like one more stupid decision I could make tonight.

He jumped the bike again, making me fall onto his back and cling to him one more time before I started frantically hitting his shoulder to stop in front of a random house.

I wasted no time getting off and handing him the helmet. "What is it when you do that?"

"Do what?"

"Make the bike jump."

"I pop the clutch a bit and it makes it jump."

"I don't like it."

He smirked, and his eyebrows went up. "I do."

I shook my head, trying not to smile back. "Thanks, I think," I said, adjusting my skirt and spinning on my heel to head down the driveway. I knew the older man who lived here, and he wouldn't care if I cut through. "See you...never again, probably."

"Hey," he yelled. "What if I do want to see you again?"

I already shook my head. Not only did I feel too embarrassed, but I still really didn't know anything about him, and the few things I did know didn't lead me to good assumptions.

"You don't."

I made it into our neighbor's backyard before I heard the bike take off, the sound of the screaming engine lasting forever until it finally faded away.

I waited a few more seconds before continuing. It was a hike to get to our house from here, but at least I felt a bit smarter for not giving a stranger directions to my house.

The mansion rose up in the night, the lights on it were a beacon of home. Unlike the other homes around us, ours sat tucked away, with a long driveway and acres of land keeping everything private compared to the few neighbors we had.

My heart hammered as I opened the door, part of me feeling like my forehead had a brand of what I had done, the other part remembering no one cared what I had done or where I had been.

My part of the house stayed empty. Six bedrooms, one office, a giant kitchen, living room, and dining room. Endless rooms on this side and not a single person in them. Our house had been split up. One side belonged mainly mine now, the bedrooms, this living room, the kitchen. The other side had been built later by my father. It had his bedroom, an office, a formal living room, and a small kitchen, which was only used when he had someone come prepare meals for him.

Okay, more like every day. Not a single person here to care what happened to me.

I huffed as I headed up the ridiculously big staircase to my bedroom upstairs, already pulling a cookie out of the box and hitting Harper's name on my phone.

"Hey. Elliot didn't lock you in a basement?" she asked.

"Nope, but I think he might have done something a hell of a lot worse. I might have, too," I said, locking my bedroom door behind me and getting into bed, telling Harper everything.

Six
Regan

Another day went by with me lying around the house. There were no events, no parties, nothing going on except endless days of no one needing me to do anything.

I had stayed around the house after college for my dad. He had made comments here and there about wanting help and not wanting me to be too far from him, and I quickly caught on. So instead of going out into the world after graduating, I came back here to take care of my dad and wait for the day he would let me step in and help him.

But he seemed to be running as fast as he could with the help of all his doctors, and I still waited.

So the most I contributed to this world was art, and even drawing didn't interest me this week. I wanted a reason to get up.

Instead of doing anything worthwhile, I kicked my feet up onto the back of the couch, watching the next episode of Dateline upside down as if it could make it more exciting.

"What are you doing, Regan? Sit upright." My father's voice startled me, making me flip back fast.

He rarely came into this living room. He seemed to spend most days locked in his office here or at his company's building in the city. Even when he was here, I rarely knew it.

Now he sat across from me, making me nervous as he cocked an eyebrow.

"Where were you last night that had you not getting home until one AM and snuck through the back of the house?" he asked, his eyes hard and angry.

"Out with Elliot. I told you I would be," I said, trying to take short breaths to control my now racing heart.

"Then why were you seen walking through our neighbor's yard to ours? He called to make sure you were okay."

"Elliot took a wrong turn and annoyed me. I thought walking through the yard would be easier than staying in the car with him any longer."

His face softened the slightest amount, but he still wasn't happy with the answer.

"You set off a dozen security alarms and sent my guys into a frenzy. I tried calling you, and you continually ignored it. I nearly had a heart attack trying to get everything under control."

"I was on the phone with Harper," I said, trying to sound as innocent as I could. I didn't want him to have any reason to get more stressed.

"This is ridiculous, Regan. I leave you home with anything you need, and yet I have to be woken up in the middle of the night with an alarm about someone walking onto my property."

"Do you have sensors around the yard or something?"

"I have them at the wall you had to climb over. I run a security company. You think I don't have this place locked up well enough?"

"I mean, I assumed, but I didn't know for sure."

"No, because you don't think about anything past your paintings or this ridiculous show," he snapped.

The words cut hard and deep. Maybe this took up a lot of my time, but it wasn't the only thing I liked to think about, and if it were up to me, I would be doing a lot more. But I didn't dare argue back. Upsetting him further would be the last thing I wanted to do. His health already seemed fragile, and the stress couldn't be good for him. Everything I had read about his disease said stress would only make his symptoms worse, and I couldn't be the reason he got worse.

I shook off the sting as my dad's phone rang. He seemed so wrapped up in being angry that he answered while still at the table.

My dad hid so much from me, and I realized this was one of those things. He rarely, if ever, took phone calls in front of me. He would glance at the caller ID and then head to another room fast before answering. I wasn't allowed to hear what he had to say or what they were calling about. The realization nagged at me, only upsetting me more.

"What?" he asked, waiting as the other person spoke. "Like I give a damn. We told you two weeks, and I mean two weeks. To the fucking hour."

He stayed silent again, his lips pressing harder together. "If I don't have the money, you're going to lose a lot more than just your business. Time is running out. You've lost yourself a day."

My mouth dropped open, the words sounding more like something I would expect from someone like Rook rather than from my suit and tie, CEO father. I could only stare as my dad got up and glared at me.

"I have to go," he snapped at me. "Stay at home this weekend. I don't need you going out and causing even more problems. You're not to leave the house at all."

"What if I need food?" I asked, dumbfounded.

"Order it. I have too much to do, Regan. I have meetings,

travel arrangements." He paused, clearing his throat. "Doctor appointments. I have a lot on my list, and you're not helping."

"You're right," I said, giving in immediately as tears welled up. "I'm sorry."

He only shook his head and pulled out his phone as he headed towards the front of the house.

I sat, staring as the door slammed behind him. I didn't want to cry. I didn't want to face how much of a burden I seemed to be to him when all I wanted to be was an asset, but I couldn't help it.

I was a failure, and I hadn't even tried to be.

As much as I wanted to follow my dad's rules and stay home, it was Hallows Night, Havenwood's annual Halloween festival, and we never missed it. I had slipped out of the house, leaving the TV on and hoping the noise would help not raise any suspicion. I didn't actually know how many cameras were in our house, and at this point, I didn't think I wanted to. I should be able to go out with Harper without an issue, though.

Harper had picked me up down the street, and ten minutes later, we were walking downtown.

"You think you can get away with being out?" Harper asked, surprised I had snuck out. I rarely went against my dad's requests, preferring to stay in his good graces, but I couldn't stand to stay in those four walls any longer today.

"I don't know. I hope so. It's like the place is mocking me. I walk around knowing I can't leave or my dad will get mad but not being able to stay and do nothing anymore because I get mad. I don't get it. I've done everything he wanted me to. Why not let me help with the business? Who else would he give it to one day?"

Harper rolled her eyes with a groan. "A man, probably."

My stomach rolled. "You think he would hand it over to a random person because he has a dick instead of giving it to me?"

"I think your dad likes powerful people and seems to think men are more powerful."

I ground my teeth together, knowing she could be right. "I can be as powerful as any man."

"I get it, but does anyone else? You hide away in the house and do what he tells you to. Maybe he truly doesn't know you can do it."

"But then the moment I try to show him, he's upset I'm not doing what I'm told. How am I supposed to win?"

She shrugged. "I think you need to decide what you want and go for it."

"Easier said than done."

As soon as we turned on the main street, I smiled. Everyone seemed ready for Halloween. The holiday had taken over—the entire street strung with orange and purple lights that draped between buildings and cobwebs that hung in each shop's windows. The cheesy, scary pop-up figures lined the street, and the screams and laughter from passersby made me smile. The main street had been closed off to cars, and we wove our way through the games, food, and vendors they had filled it with.

Harper yelled, grabbing my hand to drag me over to our group of friends.

Elliot stood with them, eyeing me as I walked up.

"Hey," I said to no one in particular.

"Where have you been?" Elliot asked, the cold tone making me sneer.

"Safe at home, no thanks to you."

"What is that supposed to mean?" he asked.

"I think it means you left your girl on the street with a robber to fend for herself. Care to talk about it more?" Harper said.

His mouth snapped shut. Whatever he had been about to say

dying on his lips. I tried to focus on the rest of the group, everyone making plans for the night and the week, but my mind kept wandering.

I heard the bikes before I saw them. My eyes jumped to Elliot, who seemed to hear them, too. He smacked his friend's chest, nodding to the road behind us. I wasn't surprised at all when he took off, his friends following him in a line as he weaved through the crowd and disappeared.

The bikes revved again, and I froze.

There was no way it could be Rook. He wouldn't really come here to find Elliot, would he? Could he even know Elliot would be here?

Then again, he knew Elliot would be with me at the art exhibit, so he seemed to be keeping tabs on him.

The rev of an engine and flash of lights caught my eye. The road had been closed, but it didn't deter the six bikes coming down it. They split off, three on one side of the street and three on the other as they drove up onto the sidewalk, none of them seeming to care as people jumped out of the way for them.

It was hard to tell the difference between the bikes. Some had different colors, but they all looked similar. A black bike with green lights took off, moving to the middle of the street and popping a wheelie as it sped down the center.

People yelled, but the riders didn't care. For one second, I wondered if it could be Rook as the bike went down the center, but I remembered his bike had pink-hued lights.

Then I saw it. The blacked out bike, the blacked out clothes, the little pink lights. I knew it was him before he even noticed me. *If* he would even notice me. He probably couldn't even remember what I looked like.

The rider stood up, his eyes scanning the crowd as one of the other bikes pulled up next to him, a guy with a girl on the back, her blonde hair cascading down her back from the helmet. She didn't seem to be paying much attention to anything, instead tapping away at her phone.

I grabbed Harper, trying to pull her away from the bikes, but she seemed too busy with the guy she was talking to. The crowd had thinned a bit more, everyone staying out of the way in case they came down the street.

The blonde girl smacked the shoulder of the guy in front of her.

The maybe-Rook looked over, and for a second I thought he was looking at me. His helmet obscured his face like always, and I almost thought I imagined it until he waved to the others and pointed directly at me.

"Harper," I hissed. I turned my back to the bikes, and heading towards the middle of the street again.

The rev of all the engines at once felt deafening, the entire group heading towards us now. The crowd around me dispersed, leaving me nearly alone in the middle of the road.

The bikes circled me. The tires screeched on pavement until I was blind to everything beyond them. One turned, speeding away before heading straight towards the group again.

My feet felt glued to the ground even as the bike barreled toward me. The engine roared louder, the rider hitting the brakes less than a foot away. The back of the bike lifted, the helmet stopping inches from my face. I held my breath, the scent of burning rubber and gasoline filling my nostrils.

"Rook," I finally said.

The bike dropped back down, and he pulled off his helmet.

Underneath wasn't any more comforting. His face had been painted, the black and white skeleton face marred by splattered red paint.

At least, I hoped it was red paint.

He smiled. The creepy makeup made me want to take another

step back, but I couldn't. Fear and excitement swirled through me until I wasn't doing anything but staring at him.

He leaned in further, our lips so close I could kiss him if I wanted. The smile changed, curving into a wicked grin as his eyes went heavy.

"Found you."

SEVEN

ROOK

Her mouth dropped open, as her eyes scanned my face, probably taking in the face paint. Or maybe the blood splattered across it.

It had already been a busy night, and I had one more thing left on my to-do list.

And now she stood right in front of me.

Her long pink hoodie clung to her hips and her thighs. The perfect curve of them made me remember my hands there, and how much I would enjoy my head between them. I wondered if there would be anything under it or if the hoodie served its purpose as a complete dress.

The night felt cool. Fall temperatures were here and made it bearable to ride with helmets and jackets on again. If she minded the cold on her legs, she didn't show it.

I had been thinking about her for days and not being able to figure any information out about her had driven me to the brink of madness.

"If you are looking for Elliot, he ran off when he heard you pulling up," she said.

I laughed, already waving Aiden over. "Shocker." Aiden idled over, pulling his helmet off.

"What's up?"

"Elliot. He's here and ran off. Which way?" I asked her. She bit at her lower lip, her eyes wide as her hands wrung together.

She still seemed nervous around me, which might work in my favor.

"Towards Hellfire Bar down the street. He goes there a lot lately."

Aiden nodded, already shoving his helmet on and heading towards Hellfire Bar with the rest of them.

"Look at you, already ratting out your ex."

"Well, if him being around means you keep showing up, why wouldn't I tell you?"

"You've been hiding from me."

"And?"

"I don't like it. You don't tell me your name. Make me drop you off at a random house. How am I supposed to find you?"

"How do you know it wasn't my house?"

"Not hard to figure out who lives there when I have the address."

She took a deep breath and straightened up her shoulders again. "What do you want from me? I don't owe you money or anything."

"I want your name."

"You can't have it," she snapped back.

The wave of pleasure rolling over me was a surprise. I had been planning to find her to see if she would continue what we started on my bike, but her words spurred a deeper part of me. A part of me which appreciated someone who liked secrets. A part of me that already liked how she had stayed to face me the night we met. And even more than those, a part of me which seemed to be entirely turned on by the rich girl playing tough rebel.

How far down could one prim and proper girl want to fall?

"My whole world is wrapped up in selling information," I said. "I find it cute how you already know how important a name could be to me."

Her nose scrunched and her eyebrows furrowed. "How do you...sell information?"

"I get valuable information. I sell it." I shrugged, leaning down onto my helmet perched on my gas tank.

"And that's your *job*?"

"Among other things."

She took one careful step back, but I rolled the bike closer to her again.

"Your name, Rebel. Give it to me."

"Why would I if you are going to use it to...I don't know, ruin my life or stalk me or something?"

I bit at the inside of my cheek, the metallic taste of blood coating my tongue when I bit down too hard.

"The last person to deny me information today is now lying on the side of the road."

"So it *is* blood."

"I thought it added a level of authenticity to the outfit."

"It adds a level of lunatic to it."

She stepped away again, creating more distance between us until she stumbled against the curb. Her foot caught, making her fall onto the sidewalk. I got off, extending my hand to help her up, but she only eyed it.

"Is there blood on them, too?"

"I'm not an animal. I did wash my hands."

"But not your face?"

"Who could ruin this work of art?" She pushed off the ground, smacking my hand out of the way.

"Going to run away from me again?" I asked, smiling as she scowled.

"Yes."

"My favorite. Run, run, Rebel. I can chase you all night."

"You have nothing better to do?"

"No, and how else would I learn who you are? You won't willingly tell me."

"Why? I don't see what the big deal is. It sounds like I made the right choice."

"I don't like being lied to. I also don't like being felt up by a girl on my bike, and she doesn't even tell me her name."

"That sounds like a personal problem," she said, smiling now.

"Oh, it is," I said, leaning down further. Her eyes moved over my face, looking at the paint and blood again. "It's deeply, deeply personal, and I plan to take care of it myself."

"How?" she asked, her words a little more shaky now.

"Run, and if I catch you within the next hour, I get your name."

"And if you catch me, but I don't give it?"

It was a question I could have only dreamed she would ask me. My chest rumbled at the thought of forcing it out of her. "I'll take it."

"Take... Take my name?" she asked, stumbling over her words.

"Take you until you give me your name."

"So if you catch me, I either have to give you my name or be kidnapped?"

She tried not to meet my eyes. I trailed a gloved hand down her face before grabbing her chin and forcing her to look at me again.

"You're so smart, Rebel, and so pretty." I leaned down to her ear and heard the sharp intake of breath. She didn't move, and I wondered if it was out of fear or want. Her hands moved to my biceps, using me to steady herself now.

I turned, biting down on her neck hard. She screamed, her fingers digging into my shoulders, pushing me away.

"And delicious," I added.

"Rook!" she yelled. I didn't move, though, kissing the spot instead as her body relaxed. I finally pulled back, looking at the angry red spot smeared with black and white paint.

"See? Beautiful," I said, stepping back.

I swung a leg over my bike, my helmet strapped to the seat behind me. I wanted her to watch my face, see my eyes the moment I caught her. Her fingers went to her neck, wiping at the paint to stare down at it as her nose scrunched.

"Hey, Rebel?" I asked, right before starting the bike.

"What?"

"Run."

Eight

Regan

My hands shook as I ran around the corner, the giddy flutter in my chest making me laugh. I knew I didn't have to do it. I could leave and he still wouldn't know who I was, but the fact that he cared so much to know my name felt nice.

I could order a car. It wasn't like it would be too hard to get one here in the next ten minutes, but I didn't pull out my phone.

Instead, I took off running down a side street. Every street in town felt safe enough, and with so many people out for the night, I didn't feel in real danger. Then again, I had a feral biker after me who seemed intent on hunting me down, and I wondered if I should rethink my survival skills.

I ran down a few more side streets until I stopped in front of a restaurant to catch my breath. I wasn't exactly a runner, and it showed as I pulled in deep, ragged breaths.

A motorcycle revved in the distance, but I had no way to know if it was Rook's or one of his friends'. The corner felt safe enough, so I stayed for another twenty minutes before I heard a bike getting closer.

My heart jumped again as I walked down another side street, keeping an eye out for bikes as I went. He had to have told all his friends to drive around town because the sound of them seemed endless. He was messing with me, making me unsure of which way to go because there were bikes all over the place.

I didn't know what I would do if Rook caught me, or if I even wanted him to, but I still wanted to play.

And I still liked the way my heart raced when I heard another bike getting closer.

For the first time in a long time, my dull life didn't seem so dull.

I started to wonder if Rook had this effect on me.

I took off again, this time ducking down a side alley. This one led to a few more hidden shops, but it was less busy than the main road. I wondered how often Rook came to this part of town and if he even knew his way around.

This part of the alley had no formal road, so it wasn't somewhere he drive up and down.

I slipped into the one shop on this road still open.

"We're closing," the girl behind the counter said.

"When?"

"Now."

I groaned, glancing back out onto the sidewalk before sticking my head out the door and into the night. I had been walking around for a while now, and I still hadn't heard Rook's bike again. It had to be getting close to an hour, and I was surprised I hadn't seen him at all.

I really thought he would be better at this. Then again, maybe he found Elliot and had given up on this game.

The girl behind the counter grumbled again, so I didn't wait any longer, slipping out onto the street and taking a left. I had come in from the opposite way, and I hoped he would still be on the other end. The town wrapped around four blocks, with a park in the middle and smaller, less-traveled roads branching out.

It wasn't big, but it should be enough to stay out of sight for a little longer.

I made it to the end as his bike roared. He had been idling down the street, revving to speed towards me the moment I stepped out of the small road.

He grinned as he got closer. The way his eyes brightened against the dark face paint made me make a quick decision. I turned back down the small alley I came from, taking off at a run. My heart raced, and I yelled out when I looked back to see Rook coming down the sidewalk toward me.

The bike screamed as he hit the throttle again and again, filling the alley with a loud echo and making my heart race. I veered into another narrow alley, my feet pounding against the pavement. The walls seemed to close in around me, the dim light casting eerie shadows that danced as I ran.

My legs ached as I flattened myself against the wall. My breath came in ragged gasps, and I tried to calm myself, listening for the sound of the bike. The alley fell silent, and for a moment, I thought I had lost him. Then one loud rev of the engine echoed off the brick walls, getting closer.

I peeked around the edge of the wall just as Rook's bike roared past. He scanned the alley, his eyes sharp and focused. I held my breath, my heart hammering in my chest. He slowed down, almost stopping right in front of me. I could see his silhouette, dark and menacing, just a few feet away. If he turned around, he would see me.

As he continued down the alley, I waited a few more seconds before slipping out from my hiding spot. I had to keep moving. The street ended, turning back out onto the main road or connecting to more alleys. I thought hiding in them might be my best bet. The crowded street would disperse the moment he followed me out.

I ran down the side alley, realizing five seconds too late that this one stopped at a dead end. Panic surged through me as I turned to see Rook's bike shut off, still rolling towards me. He kicked the stand down, jumping off to corner me.

Rook was fast, already wrapping an arm around my waist and turning me to face the wall. He pushed me harder into it, caging me in with nowhere to go.

"Caught you."

His lips found my neck, biting down on the other side now. His hands grabbed mine, pinning them on each side of my head. I leaned back against him, liking the strength of his body against mine and the feel of his chest heaving at my back. He pressed a little harder into me, my hands pinned on the bricks under his. My body flushed, heat creeping down my spine as my thighs clenched together.

"Let me go," I finally said, already regretting it before the words were out of my mouth.

"Not until you tell me. You heard the rules. If I catch you within the hour, you tell me your name. How long has it been?"

I looked at my watch. "Fifty-six minutes."

"I win. Now tell me."

"Why?"

"That's none of your business," he said, biting at my ear. "Tell me."

He pressed against me harder, the ragged breath and wicked smile letting me know exactly how much he liked this game. I did, too. I liked someone caring so much about who I was, even if it was just about my name. His wild, dangerous energy felt intoxicating, something I had never dealt with before. It gave me the type of thrill I never thought I would want, but there it was, pulling me in despite every rational reason to stay away. The fight in my head seemed almost unbearable—I knew I shouldn't feel this way about him, but every part of me liked his intensity.

"Regan," I yelled as his hand wrapped into my hair.

"Regan," he breathed. "I was already so close with Rebel. Regan what?"

I didn't answer, too scared to know why he wanted my last name.

"*Regan what?*" he asked, his hand tightening again.

"Fletcher. Regan Fletcher," I yelled.

All at once, his hands dropped from me, and Rook stepped back, breaking all contact. His nostrils flared, his chest heaving as his eyes roamed over me.

"Who are you to Cameron Fletcher?"

"How do you know my dad?"

"You're his *daughter*?" The question, filled with so much disgust, felt like a slap to my face.

"Yes. You know him?"

"No. But I know of him. I have to go."

"Why?"

"I have more to do tonight." His lips were smeared from kissing my neck, his dark hair fell over his forehead, his blue eyes wild now.

"Can't it wait?"

"No." He swung back on the bike and was about to turn it on when I ran over.

"Rook." He already had his helmet on, but he turned to look at me. I went over, pushing the visor up, and his eyes narrowed. "Why are you running away now? How do you know my dad?"

"I'm not running away. I have shit to do. Do you think I can play games with you all night? And I don't know your dad, but I know how much money he has. Stay the fuck away from me, Regan."

He nodded hard, slamming the visor down, before he disappeared into the dark.

NINE
ROOK

The entire pack came out with me tonight—four other bikes rode with mine, plus Kane in a car behind us for transport, and Evie on the back of Aiden's bike. She had demanded to come, and I wasn't going to fight it. The pickup shouldn't be too hard—just one squirrely, drugged-up messenger boy, who'd hopefully tell us where a shipment of drugs had disappeared.

Aiden's bike roared before he picked up the front. I curled my lip and hit the button on my phone, connecting to the rest of them. "Why the fuck do you always lift the bike with Evie on the back?"

"It's fun?" Evie said. "Stop trying to ruin my fun."

"She asks me to do it every time. Are you insinuating I'm going to fuck up?" Aiden asked.

"I'm insinuating that if she falls off, you'll be dragged behind my bike."

"Oh, shut up," Evie said. "I know how to hold on to him."

Mason pulled up next to me, pointing at Evie and Aiden.

"I'm thinking you know how to hold on to him a little too well, if you know what I mean."

"Don't you fucking dare, Aiden. Evie, you're riding home with Mason."

"I didn't do anything!" Aiden yelled, flipping me off.

Hero sped around us, swerving back and forth across the highway. I could clearly see the gun strapped to his back, only partially hidden by his jacket.

"Why the fuck did you bring a gun that big? It's one guy."

"You never know."

"Guns aren't part of the plan tonight. Don't get unhinged and pull it out for fun."

He groaned, dropping back next to me. "You really are a fun killer," Hero said as we turned on to the road of the club.

We were told the guy came here tonight, tucked into a corner, drinking and getting higher than a fucking plane. It would be an easy place to pick someone up, and we used it often for business, never for pleasure. I made it clear to everyone we weren't mixing the two on our own ground.

The pulsating bass of the club's music spilled out into the street as we parked our bikes out front and made our way inside. Kane stayed in the car, Evie keeping him company as they kept a close eye on our bikes.

The lights inside were dim, a haze of neon lights and swirling smoke coating us, the pulse of the music reverberating through me. As we pushed through the crowd, a pretty girl with long, dark hair and a tight dress stepped in front of me, blocking my path. Her eyes were bright with interest as she smiled up at me.

"Hey there. Want to get a drink?" she asked, her voice dripping with flirtation.

I glanced down, barely registering her words. For a split second, an image of Regan flashed through my mind—her eyes, her smile, the way she kept trying to be rebellious. I shook my head, trying to dislodge the horrible thought.

"Not interested," I said, stepping around the girl.

She huffed, stepping closer. "We could go dance instead."

"Still not interested," I said, trying to step around her again. The group had disappeared in front of me as soon as she stopped me, and I hoped they were already grabbing the guy. I liked going out usually, but not tonight. I had no reason to be somewhere that would constantly remind me of my attraction to Cameron Fletcher's daughter.

The bad taste in my mouth almost made me want to lean down and take this girl up on her offer, but I didn't. I didn't like how she looked just enough like Regan to remind me of her.

The guys came back down, one half-limp man being brought out with them.

"Rook, you coming?" Hero called out.

"Yeah, right behind you," I replied, pushing Regan out of my mind. There would be no time for distractions.

I followed them, my focus sharp again, despite the unexpected intrusion of Regan in my thoughts. We had a job to do, and I couldn't afford to let anything—or anyone—get in the way.

The garage was lit up bright inside tonight. We had left the door shut tight, the scent of blood, sweat, and gasoline filling my nostrils and making my nose scrunch. The guy strapped to the chair in the center didn't seem to mind, though. Hero stepped forward, the cruel grin on his face making the guy squirm more.

Hero reached out, grabbing his pinky finger and twisting until bones crunched in his palm. I grabbed for the other hand, choosing his pointer finger instead.

"Why a different finger?" Hero asked with a frown. "I don't like them not matching."

"Why the pinky? This one is more annoying if it's broken."

"Why would he care which fingers are useful if he will be dead before he can use them again?" Hero asked. The man screamed against his gag, and I smacked the back of his head.

"Tell us where you're hoarding millions of dollars' worth of drugs, and we let you go," I said. Our job would be getting him to reveal where his boss hid the drugs he stole from another drug lord, but my heart just wasn't in it today.

I still picked up the pliers, shoving a deep socket into the guy's mouth to force it open before getting a good grip on his front tooth and pulling.

We ran our own business in a lot of different ways, from playing messenger between bigger operations, to dipping our hands into gambling and counterfeit parts, but sometimes we were middlemen. The men in the middle of bigger businessmen when they couldn't play nice for five minutes. From finding out information to selling it, it worked perfectly for us. We made the money and never had a trail of evidence leading in our direction.

My mind wasn't here, though.

My mind felt stuck on Cameron Fletcher. The man I hated more than anyone, the one who burned my life to the ground and walked away with everything he wanted. There were no consequences for the terrible things he had done and continued to do.

Ten years ago, we had everything. My family wasn't anywhere comparable to the Fletchers, but we had everything we wanted and needed. Until one day, the business took a hit, and Cameron had been suddenly there to save us. My dad signed a partnership with Cameron in hopes that it would all be restored. They were art dealers, and I had come to learn Cameron was a fan of stealing art and selling it on the black market. What better way to do that than seeking out my parents and becoming their partner? But when my dad wouldn't give in to smuggling art through his business, Cameron stole it.

He stole their lives first. It made it easier to take over the business you owned with your partner when the partner suddenly went up in literal flames.

Everything we owned had been signed to Cameron before my parents' deaths, and he collected the moment he could. He had somehow even found a way to sway our custody since we were minors, and Evie and I had been shipped out of town before the funeral even took place.

Now I found out the girl I'd been chasing around and trying to find ended up being his daughter? The thought of it made me sick, my jaw clenching as my stomach flipped. I put my lips on his fucking daughter and liked it?

I should cut off my own lips for it. It felt like a betrayal to myself, my parents, and Evie.

I let Hero take over, and he seemed happy to step up. He threw a punch, more bones cracking and popping beneath his hand, as I headed over to the couch we'd set against the wall.

"What's up?" Aiden asked, dropping onto the couch next to me. "Don't like the view?"

"The view being a man getting tortured to death? It's great, but I have other things on my mind."

"Like the girl we had to track down the other night? Did you not get what you wanted?"

"Oh, I got what I wanted. I know exactly who she is now."

"So the problem is...what, exactly?"

I took a deep breath, trying to figure out how I could even admit this. "Her name is Regan. Regan Fletcher. She is Cameron Fletcher's daughter," I said fast.

Aiden's eyebrows jumped up as his eyes went wide. He knew the history there. He knew exactly why I hated the man.

Aiden glanced over at Evie, who sat behind the computer

across the garage. "The guy who killed your parents and tried to burn you two alive, who you desperately want revenge on, now has a hot daughter you've been obsessing over, and you find this to be a problem?"

My hands balled into fists. Aiden's relaxed comment wasn't the issue, exactly, but saying I had been obsessing over Regan felt wrong. Maybe I had gone out of my way searching for her, and I had gone to town the other night partially to find her. I couldn't be obsessing, though.

"I wasn't obsessing over her. I just didn't know who she was and I'm sure as fuck glad I found out. Her father killed my parents. He took everything from me and Evie, and now here I am trying to fuck his daughter on my bike."

Aiden tried to stifle his laugh but failed. "The irony here is great. What's the problem, exactly?"

"What do you mean?" I asked, trying to play dumb. The problem is I *had* been obsessing over her. For the first time in a long time, I felt interested in someone.

"I mean, you've been killing yourself trying to get to Fletcher for years. Are you seriously not considering using Regan to get to him? What better in to his life than his only daughter? You've tried before and never figured out who she was. Isn't this a good thing?"

I had tried to find her before, years ago, and the moment I got close, he sent her off to boarding school for four years, then college for another four years. I didn't even realize he let her come home until now. For all I had known, he killed her off, too. Why keep an heir around when, even dead, he wouldn't want to let his fortune go?

The idea of who Regan could be to me had clouded my vision until I didn't even think of the option to use her. Now, I needed to see her for who she was, the daughter of the devil.

The guy tied to the chair screamed, interrupting my thoughts and making me coil with anger. I had too much going on to hear this shit.

I flipped my knife out. "I'm so fucking sick of you bitching when you're protecting one shitty man from another." I slammed down the blade, slicing through the back of his hand until it sank into the wooden arm of the chair. He screamed, his eyes wide, looking at what I had done. "Tell us where the fuck you're dropping everything. In exchange, I'll give you five grand and tell everyone you're dead."

The metallic scent of blood filled the air, and he bit at the gag again. I ripped it down when I realized he wanted to say something.

"They will want my body."

"Great, I'll give them a body. My offer stands. Take it or you will be chained in this garage until you die. I'll have a body to give him either way."

"Fine! Fine! I'll take the deal if you let me go."

"How kind," I said, standing up. "Zack, get the information, check it out, and then drop him off at the bus station." I grabbed five grand out of the toolbox and handed it to Zack. "He doesn't get a dollar until the location is confirmed. If he lies, kill him." I turned back to the guy. "And if you ever come back, I will personally gut you."

Aiden caught up to me as I headed to the back office. "So are you going to do it?"

"Do what?" I asked, already knowing exactly what he meant.

"Use Regan to get to Fletcher."

I sat back at the desk, thinking back to Regan at Hallows Night. She had asked me to stay, and I ran off. "She might be pissed at me now. It's not like she was my biggest fan in the beginning anyway."

"That doesn't answer my question."

"Of course I'm going to do it. The girl is naïve to who I am and would give me unlimited access to Cameron Fletcher. I'd be stupid not to use her."

Aiden grimaced, looking me over. "You being stupid is really not out of the question here."

"Shut the hell up and go get Evie and the guys. Starting now, I want to figure out where Regan is going every day and what she's doing."

"What a way to woo the girl. Send a pack of bikers to watch her every move."

"Do you have a better idea?"

"Yeah, stalk her yourself. Lazy ass. We have shit to do around here," he said, grinning.

I grabbed my stuff, heading back out. "You're right. So congratulations, you're in charge of this shit show until I'm done."

"Wait, that is not what I meant."

I was already on my bike, shoving my helmet on and backing it out. "Don't care. That's what I heard."

"What did you hear?" Evie asked.

"That Aiden's in charge while I deal with something." I wasn't going to explain to her what I was doing yet. Evie had gone through her own trauma with losing everything and everyone besides me. I wouldn't get her hopes up that I could finally take down Fletcher until I knew for sure I could do it. Right now, I had to figure out more about Regan and see if I could get closer to her.

"Why does he get to be in charge and not me?"

"Because I know what the fuck is going on around here and you don't. Back to the computer, psycho. We need those files you're digging around for."

She glared at him, but I still backed out. Evie could be mad. When it came to her being safe, I didn't give a shit what she wanted. Aiden knew it and would always make her safety a priority.

I took off, heading toward the Fletcher mansion, but for the first time, I had a reason to go. The wind whipped past me as I raced down the dark streets. For the first time in a long time, I felt like I had a chance. This could finally be what I needed to get the revenge I'd wanted for so long.

Regan Fletcher would be my ticket to bringing down the man who had ruined my life, and I wasn't going to waste it.

TEN
ROOK

S talking a girl who preferred to lie in bed watching movies, reading, and ordering endless takeout was boring. It had been four days, and she had only left the house twice.

How could I stalk her if this was all she did? I was used to stalking. It's not like this is the first time I've done it; the people I follow are usually up to pretty horrible things. Torture, human trafficking, and fucked-up fantasies come to life. Even their day-to-day lives reflect it more often than not.

Not Regan, though. The girl did next to nothing.

She left once to go back to the bakery, and once to go to another art exhibit.

By the sixth day, I felt pretty confident her schedule wasn't going to change anytime soon and the stalking from afar thing wasn't going to help me anymore. It was Tuesday night now, and she was laid back on the couch, watching another old episode of Dateline. The girl seemed to have an obsession with old true crime shows, and watching them through her windows just wasn't cutting it for me anymore.

While the entire thing bored me, part of me wished I could be doing this with my night instead. The endless running around had me exhausted, and when I wasn't chasing after her or someone we needed something from, I worked at the shop, running the actual business at Maverick Moto. All the guys helped. It wasn't like I was alone in it, but somehow we had grown both our businesses overnight and we were all running ourselves ragged.

All I wanted to do now was sink into the couch, eat those stupidly good cookies, and watch an episode of *Dateline*.

I had gone onto Evie's computer earlier, grabbing Regan's number and hoping I did a good enough job hiding that I had been on it because Evie hated me messing with her stuff.

Now I stood outside Regan's window, watching as she drew on her tablet. Another episode of some true crime show played in the background. The couch she was on seemed to suck her in, and I knew I was seconds from barging through the door to sit there next to her. Just a few hours of sleep where no one could find me and ask for help with something else. My shoulders fell at the thought of a few hours next to her, watching her shows while I slept.

But instead of sneaking in to sleep on her couch, I pulled out my phone.

UNKNOWN

You can't seriously be entertained by this. I think we've watched this episode already.

REGAN

??

Who is this?

UNKNOWN

Put on a better show. Or a movie maybe? Something scary or maybe...Taken?

Seconds went by until I heard the alarm system enable.

UNKNOWN

That didn't work in the movies, and it won't work now.

REGAN

WHO IS THIS?

UNKNOWN

You're supposed to start running around the house looking for me, Rebel. Then, I jump out with a knife, you scream and run around until I catch you.

REGAN

Rook???

How did you get my number?

And how very Scream of you...the call is coming from inside the house? Are you a stalker or a killer?

ROOK

I believe I am both.

REGAN

Where are you?

ROOK

Around. And it's surprisingly easy to get someone's phone number.

REGAN

So you get all mad at me and now you're stalking me?

I laughed as her eyes darted to every window and doorway.

ROOK

I prefer to think of it as keeping an eye on you, but yes. For days now.

> You should be more observant.

REGAN

> You're creepy, you know that?

ROOK

> And yet, you keep talking to me. What does that say about you?

REGAN

> That I'm making a terrible mistake?

ROOK

> Or you secretly like it? Admit it, you're a little curious about me.

REGAN

> Curious? More like trying to figure out how to get a restraining order.

She added a little smiley face, and I smiled down at my phone.

ROOK

> Good luck. Restraining orders are for people who actually follow the rules.

REGAN

> So what's your plan? Keep stalking me until I call the cops?

ROOK

> I'm not sure yet. Maybe I'm just bored? And calling the cops has zero effect on what I do.

I had also used Evie's computer to install a security system app. One that would easily connect to Regan's house security, so I had a little control over it. It also helped me blank out a few of the cameras when I needed to.

I clicked the button, unlocking the doors all at once.

"Rook!" she screamed.

I wanted to be closer. I wanted to see if she would be shaking in fear or if she would reach out to me.

> **ROOK**
> Yes, Rebel?

REGAN
Knock it off, you're freaking me out.

> **ROOK**
> You're all alone.

REGAN
Thanks, that's really helping.

> **ROOK**
> Shouldn't this place be filled to the brim with staff and your dad?

REGAN
No, and he's away on business.

> **ROOK**
> For how long?

REGAN
A few days? Idk.

> **ROOK**
> You are so smart, but you really need to keep important information to yourself. Don't you know how many people would pay me to know when he will be out and it's only you in this house?

REGAN
Please don't tell people.

Please, Rook. I already hate being here alone. Don't make it worse.

ROOK

Does this mean you are done being scared of me? Maybe, learning there are other things more dangerous to you than me?

REGAN

Maybe you aren't as scary as you thought.

ROOK

Or maybe you're a devil yourself. Why fear what is your equal?

It wasn't a far-fetched idea. Her father could have raised her to be as ruthless and destructive as he was. I wondered how dark her world got. Did he show her he killed people? That he protected shitty people and ruined lives to make his money.

Anger flared at her, but I tamped it down. She could be naïve to the entire world or know every single detail. I needed to keep pushing to find out.

REGAN

Equal? You think I could kill you?

ROOK

Could you? No. Do you kind of want to? Yes.

REGAN

I'm done with your creepiness. Go away.

ROOK

I'm done with your clothes. Make them go away.

REGAN

Creep.

You can't watch me all night. You have to sleep at some point.

> **ROOK**
>
> You sitting around looking at a computer and watching the same old tv show is going to make me fall asleep. What are you looking at, anyway?

> **REGAN**
>
> Would you rather some trashy reality TV show?
>
> And I'm not looking at anything. I'm drawing.

> **ROOK**
>
> What are you drawing?

> **REGAN**
>
> Are you really sitting somewhere stalking me while texting to get to know me??

> **ROOK**
>
> Yes. Aren't you glad you haven't been alone all night?

> **REGAN**
>
> I would rather you either come inside or leave. Where are you, anyway?

I slipped the mask I brought back on, climbing down off the second-story balcony I had been looking into and walking back to the main living room she was sitting in.

The *main* living room, because there was more than one, had taken me the last hour looking around and getting a better idea of the layout of the house. I wasn't sure how my plan would come together to take down Cameron Fletcher, but any information I could gather would be helpful.

I stepped in front of a window where she would notice me immediately.

The scream that escaped her was a bonus.

"Rook!" she yelled. "What is with the mask?"

ROOK

There are cameras all over this place. Do you think I would willingly show my face?

"Why are you here?" she asked, loud enough I could hear her.

ROOK

Again. I'm stalking you.

She marched over, throwing the huge window open. "Aren't you doing a really bad job at stalking me if I catch you?"

"You didn't catch me. I made my presence known because I couldn't take one more silent episode of Dateline without screaming."

She leaned down onto the windowsill. "I could turn on subtitles if it's helpful."

"It would be nice. At least I would find out the ending," I said, grinning behind the mask.

"You could come in and actually listen to it."

"You're inviting your stalker in to watch TV?" I asked. Just when I felt like I was getting a glimpse inside her head, she said something like that and threw me off. I never knew if she was scared of me or interested in me? Or maybe she didn't even know.

"I'm just saying I have the TV and some more cookies, so it's not a bad deal for you."

"What's in it for you?"

"Not sitting in this huge house alone, freaking out because someone just texted me and got me all scared someone is going to break in."

I smiled again, thankful the mask hid it.

She reached out, hooking a finger under the bottom of the mask and pulling it up. Her eyes went wide, quickly looking over my face. It had to be the best look at me she had gotten so far.

"I feel like stalkers should be creepy old weirdos. What is it you're stalking me for? Do you really not have better things to do?"

"Just curious about how the other half lives," I said, looking past her into the fancy living room. "And no, nothing at all. You didn't answer my question."

"Which one?"

"What are you drawing?"

"A girl," she said, trying to avoid answering.

"Doing what?"

She turned it around, showing me the drawing on her tablet.

A girl stood facing a mirror, a rope of thorns wrapped around her with one over her mouth. The mirror showed another girl, this one perfectly beautiful, but a sinister smile on her face, with two little horns poking out of dark hair.

"It's incredible," I finally said, glad I could think of anything to say.

"It's not, but I appreciate it either way."

"Do you think I go around complimenting people on their art often?"

Her lips pressed together, the slight red hue to her cheeks making me stare at her now.

"No. I guess you wouldn't," she said, turning the tablet back around to glance at it. "I answered your question. Now, are you really just here to get to know me?"

I had too many things to do, and there was no good way to explain that I was neglecting a lot of my work to stalk her so I could either kill her dad or ruin his life.

Or both.

My phone rang before I could respond.

"What?" I snapped.

"We need you back here," Hero said.

"Why?"

"Trouble with a messenger."

"Fine. I'll be there in fifteen." I clicked off, my eyes meeting hers again. "Well, you got your wish, Rebel. I have to go."

Her eyes narrowed as she stared down at me. "Are you coming back tonight?"

"No."

Her face fell the slightest amount, and I was surprised at how quickly she recovered. Would she really rather have me lurking around than be alone?

"Will I see you again soon at all?"

"No," I said. It was a lie. I would be back another night and she would see me again, but the guilt itching its way into my brain made me tell her no. I would be using her, and she thought I came for her. I didn't know when I started to feel anything like guilt or empathy, but I wasn't okay with it.

I stalked back out to my bike I'd left hidden by the street. I had shit to do, and taking care of one lonely rich girl all night wasn't going to be on the list.

Eleven

Regan

I didn't know what I was doing. What had I been thinking? I held on tighter to Jake, my stomach churning at how stupid of an idea this had been. This felt nothing like riding with Rook. Rook had been a wild driver, but I hadn't felt like I was about to fall off every second.

Jake, on the other hand, was currently making me wonder if jumping off the back of the bike would be safer.

Every turn made me cling to him, the bike wobbling a little too much, and then he would immediately hit the gas, lurching us forward in an unsettling way.

After I found out Rook was stalking me, I had reached out to a few people, hunting down anyone who knew where bikers would be hanging out until someone connected me with Jake. He seemed to know all about what he called Syndicate, a place where bikers around town would meet up for racing and hanging out every week. He told me he would be happy to take me if I agreed to go out to dinner with him.

And I had agreed, which seemed to be the stupidest thing I had done this month, which included going with Rook.

I held on, my mind fighting with me on the conflicting emotions. It wasn't like I could deny I had an interest in Rook, even though he was obviously trouble.

He was everything I wasn't—wild, unpredictable, and dangerous. I had always been the good girl, the one who followed the rules and stayed within the lines. My life had been predictable, boring even, until now. I didn't do anything in college except study and push to graduate with honors to show my dad how serious I was, and then once I left, I was immediately faced with how short life was. I knew my dad just wanted to keep me safe, but I couldn't live my entire life locked up.

Rook represented everything wrong for me, yet I couldn't stay away. The sensible part of me screamed to walk away, to return to the safety of my predictable life, but I had already started down this path. Honestly, I didn't want to go back to that. I liked the thrill I felt when he came around.

What's wrong with me? Why would I be so attracted to someone covered in tattoos who had threatened to not only kidnap me but nearly kill me, and who loved stalking people? I felt like I was betraying my dad, and maybe even myself, but somehow I liked it?

The ride only lasted another five minutes before he pulled off into an old, abandoned parking lot. The place was already chaos, the sound of revving engines and the flash of headlights making everything one big mess. Motorcycles were parked in nearly every open area, the lights reflecting off chrome and steel, making it all blend together. A few bikers sped down the middle of the lot as they raced each other. In another area, someone spun in constant circles. The scent of burning rubber filled the air, and I wondered if they would even have a tire left after they were done. I scanned the crowd, the pulse of it all and the music making me realize just how difficult it would be to find Rook in this mess.

He had a black bike, and he was pretty much always dressed

head to toe in black. I assumed it was to make stalking easier. Then the mask and the face paint. Until a few days ago at the window, I hadn't seen his face clearly. Now I remembered it perfectly. His blue eyes, the perfect angle of his jaw, the way his dark hair would fall across his forehead, and even the way he smirked like he could kill me and be happy about it.

But I really tried not to focus on that last part.

Jake weaved through the bikes, and I looked at each face I could focus on. We parked, and I jumped off, happy to be back on solid ground.

"I'll be back in a few minutes," I yelled to Jake, running off before he could respond.

I walked through the slightly terrifying crowd to look at bike after bike, guy after guy, and I still couldn't find him. Then I came up to four bikes surrounded by people, the night not letting me see their faces well enough until they were lit up by passing headlights.

"Rook," I breathed, taking note of the women surrounding him.

And the one currently sitting on the back of his parked bike.

I took a few more steps towards him until I broke through the small crowd.

His face fell when his eyes met mine, and my heart stopped.

He didn't look happy to see me, which shouldn't have been a surprise. I wasn't sure why he was stalking me or spending time chasing me down just to learn my name, so why had I felt so sure he would be happily surprised to see me here?

I stepped in front of him, my chin tilting up as I pulled back my shoulders. "I see you found another backpack."

"I see you learned what a backpack is," he said with a rude grin.

"You work quick. You've already found yourself a new girl to put on the back of your bike when you were stalking me a day ago."

With what felt like nothing more than a flick of his wrist, the crowd dispersed and the girl on the back was gone. In less than a minute, we were basically alone.

"It almost sounds like you're jealous of me having another girl here. Do you suddenly think you have a claim over me or my bike?"

"No, not at all. Just surprised."

"How sad. I would *love* to see you stake your claim. What are you doing here?"

"I came to hang out. Is that a problem?"

"Not if it's the truth. Did you come here to find me?" The edge to his tone made me wince, but I still couldn't understand if he was happy about this or not.

"No," I said, putting my hands on my hips as I pulled my shoulders back. "I'm not interested in creeps who stalk people."

"Only the ones who hold you at gunpoint and let you feel them up?"

I fought to keep my face straight. "Something like that."

"I didn't bring a gun tonight, but I have a knife. Want me to threaten you with that?"

"No need. I'm here with someone, too."

The brief furrow of his eyebrows made me want to smile, but I held it back.

"No, you aren't."

"I am, actually. And I have to get back, so have a good night." I spun on my boot heel, angling myself in Jake's direction, when a hand wrapped around my wrist, ripping me back. A thrill went through me, my wrist burning where his hand held it.

"We aren't done," he said, his voice low and edged with anger.

"We are. You're the one who ran off two times now. I'm here with someone, so you need to let me go."

"Who?"

"What?" I asked, pretending I hadn't heard as I pulled away.

"Who are you here with?" he asked again.

I glanced over my shoulder, my eyes searching the crowd for Jake again until I saw him still by his bike. Jake wasn't exactly my type, and besides the dinner I agreed to, I wasn't planning on spending any extra time with him. And as much as I didn't want to get on a motorcycle with him ever again, I still thought it was nice he brought me.

Rook must have noticed who I was looking at. "Jake? You're here with *Jake*?"

"You know him?"

"Yeah, I know him, and there's no fucking way you're leaving with him."

"I can leave with whoever I want. I really did get a taste for you motorcycle guys after meeting the one who held me at gunpoint, you know? But I went and found one who wasn't trying to kill me."

"He wrecks his bike once a fucking week. He is trying to kill you more than I ever did."

"Too bad. I came with him. I'm leaving with him."

I made it another foot before he grabbed me again. His arm snaked around my waist, pulling me hard against him until my body was flush with his. "No, you're not."

I wiggled out of his grasp, heading fast towards Jake, who seemed to notice what was happening now. His eyes went wide, and I knew it meant an angry Rook stalked after me.

Every part of me was on fire. I couldn't believe I found him. I'd been looking, but came up with nothing and had been mad at myself for not learning more than his first name. It should have been a part of our deal when he chased me for mine. I wanted to know why he ran off when he learned my name, and why he would want to suddenly stalk me after.

Now he chased after me again, and I could only wonder if he would keep catching me.

"Stop following me," I said. He reached out again, but this time he caught the back of my neck. His fingers dug in, ripping me back and tipping my head until his mouth crashed onto mine, rough and urgent. I felt a small sting as he bit at my lower lip, forcing me to open more. My lips parted for him, letting his tongue explore every inch of mine.

The only thought running through my mind was how badly I wanted this. Despite his roughness, I had never had someone touch me like they desperately needed it, and I couldn't resist it. He kissed me hard, not caring that my lips would be bruised. If anything, it might be his goal, but I took it. I got lost in it. He hadn't kissed anything except my neck, and it had been enough to make me want more, but this felt all-consuming.

The roar of a motorcycle engine broke through my thoughts, jolting me back to reality. I bit down and pushed against his chest, trying to wiggle out of his grasp again. A metallic taste of blood coated my tongue, and I realized I had bitten down until he bled.

He loosened his grip on me, but his fingers still dug into my arm. His eyes trailed over my face as I stared at the smeared blood on his lips. A wicked grin came over him as he glanced back at Jake, and I realized how badly I had messed up.

"You took my girl on a date, Jake?" He asked, his eyebrows shooting up.

"I'm not your girl," I hissed.

"Say it louder then, Rebel," he whispered. "Tell him you didn't come here just because you wanted to find me."

I didn't say anything. Jake's eyes were wide, and they didn't leave Rook. Apparently, they knew each other well enough that Jake seemed scared of him. I wondered how many other people here were scared of him.

And more importantly, why they were.

"Touch her again, Jake, and I will kill you."

"Enough, Rook," I said through gritted teeth, pushing hard at his chest, but he wouldn't budge. "I can't believe I made a show of that. Let. Me. Go."

"Shh," he whispered, his hot breath sending shivers down my spine. "I will in a second."

My mouth dropped open, my eyes narrowing as I freed one hand enough to pull back and slap him. The sharp sound echoed, and the nearby crowd went silent. But Rook's reaction was a slow, menacing grin that only made me worry I had made a bigger mistake than kissing him.

"Don't shush me," I said, proud the words were only slightly stuttered. I always kept my mouth shut and I rarely talked back, but I didn't want him to walk all over me. I should be scared, but the way he seemed to think he was untouchable only made me want to prove him wrong.

"Cute, Rebel, very cute," Rook mocked, towering over me. "And lucky for you, I like your attitude. But if I let you go and you run right to him, we are going to have issues."

His arms dropped, letting me go, but his eyes promised consequences. As soon as he let me go, I turned, my heart pounding in my chest, as I bolted towards Jake. Every step felt weighed down by the certainty that Rook wasn't going to let this go without repercussions. And that made some twisted part of me excited.

"I'm so sorry. I didn't know this would happen. I didn't know he would be here," I said to Jake.

Technically, I hadn't known he would be here. I had hoped, but I didn't think that was important right now.

"It's alright," Jake said. "It's really alright. I didn't know you had any connection to him." He looked past me, and I knew Rook had stepped up behind me again. "Sorry, Rook. I really didn't know."

"Wait, so you won't drive me home?"

"Not a chance in fucking hell," Jake said.

"Glad we cleared that up. Come on," Rook said, grabbing my arm to drag me along with him.

"Wait, why wouldn't you drive me home? You drove me here! You would leave me stranded?"

"Pretty sure you have a ride home," Jake said, nodding at Rook.

"I came with you. What if I don't want to leave with him?"

It wasn't actually how I felt. I wanted to leave with Rook. It was almost the entire reason I came here tonight. I wasn't sure what I wanted to happen after that, but I definitely didn't want to get on the back of Jake's bike again.

I pulled at Rook, trying to slip out of his grip, but he picked me up instead, throwing me over his shoulder.

"You are such a brat. What were you doing here tonight, Rebel? Looking for me?"

"Put me down."

"Tell me the truth. If you didn't even know what a backpack was, I know you weren't riding with other guys before. So tell me, were you looking for me?"

"Maybe."

"I like that, Rebel," he groaned, the rumble of it reverberating through me. "I like that a lot."

We made it to his bike before he finally set me down.

"Looks like I'm your only ride home now tonight. Going to take me to the wrong house again or are we past that?"

"You know where I live now. Stalker."

"You know where I hang out now," he said, leaning down onto the bike. His face was inches from mine now, and the thought of his lips on me again made my heart race. "*Stalker.*"

"I'm not stalking."

"You are too, Rebel," he said, running his lips up my neck. "You run around here looking for me all night and the moment you find me, you act like the rich, stuck up brat you are. Like you're too good for me and this place when you're here hunting me down."

"I am not," I snapped.

I knew I was a little. And I kind of did stalk him, but it wasn't the same way he had stalked me. Every logical part of me screamed not to seek him out, but I did anyway.

"Are too."

"What about the girl you came with?"

"A girlfriend of one of my friends. She needed a ride here, but she's leaving with him."

"Oh."

"What? Disappointed you went feral for me for no reason?"

"I did not go feral."

"Maybe not entirely, but you were so, so close. Now I have to figure out what is going to push you over the edge." His lips pressed against my neck, his kiss sending a shock of heat to my core.

A bike pulled in, catching Rook's attention.

Then there was an entire line of them, their engines revving until the ground shook beneath me. I watched as Rook's friends headed to their bikes, everyone slipping on helmets and getting on.

The first newcomer drove past without a helmet, cocking an eyebrow as his eyes raked over us.

"Get on the bike," Rook said through gritted teeth.

"What. Why?"

"We have to go."

"I just got here."

"Too bad," he said, shrugging off his jacket to hand it to me and then grabbing his helmet. "Put these on."

"Why?"

"Because I'm about to speed and if you fall off, maybe you'll survive with these. Put them on, now."

"Rook!" I yelled, shoving them back at him. "If those are my choices, then I won't go with you."

"They already saw you with me, and I promise, they will grab you if they think it will get me to come back for you."

"Would you come get me?"

"When you have the option of getting on the bike right now? No. Either get on the bike or be fucking bait if you think that's a better option than going with me."

"You really wouldn't—"

"Fucking hell, Regan," he said, shoving one of my arms into his jacket. "Now is not the time to work out if I care about you dying or not." He forced my other arm in and zipped the jacket up before slamming the helmet on my head.

"Ouch!" I yelled.

Aiden's bike screamed as it passed us. The blonde girl was on the back again, holding on to him as he lifted the bike up onto one wheel. She made it look so easy, but I was already terrified.

Rook wasn't wasting any time.

"The second I tap your hand twice, hold on tight because your life literally depends on it," he said, getting on the bike and waiting for me to climb up behind him.

Before I could ask any more questions, chaos erupted. The new group of bikers had parked, half of them getting off their bikes and throwing punches at anyone who stood too close, while the other half spun their bikes until smoke clouded my vision. The scene had turned into a frenzied blur of screaming bikes and burning rubber.

By the time I wrapped my arms around Rook, pushing against the tank to hold myself up, he was already pulling out. The rest of his group came down the road with us, six bikes surrounding us as he headed for the highway.

He tapped my hand, reminding me to hold on tight, and I clung to him, trying to suppress a scream as the bike jumped forward. The helmet made a noise trying to connect it, and I tapped the side like I had last time.

"How's it going?" a girl asked. I turned my head, seeing the blonde waving at me from the bike next to us.

"I'm Evie, Rook's sister. Doing okay?"

"Rook has a sister? And yeah, I think so. How long does this go on for?"

"A few miles. Aiden said some of them are following us, though. You might want to let go of Rook a little," she said with a laugh. "He might not be able to breathe."

"Well, he's trying to kill me going this fast."

"Right now they are trying to get us not killed. Rook's good. He won't wreck or anything unless someone else majorly fucks up."

The bikes slowed a bit, enough I could sit up and catch my breath, but I apparently wasn't supposed to because Rook smacked frantically at my hands again.

"Get down," Evie said. "I think they are going to try and lose them before we... You know." Evie moved her thumb across her throat, insinuating they would be cutting their throats. "Just hold on and don't let go until Rook tells you to. And I'm getting off because I don't want to hear you scream."

"What do you—" The click echoed at the same time Rook took off. I did scream.

I squeezed my eyes shut, not wanting to see the speeds we were going as the wind whipped against us. Then I realized I had on Rook's helmet. He had nothing, and we were going faster than I think I had ever gone.

So I screamed again.

TWELVE
ROOK

I had barely made it another half mile down the road when the roar of the two bikes behind us grew louder. The headlights bounced off the small mirrors, and I knew they were too close now. My heart pounded, a mix of adrenaline and fear surging through me. The idea of Regan caught in any crossfire made my stomach flip in an uncomfortable way.

I decided it was time to give up outrunning them. I couldn't see anything at this speed without a helmet, and my stomach churned at pushing Regan this fast when she didn't even know what she was doing. At least she had stopped squeezing me to death a mile ago.

I signaled to the rest of them and pulled off, parking my bike far back as Aiden, Hero, Mason, Kane, and Zack pulled up next to me.

Aiden rolled to a stop, pulling off his helmet, his eyebrows jumping up as Evie grinned at us. No one would have expected Regan to show up at Syndicate. Hell, I hadn't even been expecting it, let alone expected her to be on my bike tonight.

Mason was the one to speak up, though. "Look who you found," he yelled with a grin, looking at Regan, as the other two bikes roared coming down the road. "Does she need me to take her the rest of the way?"

"Mason, if you so much as joke you're taking her home, I will —" My words were cut off as the other two bikes rolled in behind us. It was good for Mason because I at least had somewhere else to put my anger at his suggestion.

Regan looked at me with her big brown eyes and red lips, my jacket hanging heavy on her shoulders and the headlights casting her in a glow and I wished I could enjoy it a second longer.

"Mason," I said. "Take her if you need to. Don't fucking touch her, though."

He gave a sharp nod, no humor in his face this time, because he knew exactly what I meant. He would get Regan out of here if anything went wrong.

"Don't get off the bike unless one of them or me tells you to," I said, pointing at Aiden and then Mason. "Got it?"

She nodded and swallowed, her lips pursing together tight.

I had no time to talk it over with her as the two guys rolled up on their bikes. Hero stepped up next to me.

"I can take the one on the left," he said, making me shake my head.

"Just keep it under control. No gouging or mutilation. I want it over fast and as clean as possible."

I vaguely knew who they were. They were a group like us, working for anyone who needed them. Currently, they were working against us, though, and as much as I would love to bring them back to the garage to figure out who had been stealing the drugs we kept getting hired to find, I didn't have the time or energy tonight with Regan here.

We were paid extensively by anyone who hired us, and we tried to keep who we were quiet, but apparently word got out somehow we were working against them now. It didn't normally happen, but we were becoming well-known enough we would naturally be one of the first places these guys looked. We all knew it could be a consequence of what we did, and we all already knew how to take care of it.

Their boss would be expecting a report back on where we were and where his drugs were now, and we wouldn't let them live long enough to make it back.

It was a simple process which had worked for us for years.

The only difference now was, along with Evie, I had another girl here I needed to take care of. The guys looked over at both of them on the back of Aiden's bike and mine. Regan had long since pulled off her helmet, making it even more obvious how beautiful she was, which wasn't helping.

"Who's the girl tonight? Got a pretty one we can meet?"

Red hot anger sliced through me at the idea of either one of them touching her. That they would even try to get past me made me angry enough, but the thought of them finding out who she was only made it worse.

I knew I wouldn't be the only one willing to use her as leverage to get to her father. The moment anyone learned her name, they'd find a hundred ways to use her. It was probably better she rarely left the house.

She had gotten in this situation to find me, and I sure as fuck wasn't going to let anything happen to her now.

She was my pawn, not theirs.

Which meant they couldn't leave here alive and tell everyone about her. Or us. I knew it could only get worse if we let them go. Next, they would try to find one of us alone, including her, including Evie.

It had happened once before. We had let a guy go, thinking it would be the end of our fight and he would move on, but two days later, he grabbed Evie when she had been alone at the counter of Maverick Moto.

Luckily for us, Evie was a force on her own and she was already clawing his eyes out before Aiden and I walked in.

So we rarely let people walk away in situations like this anymore.

It was all the excuse I needed. I slipped the knife out of my pocket, hiding it in my fist as I threw my first punch. I hit him in the jaw, giving me just enough time to flick the knife out and ram it into the side of his neck. I made it a quick kill, the least mess I could make when we needed to get it over with and move on without a trace of us being here. Blood spurted, coating part of my shirt before I stepped back. The guy choked, the horrible gurgling making my lip curl before he crumpled to the ground.

I could never decide if I liked this part of the job. There wasn't anything particularly enticing to me about killing someone, but it made my life easier. It made every single one of us safer, and I really couldn't argue with it. With some people, I liked it more. The really disgusting ones felt like a service to the world, but for others, I tried to not think about it much.

Hero caught up in his fight, trying to fit in a few more punches before following my lead and killing the guy in front of him the same way.

He always seemed to have a thing about things matching.

I glanced back. Regan's wide eyes were stuck on me, her face paling, before I looked over at Zack and Kane.

"Put them and their bikes over the hill. I have to go." They were already on it, handling everything, as I got back on my bike.

The bikes would be over a mountain, their bodies along with them. The ground would be swiped clean so no one would see any signs of a fight or blood, and any trace of them probably wouldn't be found for weeks, if ever.

Regan didn't say a word, but she shoved the helmet back on.

I pulled back onto the highway, keeping to a little lower of a speed as I headed to her house.

Cameron Fletcher's mansion.

I still couldn't believe Regan, of all people, had to be his daughter.

She had followed me, trying to get closer like I needed her to, and now she had watched me kill the guy. The horror on her face was so clear I wasn't sure how I would recover from this.

I had seen the disgust in her eyes, the shock turning her world upside down. My stomach tightened as I braced myself for the inevitable freakout coming once she got off the bike.

"Of course you know where I live," she said, ripping off the helmet. "I almost forgot you're a stalker." She stumbled off the bike, her legs wobbly like a baby deer once again, nearly collapsing to her knees as she tried to escape. I jumped off, reaching out to help her, but she smacked me away, her wide eyes not leaving my hands. "You're insane. Stay the fuck away from me."

"Regan," I said, stepping closer. "Calm down."

"Calm down? Why would I calm down after what I watched you do?" she yelled, her hands flailing wildly.

"You already knew I did those things. You said it yourself."

"Knowing it was a possibility and seeing it are two *very* different things."

"Maybe. So what? You're running off?"

"Yeah, I'm running off. Goodbye, Rook."

I watched her run down the sidewalk, disappearing into the night. I heard the front door slam shut, and still waited.

"*Fuck,*" I said, knowing I had to go after her. She couldn't stay mad at me, not when I needed her to keep giving me access to her house and her father. If I could find something, anything, to prove how dirty his business dealings were, I would have a chance at ruining him.

I had to find a way to show her I wasn't just a monster—that there was more to me than the violence. At least enough to not put up a fight at me coming back around. I needed her to see the parts of me that were still good, still capable of something beyond destruction.

I had to keep her in my life.

So I went after her.

THIRTEEN

REGAN

Ten minutes later, I had changed and laid back in bed, trying to bury myself in pillows and forget the horrifying sight I had just witnessed.

I froze when the window to my bedroom creaked open. One black boot slipped through, followed by another. My breath caught in my throat as Rook unfurled his body and stepped inside.

I pulled the blankets up, my mind racing between screaming and telling him to leave, but I couldn't bring myself to do either. Paralyzed, I watched as Rook moved closer, his presence filling the room with an unsettling mix of fear and familiarity.

"What are you doing here?" I choked the words out.

"We weren't done talking," he said calmly. "You can't run off like that."

"Yes, we were, and yes, I can. There's nothing else to talk about."

He shook his head, setting his helmet down on my dresser before stalking towards the end of the bed.

"Fine, we won't talk, then."

I wanted to be afraid of him, to feel scared he had followed me, but a part of me was comforted by the fact he cared enough not to let me leave upset.

He stalked closer, making me move up the bed until I pressed myself against the headboard.

"My dad is home tonight. If he catches you, he'll call the cops."

"That's okay. I'm faster than them."

I rolled my eyes. "Then what do you want? You came to kill me next?"

He smiled, shadows twisting over his face in the dim light. This was absolutely what they meant when they say angel of death. He looked too handsome to kill me, but here he was, blood still on his clothes from his last victim, and I could be next.

"You shouldn't be here. You shouldn't come around me anymore. You're a monster," I said, glad my voice didn't shake now.

He grinned, stepping closer. "I don't think you know the half of it, Rebel."

He came to my side of the bed, his eyes locked on mine as he grabbed the bottom of his shirt, lifting it slowly. I gasped, my anger dying out at the sight of his burned, scarred skin, tattoos, and abs. The combination made me lose my train of thought as I tried to take it all in.

"Quite a monstrous sight, isn't it?" he asked.

My mouth dropped open as I reached out, my hands tracing around the edge of the scars. "What happened?"

"Fire, wrecks, drunken nights adding tattoos. All of it. Half of me is scarred from a wreck. I laid my bike down the first time I ran from the police," he said, pointing to the scars on his right side that were healed and faded. "The other half is from a fire."

"Fire? They had to be pretty severe burns to cause that type of scarring."

"They were," he said quietly. He hadn't moved from the spot next to my bed. Even as I touched him, he hadn't come closer.

"Tell me," I whispered.

I couldn't figure out why he chose now, of all times, to show me something so...horrific. My heart pounded as the true horror of it sank in. I did want to understand what had happened to him. Was he truly a monster, or had someone turned him into one?

"A house fire. My parents died, my sister was young. I went to her room to get her and didn't have as much luck getting out."

"Evie," I said. "She made it out okay?"

"Yeah, without a scratch or burn on her."

"Rook," I said, the sadness in my voice obvious.

"Don't talk to me with so much pity. I am fine."

"Maybe now, but at some point, you weren't. Does it hurt now?"

"Sometimes. I have days where it aches, usually after a long night of working or long rides." He gave a tight smile. "It makes it more difficult to get into fistfights now. I learned the hard way you're not as good of a fighter when half your body is more vulnerable."

The words brought a clear image of a younger Rook trying to fight. His arms swinging, his body coiled to win, until he was hit on these scars.

I pushed myself onto my knees, feeling the soft fabric of his shirt under my palms as I pulled it up and over his head before I wrapped my arms around his neck. My heart raced with anticipation and fear as I pulled him down for a kiss, tasting the mint on his breath. He hesitated briefly, but then his hands found their way to my hips, gripping them tightly as he kissed me back with a fierce intensity. A growl rumbled in his throat as he pushed me down onto the bed, pinning my wrists above my head as he kissed along my jaw.

"You feel so bad for me, you're kissing me? You think I need that level of pity?"

"Yes," I breathed.

He stood back up and grabbed my ankles. I yelped as he dragged me to the end of the bed and he dropped to his knees in front of me.

"Should I take advantage of that? Make you feel so bad for me, I take everything I want from you right now?"

"Yes," I said, trying to catch my breath.

His hands trailed up my legs, stopping at my thighs.

"And you want to be fucked by a monster? You want my ruined body on yours? You want my hands on you when, ten minutes ago, you were scared of them?"

I nodded. "Maybe you aren't the monster." He pushed at the oversized shirt I had slipped into, bunching it at my waist and smiling when he saw nothing underneath. "Maybe I am."

He glanced up at me with heavy eyes as he grabbed my hips and yanked me further down the bed until I was perched on the corner.

In one smooth motion, my legs were thrown over his shoulders and his head buried between my thighs.

I gasped at the sudden heat of his mouth against me, the way his tongue moved along me in one rough motion. He didn't hesitate, or give any light touch. There was nothing except him taking exactly what he wanted. He reached my clit, the burning need to have him moving harder and faster set me on edge, and he matched it immediately.

My skin prickled at the feel of his hand sliding up my bare thigh, leaving a trail of goosebumps in its wake. I should have hated the fast pace, but all I could think about was how badly he wanted to taste me. It felt as if he couldn't wait any longer, and I liked each confident touch.

His fingers found their way to my entrance, making me gasp

as he pushed two fingers inside. I met his intense gaze. He had angled us at the corner of the bed, giving me a full view of what him in the tall mirror sitting in the corner of my room.

I couldn't look away. The view of his head buried between my legs was better at this angle. I could see the muscles in his back flex as his arms tightened on my thighs, the tattoos moving with him.

"Keep watching. Watch how much you love to get off on the tongue of a monster."

"Stop," I breathed. "Stop calling yourself that."

"Why? You just did."

"I take it back."

"You will regret it. Don't scream, Rebel. If your dad walks in here, I will have the perfect excuse to kill him."

"He's not actually here," I said. "I lied, so you can't kill him even if you wanted to."

He almost went to say something, but his head dropped again, licking and sucking like he couldn't get enough and I couldn't take enough. My hands fisted into his hair, pulling him hard against me. He groaned in satisfaction, so I pulled harder.

I could feel the orgasm getting closer, the build-up like walking to a cliff edge, and then panic took over. Something about it felt like too much, like I couldn't handle what was about to happen.

I shrieked, flipping myself over to crawl up the bed, but Rook jumped forward, his mouth coming down over my clit again, his hand pushing me until my face fell against the mattress.

"Where the hell do you think you're going?"

My hands fisted into the sheets and I yelled against the blankets as he continued his carnal attack. He flipped me onto my back again. "Trying to run, Rebel? You're not going anywhere until you coat my tongue in cum."

"Rook," I moaned as he buried his tongue in me again. This time, I let it build, let it take over as my brain turned to nothing but screaming with need for relief. My hands buried in his hair again, pulling him hard against my swollen clit as every muscle tightened. "More, Rook, now. More," I nearly yelled, the teasing, agonizing feeling demanding relief.

His fingers pushed into me again as he covered my clit. My hips lifted off the bed as I gasped for air. The relief felt overwhelming, black dots coating my vision as my body tightened. My fingers pulled tighter, the rush of hot liquid between my legs feeling like too much as I finally fell back to the mattress.

He moved up the bed, crawling over top of me.

"What a good girl, taking what I give you. Now taste how much you like my mouth on you," he said, his lips dropping to mine, making me taste myself on his tongue. "You made a fucking mess, baby. All over my face and the bed. I would apologize, but I think it's the hottest thing I've ever seen."

I could feel my cheeks flame, but the room was dark enough to hide it. My chest heaved with heavy breaths as my hands ran down his sides, one moving over marred skin.

"Does it hurt?"

"Not much. It probably bothers you more," he whispered against my lips.

He shifted, pulling a knife out of his jeans and laying it down on my nightstand, kissing me as he did. My eyes flicked to it and back to him.

I almost asked why he set it there, but then he dropped on the bed next to me like he couldn't hold himself up anymore.

"You're tired?" I asked.

"Exhausted."

I laid there in the quiet for a few minutes before I couldn't keep my thoughts in.

"You didn't have a helmet or jacket. You gave me yours."

"Maybe that answers your question whether I care if you die or not."

I sat there in silence, staring up at the ceiling as my thoughts on the man next to me raged.

The door slammed open, making me jump. Harper's face appeared in the doorway, but it was Rook who got my attention.

He sprang up, grabbing the knife from my nightstand and moving it directly over my chest. Poised and ready to plunge it into me if he wanted.

My chest heaved, each rise causing the tip of the knife to graze against my shirt.

I kept watching as he glanced from me to Harper and back at me.

"Fuck," he muttered. "Sorry. I thought it could be someone else, Regan."

"Who is coming through my door that is going to make you *kill* me?" He had set the knife back down, but I grabbed it now. My hands went clammy. Anger and fear coursed through me. I had trusted this man enough to do what he had just done. My hands started to sweat as I held the knife. "Get out."

"Regan, relax, I wasn't going to hurt you."

"You were about to shove a knife into my chest!" I yelled.

Harper watched, still frozen in the doorway.

"I had it *look* like I was going to. I wouldn't hurt you. And no, I'm not going to hurt you, either," he said to Harper.

She didn't respond, watching wide eyed as I got up.

"No, because I'll cut you," I said, facing him now.

Rook only grinned as he slipped on his shirt. "And I'll let you, baby."

"Don't call me that."

"And here I thought you liked me being a gentleman. Especially after I made you come. Fine." He stepped around the bed, and I held up the knife.

He didn't care, though. He pushed against the knife until it pressed between us, the blade on his chest.

"Go ahead," he said, smiling. "Plunge it deep into my chest. Watch me bleed out on the floor right here. I would never bother you again, but you would have a mess to clean up depending on where you stab me." Reaching up, he grabbed a handful of my hair and forced my head back. I looked up at him, trying to press the knife harder, but scared I would actually hit skin. "I'm not going to hurt you, Regan."

He was rough as he kissed me again, biting once at my lower lip, but I stayed rooted to the ground, his hand still wrapped in my hair. "I'll see you later, *baby.*"

"Don't come back."

"Text me when you need me. For any needs." He smiled at Harper and then back to me. "Murder. Orgasms. I'm here."

"You forgot your knife," I said.

"Keep it."

"Why? Some weird gift to help protect me from you?" I asked, the words dripping with sarcasm.

He grabbed his helmet, already heading to the window.

"Sure, Rebel. All here to protect you. Not that it would be careless to carry a murder weapon around with me. *Definitely* not that."

"Rook!" I yelled.

He shoved his helmet on, waving as he slipped out the window without another word.

"Rook!" I yelled again, but he was already gone.

As the adrenaline faded, anger surged through me. I had invited Rook into my life, and now it felt like I had crossed a line I could never uncross.

FOURTEEN

ROOK

The next night, I watched from the tree line as Regan stepped out into the night. The light from the sconces on the house made her flicker in the shadows. She had dressed up tonight with her dark hair pinned up, and the red dress she wore clung to her perfectly. It would be hard to miss her, impossible even, and it would make it so much easier to find her when she got to the dinner.

The black BMW she seemed to always use pulled up, its sleek surface reflecting the moonlight. I couldn't tell from here if she had a driver or if it was her dad behind the wheel, but it didn't matter. Cameron would be with her at some point tonight.

I had found out Cameron would attend a dinner party at his country club tonight, and Regan would be there with him. From what I could gather, she was nothing more than an accessory at his parties. Most people knew nothing about her besides she liked art, and her dad was smart enough to let everyone leave it at that.

I still couldn't believe I hadn't known about her. I spent more time watching Cameron and his business than her, and he seemed to keep her locked away from what I could gather. When she did attend these things, she was invisible to others.

Not anymore, though. Now that I knew her, it would be impossible for her to be invisible. Even if she wanted to be.

I had stuck a tracker on the car even though I wasn't worried about losing them tonight. It would at least help me keep tabs on her whenever she left the house. Following her car from a distance had become a routine this week, although she barely went out. It seemed like, aside from these parties, she really didn't have much involvement in his business. I still wasn't sure how much she actually knew about her dad and his dealings, but she did like to stay hidden.

It barely took ten minutes to get to the country club's main building. I stayed back, making sure she wouldn't hear the bike rev behind them. Regan got out, moving gracefully as she walked up the large steps. Her laughter echoed in the night air as she talked on the phone before quickly slipping it into her bag.

Her face dropped for a second before an elegant smile spread across across it.

I followed her movements through the large windows in the building's foyer. A guy around my age stopped her, taking a long look to admire her dress and body before leaning in with a smile. I rolled my eyes, still watching as he flirted and touched her until she finally broke apart from him and disappeared into the dining hall.

My pulse quickened, the thrill of hunting her down again surging through my veins. I made my way to a side entrance, slipping inside unnoticed. I'd been here a few times to meet with people and knew the layout enough to know where I could and couldn't go to stay hidden. The staff here were used to serving the elite and didn't have time to pay attention to me as I stalked through the side halls down to one of the smaller rooms I knew well.

The room sat empty when I slipped in, the soft glow of a single light casting long shadows across it. Shelves of old books lined one wall, and a heavy oak desk sat in the corner, but the main attraction was the wooden pool table filling the middle of the room. I could hear the faint murmurs of the dinner in the distance, the clinking of glasses and muted conversations.

I pulled out my phone as I leaned back on the pool table.

ROOK

Come to the back office. The last door on the right.

She didn't say anything for a few minutes, but I watched the three little dots pop up.

REGAN

Why?

ROOK

Would you rather I come there?

REGAN

No.

ROOK

You have one minute.

Unless, of course, you need more time to flirt.

REGAN

I wasn't flirting?

ROOK

Liar.

Regan walked in less than five minutes later, her eyes widening as she spotted me setting up the pool table.

"What are you doing here?" she asked. The surprise in her tone should be expected, but I didn't love the way my heart rate picked up at the curiosity in her voice.

"Want to play?" I asked, holding out a cue for her.

She snatched it, her eyebrow arching. "Yes, because I know for a fact I can beat you."

"Wow, someone is cocky tonight. Is it the dress?"

"What about the dress?"

My lips curved into a smile, looking her over. "I'm pretty sure it was made to make men crawl after you. I'm surprised you don't have a little line of them begging to see what's underneath," I said, lining up my first shot. As the balls scattered across the table, I kept my eyes on her, noting every detail. "So who all is here tonight?" I asked, my voice calm as I lined up another shot. "Besides the guy you were flirting with."

She glanced at me, her eyebrow arching up again. She had every right to be skeptical, and I almost liked it more. "The usual crowd. Business associates of my father's, some old friends. And again, I wasn't flirting. Why do you ask?"

"I'm curious who my competition is," I said, sinking another ball. "Your dad seems like a busy man. Must be important to keep up appearances."

She narrowed her eyes slightly, but stepped up for her turn. "He is. Always working, always shaking hands and closing new deals. What about you? You're always busy, so what are you doing here tonight?"

I leaned over her back as she hit another ball, my voice dropping to a low murmur. "Maybe I wanted to see you."

"You expect me to believe that?" she asked with a small laugh. "You're lying."

I wanted to laugh and play it off, but I was starting to think it wasn't completely a lie.

"Okay, fine. You caught me. I wanted to know more about your father's business. Heard he's got a lot going on."

Her eyes flew to mine, and I could see the moment her guard was back up. "And why would you care about that?" she snapped.

I shrugged, trying to calm her down again. "Call it professional curiosity. After all, knowing the right people can be very... beneficial. I like information. Maybe he has it."

"He doesn't. Not for you, at least."

Her shoulders stayed squared, and I knew she wasn't going to back down again easily. "What about you? Do you know all his secrets?"

She didn't look at me, her hard gaze staying on the table as I took my turn.

"No."

"Hmm. Interesting. Why don't you?"

"Would I tell you if I did?"

"True."

She stepped up for her turn, hitting the next ball with a perfect shot. Then she did it again, and again. Finally, she sunk the last ball and won.

"I want to say you hustled me, but you were honest about kicking my ass. I think I'll blame the dress."

"Do you always underestimate women in dresses?" she asked, her eyebrows jumping up.

"No," I said, laughing now. "I don't usually, but then again, I don't know if I've ever seen a woman look so delicious in a dress."

Her nose scrunched. "What are you? A cannibal? You're always saying how delicious I look, like you would eat me."

I groaned, biting down on the inside of my cheek hard. "You literally set these up for me, Rebel." I mindlessly hit a ball, watching it roll effortlessly into the hole. "Of course I would fucking eat you," I said, leaning down until my lips brushed her neck. "And I already know you are, in fact, *delicious*."

Her cheeks flamed, and my heart flipped that this was only the start of it happening. "I don't need anyone...doing that."

"No? What about the guy out there who can't keep his hands off you? I think he's starving."

"He wants to take me out on a date. Is there a problem?"

"Not at all. Interesting, you're fine with him all over you, because what do you have this for then?" I asked, pulling out the fun little toy I had found in her nightstand when I searched her bedroom earlier. "Was this something you needed because of Elliot, or something you keep for all your really *good* dates?"

I held up the vibrator, nearly waving it in her face. Her mouth dropped open, the red on her cheeks burning brighter now. It wasn't too big, easy enough I could fit it in my back pocket, and I had been surprised to find it there.

She reached out, trying to grab it from my hands, but I pulled back, laughing now.

"What the hell? You went into my room and stole it?" she shrieked. "Give it back!"

"Yes, I did," I said, grinning harder.

"You can't break into my room, and you can't steal my things."

"I can and I did."

"But why?" Her eyes were wide and her chest heaved. She looked so mad, but she didn't seem to know what to do with all the anger. I grabbed her waist, setting her up on the table and standing in front of her.

"I went in looking for something. Imagine my surprise when I found this instead. A little smaller than me, but it really helps the ego."

"You are insane."

"Because of this?" I asked, running it up her thigh now and taking the dress with it. "On the list of insane things I do, this seems like it would barely make the cut."

"Rook," she warned, but stayed planted in place. "Give it back."

"Damn, trying to get off before the date? I really don't blame you. I'm sure these guys, along with Elliot, are a little more selfish than a girl would hope for."

"And you wouldn't be?" she asked, the smirk on her face having an edge to it. "You think the girls you sleep with aren't running home to finish the job with this? Please tell me your ego isn't that big."

I moved it between her legs until her thighs fell open.

"Again, you set these up so perfectly. My ego is big, but I have something else that's bigger."

I thought she would be angrier, but she only smiled, smacking my arm and then snatching it out of my hand. "I don't care how big it is. If you don't know what you're doing, I have no use for it."

"Hey, give it back," I said, nearly laughing. "Finders keepers and all that." I reached for it again, but she shoved it hard into her bag. "I wasn't done with it."

"You definitely were. Now I have to throw it out. Who knows what you did with it?"

"When is your date with that guy, so I know when to deliver a new one? Or should I come over after?" I slid her dress higher, showing off one perfect thigh, and continued on until I saw red lace. "Planning on someone seeing these tonight?"

Her mouth fell open. "It's not any of your business."

I grinned. "It is now."

Male voices carried down the hallway. This wasn't how I wanted my reintroduction with her dad to go, and I had no way to know who was heading this way. Not that it wouldn't be fun to have him see his daughter lifting her dress up for me, but it wasn't nearly enough, and I needed him to not know about me for a little longer.

"Saved just in time," I said, lifting her down.

"In time for what?"

"Just in time, before I laid you back and spread you out on the table as a snack."

"Oh," she said, and I smiled harder. It really didn't sound like she would be against the idea.

"Maybe a rain check?" I asked, heading towards the door to our left. It led to a small hallway, which would lead me to another door right to my bike.

"You're leaving?"

"Unfortunately."

"And you still aren't going to tell me anything about yourself?" she asked.

"Unfortunately. I'm sure you'll see me around soon."

"See you around stalking me?"

"Exactly. Have a good night, Rebel. Text me when you go on the date. I'll make sure you aren't left unsatisfied for the night."

I ducked out just as the doors opened. I could hear male voices talking to her and she responded, but the door muffled everything, and I cursed it. I had come to learn more about Regan, but more importantly, I needed to learn about Cameron. I basically failed at both.

Smiling to myself, I swung onto my bike.

All I learned is that Regan likes toys.

Which, I guess in the grand scheme of this entire revenge plan, wasn't bad information to know.

FIFTEEN
REGAN

A week went by without a word from Rook or any sign of him randomly showing up. I told myself it could be a good thing, but the loneliness that vanished when he came around quickly returned. I had endless days of being alone, unless Harper could hang out.

And me being the socially pathetic girl I am, I kept looking out the window to see if Rook would show up. Could a person really be so lonely she wanted a stalker? I guess I couldn't consider Rook a stalker anymore when I kept inviting him in every chance I could.

I groaned as I slipped on my new dress, the pink fabric hugging me, the sides and back cut out with black lace that I loved. At least I would be the prettiest pathetic girl at the ball, I thought with a roll of my eyes.

My dad had another dinner party to go to tonight, and he had invited me to join him. Excitement and a flicker of hope bubbled up inside me at the thought of him finally taking me more seriously. And possibly at the idea that Rook might show up again. I hadn't really minded him showing up or the game of pool even though I was still a little annoyed he went through my room.

Either way, tonight could end up going better than ever. Every time my dad asked me to go, I couldn't contain the anticipation. Maybe this would be the night he'd tell me I could finally start learning the business, that he trusted me enough to let me in on the secrets and responsibilities he shouldered. I imagined us talking it all out and him introducing me to his associates, acknowledging me as his equal. I imagined I could walk into a room and not just be his daughter, but be Regan Fletcher.

But there was always a shadow of doubt. Each invitation felt like a double-edged sword, bringing both hope and the fear of disappointment. The countless nights I spent getting ready, dressing up, and perfecting my smile, only to end up feeling like a decorative accessory, haunted me. I couldn't quite bring myself to believe this would be the night when I had wasted so many on the thought.

The memory of previous parties lingered—me, standing on the fringes, trying to engage in conversations which always seemed just out of reach. The sting of being overlooked and the frustration of not being taken seriously gnawed at me. Yet, despite the recurring disappointment, I clung to hope. So tonight, like a hundred other nights, I would get ready, go with him, and act like I could handle everything. Maybe this time, it wouldn't be just an act.

I clung to that sliver of hope and put my earrings in.

I would always have my doubts, but I still hoped.

That hope died fast when I made it down the stairs to find him in casual clothes with his phone glued to his hand. The sight felt like a punch to the gut, my excitement deflating instantly.

"I have to go," he said without even looking up. "I have a last-minute...appointment. The doctor called and needed me to fly to Boston for an appointment tomorrow."

"What about the dinner?" I asked, hating my voice tinged with desperation.

"You go. Shake all the hands and excuse my absence. I can't miss this."

"Aren't they expecting you, though?" I tried to keep the frustration out of my voice, but it seeped through. It wasn't his fault he's sick, but between never spending any time together, not getting any knowledge of his company, and always having to go to these things alone, I only grew more getting frustrated.

He glanced at me briefly, then back at his phone. "No one is going to mind me not being there when you are. You look beautiful, Regan. You'll be the center of the party."

"But I thought you could introduce me to everyone? I'd like to get to know who you work with and this would be perfect," I insisted, my heart sinking further.

"Yes, but the doctor seems to think I need a few more tests. I think he has some concerns from last time. Sorry, Regan. You can understand my health is more important. You seem to be more upset every time."

"Of course, your health is more important. I mean, I understand. I had just expected to go with someone. It's weird being there alone. I would have invited Harper."

"You could still invite her," he said, checking his watch and starting towards the door.

"Yeah, I guess I'll have to. I'll see you in a few days, then?"

"Back by Sunday, possibly. I'll let you know." He nearly walked out the door, but seemed to think better of it and came back, kissing my cheek once and then disappearing.

As the door closed, I stood there, feeling a mix of anger and sadness well up inside me. I had spent hours preparing, hoping tonight would be different, only to be let down once again. The disappointment was now a familiar ache, but it didn't hurt any less.

I sank onto the bottom step, staring at the spot where he had been. Why did I keep hoping for something different? I thought of all the times I had been in this exact position, dressed up and ready, only to be cast aside for another "urgent" appointment or meeting. The loneliness wrapped around me like a suffocating blanket.

I pulled out my phone, ready to text Harper, knowing she would at least try to lift my spirits, but clicked it off instead. I would go to the party, put on a brave face, and play the role I was expected to play. I couldn't run a company if I couldn't go to a party alone.

I would try again.

Like I did every other time.

I took a deep breath, wiping away the tear that had escaped, and stood up. If my father wouldn't introduce me to his world, I would have to find my own way in. Tonight, I would be the perfect guest, and maybe someone would take notice of me for who I was, not just as Cameron Fletcher's daughter.

The plan I had made of being a perfect guest was short-lived.

By the time I made it inside, I had talked myself down again, slumping my shoulders and trying to hide away.

The entire room and entrance were as grand as the people inside—rich men who didn't bother to look my way, unless they were creepily checking me out, and women who scowled when I approached their group, trying to insert myself into their conversations.

I didn't actually know anyone enough to start a private conversation, and I couldn't think of one thing I had in common enough to talk about with these strangers.

How ironic that I had started to get out of the house more,

only to have even less to talk about with people. A conversation about a game of tennis they had played over the weekend felt a little different from one about my stalker, who I seemed to have a crush on, taking me out on his bike.

I made my way to the table with the two seats reserved for me and my dad. The table was already half full, and I smiled at the others as I took a seat. They gave tight smiles back, but no one introduced themselves.

This was hell.

And further proof that my dad could be right. Maybe I couldn't handle taking over the business. He dealt with more powerful men than the ones at this table, and I couldn't even handle this.

"Are you here alone?" the guy across from me asked.

"Yes," I said, trying to straighten up. "Cameron Fletcher, my dad, was supposed to be here with me tonight."

The made grumbled something I couldn't understand and rolled his eyes.

"So he threw some lipstick on his daughter to parade around and thought that would keep them happy?" he asked with a grunting laugh. "People were expecting him tonight and they won't appreciate a stand-in."

"What a rude way to talk to the woman who could ruin your life, Williams," someone said, the voice dripping with menace. "I suggest apologizing before she lets it slip what you do on Thursday nights with all the money you skim off the top from your department."

Williams' nostrils flared as he looked past me. I turned back, meeting Rook's eyes. The playful glint in them made me suppress a smile. My eyes raked over him, the cut black suit making him fit in just enough besides that tattoos covering his hands and peaking out from his collar.

"Is this seat taken?" Rook asked, his tone suddenly casual, as if he hadn't just threatened to possibly ruin this man's life somehow.

"No," I managed to say, my heart racing.

Williams still hadn't said anything, and apparently, Rook wasn't happy with that. "Did you hear me?" he asked, pulling out his chair. The black suit making it impossible to stop staring as he sat down next to me.

"Sorry, Ms. Fletcher. It was more of a joke, but my apologies."

"It wasn't a joke," Rook said bluntly, his tone ice-cold. "And even if it was, she's not the brunt of any joke."

"I am sorry. I hope there won't be any issue with you saying anything?"

"If you would leave us alone, I'll keep my mouth shut," I said, feeling brave with Rook next to me.

"I'm going to go get a drink," Williams said, shuffling away fast and taking his still-full cup with him.

"What is going on?" I hissed as Rook leaned closer. "What are you doing here? And more importantly, where does he go on Thursdays?"

Rook smiled, his face softer now. "He takes money from government accounts and goes to the strip club. Barely a big deal in the grand scheme of things, but enough to possibly get him fired. I knew it would scare him off."

I stifled a laugh, pressing against his arm for a second. "And you being here?"

"Someone told me you showed up alone and didn't look pleased about it."

I looked around, trying to see anyone that could be here with Rook. "You have someone watching me?"

"I work with over half of this room, Regan. A hundred dollars and I could get a list of everyone here in minutes. You already know I've been following you. Is this surprising?"

"I guess not. So you're a criminal and work with tons of the upstanding people here? How?"

He took a sip of my drink, cocking an eyebrow at the fruity cocktail before taking another sip. "They are glorified criminals. They basically all do the same things I do, but they pay other people to actually get the blood on their hands."

"Please don't remind me of bloody hands," I said, my nose involuntarily scrunching.

He gave a harsh laugh, lifting his hands to show me there currently wasn't blood on them. "You don't seem to mind my hands doing anything else."

"Shh," I said, smacking his leg under the table. He grabbed my hand, forcing it onto his thigh.

"Does this mean you are finally learning discretion?" he asked, moving my hand higher.

"Well, yes, in places like this, I know how to keep quiet."

He smirked as my hand trailed over his groin, feeling the hard length of him. "Could we put how quiet you can be here to the test?"

"Rook," I said, my teeth gritted together as he moved my hand back and forth over him. "Why are you this turned on right now?"

"Because someone had to wear a dress that clings to her body. A body I've had to watch writhe and fall apart under my tongue," he said. "I'm dying to get another taste."

"Why did you come here, Rook? I can't imagine this is a normal place for you, and based on the stares, I'm going to assume everyone else agrees." I only grew more annoyed with the fake answers, and I didn't think he would be telling me the truth soon.

"Because you shouldn't be alone here."

"Why?"

"You're the daughter of one of the most powerful men here

tonight. You should be asking why you're allowed to go anywhere like this alone."

"So you are here to what? Be my bodyguard? Ironic when you're the one trying to kill me."

"You have an obsession with wondering if I'm trying to kill you or keep you safe."

"It's a legitimate concern. You could do both."

"That's true," he said. "Honestly, I'm probably putting you in more danger being here than if I hadn't come."

"How?"

"Because there are going to be plenty of conversations tonight about why I came here. I've never shown my face at any place like this. Anyone connected to me in any way is going to worry about what's happening. They are going to be worried someone pissed me off, and me being here with you will make them wonder why. There will be plenty of questions over the next few days."

"So you're not going to kill me or protect me. You are going to put me in danger and then leave?"

"I'm not doing any of those."

"Then what?" I asked a little too loud, making his eyebrows jump.

"What happened to discretion?"

I only stared and waited. He had to have a better reason to have come tonight, and I doubted any of the reasons he gave were the truth.

"Fine," he said through gritted teeth. "I came because I didn't like you here alone. That's not a lie. I also like learning about you."

"I thought you said I was boring."

"You are," he said with a grin. "But I think I might be jealous of your type of boring." He stood up, seemingly uncomfortable, as he brushed off his jacket and ran a hand through his hair. "Come on. I'm showing you how to handle this place."

"And how would you know how to handle a place like this? I'm sure they are much different people here than in the places you meet them," I said, trying to keep my voice steady despite his confession rattling me.

"Doesn't matter. They are still the same people with the same secrets." His hand moved to my lower back, sliding once down over my ass and back up. The intimate touch made my skin tingle, and I had to fight the urge to lean into him. "You're teasing a starving man," he groaned. "Let's go to another room so I can taste you again."

I tried to keep my cool, even as my pulse quickened. "Keep helping by telling me all these secrets, and maybe I will let you."

He gave a satisfied groan, the sound reverberating through me. "See, you already know what you're doing, and how to handle these people. Use everything you fucking have to make me bend. Force me into a corner, so my only way out is to do what you tell me. You are always playing a game here. Every single one of these powerful men can be backed into that corner and all of them will cower at your feet if you say the right words."

"And you know the right words?" I asked, almost in awe of his confidence. I had walked in here and wanted to hide. He walked in and wanted everyone to see him, for all of them to wonder what he was doing here.

For all of them to fear him.

"For a lot of them, yes. For the rest of them, I will someday." His eyes glinted with a dangerous promise, one that both thrilled and terrified me.

I wondered if he came here to learn secrets about me. If he came here trying to learn things to use against me one day. He would be disappointed to find out there weren't many dirty secrets to learn. So far, my dirtiest secret was him.

"So if you have the information I need to make them cower,

how do I back *you* into the corner to make you tell me those things?" I leaned in, tilting my head as our breaths mingled.

He grinned, a rumble coming from his chest, as he pulled me hard against his side. "That's part of the game, Rebel. You have to dig and dig until you find the right thing to say to make me fall."

"And how will I know what the right thing is? Do I keep threatening you until one works?"

"You could, but after one or two attempts with the wrong thing, these men would be bored and not take you seriously anymore." His eyes didn't leave mine, the intense gaze making my legs weak.

"So how do I know?" I pressed, wanting to understand the mechanics of this dangerous game he played so effortlessly.

"You train yourself. You get ruthless. The more devastating the information, the better. Could it ruin lives? Could it take away money or power? You figure out what they crave, what they need to survive in their world, and you threaten it."

"You need your motorcycle. Do I threaten to break it?" I asked, half-joking.

"That wouldn't make me bend to your will. That would get you punished." His voice dropped, making a shiver run down my spine.

I thought it over more. The ways he could punish me could range from painful torture to being tied up and forced to come. It really could be a good thing.

I ran my hand down his stomach, stopping right above his belt. "What if I told everyone here how desperate you were to taste me again?"

He smiled, a wicked glint in his eyes as he turned on me. "I would put your ass on a table and show them. I don't care if people watch. If anything, I prefer it. Let them see my head under your dress as you moan and scream for more. They would love how you wrap your fingers in my hair and force me harder against you, desperate for my tongue."

Heat swept over me, the sudden wetness between my thighs unsurprising as my body tightened with want. I had to change the subject before I did pull him to a side room.

"Well, I suck at this," I said, groaning as I slumped into him more. The weight of the night already felt heavy and being so bad at this wasn't helping my mood.

"It's a skill. You have to practice." He turned to face me, ordering us two more drinks, but my mouth watered looking at him. He always had a dangerous level of attractiveness, but the black suit took it to another level, making it nearly impossible for me to resist.

"I'll give you a few pieces of information so you can practice."

"For free?"

"Nothing is free, Rebel. But in the meantime of me waiting on that payment, let's go piss off some very rich men."

Sixteen
Rook

The backless dress she had on was already threatening to break my willpower. The feel of her bare skin under my fingertips kept going to my head, each touch sending a shock through me. We were talking with another rich asshole of a man I had never worked with, but knew all about. It should keep my attention to listen for any new information I could dig up on these people, but my entire focus remained on her.

I leaned down to her ear, ignoring the way he eyed us. He seemed to know me, enough I could see the concern on his face, at least.

"I don't work with him for a reason," I said, biting at her earlobe. "He's disgusting. Likes them so young there is an active police case being built against him."

Her eyes went wide, still locked on him. The panic that rose on his face was so clear I almost laughed. "Well, tell your dad I said hello," he said, trying to end the conversation.

She scrunched her nose. "I'd prefer not to. Do you work with my dad?"

"Well, yes? We've done a few business deals together."

"I don't think you will be anymore," she said, her voice steady and cold. "I think we prefer working with people of age... Unlike you, apparently."

My knees almost gave out from the sheer perfection of it. The way his eyes nearly bulged out of his head, the way he shuffled off so fast.

"Did I do it right?" she asked, watching in confusion as he disappeared into the crowd.

"It was perfect, and I'm uncomfortably turned on right now."

"It seems like he got scared and ran off. What would that accomplish?"

I laughed, angling her to the side of the room. "Fear. The idea you aren't going to take their shit like how they were treating you when you got here. You want to be respected, right? It's a fast way to show them you shouldn't be messed with. Do it a few more times and word will get around. Soon people are going to wonder if you are going to work with them or ruin their lives, so they will do what they need to keep you happy."

"But he isn't backed into a corner?"

"Why not? He knows you know. If you went to him right now and asked for something, he would probably give it to you. You might have to push him more, but you could remind him how much you know and that you would keep your mouth shut for a price or a favor."

"Hmm," she said, looking around at the rest of them. "And this is what you do? You spend your days finding out this information to hold on to it until it's needed?"

"Sometimes. Other times, I sell it. If you wanted to take down your biggest competitor, wouldn't you pay for information on them to do that?"

"That's scary, and efficient."

I had planned to come tonight either way. I thought it could be a good time to see Cameron Fletcher and see if he even recognized me, but when I had gotten word she came alone, I still thought it was a good idea. What better way to get closer to her than to save her from a night of being fed to the wolves?

But now, I stood here telling her more and more information, not expecting anything in return. Each time she tried to bully one of these guys, I was mesmerized. I really shouldn't be this interested in the girl I'm using to get my revenge, but she seemed to be begging to climb to the top, and no one wanted to help her.

I spent the rest of the dinner with her next to me, asking questions and me answering every single one without hesitation.

I glanced at my phone. It was almost ten at night now. I still had plenty to do tonight, and with how easily I kept slipping her information, I figured it would be better if I stopped talking completely before I said something I couldn't take back.

For someone whose world demanded tight lips, I somehow forgot all the rules tonight.

"I have to go," I said, her face falling. "I have more work tonight."

"Okay. Are you coming back around soon?"

I smirked, shoving my phone back in my pocket. "Are you asking if I will be stalking around your house soon?"

She bit at her lip, looking at the crowd instead of me. "Maybe."

"Then my answer will also be maybe. Leaving soon?"

"Yeah, I'll text the driver to come back around and get me."

"Alright. See you later, Rebel."

She watched as I headed back out, but I fought not to look back.

I thought I would be fine to get to my bike, change, and head back out to get work done, but I got on and pulled out in the wrong direction, turning left when I should have been turning right. My hands gripped the handlebars tightly, knuckles white with tension. Every instinct told me to turn around and go back.

To spend one boring night with Regan and see if I liked it as much as I thought I would. But I couldn't afford to be weak. Not now.

I knew she wouldn't be too far behind me and, with adding a stop, I needed to be quick.

Each moment I spent near her chipped away at me, and I had to remember why I was doing this. My parents, my sister, our ruined lives—Cameron Fletcher caused all of it, and Regan was only my ticket to him, nothing more.

I made my first stop at the bakery and headed back out, racing through traffic until I pulled up in front of the giant Fletcher Mansion. The sight of it brought back memories of everything I had lost and everything I kept fighting for. The contrast between my world and hers was stark, and I needed to remember it.

It took me less than five minutes to get in, set the box on her pillow, and slip back out. I stood there a second too long, looking at her peaceful room, and a pang of guilt hit me. Could she really be this innocent in all of this? Could she really have no clue how deranged her own father could be? She seemed more than shocked at what I did. Wouldn't it be less surprising if she knew her dad was worse?

As I drove away, I couldn't help but feel a mix of satisfaction and dread. I kept getting closer to her, closer to my goal, but I wasn't sure how much longer I could keep them separate enough. Technically, I wanted to be around her, and it worked perfectly for my plan, but it didn't stop the small gnawing in my gut that she would hate me soon.

I shook my head, trying to clear the confusion. This wasn't about me or her—it was about justice, about righting the wrongs done to my family. But as the mansion disappeared in my rearview mirror, I couldn't shake the thought that the line between my revenge and this obsession was blurring, and I worried I might be losing more than just my focus.

SEVENTEEN
REGAN

Rook was still following me. I hadn't been sure if he had truly grown bored with me, but then I got home last night to find the box of cookies on my pillows and knew they were from him.

So instead of waiting around for him to show up again, I decided it was time that I did a little stalking myself. I didn't know much about him, and I couldn't find anything about when the next Syndicate bike night would be. He had mentioned that he and his friends owned a motorcycle shop in town and I knew what his bike looked like, so I felt like I had a pretty good chance of finding him.

The driver pulled up, and I slid into the back seat. He had driven me a few times, so I knew him well enough, but I still leaned forward, ready to give him instructions. "I have to do something today that I would prefer my dad not know about. Is that an issue?"

"No, ma'am. Not an issue at all. You called me for the day. I work for you today."

"Perfect. I want to start by driving past a few shops. Then we might be out for the day. I'm not sure yet."

"Not a problem," he said, pulling out. "Just tell me where to go first."

We drove around for another two hours, and I still had no luck. We had gone past three different mechanic shops which were definitely not Rook's, and I got more frustrated with each one. We were headed back across town when I saw the bike a few cars ahead of us.

"Wait!" I yelled before the driver turned. "Follow that guy."

"On the bike?"

"Yeah, stay close to him."

The bike wasn't blacked out like Rook's, but something about it still caught my attention. Then I realized the helmet and jacket matched the one Rook wore. It wasn't a far-fetched idea to think he had multiple bikes, but I still wasn't sure it could be him.

We followed for a few blocks, watching as he weaved through traffic before we would catch back up to him. Another three blocks and we were right behind him, waiting for the light to change so we could turn left.

The rider hit the kickstand, leaning the bike to get off. I held my breath as he walked back to my car, opening his jacket and pulling out a gun as he used it to tap on the driver's window.

"Why are you following me?" he asked, setting the gun along the windowsill.

"He's not looking for anyone!" I yelled, feeling bad for my driver. "I am!"

His head cocked, the helmet still not showing me if it was Rook, but I was almost positive it was. He stood back up, taking a few steps to the back door and pulling it open. He leaned down in the open door, not saying a word as he watched me.

Finally, he pulled off the helmet. Dark hair fell over his forehead, the angry, tired look in his eyes almost making me feel bad for how tired he seemed.

"Rook," I breathed in relief.

"Are you stalking me, Rebel?"

"Trying, but you are hard to find."

"Yeah, I do that on purpose. You going to keep following me?"

"Yes."

He smirked. "Interesting. Fine." He slid out, slamming the door shut. The window to the driver had stayed open, and Rook leaned down to him. "I suggest staying back at the next stop. I would hate for anything to happen to her."

The driver only nodded, quiet as Rook headed back to the bike and got on. The light had already changed back to red, but Rook took off anyway.

"Follow him!" I yelled, watching him speed down the road.

We stayed close for another ten minutes before Rook pulled up to a warehouse. He swung off his bike and glanced back at me. The small cutesy wave was a harsh contrast to the gun in the other hand. I stayed frozen in my seat, watching as he walked in. He was gone for maybe ten minutes. One loud pop echoed around us, and then he walked out, getting on the bike and pulling out like nothing had happened.

"Was that a gunshot?" I asked, not really knowing if the driver would give me an answer.

"I believe so," my driver said, pulling out after him, winding through town until we pulled up in front of one of the motorcycle shops. I felt like I had barely taken a breath the entire time, the anticipation killing me.

Rook parked the bike and got off, heading inside without a glance back at me, but I caught up to him fast.

"You shouldn't be following me, Regan. You won't like anything that you learn."

He swung the door open, and I ran inside, following after him into the front of a motorcycle shop. Maverick Moto. It had been on my list, but I had found Rook first. I glanced around. The place was nicer than I had been expecting. No one would know the terrible things the people who ran it did.

"You've been stalking me. It's only fair that I stalked you a little," I said, nearly yelling as he walked behind the counter.

He turned, the rage on his face making my mouth go dry. He was fast, stepping around the counter and behind me before I could say another word. One arm wrapped hard around my waist, the other hand clamped over my mouth as he walked me through the back door into an open garage, my legs nearly off the ground as we went.

"If you're going to be in my life, you are going to have to learn more discretion," he hissed. "I've already made this clear."

I bit at his hand, but he didn't react, so I bit down harder.

"That will do nothing, Rebel. Well, not nothing, but I don't think your desired effect is getting my dick hard. Are you going to keep your mouth shut now?"

I nodded, and he finally dropped his hand. I threw my elbow back, hitting him in the sternum, which gave me a second to break free and face him.

"Who said I wanted to be in your life?"

He shook his head and clutched his chest for a second before that dark, menacing smile twisted back on his face.

"You did when you stalked me. You are such a brat. And unfortunately for you, I like when you get rough," he said, grabbing me again. He spun me, leaning down and throwing me over his shoulder before I had a second to react.

The skirt I was wearing fell to the side, leaving one leg exposed to him. I couldn't see him, but I felt the moment he turned and bit down on my thigh.

I yelled out, the pain radiating before he kissed it once. "Sorry, baby. Those damn intrusive thoughts won when I saw this beautiful ass."

He stopped, bouncing me once to readjust his grip before heading back down the hall.

"Rook!" I yelled. He smacked my ass in response before setting me down. "What was that one for?"

"Stalking me." He sat back behind a desk, watching me as I took in the room. His bike was parked in the corner of the office, and he eyed me as I walked towards it.

"Why is this in here?"

"I used a backup bike today because I was trying to not be recognized. And I don't risk any client or customer walking in and fucking with my things while I'm gone. I don't trust anyone who walks in here."

"Including me?"

"I haven't decided yet."

"But you still let me come back here?"

"I didn't have a choice when you're yelling out my personal business."

"So if I would have walked in and said hello, you wouldn't have brought me back here?"

I reached out, ready to run my hand over the bike, but he stopped me.

"Touch my bike and I touch you."

I felt brave. The way Rook always pushed me to be scared of him had worked—until now. My hand dropped, my fingers running along the handles to the tank.

"It's honestly crazy how fast you go on this. No seatbelts, nothing around you to hold you in if you crash, but you willingly do it." I moved to the back, the small seat where I had sat looking as ridiculous as it felt under my ass. I still hadn't sat where he usually did. I looked back over my shoulder at him, his face unreadable as he watched me, but I smiled.

"Why did I come home last night to find my favorite cookies on my bed?" I asked, lifting my skirt up and swinging my leg over the giant bike to hop into the seat. It was leaning to the side, the kickstand holding it up as I put my feet on the pegs.

He sat back in his chair, his eyes heavy and unwavering as they locked onto mine. The intensity in his gaze sent a shiver down my spine.

"How would I know?" he asked.

"Because you're the one that put them there."

"Can you prove that?"

"No, but I don't know anyone else who would have done that for me."

"Interesting," he said with a smirk. "But you also think I'm going to kill you?"

"Yeah, I've wondered."

"Yet you came to hunt me down. To what? Sit on my bike? Pretend you belong there? Why follow me and come here?"

I leaned back, my hands propping me up on the small seat behind me.His dark gaze stayed fixed on me, his lips curved into a sly smile.

"I wanted to say thank you."

"For breaking into your house? Anytime."

"You know that's not what I meant. I thought if I touched the bike, you were going to touch me?"

"Oh, I will."

"When?"

"When you beg for it."

"What if I don't?"

"Then, whenever you demand it. What are you wearing under

that?" he asked, nodding to the long skirt I had on. I went with something that made me feel a little more stalker-ish than one of my normal outfits, and settled on black boots, a long silky skirt, and a t-shirt.

"Nothing," I finally answered, feeling even more daring.

"Lift it all the way."

I had already bunched it at my hips, but I lifted it higher now, not even hesitating to follow his command.

"Good, now lean back and spread your legs more."

I couldn't help the thrill that ran through me. "For what?" I asked, breathless.

"So I can watch you get yourself off." There was nothing but confidence in his tone. Then again, pushing boundaries seemed to be fun for him.

"Here?"

He leaned back in his chair, his eyes heavy as he watched me. "Yes, right there."

"And you are going to sit there and watch?" I asked, still not believing this was what he was asking me to do.

"Yes."

"I'll be so on display."

"That's the point. You're mine to be on display for. I want to watch your face when you come. Mine was too buried in you to see last time."

"You think I'm yours?"

"I think you're in my office, on my bike, getting yourself off to the thought of me touching you. What else do you need to be considered mine? Go ahead, Rebel."

A shiver ran through me at his words, and without another thought, my hand moved down and pushed my skirt up out of the way more. "What am I supposed to be getting off with?"

"You don't like your fingers? You want to be filled better than that?" he asked, smiling as he stood up and stalked around the table to me. "Oh, that's right. You like toys, don't you, Rebel? You like to be stretched and filled."

I nodded, hoping that would mean he would come fill me himself, but he only clicked his tongue.

"Such a greedy thing. Reach into that bag behind you."

"For what?" I asked, already reaching back.

"Just grab what's in the bag," he said, smiling.

I listened, pulling out a new wrench. My eyes went wide as he stepped up next to me. "You want me to use *this*?"

He laughed, taking it out of my hand. "I had something else in mind, but let me see if this will work." The cool metal trailed up my thigh. "Is this going to get you off? Is this going to make you come hard until you cover my bike?"

His words spurred me on, making me wet as he ran one hand over my thigh.

I shook my head no, my mouth dropping open as he moved the wrench higher. I hissed as it pushed against my entrance. "Rook, that's cold."

He pushed more, the handle slipping into me with ease.

"Get yourself off, Rebel," he said, moving my fingers over my clit. "Think about how much you liked my mouth on you."

My fingers moved in slow circles, my body already coiling, desperate to feel the relief I knew would come.

"Such a pretty slut, desperate to get off again, aren't you?" he asked, pushing the handle of the wrench deeper. "But it's still not enough for you. You want to be filled and stretched hard."

I could only whimper. My hips pushed to take more as I continued the agonizing circles around my clit. The orgasm was teasing me, making my head fall back and my hand move faster.

"Is this enough? I want you to have my bike dripping."

I shook my head again. "No," I breathed with a moan. "Not enough."

He leaned down, his tongue swiping deep against me as he

reached into the bag to pull something else out. I pushed up, burying his face more before he pulled away with a laugh. "That pussy is so desperate to be filled. I can't wait for you to come all over my cock. You're going to cry and scream when I fill you. When I bury myself so deep in you and fill you. My pretty little slut used and covered in cum."

He grabbed my hand, replacing the wrench with a brand new vibrator in it before stepping back.

"Use it," he demanded. "Let me watch you stretch yourself around it and make my bike drip."

I didn't even care if he told me to or not. My body was so tight, so needy, that I was desperate to get off. I leaned back, my hand still rubbing my clit as the vibrator clicked on and I pushed it hard and deep into myself.

I cried out, already ready to come. Rook stepped closer, his hand wrapping around my neck and forcing me to lean back more.

"Don't come unless you know you will coat my bike. Don't waste my time on a quick orgasm that barely gets you off. I want it dripping so much I could lick it off the floor or I want nothing at all."

His hand tightened on my neck, cutting off my air just enough to make me feel a little high. I picked up my pace, fucking myself faster now as I rubbed my clit harder. It took seconds, then white stars exploded as my eyes snapped shut. My body tightened and shattered, the same rush of liquid coming as I gasped for air against Rook's hand.

"That's good, baby. You did perfect. Look at my bike, it's fucking soaked. I want to get on my knees and lap it up, but I'll just clean you off instead."

He leaned down, sucking and licking every inch of me until he pulled away.

"Come on," he said, pulling me off.

"What about the mess?"

"Mess? That's a goddamn work of art. My bike won't be cleaned ever again."

He dropped down into his office chair, pulling me in front of him. I stood awkwardly, still on a high from my orgasm and not sure what to do after putting on such a show for him.

"On your knees," he said.

I listened, dropping down onto my knees and immediately reaching for the button of his jeans.

His hand caught my wrist, the scowl on his face unreadable. "There's scarring on my legs, too. Just so you don't start screaming about it."

I nodded, still working to take off his jeans. "I wouldn't scream."

The button finally gave, his jeans falling open, and I was quick to reach in. I pulled out his cock. The length alone made me nervous if I would fit it all.

"So eager to get my cock, aren't you, Rebel?"

I nodded, licking my lips as I stroked him once.

He grabbed my chin, his fingers squeezing my cheeks. "Have you ever had this mouth used and fucked? Have you ever had a man worship it with his fucking cock?"

I tried to shake my head, but he forced it still. "No. Nothing like that," I whispered.

He leaned forward, looking me over and squeezing my face harder until my mouth opened.

"It's about to be used," he said, letting a line of spit drop from his mouth to mine. "And you will not stop until your throat is coated in cum. Understand?"

I nodded again.

He pulled my face closer until my lips met the head of his cock, and then pushed his fingers deeper into my cheeks, hollowing them out as my mouth wrapped around him.

He groaned, his hand sliding around until he had a handful of my hair. "Oh, fuck," he muttered as he pressed me further down onto him. "I want to see you take it all. Fucking choke, baby. Show me you want it all. I promise every inch you bury in that throat will be buried in that pussy one day."

I moaned against him, pulling him deeper down my throat. I wanted it all. I wanted to get him off better than he ever had before, and I wanted him to be desperate for more like I was for him.

"Good girl. I like hearing you struggle to take it all," he groaned, thrusting hard once before slowing. "You're so eager to please me, aren't you? I like watching what you like and now you're doing the same for me. I want your hand wrapped around me, and I want you to suck until your mouth is sore."

I listened, wrapping my hand near the base and pulling the rest into my mouth. I moved in tandem, my hand slick as spit ran down his length. He groaned, pushing in rhythm with me until he pulled my hand away. "Take it now, baby." I slipped him deeper as cum coated my tongue. He held me in place, making me swallow every drop so I didn't choke.

I kept sucking, not knowing exactly when to stop until he grabbed my hair and pulled me back. "Trying to kill me?"

"Just making sure you were done," I said, pulling back to catch my breath. His thumb swiped over my lip, wiping away anything that had dripped before he fixed his jeans.

"Come on," he said, pulling me up and onto his lap. "Let me catch my breath."

"Hopefully that means it was okay for you?" I asked, cringing at the question. I didn't think I wanted the answer to it.

He gave a quiet laugh, smoothing out my skirt. "Best I've ever had. Don't get all shy now. I just watched you cum all over my bike. There's no being shy about that."

"There is, if I worry that I pale in comparison to the other women you run around with."

He laughed again, the soft exhale tickling my arm. "Isn't it funny how we always build up interactions in our mind? We think they are good, maybe great even. Until you have the really amazing thing, though, it's hard to make an accurate comparison. Then, once you have the amazing thing, it would be impossible to go back and think that first thing was even okay, let alone great."

"You lost me," I said, suddenly under the impression that I could be the amazing thing he was talking about until my anxiety kicked in and I thought I was being stupid for thinking he could be saying that about me.

A thump jolted me out of my thoughts and we both looked towards the door.

"Rook! We have to go," a guy yelled from the other side of the door.

"I'm not going anywhere," Rook said, running a hand up my neck.

"We don't have a choice. Now, Rook."

"Fuck," he mumbled. "I fucking hate this place sometimes. Come on, I'll bring you up front."

"I can walk myself," I said, a sting of rejection making me glare at him.

"And I can walk you up front."

"If you walk me up now, looking like this, people are going to make guesses about what happened."

"Yes, they are, and I'm thrilled that some of those guesses will be right," he said, pulling open the door. "Little rebel girl likes to get off on motorcycles and get on her knees," he said, coming up behind me and pushing me out of the office. "She likes to suck until her mouth is full of cum."

"Rook," I hissed. "Shut up before they hear you."

"No, I want the world to know you hunted me down to be my pretty little slut."

"I did not!" I yelled, and two of the guys glanced our way.

"For me, you are and will be."

"What if I don't want to be yours?" My teeth ground together as the ache between my thighs grew.

His hand wrapped into my hair, bending me over the bike next to us.

"Then I suggest not hunting me down to swallow my cock," he said, his other hand sliding down my side. "It really gives mixed signals."

"Rook, people can see us."

"So? What are they going to do about it? They already know they can't touch you."

He pulled me back up, spinning me around to face him so he could kiss me.

"Why?" I asked, trying to catch my breath again.

"Because you're mine. Off-limits to them. Off-limits to anyone until I'm done with you."

"Until you're done with me?" I rolled my eyes, but my stomach fluttered. "How romantic."

"Isn't it?"

"And if I want to be with someone else?"

He stepped back, his hand moving to my lower back as we headed out front. "He's going to really hate you when I cut off every part of him that touches you."

"You're not serious."

"A week ago, you were terrified of me for doing similar things. Now, you seem to think of it more as a joke."

"I think my humor is a coping mechanism," I said.

"So if I start laughing when I cut off body parts, does that count as therapy?"

"No, going to therapy counts as therapy. Cutting people up counts as murder."

We made it to the car, and he opened the door for me.

"Could you imagine the depression I would give a therapist?" He leaned down, kissing me once. "Thanks for stalking me. I never realized how fun it could be to be on the receiving end. I'll talk to you later."

I got in and pulled out, looking back a few times as waves of heat washed over me. My mind raced with thoughts of him, each one only making me more interested in a world I never thought I wanted, but now couldn't resist.

EIGHTEEN
REGAN

I sat back with my tablet, clicking Dateline on while I worked on my next drawing.

Unlike all the other days I'd done this, today, I didn't feel dull. Maybe what I was doing wasn't all that different, but it didn't feel as boring now. I suddenly felt oddly good about the pace of my life.

Things had changed, and this felt more like a break from the chaos more than another boring day of my life. The nagging need to find more excitement in my life finally quieted now that I was at least trying new things.

My dad stormed into the room, the anger etched on his face making me immediately shrink back into the couch. I hated when he was mad at me, and I knew I would always go overboard to make him not mad at me anymore, even when I didn't want to.

"What happened at dinner last weekend?" my dad demanded, his voice icy as he stood in the doorway of the living room.

My stomach flipped, memories of every second with Rook flashing through my mind, but I tried to calm my face. "What do you mean?"

"I mean, why did one of my biggest clients just pull out of his contract, which had a large fee if he did so, because of you?"

"He said he did it because of me?" I asked, trying to keep my voice steady, already knowing exactly who he meant. The guy I told we wouldn't work with anymore because he liked underage girls.

"He did. Could you explain why and who went with you? Because I heard a few things about that, too."

"Oh," I said, my hands going clammy as I tried to think of any excuse. "I saw a friend when I got there, and we ended up hanging out most of the night."

"And this friend's name?" he pressed, his eyes narrowing.

I hesitated, unsure if I should tell him Rook's name. Technically, my dad could be on the list of people Rook worked with. He could also be on the list of people Rook knew secrets about. Neither option seemed great.

"Jake," I said, hoping the lie would hold. "I don't know if you know him or not."

"No. I don't think I do. And he was causing trouble with you?"

"We were just having some fun. Some of those guys suck, and I politely pointed it out. We weren't causing trouble."

"We don't *politely* point anything like that out, Regan. We keep our mouths shut and work. Those are men that give us business, and pay us to do business."

"But what business are you wanting to do with disgusting old men?" I almost yelled, frustration bubbling over. "Protecting them or their stuff? That's gross. Just let them fend for themselves if they are going to be disgusting. He's a literal pervert. Why would you want to work with him?"

"If I cared about everything people did behind closed doors, I wouldn't be able to make any money."

My stomach churned. I had watched Rook stick a knife into a

man's neck and even he wouldn't do business with this guy because of the terrible things he did. Rook couldn't really have better morals than my dad, could he?

"So what? I'm just supposed to deal with these guys, knowing what they do behind closed doors? I'm supposed to find respect for them, knowing those things?"

"Yes, actually. You are, because you are no one to them. They have the power, not you. You are a damn spoiled little girl in comparison and they don't care who the fuck you are when you bring their shit out into the open," he yelled. I coiled back further, not expecting the angry, hateful tone. For all the things my dad did, he rarely screamed at me like this. His attacks were more calculated than uncontrolled rage. "You think they wouldn't ruin you if you are trying to tell people their private business?"

I kept quiet, taking in the words that were exactly the opposite of what Rook told me. To him, the secrets were power. To my dad, they were ruination. I didn't understand how two seemingly powerful men could have such a drastically different outlook on the same thing.

Rook had given me secrets, and the men seemed to run from me in fear of those secrets being told. To my dad, the secrets these men kept were power, but power *over* him.

"I wasn't trying to upset you. You should calm down before it causes you any issues."

My head was swimming in information as my dad continued to yell at me.

I wondered if that was the difference between an upstanding business like my dad ran, compared to the less than legal business that Rook seemed to run.

I wasn't sure, but I did know that he was calling me a spoiled little girl, and it was a harsh reminder that was all he saw me as.

"I don't want to be a spoiled little girl. I'm an adult. I'm a full grown woman and I would like to be treated like one," I demanded. "I have asked over and over to help you. I hate sitting around here. I hate that you're hurt and suffering when I could help. I could help and do the right thing by you. I'm *trying*. I want to learn, but if I'm kept in the dark with you and your company, there's really nothing I can do."

"And why the hell would I want to tell you anything if you insist on talking about business to others when you don't even know what the fuck you are talking about?" he screamed. "Do you know how much money you cost me? How much we've lost now, thanks to you? Now, I'm the one that has to fly out, go to his boss, and try to fix this. Why did you think talking back was a good idea?"

"Because he's gross, and... Jake said he wasn't a great person."

He stomped closer and, for one beat of my heart, I thought my dad was going to hit me. He never had before, but there was something different on his face as he came over. The unhinged, wild look in his eye as his hand twitched at his side.

He seemed to change his mind, stopping a foot from me. "You think you should listen to Jake over me? That his opinion is more important than mine? I want you to listen for once in your fucking life. I don't give a fuck who is a good person and who isn't. If they pay us, I don't care. They pay for our lifestyle. For you to sit around here with everything you want, to watch your stupid shows and color on your tablet. You will not talk back to them. You will not care about their business outside of work, and if you think I will give you my company just for you to ruin it because you think you are better than them, when you have never had to deal with the world, you are wrong. You are supposed to inherit this business, Regan. You can't be a little girl anymore, and I don't need a little art girl either. I need a cut throat daughter who understands the world isn't perfect and beautiful. Do you understand?"

I nodded. "I understand. It won't happen again," I said. I

understood what he was saying. "I can't sit around doing nothing, and if I want to run a business, I have to keep my own thoughts out of it."

His shoulders sagged as he took a deep breath. "This," he said. "This is the daughter I want to give my company to. I'm glad you understand. I know you are smart, Regan, but you have to use those smarts in the right way. We aren't here to be the judge of people's lives. We are here to get paid to protect them or their property. These aren't little home alarms, this is high-level, dangerous work for men that can be dangerous. They aren't people whose buttons you should push. It's not something a quiet, shy girl can run if she wants to sit in the corner and judge people. Do you understand, Regan?" he asked, the words a little too condescending, as though I wouldn't be able to comprehend how important all of this was.

"Yes," I said. "Yes, I get it. I thought I was doing the right thing. It won't happen again."

"Good. Until I clean this mess up, I want you to stay home and not cause more problems. Are you able to handle that?"

"Yes," I said, trying to pull my shoulders back, but the weight of it all made me slump. I tried to do something good, and it made him more pissed off than I had ever seen him.

"Good. I'll be gone for a few days. Stay here and don't cause trouble, and we will be fine."

"Will you let me help with the business more, so I don't make any more mistakes?"

He grimaced, pulling out his phone as he headed towards the door. "Let's see how things go for a bit, and we will talk about it when I get back. Alright?"

"Yeah, alright," I said, a little more defeated. I understood I had messed up, but to be told that I had to keep waiting really sucked. "Love you," I said, halfheartedly.

He stopped, looking back at me with his eyebrows furrowed. "Love you, too. Have a good weekend."

He left in seconds, and I was surprised when anger boiled up. One more week of sitting around. One more week of being told to be good and then I might be thrown a bone. If he wanted a cut throat daughter who could handle a business, would she really sit around here quietly?

I pulled out my phone, already calling Harper to come over. There was no way I would sit around doing nothing this week.

The next morning, I paced my room, the heavy weight of my curiosity making it hard to think straight. Harper sat cross-legged on my bed, watching me pace with her eyebrows up. She had stayed up most of the night with me, listening to me rant. The ranting went from me nearly in tears about making my dad upset when he was sick to me nearly yelling that I wanted more. Harper dealt with it all until we sat and made an actual plan.

"Are you sure you want to do this?" she asked for the third time. "I mean, it's your ad's office."

I stopped pacing and turned to her. "I have to. If he isn't going to let me in and show him I can handle things, I'm going to have to do it myself. His doctor's appointments are becoming more frequent, he now has a rage issue, apparently, because I have never seen him as mad at me as he was last night, or when he had that phone call last week, and on top of all of that, he still won't give me a sliver of information about his company. What if he's being secretive about the appointments because he's getting worse? What if he passes away and I know nothing?"

"And figuring all that out starts by breaking into his office?"

"Do you have a better idea? I've been waiting around, hoping he would notice, but apparently, I'm failing him. I have to take some sort of initiative."

Harper gave a sharp nod and stood up. "Alright, then, let's do this."

We headed down the hall, the house feeling eerily quiet even though it was always this way. My heart pounded in my chest as we reached the door to my dad's office. I reached up, punching in the code as Harper turned the key.

He didn't know I had the key to the door, but one day I had found the spare in his hiding spot. The beautiful antique-looking key was too hard to resist keeping. I didn't even know what it was for until I saw his identical one a few years ago.

The lock clicked, and I swung the door open.

The office was dimly lit, the heavy curtains drawn to block out the afternoon sun. We slipped inside, closing the door quietly behind us. I glanced around, taking in the imposing desk, the walls lined with bookshelves, and the faint smell of polished wood and leather. I had been in here so many times in my life, but never without my dad in there with me.

"Where do we start?" Harper asked, her voice barely above a whisper.

I pointed to the large oak desk in the center of the room. "There. He keeps everything important in his desk."

Harper started rifling through the drawers on one side while I tackled the other. My hands shook as I sifted through papers, trying to stay quiet and efficient.

"What exactly are we looking for?" Harper asked, glancing over at me.

"Anything that seems out of place," I replied, my voice tense. "Something that might explain why he's so secretive about the company? Papers from doctor's appointments? Anything."

After a few minutes of searching, I pulled open the bottom

drawer on my side and found a small locked compartment. My heart skipped a beat. "I think I found something."

She came to my side, looking down at the small lock. It didn't look all that complicated, and my eyebrows shot up when Harper pulled out a bobby pin from her hair. "Let's see if this works," she said with a grin.

"How do you know how to do that?"

"You think we sit around watching true crime and I haven't tried a few things? The better question is, how have you not tried to do this?"

After a few quiet moments, the lock clicked open. I carefully lifted the wooden lid, revealing a stack of documents.

"Weird place to store more documents."

"Really weird. And with how security-crazy my dad is, I don't think he would leave really important documents in a place like this."

"Okay, then, what are they? What kind of documents is he locking up that you don't think are important enough?"

I pulled out the documents and scanned them, my eyes narrowing with each line. They detailed a series of names, addresses, and shipments. The addresses were recognizable, places around our smaller town, Havenwood, but a lot of them were in the city of Valeport that we connected to, and ones in the actual boat port.

There wasn't much information past the dates and port names, but a few had smaller amounts of money marked next to them.

"Maybe shipments he had to help keep safe?"

Harper shrugged. "It's plausible, but weird. Does he do security for literally anything?"

"I don't know. I guess I assumed only people and buildings." I pulled out the next page. The transactions were a lot bigger for a few of those. "These all have weird names next to them. *Starlight,*

Black Pearl, Silver Bullet. Those sound like nicknames or something."

"For what? A fucking pirate ship?" Harper asked. "What does that mean?"

"It could be boat names, maybe?" I pulled out my phone, taking a quick picture before flipping to the next page. "Don't these payments seem a little high for a security company to make from one shipment being watched?"

"I would say so, but then again, what do I know about what he would charge? Maybe they were more important items."

I flipped to the next stack underneath these, the lab results and notes from doctors making my throat tight as tears bubbled up. I hated facing that my dad was sick. That in a few years, I could be all alone.

I was already so alone. What would I do when he was really gone?

The lab results all showed numbers next to them, each one green besides a few random ones that were in the red.

"Why would he keep those locked up?" Harper asked, looking them over with me.

"I don't know. He's shown me plenty of the lab results before. I think he's even shown me these."

"So what's the secret? Is he worried someone is coming in here to steal lab results?"

"I mean, he hasn't wanted many people to know he's sick."

"Is he getting worse and doesn't want you to know?"

"I don't know. Set it down. I want to take some pictures of these."

Harper laid them out, helping me snap a photo of each one.

Something banged outside, making us both jump.

"We should put it back," she said. "Being in here freaks me out."

I nodded, but my mind was racing. This document raised

more questions than it answered. I laid the papers back in the compartment and closed the drawer.

We quickly made sure everything was exactly as we had found it before we slipped out of the office. My heart pounded with a mix of fear and adrenaline as we made it back into the hallway.

"Okay, what are you going to do?" Harper asked.

I swallowed hard, flopping back on the bed. "I think I need to keep digging. I mean, right? I've been patient and waited around for years for my dad to let me in, and he hasn't. I either need to be let into whatever he's doing or move on with my life. Can I move on with my life? It's not like I can leave when I know how sick he is, but I can't stay locked up in this house just waiting for him to pass away. That seems so gross."

"If I were you, I would dig and figure out what's going on and why he won't let you help. Or at least, that's what I would want to do. But you should be careful. Your dad... I don't mean to be a dick, but he freaks me out sometimes."

"After yesterday, I get what you mean. He's all perfect and powerful and it can be a lot. He's definitely not someone I want to be pissing off. If he doesn't care if I take over the business, he needs to tell me. I can't waste any more time doing nothing, and if this is going to cause issues between us, I would rather spend the time we have left together doing things we both like doing instead of him avoiding me or making me parade around at parties for no reason."

"Is that why you're always doing what you're told? You're scared of him?" she asked.

It wasn't like it was something we hadn't talked about, but she had never asked me so bluntly. It honestly wasn't even something I thought about so bluntly.

"I guess, in a way. Not that I've ever thought he's going to hurt me or anything, but just make my life hell if I start going against the things he wants from me."

"And the things you want from you?"

"I'm starting to think those two things are at odds with each other."

We hung out for a few hours around the house after ordering food, but I was growing restless. The words my dad said to me could have been a knife to the chest. I had done the right thing, and now I had ruined something for him. I hadn't been trying to. Rook had just been helping me get better at dealing with those situations.

"He really told me to not cause *more* problems?" I said for what felt like the hundredth time, making Harper's eyes jump to mine.

"You good, babe?" she asked.

"No," I demanded. "I'm not. He told me to stay home and not cause more problems. I rarely cause problems. I sit around here all the time doing nothing and not causing any issue, and the moment I stir things up a little, he freaks out. Not like gets a little mad, he full on freaked out."

She grinned, sitting up more. "Okay, hear me out. What if you *do* stay home but cause problems? Is that acceptable?"

"I wouldn't see why not," I said, laughing. "What are you thinking?"

"A party?"

I thought it over. I wasn't a huge fan of parties because of all the people, but it would be a way to have some fun without leaving.

It would also be a good excuse to see Rook.

Twenty minutes later, Harper walked into the kitchen with her phone in hand.

"Alright, we have, like, twenty people saying they are coming, which means forty because you know they are all bringing someone or an entire group. Did I miss anyone?"

I tapped my phone, the message to Rook sitting there unsent.

"I have someone I kind of want to invite."

"Who?" she asked, a smile growing on her face.

"Rook."

"Biker boy? I thought he freaked you out."

"I mean, he does sometimes, but I don't think he actually wants to hurt me. He seems to... care about me, maybe? I'm not sure, but he's been almost sweet to me."

"That's almost hilarious. I'm still a little scared of him after the whole knife to the chest thing, but in a still laughing way, you know?"

"So, you would be okay if he came? He would probably bring his friends."

"I mean, are they going to kill someone while they are here?"

"I don't think so."

"Don't *think* so? Is there a way to get a guarantee?" she asked, fighting a smile.

I shrugged. "I guess I could ask."

She sat up straighter from her perch on the stool, smiling as she laughed. "Oh my god, please ask that. I need to see what he says."

REGAN

Hey.

ROOK

Hello.

REGAN

If I ask you to do something, can you promise not to kill anyone?

Harper howled with laughter, nearly falling off her seat.

"Shouldn't you be freaking out? I freaked out. He actually does this, Harper."

"To who? Like strangers on the street? Or bad people?"

"I don't know. Both? So far that I've seen, it's just with problematic people, but I don't actually know how often this happens."

My phone dinged, and she sat back up.

ROOK
Seems like a setup.

REGAN
Or what normal people do??

ROOK
I might be able to take a night off for you.

"You're flirting about killing people!" Harper screamed, laughing harder. "You little freak. What is going on? One day you're with douchebag Elliot, and now you're flirting with a hot tattooed biker man who scared you to death because you thought he would kill you." The phone dinged again. "I hope that's a text saying he's coming because I can't wait to hear this in person."

ROOK
You going to tell me what you want?

REGAN
I wanted to invite you over, but no murder allowed.

ROOK
Where?

REGAN
My house. My dad is out, so we are having a party.

ROOK

Such a Rebel.

What's in it for me?

REGAN

Nothing except having fun.

And seeing me.

ROOK

Fine. This is for all of us to come, or just me?

REGAN

Everyone's invited, but if you all aren't on your best behavior, I will personally be kicking you all out.

ROOK

One little rebel against six bikers? And Evie? Good fucking luck.

Harper leaned over my shoulder, reading the texts, and blew out a hard breath.

"Six hot bikers is a party I for sure want to go to."

I glared over my shoulder at her.

"Fine," she said, rolling her eyes. "Take Rook out and make it five. I don't care. I'm still in."

REGAN

Are you coming or not?

ROOK

We'll be there, Rebel. I'm sure you'll hear us coming.

REGAN

One more thing...Could you possibly get into his cameras to shut them off for the night? He changed the password after I snuck through the backyard and now I can't.

ROOK

Ahh, finally, the real reason you wanted us
there.

REGAN

No! I did actually want you to come. I just
thought you might have an easier time getting
in than I would since you seem to have
already broken into it.

ROOK

We will put up dummy footage. Give me
twenty minutes before you flood the place. I'll
be there in thirty.

"Okay," I breathed, my hands suddenly turning clammy.
"They are coming. Him and his entire friend group are coming
here."

Harper jumped up. "Then let's go. We have a party to start."

Nineteen
Rook

arlier that day

E I pulled up to the curb and threw my kickstand down. This was the last thing on my to-do list before I could go home and be done for the entire night.

I would get to relax with no other job to do for a few hours. The thought alone made my shoulders droop. I was still exhausted. Nothing had slowed down and, with adding all the shit I had to do with Regan to my list, I was only busier than before.

Not tonight, though. I might even put on a ridiculous true crime show and sleep. The thought of doing that with her crossed my mind, and I shook it off as I pulled off my helmet and looked around. The informant wasn't here yet, which was fine. I preferred getting here first.

I had someone tailing Cameron still. I always had someone tailing Cameron. From the moment I had a few extra hundred dollars in my pocket to give someone to keep tabs on him, I'd had someone tailing Cameron. He had brought me useful information over the years, and I knew a few of his business dealings. Mostly stolen items he resold on the black market. Sometimes, there was the occasional bigger deal for him. I think one time, he transported an entire cargo ship of exotic animals into the country, but none of it was what I was looking for. Nothing he did felt like enough to ruin him the way he had ruined me.

Yeah, I could send him to prison, but there was always the chance that he could thrive there. I needed everything taken from him. I needed him to know there was nothing left for him on this entire fucking planet. I needed him to burn and suffer the way my parents had.

And no matter what information I was given today, it probably wouldn't be enough to do that, but the compulsion was still there. It was always nagging at me. I couldn't leave Cameron alone, and I would never be able to until he was dead.

Now the only difference was I had his daughter, and she kept falling perfectly into my trap.

The informant finally appeared. He was a wiry man with a nervous twitch. He always dressed normal, looked normal, but nothing else about him was normal. He was smart and fast, always able to slip around the city unnoticed, and he stayed my top guy for getting accurate information fast because of it.

"You want to tell me why I didn't know Cameron's daughter came back around last year?" I asked.

The informant cocked an eyebrow. "She involved in his business?"

"No."

"Then how the fuck would I know? You have me running around for him and his business. And before you ask, I don't know if he's got a wife or mistress either. I'm going to need paid more if those things need checked."

I shook my head. I could figure that all out myself, and I could only be mad at myself for not keeping a better eye on Cameron's personal life.

"Got anything useful?"

"Yeah." He nodded, pulling out a cigarette. "I got something, but I don't know what the fuck it is."

"Alright, I'll still take it," I said, pulling a thousand dollars out of my pocket and handing it to him. He didn't count it. We had grown some sort of trust after years of working together. I knew he would give me true information, and he knew I wouldn't stiff him any cash.

"Cameron's got something big going. I think it's something bigger than ever. He's meeting with a few people in the city."

"Who?"

He handed me a scribbled list of four names. I knew every single one of them. "These are the guys I'm working with," I said, wishing I hadn't. They were the reigning drug lords of the city and the exact guys I'd been working for as an in-between. Two have had shipments go missing and the other two were about to declare an all out war between the others before they had anything go missing.

"Is he offering security?" I asked. It wouldn't be far-fetched to think Cameron would be trying to get an in to the drug business, but this was a weird way to go about it. Once you worked for them, you would never rule them.

"I have no idea. He goes into the building, stays for twenty minutes, and leaves with his guards."

"How many now?"

"He's upped it. Has about four men with him at all times now."

I nodded, knowing he always traveled with one or two, but him adding two more wasn't a good sign either. It also wasn't a good sign that he wasn't guarding their house. Regan sat there, alone, every fucking day, with minimal security. He needed four grown men to protect him, but she was left on her own?

It's not like everyone didn't know where his house was. He basically had a sign with his name on the gate.

How the fuck was he protecting her?

"It sounds like there's another meeting going on soon, but I can't find details yet."

"What kind of meeting?"

"At least two of those guys have agreed to a meeting with Cameron."

"When?"

"Like I said, can't figure out where or even about what. It's being kept quiet."

"Which two is he meeting with?"

"Asher and Cross."

"One that's been robbed and one that hasn't."

"Like I said, some good information, but I'm not sure what to do with it."

"I do. Thanks. No need to wait until next month. If something comes up, text me as soon as you learn it. If Cameron is wrapping himself up in this at the same time shipments are going missing, I need to stay on top of what he's doing."

"You got it. Talk soon," he said, before disappearing around a corner.

I waited, the information he gave me bouncing back and forth in my mind. Something was going on, and it felt like the tensions were rising. Drug lords were bad enough to deal with, but pissed off drug lords who were ready to blame someone for millions of dollars in stolen drugs were worse.

I pulled my helmet back on before hitting the bike on and pulling out. I had to get back to the guys and tell them what was going on before I found Regan.

She couldn't stay alone in that house any longer, and if her dad wasn't going to keep her safe, I would.

I finally sat back on the couch after talking with everyone. They all knew what was going on, but we couldn't decide what to do next.

ROOK

You alone tonight?

REGAN

Harper's here. Why?

ROOK

Just wondering.

Since she wasn't completely alone, I decided I was still taking the night to sit. I clicked on the TV, trying to not let myself turn on her stupid crime show and failing.

I was getting pathetic now.

As if Regan knew I was still thinking about her, she texted me, asking us to come over for a party.

I showed Aiden, who groaned but nodded.

"We should go," he said. "If he's not home and everyone is drinking, we might get into his office. Evie could get into the computer and figure out what's going on."

"True."

And I wanted to see Regan.

Or more like I wanted to sit back and do nothing with Regan next to me.

But Aiden was right. With Cameron on the move with things, we didn't have time to wait around for the next bit of information to come to us. We had to go looking for it. Nothing was adding up to make sense with Cameron, and as soon as we thought we found the missing piece to make it click together, he would do something else that didn't make any sense. The shipments, the stolen items, his business, and now meetings with drug lords. We had to figure out how they all came together.

Not only for my own revenge, but this meant his business would be mixing with ours. We worked with these people, and there was no way I could go in blind to any situation when Cameron Fletcher was involved.

Having access to his private office and computer could change that. I had a strange feeling in the pit of my stomach, and I didn't know if it was because my world had collided with Cameron's too much or because of how excited I was to be going to his house to see his daughter tonight.

"I think I've lost sight of what the fuck I'm supposed to be doing," I said, running a hand down my face.

"Maybe because you're hanging out with a hot girl, stalking her, and sneaking into her room, but not getting laid."

"You think I should sleep with the girl I'm using to ruin her dad's life, and hers, inevitably?"

He shrugged. "Doesn't have to be her, but yeah. You've been waiting years for this opportunity. You can't fuck it up because of something so stupid."

I thought it over, trying not to think of Regan on her knees in front of me and failing. Touching her again was taking over my thoughts and it could be fucking up how clearly I was thinking about the real issues.

"Maybe you're right. We'll go tonight, search the house, and I'll figure the rest out."

What I needed to figure out was how to put more distance between Regan and me while staying close enough to make my plan.

Or more accurately, I needed a fucking plan.

"Get ready," I yelled to everyone. "We're going to a party. And try to make yourselves look decent. We can't look like a pack of wild animals."

"What?" Evie yelled, crawling over the back of the couch and shoving herself between me and Aiden. "We're all going to a party?"

"Regan asked us to come."

Evie's eyes narrowed. "She invited us or you did? Because there is a big difference."

I flipped my phone to face her. "It says, if you guys want to come over, my dad's out, so we are having a party."

She screeched, jumping back over the couch. "I'm going to get ready. Oh my god, people that aren't you guys that want to hang out? Hell yes."

"So... I'm going to be a little busy with Regan, and we need a few people that can look over the house," I said to Aiden. "You know Evie's going to be partying until the second she gets to the computer."

Aiden groaned. "Fine. I'll watch her, but I swear if she acts up, I'm bringing her home."

"You could make her walk. Just follow close on the bike."

"I think I might do that," he said, disappearing down the hall.

I wasn't far behind, heading into my room to change. I pulled off my shirt and caught sight of my left side in the mirror. I didn't think about it much. I didn't really care what people said about it, and until Regan, I hadn't bothered to ask any girl if it would bother them.

I didn't care even when I saw their faces twist in disgust.

But Regan's face hadn't. Hers had dropped in sadness. Then she seemed more than happy to touch me.

I didn't know what was happening to me now. The whole thing felt easy at first—use her to get access to Cameron until I found information that would ruin him.

Now I was too preoccupied trying to fuck Regan half the time. I couldn't focus.

Maybe Aiden was right. I needed to sleep with her and move on.

Which could be convenient, considering I would be at her house most of the night.It could be my plan now. I sleep with Regan while the group looks for a way into Cameron's office.

I would get two things I wanted, and instead of running around trying to fuck with people, I could get to lie down and relax for a few hours.

I walked out, finding half of them ready to go.

Then Evie walked out.

"What the fuck are you wearing?" I asked, looking at the glittering dress that was less of a dress and more of a piece of fabric.

"And what the fuck is that?" Aiden asked, pointing to the knife strapped to her thigh.

"An accessory? It's cute."

Aiden looked at me and back at her. His mouth dropped open. "You little psycho. Of course you think a knife is cute. You're going to scare everybody at that party. These people aren't like our friends."

She shrugged, pulling her long blonde hair over her shoulder. The small chain holding her dress up seemed way too thin.

"Keep the knife, but maybe put some clothes on?" I asked.

"You two suck. I'm wearing this."

"You are riding on my bike, Evie. Everyone will see your ass," Aiden said.

She stomped over to the door, grabbing Aiden's leather jacket and slipping it on. In her defense, it did fall to her mid thigh, covering everything.

It was good enough for me.

"Problem solved," she said. "I'm going to a party that isn't full of biker boys with one brain cell. These are Regan's friends, so I have to assume it's all rich, sophisticated men. I have to look good."

"Husband hunting?" Aiden asked.

Her sweet smile was a lie, and we all knew it. "Have to find someone to sink my teeth into."

"Or your knife," Mason said, walking past her to the garage door.

"That too. Come on. We need to go," she said.

I only shook my head, grabbing my jacket and helmet to head out to my bike. I didn't care if Evie wanted to kill someone, Aiden could take care of it. I wouldn't care if they wanted to go on a damn rampage. All I had to do tonight was keep Regan occupied.

I shoved my helmet on with a smile.

Who would have ever thought getting revenge on the person who ruined my life would be so much fun?

TWENTY

REGAN

The rumble of their bikes came long before they actually pulled in.

Harper jumped up and down.

She was more excited than me for all of them to come. My hands wrung together, wishing I could find anything else to pay attention to besides the sounds of their bikes getting closer. They had to be coming up the driveway now.

Rook would be here with all his friends, around my friends.

"What was I thinking?" I asked, grabbing Harper's arm. "Did I just make a terrible decision?"

"Maybe," she said with a smile. "But I think it's going to be a really *fun,* terrible decision."

The bikes revved, and my eyes went wide as I watched six of them drive down the path around the house and park on the back patio.

I ran over to Rook, already knowing his bike now. My face heated at how well I knew him and his bike, but I pushed that aside as he pulled off his helmet. His dark hair was tousled from the ride, framing his sharp jaw and piercing eyes. Tattoos peeked

out from under the sleeves and collar of his hoodie, and his confident, dangerous aura made my pulse quicken.

"I told you to park in the front," I said, trying not to melt at
the sight of him. He seemed to look hotter every time I saw him.

"Well, hello to you, too, Rebel. I'm not parking my bike out
of my sight when I don't know anyone here."

"No one here is going to mess with your stuff."

"Can you guarantee it?"

I knew most of the people already here, but not everyone.
Friends of friends that I couldn't assure him didn't know him or
wouldn't mess with the bike.

"No," I growled. "Keep it out of the way, though. If someone
messes with it back here, it's your problem."

"A little ray of sunshine today, aren't you? I thought you
would be happy we were here. Was I supposed to decline the
invitation?"

"I don't know. I mean, no, I wanted you to come. I'm just...
nervous. You're nothing like my friends, and they are nothing like
yours."

He set his helmet down and threw his hands over his heart
with a frown. "Aww. We're just star-crossed lovers. Will this turn
into a street fight, or are you and I going to kill each other at the
end in the name of true love?"

"Ha. Ha. You make jokes now until you want to punch one of
these guys. Then what?"

"Then I punch them and kidnap you. Actually, that sounds
like a great plan. Better than the one I had."

Evie slid off the back of the other bike, which I was pretty sure
was Aiden's, and came to stand next to Rook with a grin.

"Hey," she said. "Nice to meet you not on the back of the
bike."

"Evie, I'm assuming?"

"That's me. Thanks for inviting us. I rarely get out around

people who aren't..." Her voice trailed off as her eyes glanced around us. "Doing the things we do. You know?"

"Well, I'm glad you could come."

Evie shrugged off the jacket, revealing her dress and, apparently, her knife on her leg.

Harper stepped up next to me, her mouth dropping open.

"I just came to introduce myself, but oh my god, I'm obsessed with you," she said to Evie.

Evie's smile widened. "Well, then, I'm obsessed with you, too. Can we meet everyone?"

Harper agreed, grabbing her arm and heading off into the crowd. Rook watched them for a second before looking back at me.

"Thanks," he said quietly.

"For?"

"You two being nice to Evie."

"Why wouldn't we be?"

"I don't know. She has trouble with girl friends. Between her level of crazy, the way she dresses, and hanging out with us almost exclusively, girls tend to either not be nice or try to use her."

"Use her for what?"

His face hardened, his lips pressing together hard. "To get to us. She's had some shit friends that used her because they liked one of us. Then some that used her just to get in the group. She's given up a bit, and I think she's been a little depressed about it. She couldn't believe she was invited today." He smiled at me, and my heart stopped. It was a real smile, not those evil little grins he liked to give me. "I had to show her your text to prove it."

"Oh," I said, looking over at Harper and Evie. I wasn't sure what I would do without Harper. Even with all the guys around, sometimes you needed other girls. "Does that mean she'd like to hang out with me and Harper sometime?"

"I'm sure she would," he said. "Can't promise she won't cut anyone, but she would probably like a break from us."

"Who wouldn't?"

He laughed again, stepping closer to me now. "If you wanted a break from me, why ask me to come over?"

"It's a party. Everyone is invited."

"Of course, and you always invite people like us to these things?"

"Sometimes," I said as he leaned down.

His hands rested on my waist, pulling me closer until his lips were at my ear. "And do you let these people stay in your bed at these parties?"

"No." My fingers fisted into the hoodie he wore, wishing he would go a little lower to kiss my neck.

"Thankfully, you're making an exception tonight."

"I am?" I asked, my eyebrows jumping up. "Says who?"

"Me."

"What if I say no?"

"What if I say I don't care?" he asked.

His hands wrapped around the sides of my neck, pulling me in until our lips connected. Each slow flick of his tongue made me open more, my body falling against his until he had to hold me upright.

"Based on that kiss, I don't think we have a problem. I'm going to find a drink. You can find me."

"Excuse me?"

"Problem?" he asked, stopping to face me.

"Yes. You came to my party, asked to stay the night with me, and then casually tell me I can come find you if I want? Why wouldn't you be hanging out with me all night?"

"I said you could come find me if you wanted."

"So I have to chase you now?"

He grabbed the back of my neck, pulling me in again until our lips were a breath apart.

"Why wouldn't I want you to when it worked out so great for me last time?"

"It's not going to happen this time."

"I bet it will."

"I bet it won't."

"I will take that bet, Rebel. I bet you by the end of the night, you will be begging for me to take you up to your bed. I bet you will be ready to drop to your knees and be my pretty little slut again." He ran a finger over my bottom lip, smiling, before he leaned down to kiss me. "I can't wait to see you beg for me," he whispered. "I'm sure I'll see plenty of you soon."

Before I could respond, he took off, disappearing into the crowd and heading towards the bar.

If he thought I would be waiting around chasing after him, he was about to be in for a shock.

After another hour of walking around, having a drink, and talking to a few friends, I headed over to Evie, who was sitting and watching the party go on around her.

"Having fun?"

"A lot, actually. Thank you again."

"Anytime. I wondered if you would want to come over again. Maybe hang out with me and Harper one day?"

"Did Rook force you to ask me?"

I laughed, leaning on the bar top next to her. "Not at all. I'm the one that brought it up, actually. "

"Oh. Well, then, yeah, I would love to."

"I'll text you next time we go out. Do you have a bike?"

"Ew, no. I ride with Aiden usually. Rook takes me sometimes, but no one really wants to be that close to their brother."

"So you don't want to drive one and they don't care?"

"Why would they care? The only time they care is when they

want to take someone home, and apparently Aiden has no game because that is a rare occurrence."

"Um, have you seen Aiden? I don't think he would need any game if he wanted to take someone home."

She glanced over at him, but then her attention quickly went back to her nails. "Yeah, I guess."

"Maybe he just likes taking you home."

She rolled her eyes. "Doubtful. He feels obligated. Rook has basically made him my bodyguard. He's forced to be around me."

"I don't know. I'm sure he could say no, but I don't know much about your friend group."

"Oh, well, you know Rook. Aiden is and has been his best friend for the last ten years."

I looked over at Aiden. Confidence radiated off him. He was muscular, and his dirty blonde hair was cut shorter, but it was still a mess. Not quite like Rook's messy hair. He had one of those smiles that made girls lose their minds and tattoos that snaked down his arms. He had that same quiet authoritative look like Rook had, like people would respect him when he walked into a room, and I wondered how they had gotten that.

He glanced over at Evie again, a scowl crossing his face before he glanced back at the girl he was talking to. Evie noticed, but continued on. "Hero is over there at the bar with Mason. He has been with us for a few years now, and Mason, too. Those two are close, but complete opposites."

I turned my attention to them. Hero was taller, and thinner, but still muscular. The first thing I noticed about him was green eyes. I didn't know that I'd ever seen such green eyes on a guy, and while he was good-looking, too, something about him made me uneasy. She pointed out Mason next to him. He looked more like Rook. Dark hair, dark clothes, tattoos covering his arms and one on his neck. He seemed funny, but the dark, brooding thing really made me keep my distance still.

"Zack and Kane are the two over there by the pool," Evie continued. "They have been around for less than a year, so everyone still keeps them out of the loop a bit, but they are funny." Those two looked less like the group, and I wondered if it was because they were newer. They had fewer tattoos, less of a menacing look, and while they both were apparently fine with the killings and hiding bodies, they both seemed friendlier.

"And you?"

"Well, Aiden *lovingly* refers to me as psycho. I don't get out much, and really the only thing I'm good at is computers, so, you know, not much."

I laughed, smiling when she turned to me. "You are saying this to a girl who is basically locked in her house watching TV and drawing all day. I think that's a lot. I think that's plenty, and it sounds fun."

She gave a tight grin, but jumped up. "I'm going to find another drink and bother Aiden a bit more. Good luck with my brother. He's...a lot, but he's the best. Promise."

I searched for his face in the crowd. It had been a while since I'd seen him, and I tried not to wonder if it had been on purpose or not.

My heart sank when I didn't find him, but I ignored it. He was ignoring me, I could ignore him. I grabbed another drink, taking it to my friends and quickly downing it.

Somehow, another hour went by, and I had lost count of how many drinks I had thrown back. Soon, I was bleary-eyed, trying to make it around the pool, realizing immediately he would find the farthest spot and sit there.

I saw Rook right away, and I didn't love what I found.

My stomach rolled and my hands clenched at the girl leaning over to touch him. It was innocent enough, the hand on his arm. He sat back, saying something to her, which made her laugh.

Did he really come to my party and say he was staying the night with me, only to flirt with other people?

Or maybe this was a part of his game.

My palms grew hot and itchy as I watched. I needed to get closer and hear what they were saying. Maybe he wouldn't even notice if I sat down near them.

His bright eyes locked onto mine the moment I stepped closer. Someone came and sat down in the only open seat making the panic of embarrassment bubble up in my chest. There were no open seats now.

Rook's head tipped with a smile before he kicked out his legs more and patted his lap.

I would have to walk over, in front of everyone, and sit on his lap. It wasn't just a seat, and I knew it. It would be a clear show that I was here with him.

He wanted to challenge me to be a rebel, and just like every time before, I would take it.

TWENTY-ONE
ROOK

Regan didn't look happy with the seating arrangement, but she still made her way over until she stood in front of me, her hands on her hips like I was in trouble.

"What are you doing?" she asked.

"Hanging out? Was there something else I should be doing?" I smirked, cocking an eyebrow at her.

Technically, there was something else I should do, but I didn't think she would stay up in her room with me all night right away. Mason and Zack were walking the house, noting anything they could easily find as Aiden, Evie, and Hero planned to break into Cameron's office once I got Regan out of the way.

So my job now was making sure the moment we went to her room, we wouldn't be leaving until morning.

I had already been pretty sure she would be interested, but I made her find me just to be certain. If she asked me over and hunted me down, there really wouldn't be a question about me succeeding.

"Why did I have to find you?"

"Sit down," I said, not liking the way everyone around us

could hear what we were saying. The girl that had been trying to reach out to me every second glared now.

"There are no open seats over here. We can go somewhere else."

I leaned forward, grabbing her hips and pulling her down. She nearly fell, but with a little adjusting, she got herself draped over my legs.

"Hello, Rebel. Looks like you found a seat."

"I think I was forced onto this seat."

"Uncomfortable?"

"Only because everyone is looking at us. I need another drink," she said, reaching for mine next to me. I didn't mind, but still laughed as she threw back the entire thing.

"Need another?" I asked, and she nodded. "I would have thought you loved the attention. Aren't you always in the spotlight, being one of the richest heiresses here? Or are you the only heiress here?"

"I don't give myself that title."

"What title do you give yourself, then? Because you seem to not like any of them."

She leaned in, her eyes narrowing as her nose nearly touched mine. "Regan."

"Rebel?"

"I don't mind that one."

"Pretty. Little. Slut," I said, my lips against hers now.

She sucked in a breath, wiggling in my lap. "That one is... interesting."

"I'm sure you'll find it quickly becoming a favorite."

"And why would I do that?"

I trailed my hand up her thigh, running my fingers over the lace of her underwear. "Because I think you will like what happens every time you hear it."

"It sounds like you're trying to train me like a dog. Is it like, I hear pretty little slut and I come running?"

"No running involved. You'll just come."

She smacked my chest but laughed. "You get a girl off one time and your ego is bigger than this house."

"My ego was already that big."

"That's true. You seemed that way the night we met."

My fingers trailed up and down her thigh, the delicate skin making me relax. I thought back to meeting her. What were the chances that I would meet the daughter of the man who had killed my family and feel something for her? Even if all I had wanted to do was sleep with her, was the world mocking me for everything it took away?

Her hand cupped my jaw, making me look at her. The lazy smile on her face made me realize how much the alcohol was getting to her. I wasn't sure how much, so I decided to ease into my questions or trying to get upstairs.

"Alright. I'm here and don't know anyone. Tell me everyone's secrets," I said.

"Secrets aren't free."

"That's true," I said, pulling her closer. "What would you like in exchange, Rebel? Name your price."

Kane brought us two more drinks, and Regan reached out for hers, not wasting any time opening it.

"I want to know one of your secrets for all of theirs. A good secret, not some silly one."

"You already know one of my secrets," I said. "A very large secret."

"Do you mean this?" she asked, running a hand over my side. The hoodie covered everything, but she knew what was underneath and how it got there. "Maybe, but you gave that to me of your own free will."

She wasn't wrong. I had given it up to make her want to keep me around, and it had worked. "You are getting very good at this," I said. "Fine. When my parents died, Evie and I were shipped off to a stranger. We were told they were family, but they weren't. I was older, around fifteen, and Evie was about ten. We decided we didn't want to be there anymore. The couple were terrible to us, so we did something about it. We started with harmless pranks and quickly amped it up to more harmful things. Some were enough to send them to the hospital. The couple got so scared of us, they shipped us back."

"Back to the burned house?"

"Back to this town. We were basically dropped on the street in front of that burned up house and forgotten about."

"What did you do?"

"That's more than one secret, Rebel. Now tell me theirs."

She huffed, but leaned in and started pointing everyone out, telling me whatever secret she could think of.

Another hour went by before I was almost bored. Unsurprisingly, the rich kids all had similar, boring secrets. From crashing daddy's cars to drug charges to almost getting kicked out of school until their parents paid someone off, they were all the same, and all boring.

"Why do you want your dad to let you take over his company?" I asked her, wanting to know more about her and less about them.

"Why wouldn't I? Wouldn't you?"

"I meant, what is the reason? You want the money, the power, the status? What?"

I groaned as she wiggled again, her ass rubbing hard against me.

"All of it," she whispered. "I want to be in charge of my life. I want a legacy for our family. I want money to do whatever I want with. I want people to look at me and not see a boring little rich girl. I want people to stop watching my every move just to criticize me for them."

"You want them to fear you."

"Not quite fear, *Mr. Serial Killer*, but more like...respect me."

The idea that she could want a sliver of the life I wanted instantly made me hard.

"Do you know secrets about my dad?" she asked. The question felt like a knife to my chest. Her dad was the reason I came back for her in the first place and the only reason we were together tonight.

Now his daughter was in my lap, and I would be taking her up to her room, in his house, to fuck her only to keep her occupied, so my friends could tear the house apart.

"Yes," I said. "Plenty."

"Would you tell me?"

"Maybe a different night. Have you told him about me?"

She nodded. "A little, but I didn't tell him your real name."

My heart twisted. She was keeping my secrets. She was doing everything I fucking needed her to do so I could use her to ruin him. "Why?"

She sighed, sinking deeper against me as her face fell. "I didn't think you would want me to."

I leaned my head back, closing my eyes as my hand still moved over her leg.

The revenge-focused part of my brain suddenly short-circuited. Could Regan actually be loyal to me over her own father? I had never considered it a possibility, but here she was, lying to him to protect me.

I kept my eyes closed, thinking over her confession. "Tell me if someone suddenly decides they want to kill me," I mumbled.

She gave a small laugh, adjusting on top of me. "I can move, Rook."

I didn't open my eyes but grabbed on tighter, holding her in place. "Don't."

Luckily, she listened, her fingers moving up my chest and tracing over tattoos on my neck.

I had no ideations about love. There was never any dream of falling for it one day.

But this felt like something it could be. Someone who wasn't going to tell our secrets, the moments between us all our own. Someone who would always have my back and always face the world with me. Someone who would let me sit here in silence, posted up on my lap to warn me if there was a problem.

Someone who would give me five fucking minutes of peace.

I didn't know how long I sat there, the party carrying on around us, but I didn't care until I heard another drink open.

My eyes flickered open, watching her as she took another long sip.

"Getting drunk?"

"I think so. How many have I had?"

"I don't think I could keep count. What's wrong, Rebel? Too nervous about me staying here?"

She groaned and drank more. "Don't remind me."

"Am I really that bad?" I grinned, already knowing she thought I was.

She leaned back, mumbling something, but I couldn't make out the slurred words.

"Alright, Rebel. I think it's time to get you upstairs."

"No, I think I'm alright," she said, the gagging sound after it not convincing me.

"Sure. Let's go be alright in your room, then." I picked her up, sweeping her legs out from under her. "Try not to puke on me."

"I'm not going to puke." Her voice was unsteady, and I knew she had to be fighting back the urge to gag again.

"Right. Do you always throw back more drinks than you can count, get unsteady on your feet, and then start gagging?"

We headed inside, but Aiden stopped me, nodding that he needed to talk to me. I set her down on a kitchen stool, making sure she would sit up on her own. "I'll be right back, Rebel. Try not to move."

She mumbled again, leaning back in the chair.

Aiden waited near the open kitchen arch, turned away from her. "There's a pretty serious lock on her dad's office door. Hero isn't sure if he can get inside."

"Hero has never had an issue with locks."

"This one is set up with a key and a code. You have to have both to open it."

I sighed, glancing back to make sure Regan had stayed still. "Get Evie on the code, and Hero on the lock. You, Kane, and Zack can keep looking around. She'll be busy for the night."

Aiden glanced back and laughed. "Wow, you really misunderstood the whole 'keep her busy in the room' thing. I meant sex, Rook, not get her so drunk she passes out."

I hit his arm. "Asshole. She got nervous and drank too much."

"Nervous? Or just has to get drunk to handle looking at your face?"

I looked back again, and she was a little more pale than before.

"Alright, fuck off, I'm taking her upstairs. You should have a few hours, but keep your phone on you. Where's Harper?"

"Her friend?" Hero asked. "The one currently making out with Zack?"

"Apparently, we should have put Zack on the whole seduction thing, because he's already out there closing the deal, unlike you."

I nearly hit him again, but the whine of an alarm filled the house. I heard a curse from Hero. Evie ran into the room, eyes wide.

"I triggered an alarm," she said. "I don't know what happened, but I triggered it."

"How do we turn it off?"

"We need the code or I'm assuming the police will be here in ten-ish minutes."

"What the fuck?" I muttered, looking back at Regan. Her eyes were wide now, looking around the house. "Regan," I said, running over and helping her up. "Someone accidentally hit the alarm. Can you turn it off?"

"There's a different code to turn it off," she slurred.

"Okay, do you know it?" Her eyes narrowed, but she let me help her to the office where I planted her in front of the alarm code box. "Here, baby, can you type it in?"

"Are we still calling me that?" she asked, her hand reaching up and holding onto the box. I planted myself behind her, nearly holding her up.

"Yes, we are," I said, laughing. "Do you know the code? Can you turn this thing off?" She grumbled, hitting the key code once, but nothing stopped. "You know the code?"

"Mmhmm," she mumbled, hitting the keypad again. The alarm beeped again before going silent.

She spun, running right into my chest. I leaned down, picking her up before she completely fell over. "I'm done," I said. "Be more careful, because that was way too fucking close. If you can't get in, do what you can to get a bug near the door or something. We need something to give us more information on what he's doing."

"Rook, I still don't know what happened. I really don't know if I can do this without triggering it again," Evie said.

"Then do as much as you can. You saw the shutoff code she used. Try to get the door open, but don't let it go off more than another one or two times. I'll pick up her phone if the alarm company calls her, but we can't raise too many red flags because I don't know when it will call Cameron." Regan mumbled again, and I headed up the steps. "Text me if you make any progress. I'll let you know if anything changes on my end, but I think we are good with her for the night."

"I'm going to puke," she mumbled. I picked up my pace, trying not to shake her too much as I made it to her bedroom door and headed into the bathroom I knew she had off to the side.

I barely set her down before she leaned over the bowl, puking.

I hid my laugh as I sat down next to her as she continued.

"When I planned to keep you locked in your room all night, this wasn't what I had in mind," I said, brushing her hair back again.

"No? What were your ideas? Ritualistic killing? Violently torturing a man to death? Starting a cult?"

"Well, those weren't my first ideas, but I love where your mind is. A cult could be fun. Would you like to be the leader? We can start with ritualistic killings immediately. Should I assume the attitude means you're feeling better?"

"No. I feel worse. Why are you still here?"

I had been asking myself the same question. I could probably go. It wasn't like she would be getting far from this bathroom for an hour or two at least, so they would still have time to search if they got in.

"Thought you wouldn't mind company."

"I mind. Nobody that has watched while I did...other things needs to watch me do this."

I laughed as she crawled back over, and I handed her the bottle of water I had grabbed from the kitchen as I leaned back against the wall.

"I can handle seeing you throw up."

"Oh, that's right, you see guts for a living. This should be nothing for you."

"Honestly, guts and vomit. A lot of people vomit when you

cut into body parts." She gagged, leaning back over like she might puke again. "I'll assume you're not a big drinker, then?"

"Yeah. Also not big on cutting off body parts, so could we keep that out of the conversation?"

I smirked, kicking my legs out before pulling her across the floor until she was leaning back against me between them. She groaned and her head rolled to the side to look at me. "Why are you being so nice? You're always being so nice. Are you always this nice to people you're trying to sleep with?" she asked with a quiet laugh.

I smiled against her hair, my lips pressing against her head. "No. I usually don't spend more than a few hours with people I sleep with."

"Oh." The word was barely a hiccup. "What are all your friends doing downstairs?"

"Why is a drunk girl asking so many questions? Doesn't that brain shut off at some point?"

"Not when there are so many things going on. I spend enough time alone with no one to answer my questions."

"I think I would kill to have more time alone."

She laughed again. "Bad choice of words. I have too much alone time, and too many questions."

"I can always try to answer any of your questions, but you might not always like the truth."

She gave an exasperated sigh and grabbed my hands, pulling them to rest them on top of hers, apparently inspecting the tattoos.

"But it's the truth, so I do like it. I get left in the dark with so many questions unanswered. I would rather know an ugly truth than be completely naïve."

I stayed quiet, thinking about how little she must be told. How little her dad wanted to involve her. Before I could find anything to say, she went heavy in my arms, nearly on top of me as she fell asleep.

But instead of getting her into bed or moving, I stayed right there. From in here, the house was quiet. I felt an unexpected sense of comfort holding her, something I hadn't felt in a long time. I could hear her soft, steady breaths, feel the rise and fall of her chest against mine.

Every part of me wanted to stay in that moment, so I held her tighter, my thoughts slowing down. The troubles of the outside world seemed to fade away. I found myself sinking into a calmness I didn't know I needed, and before I knew it, I had drifted off to sleep, too, holding her close.

Twenty-Two
Regan

My tongue grated against the roof of my mouth like sandpaper.

I blinked, trying to get my bearings before I realized I was back in my bed, but more importantly, I wasn't alone.

I rolled over, not expecting who was next to me.

"Harper? Where did Rook go?"

Her head popped up, looking around in a daze. "I think he left after he dumped you into bed with me."

"Last night?"

"I came in around two in the morning, so after that? I don't know. I wasn't looking at the clock."

It was eight now, so he had stayed with me most of the night. I hadn't heard the bikes, so I slipped out of the room. Each of the rooms I checked in was empty, but the beds were all a mess. Obviously, his friends had stayed the night.

The back patio was empty of bikes, but trash from the party had been thrown everywhere. I groaned. I should never throw another party simply because I didn't want to be alone here. Or because I was mad at my dad for always leaving, no matter how much I needed him.

But Rook had stayed. He even stayed while I was too busy throwing up. As much as I wanted to find it sweet, it made me more nervous about what he wanted from me.

I went back up to my room to get dressed before shaking Harper a little.

"I'm heading out for a bit. You good?"

"Mhhmm," she mumbled, burying her head in the pillows.

I grabbed my bag, heading out to my car. I didn't drive much, but I loved my car. The BMW M4 was wrapped in hot pink, and it was exactly what I had wanted. My dad had given it to me years ago when I graduated from high school, but I had rarely needed it at college. Then, when I came back, he had insisted on me getting driven everywhere, so I let it sit even longer.

But things had changed for me now. If I wanted to be in control of my life, getting in control of taking myself places would be an easy first step.

I headed into town first and then parked myself in front of Maverick Moto. The shop was already open for the day. I held the box of donuts in one hand, and my phone and keys in the other.

Mason grinned when I walked in. Aiden stood next to him with a grin on his face, too.

"Hey, there," Mason said with a laugh. "Heard you had a great night."

"Real great night," Aiden said. "Are those *sorry for puking on you* donuts for Rook?"

"I did not puke on him!" I yelled, my eyes wide, hoping he was kidding.

They both reached over, trying to open the box. I smacked at their hands, their eyes going wide and mouths dropping open.

"After those comments, I don't think you two deserve any donuts."

"Aww, come one," Mason said. "We're hungover and forced to work today."

They both pouted, waiting patiently for donuts. "We're kidding, Regan. We thought it was funny that Rook was playing nursemaid all night."

"I don't like that either. Still no donuts."

"Okay, how about Rook is all about you to the point he would rather hang out with you puking than go out riding? It's a big deal. We get to make fun of him until he tries to kill us."

Aiden reached out, waiting for me to hand him the box as he flashed that perfect smile. "You really think that sweet smile is going to get you a donut?"

"If you give me a donut, I won't tell Rook how sweet you think my smile is," Aiden said, laughing.

As if he heard us, Rook stepped out.

I couldn't move, the heat spreading over me until my cheeks were hot and my thighs clenched. How did he still look good after a night of no sleep and taking care of me? His dark shirt clung to him and his jeans hung low on his hips. Two full arms of tattoos and ones creeping up his neck seemed to turn me on more, and I couldn't believe I had been so nervous to spend the night with him that I got drunk instead of taking a chance at sleeping with him.

"Regan? What are you doing here?" he asked, coming around the counter to me. He immediately flipped open the lid to the donuts. "Delivery?"

I nodded, and he didn't hesitate to grab one.

Aiden and Mason groaned. "We try to grab one and she wants to take an arm off. You take one and she's fine. I see you're picking favorites," Mason said.

"Of course she's picking favorites," Rook said. "If you think you even had a chance to be the favorite, you need your ass kicked." He walked us out of earshot of the guys, leaving the box behind as he turned to me. "What are you doing here?"

"I came to apologize."

"Apologize for what?"

"Um," I said, looking around to see if anyone could hear us. "Getting so drunk that I couldn't even handle getting myself to bed?"

He smiled, another true, genuine smile, and I wondered if my legs could give out just from that.

"There's nothing to apologize for. You're allowed to have fun."

"But you kind of implied you wanted to do other things."

"And it got you so worked up you had to get drunk to get out of it." He laughed now, and I smacked him.

"Rook, I did not," I hissed. "I mean, I didn't do it to get out of it."

"It's alright. You were having too much fun being a rebel. What are you doing later?" he asked.

"Tonight? I have a date," I said. It was a lie, and one I didn't know why I was telling him, but part of me wanted to see his reaction. Maybe it would help me figure out what he wanted from me. If this all revolved around sleeping together, or more.

His scowl made me laugh, and I wondered what terrible things were on his mind. I nearly scolded myself for how giddy it made me that I knew he was thinking dark, dangerous things all because I would be going out with someone else.

"With who?"

"None of your business."

He grabbed the back of my neck, dragging me closer. "You are always coming around here being a brat," he said with a shake of his head. "It absolutely is my business. What the fuck do you think you are doing going on a date with someone?"

"I'm a free woman."

I wanted to pull away, but there was a part of me, a dark and twisted part, that liked his possessiveness. I wanted to be wanted, to be *needed* by someone, and Rook continued to give that to me. It was a dangerous game, one that I knew I couldn't win, but here I was still playing.

"Maybe you shouldn't be," he growled. One arm circled my waist, picking me up just enough that my toes could barely touch the ground as he dragged me towards the garages in the back.

Fear involuntarily bubbled in my throat. I knew Rook could be violent. I knew he could hurt others, kill them, and I had let myself get comfortable with that. I had let my guard down and then walked right into his hands. But he had taken care of me all night. His touch had been gentle, and him being with me had been a comfort. I didn't think he would hurt me, but now he was dragging me down the hall like he wanted to.

His grip was firm on my waist. The other still wrapped around my neck. His fingers dug into me, and for the first time in days, I wondered again if I had misjudged him. It was easy to hide who you truly were for the days we hung out. It's not like he had let me into his life at all.

The possibilities of what he could do, would willingly do, twisted my gut with dread and excitement.

We made it to the office before he said a word.

"Lie down," he ordered, pushing things across the desk.

"Why? What are you going to do?"

That sinister grin came over his face, the one I knew from the first night we met, and my heart raced.

"Lie down, Regan."

I listened, too scared to find out what would happen if I didn't.

He pulled out a black marker before he pulled my shirt up and my leggings down. "I'll be nice and give you this one for now," he said, moving my head back down when I tried to watch.

"But if you wash this off before your date, the next one will be permanent."

He leaned down over me, the marker pulling against my skin as he wrote on my lower stomach. It almost tickled, but the hard push of the tip made me hold my breath.

"That's what you are doing?" I yelled, looking down at his name scrawled across my lower stomach. My head fell back against the desk, and I let out a heavy breath. "Dammit, Rook, I thought you were about to cut me open or something."

He laughed and jumped up onto the desk, coming down over me. "Why would I kill you?"

"I don't know. Maybe this is your murder room or something."

"This would be a pretty shitty murder room. There are papers, my bike, the desks. Who would clean it up?"

"All this because I had a date?"

"No, all of this because I told you that you are mine, and you didn't listen."

"So I'm supposed to go out with him, but apparently, not get undressed in front of him?"

He shrugged, kissing down my neck. "You could technically get undressed in front of him, but he's going to have questions. And I will be there to answer every single one. There is a third option."

"Which is?" I asked, my face flushed, the heat creeping up my spine from him kissing me.

"You go out with me tonight instead."

"You're...asking me on a date?"

"We're all going out for a ride tonight, and then a movie. You could come with me."

"So not a date?"

He sighed, leaning his head down onto my shoulder. "Whatever you need to call it to make you go with me."

"That's not an answer," I demanded. I stayed still underneath him. One minute, I was scared the man could kill me, and the next, I was demanding he tell me if we were going on a date or not.

He moved down my neck, kissing his way to my collarbone. "It's enough of an answer. Are you coming with me? Or are you going out on a date, so I have to follow you all night?"

"You wouldn't."

"I absolutely would."

"Fine. I'll go with you, so one, you don't stalk me more, and two, I don't wake up tomorrow with a permanent tattoo of your name on me."

He gave a satisfied groan, dropping to kiss me. "I change my mind. Please go on your date. Stalking you, killing him, tattooing my name on you. It sounds like my dream date."

"I'm going with you!"

"Fine," he said, pressing his groin against mine. "Then get out of here so I can get things done, and I'll pick you up later."

"You're really going to take me out and let me see some sliver of your life?"

"I am," he said as he got up and kissed his name written on me. Then he was pulling me to my feet with him. His arm wrapped around my shoulders, walking me back out front to the shop and then to my car. "You drove here? I assumed you had a fancy ass driver waiting out here."

"Nope, just me and my car."

"Do you drive it often? I've never seen it. I love it, but I've never seen it."

"You seem shocked, and I'm really glad I'm the one surprising you this time. And to answer your question, no, I haven't driven it in years."

"Why today?"

"It felt...rebellious," I said, smiling as I got in. "I'll see you later?"

"You'll hear me coming, Rebel."

"Or you can text me like a normal person," I yelled, putting down the window as I started the car.

"No," he yelled, grinning as I backed out. "That fun new tattoo you have better be there when I see you tonight."

I couldn't find anything to say as I pulled out, glancing back more than once to see Rook still there, watching and waiting as I left. I would see him in a few hours, and I already wished it wouldn't be that long.

I felt like I was losing my mind. One day, I had been living my perfectly normal life, and the next, I had gotten on the back of a murderer's motorcycle and had been chasing after him ever since.

I didn't know if this was a slow descent into madness or if I had tripped and fallen into it immediately. But either way, I liked it.

TWENTY-THREE

ROOK

I wasted no time grabbing everything I needed and heading to Regan. She had texted me three times, each one demanding to know when I would be there, but I hadn't told her.

Instead, I pulled up on my bike around six and revved it loud. I knew the echo of the engine would make it into the house and I knew she would be listening. It barely took two minutes before she headed out to me, waving her arms to stop.

"My dad is home," she yelled. "Don't do that again or he's going to come out here and interrogate you."

My heart raced immediately. Cameron Fletcher was right inside. Not only inside his house, but in a house I now knew well. One I could get in without him knowing and kill him.

I ran my hand along the gun in my side pocket. It would be so easy. It would be over in less than ten minutes, and I wouldn't have to see Regan or keep up this game anymore.

But I already knew it wouldn't be enough. I wanted him to suffer. I wanted the last hours of his life to feel like the last ten years of mine had felt. I needed him to know an ounce of the pain I felt at what he did to us.

So instead of stalking in there, I would take Regan out. I would make sure I actually tried to learn everything I could and understand what Cameron cared about, so I could take it away.

Even if I had been failing at learning anything new about him.

I reached behind me, grabbing the pink and black helmet off the seat and handing it to her.

"What's this?"

"Your helmet."

"*Mine?*"

"Yes, yours." I turned it around, showing her the small pink name running along the side. *Rebel.*

"You put that on there?"

"Technically, Evie did. She has all that computer shit and printed it out."

"And you told her to? Or she did it for me?"

My palms were hot at her demanding an answer. I didn't mind doing things for people, but the entire show that came after made me anxious.

"I did," I said fast, pulling the matching jacket out of the backpack I'd brought. "This, too."

"Rook," she whispered as she held it up. It was a simple black leather jacket. We all wore similar ones, and hers wouldn't stand out any more than ours. Our helmets were all different. I kept most of my favorite ones a plain black, but we all had a variety.

"These are actually for me?"

"They are. I was getting pretty annoyed with mine getting taken every time," I lied. It never bothered me, but I wanted her to have her own that actually fit.

She bit at her lip before stepping forward. Her arms snaked around my neck and her lips found mine. The hot, desperate need to sink into her came over me. Like she could read my thoughts, she deepened the kiss, pushing harder against me as her tongue moved faster against mine. Her hands slipped under my shirt and ran over my stomach, hitting scarred skin, and she hesitated for a second before continuing.

"Better get on the bike," I whispered, already moving down her sides to reach for the button on her jeans.

She smacked my hand away and pushed the helmet on. I had already hooked up an earpiece in it, but I stayed quiet as she got on.

Her arms wrapped around me, and I took off. The bike rumbling beneath us as I pulled out and headed towards the highway.

"Helmet feel okay?" I asked after I realized she was mumbling something to herself.

Her arms tightened as she leaned down further. "I didn't know you could hear me. Please tell me you didn't hear all of that."

"I didn't, but now I'm curious about what you said."

"Nothing. Nothing at all. Where are we going?"

"First," I said, taking a turn a little faster than she was used to, "we are going to teach you how to ride on the bike the right way. Then, we are going out with the group. Evie planned some night out, and we are going."

"Where to?"

"You'll see. For now, just learn how to be on the bike without falling off or killing me."

We drove for another two hours. I spent plenty of time making her go around curves and turns, speeding up and slowing down. She screamed when I slammed the brakes, the bike tipping forward just enough to make her fall onto me more as she cursed.

"What are you doing?" she yelled, holding me tighter. "*Don't* do that again."

"Okay, I won't," I said, smiling. "You better hold on very, *very* tight, Rebel. I would hate to put that helmet to use the first day."

"What—"

Her words cut off as I sped up and pulled the bike onto the back wheel. She screamed again, holding on tighter as I kept it up. I made it another hundred feet down the road before dropping back down. Her hands let me go the second she was steady, smacking at my shoulders.

"Why. Would. You. Do. That?" she yelled, a smack coming with each word.

"Because you did fine. I didn't think you would fall off. Not completely, at least."

"You're the worst."

"Yet you get on the bike every single time."

That seemed to shut her up, but her arms held onto me still.

I stayed on the winding road, leaning the bike back and forth until she finally leaned with me and relaxed. Soon, her arms weren't grabbing me in death grips and her body wasn't a board behind me. We kept going deeper into the forest, the trees thickening as we made it to the next town and made our way up the small mountain.

"Are we going somewhere specific?" she asked, her hands moving from the tank to my legs as the road straightened out.

"Yes. Like I said, something Evie set up." Her hands moved higher up my thighs, reaching my groin. "Rebel," I said, trying to hide my groan as her hand moved over me.

"Yes?"

The bike slowed as she continued her exploration. Soft hands slipped under my shirt, my stomach clenching at the touch. She moved over the scars, her fingers trailing over them with a softer touch before going up and over my chest. I was glad the bike would hide the shiver that ran through me. Her nails glided down. The light scratch over my stomach to the top of my jeans made me want to lose my mind.

I sat up more, and she took the invitation. Once again, she surprised me. Every time I thought she would retreat, Regan pushed forward and acted like the rebel I knew she wanted to be. Ever since the first night, she had taken every challenge to do whatever I asked of her. I should have known she would push this, too.

Her hands ran over my jeans, my cock already hard from being felt up by her. I rarely had anyone ride with me. It wasn't that I was uncomfortable with someone on with me, I just didn't prefer it. Regan, though, was finally getting the hang of it. She was also getting the hang of feeling me up when I sat defenseless to her hands.

It was a blissful torture, and I didn't want it to stop.

She ran over my length again, a small appreciative moan echoing through my helmet and turning me on more.

"Is this because of me or do you just really like riding your bike?" she asked, almost laughing.

"I do like my bike, but I promise that's not what I'm currently thinking about fucking."

She froze, her hand resting on my cock before she pressed the slightest bit harder. I groaned, wanting to press into it, but I couldn't in this position.

"You are going to hate the moment I stop this bike."

"And why's that?"

I swerved the bike back and forth between the lines. Night had fallen, the moon already coming up now.

"Because I'm going to catch you, Rebel," I said as her other arm draped over my shoulder, her fingers brushing along my neck. "And I'm putting every damn inch of this to use when I do."

The abandoned house finally rose in the night, the darkened windows and sagging porch looking as bad as I remembered it. We came here once in a while. It used to be more for partying. Now it was when Evie wanted to change things up for whatever event she needed us to celebrate.

The cool night rushed over me as I pulled off my helmet, the scent of decay and damp ground making me relax. I liked it here, the calm, quiet making me feel at home.

"*This* is where we are going?" Regan asked, swinging off the bike.

"It is."

"Why? This is...creepy."

"I'm pretty sure that's the point. Scary movie, scary place."

"You brought me all the way out here to watch a scary movie in a place where scary movies take place? And you somehow thought I would stay?"

"Where would you go, Rebel? You're here all alone without a ride home. You are stuck, miles from another house, and miles from anyone who could help you."

"Stop it," she said, backing up and putting her hands on her hips, but I could hear the small shiver of fear in her tone.

I swung off, setting my helmet down. "They say a deranged doctor lived up here and did experiments on humans. That there is even one of them still living up here today. Do you think he's in the house? Or maybe the woods?"

"Okay, what if I'm too freaked out for this?"

"I thought I was the monster? Who else would come grab you besides me?"

"I don't know. Maybe the half-human monster thing. At least you are all human."

"Then you better let me be the one to catch you. Run, run, Rebel."

I stalked towards her as her eyes went wide. I knew she wasn't that scared of me anymore. She wouldn't have gotten on the bike if she had been, but I still liked the way she took a deep breath, the way her nostrils flared and chest heaved. Her hand pushed at her hair, tucking it behind her ears.

"Rook," she breathed, taking a step back towards the woods.

The clear line of trees surrounded the house and as soon as she disappeared into it, I could run after her.

A gust of wind came. The old door on the front of the house opened and slammed back shut, echoing around us.

She jumped and took off, disappearing into the woods.

My stomach flipped, my heart already racing. The thrill of catching her pulsed through me, but I tried to tamp it down just long enough to let her get a head start.

She was mine, and there was no chance I wouldn't catch her.

I would always catch her.

Twenty-Four
Regan

I mumbled a string of curse words as I ran into the woods. I wasn't going far, just enough to circle around the house and come back out on the other side. There was no way I was going to risk getting myself lost in these woods, but I was still going to play along. I wanted to play. I wanted to feel how bad he wanted to catch me.

I didn't hear him behind me, but really, anything past the rush of my heart was gone.

I made it around the back of the house to find an old dresser sat near one wall, the long drawers and tall mirror giving me a perfect place to hide. I slipped behind it and crouched down. My breaths came in shallow gasps, my heart pounding like a drum. I strained to hear any hint of Rook approaching, but the silence wrapped around me. The anticipation of him catching me coiled in my stomach, mixing with the fear and exhilaration.

A twig snapped, catching my attention as I held my breath. I could hear his footsteps now, the slow calculated movements making me a little more scared. He wasn't mindlessly running after me. He was taking careful steps as I stumbled around the forest. Rook was a predator, and I would always be the prey.

It should disgust me, but there was no denying how excited I got every time he wanted to catch me. He would always come after me.

I peeked out from behind the dresser just in time to see him round the corner and scan the area with narrowed eyes. Our gazes locked, and he smiled.

"Hi, Rebel."

Without hesitation, I jumped from my hiding spot and bolted past Rook, his hand outstretched just enough to grab me. One hand wrapped around my waist, pulling me to him and spinning me until my back slammed against his chest. The other hand wrapped around my neck.

"Rook!" I yelled, but he held me close. My body pressed hard against him, and I leaned into it.

"Got you," he whispered, his lips already dragging down my neck. He bit down, making me arch into him. Heat flooded me, my thighs pressing hard together as he squeezed my neck a little more. "I'll always get you. How scared are you, exactly?"

"Scared enough that if you let me go, I'm going to scream."

"You're going to scream either way, Rebel."

He unbuttoned my jeans, pulling them down to my knees before he pushed me forward. My forehead was nearly against the dresser mirror now, and I watched in it as he ran his hands down over my hips.

"Did you enjoy your game on the bike?"

"What game?" I asked, trying to sound as innocent as I could.

He laughed, the deep rumble making me freeze. A scream came from inside the house, the wind whistling through one of the broken windows, adding to the eeriness and making me shiver.

He dropped to his knees behind me. "Did you like trying to

fuck with me on the bike, Rebel? Or were you just disappointed that we didn't stop *to* fuck on the bike?"

"Yes," I said, nearly holding my breath as his fingers trailed down my hips.

"Yes, to which?"

"Both."

He groaned and hooked a finger under the band of my underwear, pulling them down and taking my jeans with them to my ankles. He unzipped the jacket, pulling it off and pushing my shirt up.

The cold air rushed over my breasts, making me gasp.

"Bend over," he said. I did, bending over the dresser as he forced my legs wider.

I gasped as his head buried between my legs. His tongue moved along me, his fingers digging into my ass to spread me open more. Each swipe of his tongue made me want another.

He pushed me forward further, holding me against the dresser. My heart pounded in my chest as my back arched. He continued, but I wanted more than just his mouth. He gently sucked and licked along me again before he pulled back.

"Are you ready for me now, Rebel?" he asked, his voice deep with lust.

"Yes," I nearly whimpered, feeling his warm breath on my lower back. He stood back up, his fingers trailing up my thigh and between my legs. I moaned as fingertips brushed over my sensitive clit, making me tighten. "I need it, Rook. Please."

He laughed, but I heard the zipper on his jeans. "I like you begging. Do you finally like being my pretty little slut?"

"Only if you give me some sort of relief and not just tease me."

I could feel his cock press against me now. He slid it back and forth through my wetness, teasing me more.

"I want to hear it before I give you anything else."

"Hear what?"

"Hear every detail about how you like being mine. How you like to be used and filled as my pretty slut."

"I like it. I like you making me get off on your bike, and you. I like getting on my knees for you." My breathing was ragged now, my heart pounding as I met his eyes in the mirror. The wild look in his gaze made me continue. "I like being naked and spread over this thing, knowing I will be filled and stretched until I want to cry."

He pressed forward, the tip of him sliding into me, and I arched, wanting more. He grabbed my hips, keeping control as he went deeper.

My fingers dug into the wood, my body tightening as he slowly filled me. The sting of his size made my eyes squeeze shut.

"Your perfect pussy is stretched, baby. It's taking me so good." He kept going, and I wiggled as he went a little deeper than I planned for. "You're so fucking tight. Does it hurt, Rebel?"

I nodded, trying to breathe as he continued. My head fell against the dresser. Somehow, the pain felt good. The sting of me wrapping around him as I tightened in need made me wetter.

He pulled out, pushing into me faster once. "I want it to sting, baby. I want you to suffer for me. I want you to remember me buried in you with every step you take tomorrow."

"Yes," I breathed. "Give me that."

"I want to slam into you, but I like this view too much." His hand ran over my ass, a finger pressing against the opening. "This is mine, too. I want it all, Regan. I want all of you."

I didn't say anything, not wanting to think about his words besides him wanting all of me. Moonlight streamed onto the mirror, bouncing off of it and giving me a full view of what we were doing. The shadows danced over his face, leaving half in the darkness and half in an eerie glow.

He pushed into me again, harder this time. He didn't stop or slow down. Each thrust was met with a moan from my lips, and I pushed back to match his pace. The satisfaction of him filling me only turned me on more. The sensation was overwhelming. He groaned in pleasure as his hand reached between my legs, teasing my already sensitive clit.

As I gasped for air, the orgasm built. I arched my back, gripping the dresser for support, and my eyes found him in the mirror again. He looked beautiful in the light, the pleasure on his face so clear, and my heart flipped that I was the reason it was there. My orgasm was getting closer, and I couldn't handle it. I needed more. He must have read my thoughts because he picked up the pace, slamming into me harder and faster.

I moaned, and his hand wrapped around my neck, pulling me back to him.

"You are all mine, Rebel. Come all over my cock and make me yours."

I gasped at his words, my orgasm unstoppable now. I screamed out his name as I was sent over the edge, feeling the waves of pleasure crash against me, leaving me breathless.

My nails dug into the dresser, trying to hold on as the world faded away. Stars burst in my eyes, my body shaking hard as I came. I looked in the mirror back at him. His dark hair had fallen over his forehead as his mouth dropped open with a moan.

His hips thrust harder, his breathing growing ragged. "You're so fucking tight, Rebel," he said, his voice hoarse now. "I can't last any longer."

"Good, don't," I said.

He grinned, his eyes filled with that hunger for me. With one final thrust, he let out a deep groan, filling me completely.

My body shook, another shiver running through me as he leaned onto me.

"Fuck, Regan. I should have planned this out better, so I could lie down after that."

"You better be able to drive me home because I think I'm the one that won't be able to walk, and you have to drive a motorcycle back."

He groaned, pulling out of me and fixing his jeans. "Don't even remind me of that right now. All I have to do first is sit with you and watch a movie." He grumbled again. "And now that I say that, I wish I would have planned this out, so I could do that in a bed, too."

Rook spun me to face him before trying to help me clean up what he could and pulling my jeans up.

"You okay to go inside?"

"If it means sitting down, yes," I huffed, my body still buzzing from the orgasm.

He wrapped an arm around me, leading me inside to what I could only guess had been a main living room at some point. He pointed to a seat near the back. Someone had set up a variety of camp chairs, blow up chairs, and even a blow up mattress that Evie lay back on with Aiden next to her. We were apparently headed to a ridiculously big bean bag chair.

"This is...insane. You guys brought all this here?"

"Yeah, Evie wanted it. She likes to go all out," Rook said.

"All out for what?" I asked Rook, but Mason turned back to us, cutting off our conversation.

"Wow, nice of you two to join us," Mason said. "We heard screaming, but weren't sure if it was you two, someone getting murdered, or the haunted freaks hanging out here."

"Great," I mumbled, ready to curl into Rook. "Now your friends are going to be giving me comments all night."

"Tell him to shut the fuck up," Rook said, a smile on his face as he wrapped his arms around me.

"What? No. He's your friend. You do it."

"I would if you needed me to, but you really don't need me to. Tell him to shut the fuck up or you're going to make me hit him.

You're in charge, Rebel. Tell him now. Say it like you mean every word and then some."

It was another challenge. One more way to make me rebel, but this time, it was completely for me.

I faced Mason, trying to not let my voice shake. "Shut the hell up, Mason."

Mason's eyes narrowed, looking me over. "Or what?"

"Or I'm going to tell Rook how upset it makes me until he comes over there and makes you regret even opening your mouth."

Mason stared a moment longer before his face broke into a wide smile. "You show up and immediately have a fucking guard dog. Not fair," he said, but sat back, still smiling.

"A guard dog?" I asked, looking over my shoulder at Rook.

"Woof," he whispered, his breath tickling my ear.

"And that's it? I say the word and you hit him?"

"Pretty much."

"But he's your friend?"

"No friend of mine is going to disrespect you and there be no consequences. Mason is joking, so that should shut it down, but I promise, if you felt it was serious, he and I would have an issue."

"And he would hit you if the tables were turned?"

"I would imagine."

I leaned back into him, pulling the blanket Evie had handed me higher on my chest. "Evie, you really went all out on this. It's creepy, but not gross. You did amazing."

She smiled, leaning back in her pillow to face me more. "Thanks. I really don't have a lot to do around the shop sometimes, so I like to plan some fun stuff for us. It gets me out of the house and out of being trapped in a dirty garage with all these guys."

"What all do you do at the garage?" I asked.

Evie looked at Rook, and I could see the question. She was

waiting for him to give his approval, waiting to know if I was allowed to know things or not. I held my breath, already preparing myself to once again be left out.

Rook shifted behind me, and Evie looked back at me. "All the computer stuff. I'm really good at getting documents we need or getting into digital places we need to go. I run the website, the socials, the client list, everything like that."

They seemed like two different things, but I didn't want to ask a hundred questions the minute someone let me in.

"Oh, that's really cool. I don't know how you get bored with all that."

She shrugged. "You get good enough at it and it's just the same thing each time." The movie blared that it was starting, and she turned to it with a smile.

Rook's lips were at my ear. "She's essentially a hacker. She is very good at getting into *any* digital place we need."

"Interesting. Can you do any of that?"

He laughed, quietly. "Not even a little."

The movie boomed. The classic slasher film was actually one of my favorites. As much as I hated a lot of horror movies, the classic slashers were always good. Rook's arms tightened around me, sinking me further against him.

"Freaking out?" he whispered.

"Not at all," I said. "I'm apparently sleeping with the monsters now. What do I have to be scared of?"

TWENTY-FIVE
ROOK

Two days later, I was sitting in the garage with Aiden.
"What are we going to do?" Aiden asked, looking back over the paper. The place we lived together had officially sold, and they wanted us out in two weeks.

"About what?" I asked, my mind wandering from what we were talking about. I'd been too busy looking at my phone, wondering why Regan hadn't responded. I texted her yesterday and hadn't heard a word since. I'd been so busy working that I hadn't been able to go check on her, but it didn't seem like a good sign that she was ignoring me after we slept together. "Move? If they are selling the place and want us gone, what else would we do?"

"There's seven of us, Rook. Where the fuck are we supposed to move to?"

"Buy an entire apartment building? How the fuck would I know?"

"You want your name stamped on the mortgage? Do you want someone digging into us for five seconds and finding out where we all live? Unless we own the entire building, we don't have any good way to make sure it's safe enough."

"Pay cash. Buy a damn house. I don't care."

"Rook."

"What?" I yelled. "We have the shop. We'll stay here if we have to for a while until we find somewhere."

We had the garage door open, trying to get a little fresh air in the place after Hero dropped an entire can of cleaner earlier. A figure stepped into the open door, and we both jumped up, not expecting anyone back here this late.

The light spilled onto her, and I could finally see the girl's features. "Harper?"

"Hey," she said, taking one step into the garage. Her face was red and tear-stained, but she still straightened her shoulders to face us.

My heart thundered in my chest, wondering why Harper would be here, crying and upset. Regan hadn't messaged me, and now this.

Panic bubbled, and I clutched my phone hard. "Regan?"

"Not here, but she's fine."

"Okay," I said, taking a deep breath. "What are you doing here, then?"

"I need...help, and from what I've seen and heard, you guys might be people who could do what I need."

I glanced at Aiden, who raised an eyebrow. "We probably could," he said. "But you're going to have to be more clear."

"I'm being harassed, followed a lot. A guy won't leave me alone."

"And that is making you come to us to do what?"

"He pretty much attacked me tonight. I started a new job because I need some cash since my parents split, and I can't exactly be away from him since he's my manager."

"How bad?" Aiden asked, nodding at her.

"Bad enough that I think if something doesn't happen right now, there will be a next time and I will be in the hospital."

"And why wouldn't someone like you go to the police?" I asked.

Harper's family was wealthy. Since the divorce started, it seemed that most of that money had been tied up with a fight between her parents. Evie had dug up plenty of shit on them, but even with a string of public crimes, they were still a highly respected family. Between the divorce and one very private court case for fraud, most of their more liquid assets were frozen solid.

"There's been issues since my parents got divorced. They have all these ideas that I'm depressed and since they pay my tuition, I'm forced to go to therapy every week. I'm worried they will label me crazy and not do anything about it. They also don't know I got a job."

"Fair concern. Why not just quit?"

"I struggled to find this job. No one really believes someone with my last name would need a job, so they don't take me seriously. I'm looking for a new one, but he found out I would be leaving and it escalated. Fast. I think even if I never went back, he's going to be bothering me."

"Hard to argue that being possible. A rich, beautiful woman," Aiden said. "People would do depraved things if they thought it would get them a chance at that money, or you."

"And why would you think to come here?"

"Regan told me some of what she's seen. And she seems to trust you. A little, at least. I thought you might be willing to help me."

I wanted to ask more about the part of Regan trusting me, but I couldn't bring myself to say the words.

"What do you want us to do?" I asked. Aiden wasn't wrong about people trying to get close to her for the wrong reasons. And

if she felt like he wouldn't stop even if she left, she was also probably right.

"Stop him? Scare him? I don't know. Don't you break legs
and gouge eyes out or something?"

"You want his eyes gouged out?" Aiden asked, the disgust on
his face clear. "Where's Hero? I don't need to be there for that."

"He hates the eyeball stuff," I said, smiling. "We prefer cleaner
methods usually, but I guess we can take requests."

"Okay, no eyeballs, but is there something you can do to help?
I don't want to walk around looking over my shoulder every
second of the day and night."

I didn't answer. It wasn't a hard decision. I really didn't have a
problem helping her, and it was something we did enough that it
wasn't an added stress, but I debated asking something in return.

I wanted to know what Regan was doing now, what she had
been doing, and if there was a reason she wasn't talking to me.

If I did, though, it might seem like I cared about Regan.

But this would take up one more night of my life, which
meant not going to see her.

"It would help Regan, too!" she said fast. "If this guy is
following me, he would inevitably follow her. We're together
almost every day."

"I was already going to agree, but way to fight for it," I said
with a smirk.

"We're going to need all the information you have," Aiden
said, looking at me. "Maybe we can get him tonight? We have...
other things to do tomorrow."

Other things being looking into one name that kept coming
up on Cameron's paperwork. They had managed to make it into
Cameron's office the other day, but there wasn't much to find.
The man was smart, and besides some papers on his desk, everything was locked up tight. We hadn't managed to get any further

into his safe or records. We did get a bug put in his office, though, and hopefully that would help once he was back in town.

The one thing we had found, though, was a mystery. A name, Candy Collins, kept coming up, but we couldn't find a single trace of her besides an address to an old warehouse in the next town over. There was no birth record, no home addresses, nothing. We couldn't figure out if she was an escort for Cameron or some made up person he used to keep his business hidden. Maybe both.

It wouldn't be the first time a man was a little too trusting of his mistress.

We had found one paper with tomorrow's date and a time on it, but no indication of where anything was happening. The warehouse had seemed like the best bet.

Aiden and I would go to the warehouse. Hero and Mason would try to keep tabs on Cameron, and Zack and Kane would be parked outside of the Fletcher mansion, just in case. I had little concern that any business was happening at that house. From what Regan said, she was there alone ninety-five percent of the time, but I didn't want to risk it.

Harper was already telling Aiden the information as he tapped at Evie's computer.

Twenty minutes later, we had all the information we needed on the manager. I grabbed my keys, deciding to take my car. Shoving a guy into the trunk was a lot easier than figuring out the logistics of him on our bikes. We'd done it before, but I preferred to make my life easier.

"Stay here," I said to Harper. "At least then you can make sure we have the right guy." I yelled for Hero, who appeared from the front. "Can you stay with her until we're back?"

He nodded, heading out and dropping onto the couch opposite of her, already ignoring her and tapping away at his phone.

Aiden headed to the car, and I followed, but I stopped at the open garage door.

"Harper," I said, getting her attention. "Is Regan ignoring me?"

"Yeah. She's all freaking out after the party and whatever date you two had. I don't know what happened, but she's been all anxiety, all the time. Give her another day or two."

I nodded, heading out to the car. At least I had something else to focus on for a few hours.

The guy screamed and squirmed when I opened the trunk.

It had barely taken two hours, and we were back at the garage.We had been dealing with so many powerful, dangerous people, I had almost forgotten how easy it was to take a normal person.

He had been camped out in front of his TV, watching a split screen. Porn on one, camera footage on the second. We barely had to break in, finding the side door unlocked, and he was too busy getting off to hear us walk up behind him.

"If we ever, and I mean *ever*, have to pick someone up who is actively rubbing his fucking dick again, I will riot," Aiden said, getting out of the car. "I fucking mean it, Rook. I would rather take my own eyes out than watch an old, nasty man flailing around to pull up his pants, screaming, with a boner. That image will forever be burned in my brain. I would rather the eye gouging."

I laughed harder now. It had been a pretty fucking awful sight. "You mean to tell me you would have rather waited? You wanted to see that and then possibly get something on your hands?"

"Oh, fuck. No. Pervert cum." He gagged out the words. "Oh

god, that's worse. That's so much worse," he said, bending over to take a deep breath.

I nearly gagged at the thought myself, but quickly pushed the image aside as I popped the trunk.

"Hey, pervert," I said. "I saw your TV setup and thought you might like to see her in person."

I grabbed him by the little ponytail he had, lifting his top half as his bound feet kicked wildly. He screamed as Aiden grabbed his ankles to help lift him out.

"This is the easy part, man. Might as well save your breath," Aiden said. He stopped, pulling one of his hands away to inspect it. "This is disgusting. Now I feel like I'm touching pervert cum no matter what I hold on to."

"I can't imagine he's getting off on his ankles."

"You saw that setup. He'd glow under a black light. No amount of cleaning could clean up what he's been doing in there," Aiden said.

"Please stop talking or I'm going to drop him," I said through gritted teeth. Now I was the one who didn't want to be touching him.

"See, not very fun when you think about it," Aiden said as we hauled him into the chair. We had it set up under one of our lifts. It made it easy to put people in any position we wanted them in.

Harper came over, her eyes wide, the slight fear in them pissing me off further. "That's him."

"Perfect!" I said with a smile, turning to him. "It's your lucky day, well, kind of. We got the right guy."

Aiden smirked, reaching up to high-five me. I almost high-fived back, but stopped midway.

"We should wash our hands first."

"Definitely agree," Aiden said.

"Aren't you just going to get blood on you?" Harper asked, making the guy's eyes go wide.

"Blood and whatever nasty shit is on him are two very different things."

Hero stepped up to the guy, looking him over while Aiden and I cleaned up.

"This is the guy that's touching you?" he asked. The guy fought against the ties as Harper stepped up next to Hero.

"Constantly trying. He was groping me all day at work and when I left for the night, he attacked me in the parking lot and tried to assault me."

Hero flicked the guy's eyeball. The weirdo loved taking eyeballs out and I could never understand why. I didn't question it, but I didn't know why.

"You think you are so nasty that women won't touch you, so that gives you the right to force them into it?" he asked.

The guy violently shook his head no, and I laughed. "No? What about those creepy cameras that are obviously hidden in the bathrooms?"

"Eww, you are sick!" Harper yelled as her mouth dropped open. "What do we do now?"

"We make it hurt so he remembers not to do it again."

"Where do I start?" she asked, making us all turn to her in surprise.

"Are you sure you want to help?" I asked as she stepped closer.

"Very sure," she said.

Hero reached next to the couch, pulling out a bat and holding it out for her. She grabbed it, pulling a little too hard. When Hero let go, the bat did, too, smacking him in the face.

"Oh my god," Harper said. "I'm sorry!"

Hero groaned, grabbing his chin as Aiden and I laughed.

"Him!" Hero yelled. "You hit him. I'm not the fucking pervert."

"I didn't mean to," she said, looking at me.

"He probably deserves it anyway. Are you sure you can do this? I don't need vomit on our floor."

"I won't vomit."

"You're cleaning it up if you do."

She lifted the bat onto her shoulder and stepped up next to him. I thought she would take a few deep breaths, maybe even yell at him first, but she only raised the bat.

"Fucking angry girl with a bat. Fucking Harley Quinn shit," Hero mumbled, sitting back on the couch. His lip had split a little, blood pooling, but otherwise, he was fine.

The bat connected with the guy's legs, and he screamed against the gag.

I smiled, looking over at Harper, who was panting, but it wasn't her that caught my eye.

It was Regan, standing in the open garage door, her mouth dropped open as she took in the scene. I was sure the last thing she had been expecting was Harper here with us, doing this. She didn't say a word, but she spun on her heel, running back into the night.

Twenty-Six
Regan

R ook had texted me yesterday, but I ignored it. I was still spiraling from the night at the abandoned house, and honestly, every day I'd spent with him leading up to that.

It seemed like anytime he got close to me, I lost all common sense and gave in to exactly what I wanted to do. I didn't care about what came next or the aftermath of what we did.

Until I woke up today and had a full freak-out over it.

Rook wasn't anyone I could keep hanging around. He wasn't someone who was going to date me or be loyal to me. He told me I would be his until he was done with me, and I knew that would be true. The only problem was I wanted to be with him. I couldn't make any sense of all of it, but I wanted to be around Rook. I wanted to sleep with him, go out with him, get to know more about him.

I wanted to date a killer, and I wasn't sure how to handle it.

He wouldn't even think twice about walking away from me, and I knew it, but that didn't seem to persuade me to stop liking him.

I paced my room for the thousandth time, trying to decide if I should even let the entire thing continue or break ties now.

That line of thinking had me grabbing my bag, calling for a car, and driving to the other side of town. What I needed to do before I went out of my mind was talk to him. I needed to make sure he really didn't want to be together, and that this was just fun.

I tried to push away the hope that he could want this, and then realized how stupid it was to think someone like him would want to be with me, or honestly, that I would want to be with someone like him.

Maverick Moto had been closed for hours, but I knew Rook might be here this late. I headed around the back, seeing the garage door open. But when I stepped in front of it, I couldn't even understand what I saw.

Harper with a bat, a man tied up in front of her. Rook and Aiden stood next to her. Hero was leaning back on the edge of the couch, watching as she yelled and swung.

It was like my mind couldn't comprehend it. I logically knew what they were doing, but I couldn't piece together how this entire scenario would happen.

Rook grinned as the bat connected. Hero yelled out and Aiden laughed when the guy screamed.

Then Rook saw me.

"Regan," he said, apparently as shocked to see me as I was to see this.

I spun, taking back off into the dark to the waiting car, not looking behind me as I prayed I wouldn't hear a bike catching up.

By the time I made it home, I had already missed seventeen calls from Rook and Harper.

They tried again.

And again and again.

I couldn't talk to them yet. My brain was still racing, trying to piece together what I saw.

Not only the idea that Rook and Harper knew each other well enough to hang out, but to, apparently, know each other enough to torture a guy together. I wasn't sure that any amount of thinking about this would make it make sense.

I heard Rook's bike pull up ten minutes after I made it to my room, but I hid. I couldn't face him, not when I could barely get my thoughts straight.

The front door slammed, and I could hear him stomping up the steps.

"Regan!" he yelled, sounding more mad than concerned.

I stayed quiet, not moving from my spot in one of the spare rooms. I knew if I saw him now, I would give in, and I couldn't do that.

He stomped through the house, walking past the door I was behind a few times as he yelled for me more.

Another ten minutes went by before the house went silent. I pulled the door open, peeking out into the hall. I didn't hear or see anything, so I stepped out.

His bike started, the rumble echoing into the house and making me freeze.

When the whine of the bike finally disappeared and the house went silent, I walked back into my room and screamed. The red words dripping down my window made my heart race.

Call me.

My hands shook as I pulled out my phone, hitting Rook's name.

"Is this your blood or someone else's?" I asked the second I heard the call connected.

I could hear his bike faintly in the background. "You are

home. Should I turn around or are you going to hide from me again?"

"Is it yours or someone else's?" I asked again.

"Does it matter? It worked. You called."

"Whose is it?"

"Mine. Why are you hiding from me? What you saw wasn't—"

"I know exactly what I saw. My best friend and the guy I just slept with, killing someone *together*. What kind of fucked up idea is that? I don't even want to know how you talked Harper into that. Let alone what you think you are doing with Harper. I don't want to see you right now, so don't you dare come back here. And you know what? You're going to respect that, Rook. You are going to respect that I don't want to see you and leave me alone right now."

"Regan, that is not what happened. We were—"

"Shut up and don't call me again. And don't come here to do this creepy shit ever again, either."

I hung up, throwing the phone onto my bed before I followed, flopping down onto my stomach.

Maybe this was the sign from the universe I had been looking for. Like a big, light up neon sign telling me that trying to date a serial killer might not be the best choice in life.

Morning light streamed in and I heard the door to my room open. I didn't look up, already knowing it was either Harper or Rook.

"We need to talk," Harper said. I peaked out from under the blankets, seeing her standing at the end of my bed with her hands on her hips.

"I know."

"I should have talked to you first. I should have brought you with me," she said.

I sat up, pulling the blankets with me. "I don't get why you didn't. Or what you were even doing? Did Rook make you do something?"

She sat down, already shaking her head. "No, nothing like that. I have a job," she blurted out.

"With Rook?" My eyes felt like they bulged out of my head. He couldn't have really hired Harper, right?

"Oh my god, no. No! Down at a little shop in town. I've needed some money with my parents dealing with their divorce, but the manager is this creepy old man. Well, you saw him. He..." Her words died out, her lip curling. "He was trying to feel me up, and I was worried it wasn't going to stop."

"So you went to Rook?"

"I just didn't know how to explain any of it, and I knew you would freak out. Rightfully so, but I just needed to know he wasn't going to bother me again. I remembered what you said about Rook and his friends, and you seem to trust him enough, so I thought it wouldn't hurt to ask if they would help me."

Tears welled in her eyes, but she took a deep breath.

"Harper, I'm so sorry. Why didn't you tell me you needed money? Or got a job? Or needed help? I feel like such a shitty friend. I didn't know any of this."

"No, it's not your fault at all. It's all just been so much, I haven't known how to talk about it. You didn't do anything. You are literally there for me every day," she said.

"But I should have noticed something was going on."

She smirked. "You think I can't hide my issues? Yeah, right."

"That's true. The master at hiding your emotions. So Rook and them took care of things for you?"

"They did, and as you saw, I even took care of things a little myself." She smiled, her shoulders rolling back.

"You liked it?" I asked, already seeing the answer on her face.

"I liked being in control of the situation. When he was grabbing me in the parking lot, I felt so helpless. I always pride myself on handling things, and it felt like there was nothing I could do. I liked being able to stop him. I mean, I obviously had some help, but that didn't matter to him when he's tied up and begging me to stop. Tables really turned on that asshole."

"And what happened to him after?"

She shrugged. "I don't know. Hero was pretty pissed and I'm pretty sure he cut one or two things off. Rook—"

"Rook, what?" I asked, interrupting as I held my breath.

Her lips pursed together tight as if she was holding back a laugh. "Rook tattooed 'pervert' on his hands. He won't be able to hide from anyone."

My mouth dropped open. "Oh my god," I said, lying back.

"Are you mad?"

"I'm mad that I'm almost jealous that I missed it." I sat back up in disbelief. "I'm basically sad that I missed a man getting tortured? What is wrong with me?"

"I mean, I liked being there and helping a man get tortured, so if there is something wrong with you, there is something wrong with me. Does this mean you're not mad?"

I spread my arms, forcing her into a hug. "No. I wish you would have told me, but I get that sucks to talk about. Maybe let me in on it first next time you go talk to Rook about torturing someone?"

"I can absolutely do that," she said with a grin.

I huffed, realizing how little I knew about what was going on around me. From not knowing Harper had a job to not even being sure what my dad's company was doing. Not only was I locked away from the world around me, I was shut out by the people I loved. Maybe not on purpose, but I had been shut out.

I didn't want to be shut out or protected from the truth any longer.

"Tell me everything, Harper. Good, bad... Murdery. Just tell me. I've been kept from so much and you're my best friend. I support you, even if that includes cutting off body parts with Rook. Actually, please tell me if that's going to happen, so at the very least, I can be mentally prepared."

She laughed. "I really don't think that's going to be a common thing, but I will for sure let you know if it will happen again. Would you maybe want to hang out for a while?"

"That would be great. Do you care if I draw?" I asked, surprised at how excited I was to finish the drawing I had been working on.

"Not at all. Dateline?"

"Please."

She sat back, sinking onto the bed next to me. I wasn't sure if I was caught up on everyone's life yet, but I felt like I was getting closer.

TWENTY-SEVEN
REGAN

My phone chimed for the hundredth time, and like all the times before it, I opened the text and shut it, not ready to read whatever Rook had to say. It had been two days since I walked into the garage, and while I wasn't nearly as mad about the situation after talking to Harper, I still wasn't sure what I would do about Rook.

Another minute passed before his name popped up again, calling this time.

"Will you please stop calling me?" I said through gritted teeth. "What is your problem?"

"You," he said, the word drawn out. "You're my problem. You keep being my problem."

The words were just slurred enough that I paused before ending the call. "Are you drunk?"

"A bit."

"And why are you calling me?"

"Because I want you to come here."

"Where?"

"Hellfire Bar."

"And if I don't?" I asked, already knowing he would have a plan if I didn't.

"I will go find my bike in the parking lot and come there because they want me out."

"You can't drive it drunk. And what the hell are you doing to get yourself kicked out of Hellfire?" I asked. The place was notorious for trouble, and I imagined it would take a lot to get thrown out.

"Can and will. And the owner is mad because I want him to pay his tab with me before I pay mine with him."

"If I come get you and take you home, will you stop calling?"

"If I remember not to."

"Fine. I'll be there in twenty minutes. Don't move."

I quickly changed into jeans and a hoodie, grabbed my keys, and pulled out of the garage, heading straight for Hellfire Bar. I knew the location of Hellfire Bar enough, but I had never been inside.

I walked in expecting a mess, but it was worse than I had been expecting. The music blared, people dancing in the center of the room, girls screaming and guys grabbing to drag them closer. The dark lights made it impossible to see everything clear enough, and it was starting to make me uneasy. I didn't like going to a place I didn't know well, and being here alone only made that worse. I scanned the crowd, not seeing Rook.

It took one more lap around the bar before I found him tucked away in a corner booth. He held up his head with a hand as he looked at the person across from him. I couldn't see who it was as I walked up behind the booth, the tall backs hiding them completely. He seemed a little bored, and I wondered if one of his friends had come out with him. I turned the corner, blood draining from my face as I saw a beautiful woman across from him.

She dressed up to get any man she wanted tonight, and it seemed obvious enough that she wanted Rook.

I stopped a few feet away, listening as Rook spoke, the words even more slurred than when I had talked to him on the phone. Three empty shot glasses sat in front of him, and I'm sure more were littered around the bar because of him.

"Like I said, I have a girl. I don't need a stranger to get my dick wet," he said, his dark hair falling over his forehead. "Didn't I tell you that already?"

I couldn't hide my snort of laughter. "You think I'm yours?" I asked, his attention snapping to me. "I thought that ended days ago."

"Regan," he said, pushing himself up and kissing me before I could stop him. Even drunk, I didn't mind it, but I was still a little mad, and that didn't need to change yet.

"Come on," I said. "I'm not in the mood to hang out here tonight, and our ride is out front."

"You still mad at me?" he asked, not giving me time to answer. "You should be. I'm using you, baby. It has nothing to do with Harper. I didn't even know Harper until she walked into your room."

"How are you using me, then?"

Rook grinned, ignoring my question and throwing an arm around my shoulder before looking back at the woman in the booth.

"Told you I had a girl." I tried not to laugh, the mocking tone almost sounding like he would stick out his tongue at her next.

"You do not," I said, walking him towards the door.

I realized his bike would be out there and stopped, grabbing his phone. I made him type in the password, which I memorized, and I quickly found his texts with Aiden.

ROOK

It's Regan. He's drunk and I'm taking him home because he's getting kicked out of the bar. Can you come get his bike? I'm guessing it can't be left here.

AIDEN

Well, fuck. Yeah, we'll be there in twenty. You can leave when you need.

ROOK

Thanks.

AIDEN

Need help with him? I heard you're not his biggest fan lately.

ROOK

I got it. He might wake up with a black eye, but I've got it.

AIDEN

Give him two.

He doesn't get drunk much, so I'd like to say go easy on him, but he doesn't exactly deserve it. Maybe don't kill him?

ROOK

Pretty sure you guys are the killers, not me.

AIDEN

You'd be surprised by how easy it comes when they threaten something you care about. Don't rule it out. Text me if you need help.

A guy pushed past me, his shoulder knocking me over into Rook.

"Hey, what the fuck?" Rook yelled. "Watch where you're going." He went to pull away from me, but I grabbed on, yanking him hard towards the door.

"Get in the car, Rook," I yelled, pushing him out onto the sidewalk towards my car.

He listened, ducking into the passenger seat and waiting as I ran around to the driver's door. The second the door shut, he grabbed me again.

"My fucking girl," he mumbled before biting at my neck. He kissed and licked his way to my ear before moving his way back down. My stomach flipped, and I leaned back, giving him more access.

"Enough," I said, catching my breath as I pushed him back into his seat. He sat back with a huff, and I rolled my eyes before shifting the car into gear.

By the time I made it to the next block, he was leaning back over to me. He reached down, his hand sliding between my legs as I started towards the house. "I'm driving. You need to knock it off."

"You feel me up when I'm driving the bike. What's the difference?"

"The difference is that I don't know how you manage to keep the bike upright. I will not keep the car straight," I said through gritted teeth as he continued.

"You can do it, Rebel. Let me keep kissing you. I feel like it's been months since I had my lips on you."

"It's been days, Rook. It hasn't even been an entire week."

"I still think it's been too long."

It wasn't a far drive to my house, but I stopped, grabbing water and a coffee before sliding back behind the wheel and handing them both to him.

"Here. Start drinking those now so I can actually get you in the house."

Ten minutes later, I parked in the garage attached to my house and shut the car off. Rook perked up, already dragging himself out of the car and around to me. His hands hooked under my ass, lifting me up as he kissed me.

"I don't know how drunk you are exactly, but lifting me is not a great choice."

"Then get me to bed or I'm laying you out right here."

"I'm getting you to bed now because if I don't, I worry I won't be able to at all. Come on."

I helped him up the stairs to my room, his lips not leaving my neck the entire time, which didn't help my attempts to keep us both upright.

"I fucking missed you," he mumbled against me. "I've thought about you every fucking second for the last two days."

"You were stalking me, Rook. I don't think you gave yourself enough time to miss me."

"Watching you through windows and a hundred feet away is not the same as this." He turned to kiss me, pulling me to a stop. "I helped Harper because she is your friend and asked for help. That guy was fucking with her, and based on what we found, about to fuck with her more."

"I know, Rook, I'm not mad. You helped her. It was nice of you, actually. Harper explained it all that night."

"Then why the *fuck* haven't you responded to me?"

"I've just needed...time."

"Time for what?"

"To figure out what I'm supposed to do with you."

His eyes went clear for a second. "You can hate me, Rebel. Hate me for using you, for fucking you, for taking from you."

"Why? What have you done?"

The hazy, drunk smile took back over and he swayed into me. "I'm trying to ruin your life, and I'm going to succeed. Now punish me for it. Scar me for life, for going against you. Ruin me. Make me regret it. Make me *stop*."

"Rook, what are you talking about? You're not ruining my

life. I mean, the stuff with Harper was a bit eye-opening, but it didn't ruin my life. I'm not even that mad, just shocked."

"But you should hate me," he said again. He pulled off his shirt first, then fumbled with his jeans and shoes.

"Should I take you home, then?"

He looked around my room, taking it all in, before looking back at me. "I'm not home?"

"No, you are in my room."

He shrugged before falling back onto the bed. "This can be my home now."

"No, it can't. I can take you home," I said again, realizing that I didn't actually know where he lived. He went quiet. I felt pretty confident I wouldn't be able to get him upright again tonight.

I changed into shorts and a t-shirt before lying down next to him, not surprised when he reached out to drag me closer. His hand slid down me, slipping under the waistband of my shorts.

"You're drunk, Rook. We can't do that."

"Yes, we can," he growled. "Use me. You have full permission to use me for your pleasure. I barely deserve to be used like that. I don't even deserve to get off. Please, fuck me, hurt me."

His hands wrapped around my hips, lifting me up and on top of him as he rolled onto his back. He grabbed my wrists, bringing them to his throat.

"I need you," he said.

"Stop," I said, ripping my hands back. "You aren't in charge here, and if you want me to punish you for being a terrible person, that's not your decision."

His hands dropped, resting on the bed above his head. "Okay. You're in charge."

"You're going to give up the control, just like that?"

"To you? Yes. Only you. I would bow at your fucking feet, Regan. You always have the control."

He groaned and pushed his hips up, lifting me with him. I yelped, but quickly settled when I felt how hard he was already.

"Is that for me?"

"Yes," he said, his throat tight. "All for you."

"This cock belongs to me, doesn't it? That's what you were telling that girl at the bar, weren't you? That it belongs buried in me and no one else."

"Yes, so let me fucking bury it," he said through gritted teeth.

"I can't. You said you weren't good. You said you've used me. That you're going to ruin my life. Is that true?"

"It is," he groaned. He reached up, grabbing my hips and trying to pull me onto his cock, but I stopped him. "I'm taking everything from you."

"What if I tell you not to?"

For a second, he seemed to contemplate it, but his jaw tightened and his eyes closed. "I still might have to."

I reached over, pulling out the handcuffs Harper had given me as a joke. I had thought she was ridiculous even for a joke, but now I might have to thank her.

The pink fuzzy cuffs slipped around my headboard and then slapped around his wrist. They could barely count as metal, but they would work. His eyes flew open, fighting against them for a second before he smiled.

"So what now? Do I lie here and trust that you aren't going to kill me?"

"Yes."

"I don't love that."

"I do," I said, grinning as I leaned down to kiss him. He reached up to meet my lips but couldn't sit up all the way with the cuffs. "Are you sure you want this, Rook?"

"Like I've never wanted anything. It's all yours. Whatever you want. I'm fucking yours, Rebel. I shouldn't be, but I am." I repositioned him at my entrance, letting his cock move along me. He groaned, lifting his hips up. "Please, Rebel."

"Maybe I should use that toy you gave me and just make you watch."

He laughed, the sound clearer now than before, but I knew he was still a little buzzed. "I think I'm forever stuck between loving you taking control like a fucking queen, while also wanting to make your ass red for trying to tell me what to do."

"I'm mad at you still, so I do get to tell you what to do. Don't you dare come until I do, Rook."

I dropped down, taking him slow as my body stretched around him. His hands fumbled with the handcuffs, desperately trying to reach out to me.

I ran my hands down him, appreciating every scar, tattoo, and muscle. "I like this. All of this," I said, moving back up his stomach to his chest.

"You don't need to lie. I'll get you off either way."

"I wasn't lying. I like all of this."

He writhed under me, his hips bucking in a desperate attempt to take control. But I was the one in control, and I reveled in his submission. As I increased my pace, my hips rocking faster and harder, his breath began to come in short bursts.

"You're so fucking beautiful," he grunted, his voice rough with need.

His words only fueled my desire, making me move against him, teasing him with each slow, calculated thrust.

His breath came in ragged gasps, and the muscles in his thighs tensed as he lifted his hips to meet mine. I slowed my pace more, enjoying the way pleasure ripped through me every time I moved.

I pulled away before dropping down, taking every inch slowly. Then I picked up the pace again.

"Oh, fuck. Please. If you keep doing that, I'm going to come."

"You aren't allowed."

He nearly whimpered and pulled his hips down, trying to break away from me.

I dropped again, taking all of him again with a satisfied moan. "What do you think you're doing?"

"Trying not to come," he said through gritted teeth.

"Oh, I didn't say you could pull away."

I lifted again, riding him faster now.

"Regan, please. I can't stop it if you keep going." He sounded like he was in agony, and I loved it.

The control, the freedom, and knowing that he would do everything he could to listen to me.

I leaned down, my breasts pressing against his chest. "You're not allowed to come, Rook," I said. "Not until I say so."

His arms ripped down, breaking the handcuffs as he rolled on top of me. He picked up my hips, slamming into me hard as he groaned.

The power of it made me hungry for more, and I reached up, my hand wrapping around his throat. "You don't come until I do."

"Fuck, baby, please," he begged, still not stopping the thrust of his hips.

"Make me come, and then you get to," I said, smiling as his head dropped onto my shoulder.

He lifted me back up again with a low growl. He thrust into me harder, each stroke sending a jolt of pleasure through my entire body. His cock filled me completely, and then he reached down, finding my sensitive clit and moving circles around it.

My body tightened before I finally found release. My nails dug into his back as I held onto him, losing my breath as stars burst in my eyes. I arched up, taking more, as his pace quickened again.

"Come on," he said, lifting me off the bed. "I have a horrible

fucking hangover already ready to kill me and just had the best sex
of my life. I need to clean up and lie down."

I laughed, sliding my arms around his neck as he carried me to
the shower. He turned on the water, letting it warm up before
stepping inside, still holding me. The water washed over us as he
set me down.

"Thank you for coming to get me," he said. "I don't know
that I've ever had to call a woman to rescue me, but I might have
to do it more often." He smiled as he kissed me before spending
the next few minutes cleaning us up.

Soon, he was carrying me back to bed, and I wasn't sure if I
had ever felt so content.

The morning light streamed in as I stayed in bed, Rook sleeping
next to me. I grabbed my tablet and continued working on one of
my drawings while he slept. It felt nice to do what I always did,
but with the comfort of not being alone.

An hour went by before he rolled over, groaning as he lifted
his head with bleary eyes.

"Regan?"

"Yes?"

"Oh, thank fuck," he said, dropping his head again.

"I'm going to assume you remember nothing?"

"I remember all of it, but I was pretty worried you were a 'not
going to forgive me' type of pissed, so I thought I might have just
imagined it was you."

"You thought you went home with another girl and just
pictured her as me?"

"It was a concern, yes."

"Why?"

He rolled over, throwing an arm over me and snuggling into

my side. "Wouldn't want to go home with anyone else," he mumbled.

"Again, why?"

"Do you think I wouldn't be loyal?"

"You wouldn't have to be, since I wasn't talking to you."

"It's not really something I'm interested in," he said, rolling over to look at me. He glanced at the tablet in my hand. His eyebrow cocked, and he grabbed for it before I could stop him.

This one was a pile of skulls, built up into the shape of a tree trunk where the tree bloomed from. Branches crawled across the screen until bright pink flowers burst from them.

"You make very dark drawings for a girl who loves bright shit so much. Very morbid. I love it," he said, sounding genuine.

"You do?"

"One hundred percent love it and would get that tattooed on me."

"You wouldn't."

"I would," he said, glancing at it again. "I will."

"Don't even think about it," I said, turning it back to face me.

"I don't need to think about it. I've already decided. What time is it?"

"Around eight. I texted Aiden that you might be a little late."

He groaned as he rolled over, looking up at the ceiling. "I take a night off and I waste half of it out at a bar rather than here in bed with you. How stupid."

"I wouldn't say it was all wasted out of this bed. We spent a good bit of time here."

He grinned, rolling us until I was under him. "That's very true. If I leave to go to work, can I come back tonight?"

"Or I could come to your place?"

His face fell and lips pursed. "You can't. Not now, at least."

"Why not?" My stomach tightened, the anxiety from everything he hid making me panic.

"Not for any of the terrible reasons you are thinking. You just can't right now. Maybe in a week or two." His fingers brushed my hair back, but it wasn't as soothing as I hoped.

"Oh," I said, pushing away. "Got it."

"Don't. It has nothing to do with you and everything to do with some problems we are having there."

"But I can come over soon?"

"Yes, you can. I have to get to the shop today, though, then some...jobs later tonight, so I'll be here late."

"Alright. You know how to get in. I might be asleep."

"Yes, I do know how to break in," he said with a grin. "Text me, Rebel. I'll see you later."

The bedroom door closed behind him, and I sighed, leaning back against the pillows. I still had plenty of questions, but I knew I had already forgiven Rook. Forgiven or not, I already knew being with him would only make my life more complicated from now on.

Twenty-Eight
Regan

I walked up to the back of the garage two days later, smiling when Rook turned to look at me, his eyebrows jumping up.

"I wasn't expecting you here. Stalking me again?" he asked, leaning down to kiss me.

"Nope. I didn't come to see you."

He scowled, looking around at the other guys. "What the fuck does that mean when you are dressed like that? Who are you coming to see?"

"Are you saying I look bad?" I asked, looking down at my new dress.

His hand slid over my hip, pulling me in. "You look beautiful. So beautiful that I will be very jealous if it's for any other man."

"It's for me, not a man."

Evie ran out from the front, heading right towards us. She reached up, pushing Rook out of the way, and making him stumble back.

"Come on, I've been stuck here all day and need a break," she said, smiling as she headed to the door.

Rook grabbed my arm, pulling me hard against his chest. "You're going out with Evie?"

"Yeah. We're picking up Harper and going out for the night."

"Where?"

I shrugged, and he scowled more. "I don't know, around town."

"But where?"

"I don't know yet."

"Fine, don't tell me. I can track Evie's phone anyway."

"That's creepy," I said, looking up at him. He smiled, the bright blue of his eyes looking more clear now.

"We all have it set up on Evie's computer that we can look at everyone's locations if needed."

"Well, it's not needed. We are going out for a drink, maybe to dance, and to hang out. Nothing dangerous or deadly." I looked past him to the bikes and the toolboxes that seemed to hold more than just mechanic's tools. "Unlike you."

His hands cupped my chin, making me look up at him. "When you look like that? I'm definitely not the one being dangerous or deadly tonight. You're going out with Evie, so yeah, you're going out to cause trouble. Text me if you need anything. *Anything*, Rebel."

"I don't think I'll need any help with anything tonight. Who knows who I might meet? Evie seems like she could attract a lot of fun people," I said, smiling to further I push his buttons.

Rook's lips twisted into that wicked smile, his eyes growing heavy. "I think you're trying to insinuate that you could meet another guy. Maybe go home with him? Or invite him home with you? Hilarious, if you really think I would let it get past the doors, let alone all the way to a bedroom."

"You couldn't stop me if that's what I wanted to do."

"Stop you? No, baby, you're a goddamn queen against me. I can't, and won't, stop you." He grinned, bringing me closer until my lips were almost at his. "But I would stop him. And you really won't want to make out with him, let alone do anything else, when I rip out his throat and leave it on your pillow. So much blood and not enough breathing."

"Rook," I warned, scrunching my nose at the thought.

A rumble came from him as he finally leaned down, closing the distance between us to kiss me. "I love when you say my name like that. Like you kind of want to wrap your hands around my throat."

"I kind of do," I whispered, kissing him again.

"Oh my god, you two," Evie groaned. "Can you please wrap this up so we can go? You can literally get a room later."

"I'll be in your room later," he said.

"I'll be okay with that. Actually," I said, leaning in further. "I have something I need to talk to you about. Something I think I need help with."

I had spent hours searching for any information on the logs my dad had hidden in his desk, but I hadn't found a single clue. If they were related to boat shipments, I came up empty. Looking into going rates for security firms also gave me nothing about the type of high-level security my dad seemed to provide. My last hope was that Rook might have the information I needed and would be willing to share it.

He brushed my hair back, looking over my face. "Anything you need. Do you want to talk about it now?"

Evie gagged and grabbed my arm, pulling me towards the door. "It's girls' night, Rook, she can talk about it later."

"Fine, but you know where we are if you need us."

He kissed me again before I broke away and headed back out to the car that waited out front. Evie slid into the back, looking at the driver.

"I feel so fancy. A driver in a car and not on a bike? I'm a damn princess tonight."

I laughed as we headed to get Harper. "It can be a nice change. I surprisingly don't mind riding on the bike now, though."

"Don't mind the bike or don't mind the rider?" she asked with a laugh.

"Is it weird for me to talk about since he's your brother and all?"

"I don't care much. I think it's cute he actually has someone he likes, but for the love of everything, *do not* tell me any details."

"Does he not have a lot of people he likes around?"

"Not even a little. He likes work, and more work, and riding. That's about it lately. He spends more time working and worrying about all of us than doing anything for himself. He's a protector to a fault. I swear he barely even sleeps anymore."

"Is that why he looks like he might pass out half the time?" I asked, trying not to smile.

"Yeah, they've been so busy that he gets a few hours here and there. Has he shown you his...scar?"

"Yeah, he showed me."

"Then you could see why it hurts him a lot. I think he ends up working more because he can't sleep with it aching. He never complains to us about it, though."

I was quiet as Harper slid in next to us and they immediately jumped into finishing a conversation they had started through text.

I didn't understand Rook. It seemed like he was always violent, but I could see what Evie meant about being a protector. He definitely didn't want to let anything happen to me.

With the driver, it made it easy to pull right to the doors to get out, and the door guys looked us over once before waving us in.

"I love going out with you guys," Evie said. "Do you know the looks I get when I'm surrounded by the guys? No man is approaching me when they are around."

"Does that mean you don't have a lot of boyfriends?" Harper asked.

"Not really. I mean, I've gone on plenty of dates. There was one guy I started seeing, but then Rook and Aiden made it pretty clear that I shouldn't be."

"Why?"

"I mixed business with pleasure and it started to affect our business. I had to stop seeing him, but I don't know if he was even my boyfriend."

"I'm sorry," I said, linking my arm in hers. "That sucks."

"It's alright. I don't think I need one anyway, right? What good will that do me?"

The neon lights cast a vibrant glow on our faces as we made our way out of the hallway and into the club.

"It's fine. Tonight's about forgetting our troubles," Evie declared, linking arms with Harper now. "Let's dance, drink, and have fun!"

The club was packed, the music loud as it thumped through me. I had only been to a club one other time and quickly found out they weren't for me, but with Harper and Evie, I was already having a better time. We weaved through the crowd and found a spot at the bar before ordering drinks.

"To a night of fun and forgetting," Harper toasted, raising her glass.

I took a long sip, savoring the sweetness of the drink. It felt good to be out, to be out with girls who I could complain to or forget my problems with. To not be worrying about my dad, or his company, or even Rook. I could just be here, and that was it.

It took less than five minutes before Evie dragged us out to the dance floor. I stayed with them, dancing endlessly as the music played on. My heart leapt at every guy that approached me, and I wondered how taken I was exactly. I knew Rook wouldn't be happy if I danced, or did anything else, with another guy, but that didn't exactly mean we were together exclusively.

As if the men around me could hear my thoughts, a guy came up, wrapping an arm around my waist and pulling me into the crowd more.

"Hey, there," he said, his lips so close to my ear that I could feel the heat of his breath.

I looked over my shoulder as he held me tighter. Fear and anger coursed through me as he kept moving, dragging me towards a corner of the dance floor.

"What are you doing? Let me go!"

The stranger spun me to face him, letting me get a better look at his face. He wore slicked-back hair and a button-up shirt open at the collar. He looked like any other guy in this place, but something made him think he could grab me and drag me across the floor.

"You need to get the fuck off me," I said, pushing at his hand.

"Or what? I didn't see your boyfriend here tonight."

My heart hammered in my chest, trying to think of a good way to get away.

"I don't have a boyfriend," I said, pushing away from him again.

"No? Did I get something wrong when I followed you here from Rook's garage after you were kissing him goodbye? How cute, by the way. I heard you like Rook's...bike," he said with a grin. "Maybe I should take you on a ride on my bike."

"Not a chance," I said, wanting to shrink back. The fact that he knew I was ever with Rook made my blood run cold, and I realized this was more than a pushy guy hitting on me in a bar. My eyes darted around, looking for any sign of Evie or Harper, but I didn't see either of them.

I didn't like confrontation, even on a normal day. The way people got pushy always made me uncomfortable enough to run away, but that wasn't who I wanted to be anymore. I *couldn't* be that person anymore.

I needed Rook here, but I couldn't act helpless now. I kept going to hang out with Rook and I knew what type of problems could go along with that. I could either run from them, and then run from Rook, too. Or I could handle them, even if it meant calling for help.

The guy stepped closer, wrapping an arm around my waist to pull me in. He whispered something, but the music drowned the words out.

Panic welled in my throat, and I reached for my phone. The only way to look at it, though, was to wrap my arms around the guy so I could hold it up enough to hit Rook's name.

The FaceTime connected and Rook's grinning face filled the screen, before he saw what was happening.

Help, I mouthed.

His face hardened. His eyes narrowed as he headed to his toolbox with me still on the phone.

I moved to my texts, sending him one fast, as the guy seemed to think we were dancing.

"My name is Victor," he yelled, his arm tightening on me.

Regan: He knows I'm with you.

Rook: Dead.

Rook: Kick him hard and find Evie. Now.

I switched back to the FaceTime, already seeing him on the bike. He clicked it on his stand before slipping on his helmet, not disconnecting the call. The guy stopped, grabbing my wrist, and I used my other hand to slip my phone into my pocket.

I kicked up. My knee connected with something, but he only held on tighter.

"Fucking bitch. We knew you would all get stupid about this."

"All?"

"All you girls. Come on, we need to get upstairs."

Before I could protest further, he dragged me through the crowd. By the time we made it to a set of steps, I could see Evie and Harper being manhandled by two other men. The three of us were forced up a narrow staircase, the music and lights of the club fading into the background as we were taken to a back office.

The room was dimly lit, with plush furniture and a large window overlooking the dance floor below. The men shoved us inside and closed the door, standing guard with menacing looks.

My heart pounded in my chest as I took a deep breath, trying to stay calm. I glanced at Evie and Harper, who both looked annoyed.

"I already called Rook," I whispered. "They're on their way."

Evie grinned up at the guys holding onto us. "Oh, you're fucked," she said.

An older guy came into the room, and Evie scowled.

"Cross?" Evie said, stepping back. "Why did you grab us?"

"Now you know these guys?" Harper asked.

She gave a tight smile, leaning over towards us. "The guy I kind-of dated that mixed business and pleasure was Asher. He's a competitor of this guy, so I inevitably know all about them."

"How are they competitors?" I asked.

"They are both drug lords in Valeport and hate each other," she said with a roll of her eyes. "Cross hates us."

"I hate you," Cross interrupted, "because you sided with Asher when you shouldn't have."

"I don't know. I think it worked out fine for us."

"Wait," I said, surprised I was saying anything. "What does that have to do with us?"

"I need your guys to look into the theft of my drugs, and they aren't responding," Cross said, not meeting our eye now.

"Then get the hint," Evie said. "They don't want to talk to you or work with you. You're a snitch, and a pig."

"They don't exactly have a choice now. They have to come here to get you and then we can talk."

"Asher isn't going to love this, either," Evie mumbled.

"Fuck Asher." Cross sat back, looking us over.

"Can I get that on a recording?" she asked. "Just want to keep him in the loop."

"Asher can go fuck himself. We all have shipments going missing and he doesn't? You can understand why he is quickly moving up to the top of my list of who did it."

"Like he would want your shitty ass drugs."

"Shouldn't you...I don't know, be quiet or something?" I whispered to Evie.

She rolled her eyes again. "Seriously, don't worry about it. He can't kill us. He wants the guys to help him figure out what's happening, and no one has the connections like we do. Rook and Aiden have been trolling this city for information for nearly ten years. They know exactly where his shipments are and he knows it. If we are dead, he's dead with no information. Right, Cross?"

His lips tight in what I could only assume was supposed to be a smile. "This is a friendly meeting."

I yanked at my arm that was still being held by Victor. "Then get your hands off of me," I said, pulling again.

Rook stepped into the room, scanning it fast. His eyes landed on me, flicking once to Evie and Harper before turning back to me. Aiden, Mason, Hero, and Zack were behind him. Zack and Mason turned, facing the door they came through as the rest of them looked everyone over.

Rook pulled out his gun, aiming it with a steady hand and pulling the trigger without another word.

Victor fell, blood splattering on the side of my dress as he went down. My lips pressed hard together as I suppressed my scream.

And the bile rising in my throat.

"Rook!" Cross yelled.

"I will continue unless you get your hands off them," Rook said. Hands dropped from Evie and Harper.

As if she didn't care what was happening around us, Evie stepped out, walking across the room to stand by Aiden and Rook. I followed, and Harper sneered at Cross as we walked over with them. Rook's arm snaked around my waist, pulling me hard against him before he shoved me behind his back.

"You're fucking lucky I don't kill you," Rook said. "If you thought for a fucking second this would help your chances of getting our help, you're wrong. I know exactly what you're doing and I don't give a fuck if your shipments go missing."

"Rook, I need help. We have looked everywhere, asked everyone, and not a word."

"And I'm going to make sure it stays that way now. You think you can bother them and I will suddenly do your dirty work? Go fuck yourself. The only reason I'm not killing you is to not start a war. Do this shit again and I won't care."

Cross went to stand, but Hero raised his shotgun with a grin.

Rook turned to us, nodding towards the door. "Go. Out of the room. Stay with Zack, Kane, and Mason."

I grabbed his arm, pulling him back. "Rook, I'm—"

"I'm coming. Just go."

Zack put an arm around my shoulders, smiling as we walked out.

"What is he doing?" I asked.

Evie walked up next to me, grabbing Zack's hand and lifting it off my shoulders until he dropped it. "No need to touch her, Zack."

He rolled his eyes. "I was walking her out, not feeling her up."

"Close enough." Evie linked her arm in mine again, Harper on my other side. "I can walk her out just fine."

"Really? You managed to get yourselves all kidnapped, basically," Zack snapped.

Mason came up behind us. "Just walk them out, Zack. No need to piss anyone else off tonight."

I smiled back at Mason, but I looked over his shoulder once.

"They aren't killing him, if that's what you're worried about."

"I was more worried about them getting hurt."

Mason smirked as we headed out front. "They won't. You want on the bike or in the car?"

"I don't have a helmet," I said, heading to the car. Mason pointed at Rook's bike, my helmet sitting on my seat.

"Oh," I went over, seeing that he had mine strapped to the back.

It was less than a minute before Rook came out. "Riding with me?" he asked, not stopping as he swung over the bike.

"If you don't mind."

"I prefer it. Come on, Kane will take Harper home safe."

I got on, relief washing over me as I held onto him.

"You know, you might never be in trouble with anyone else, but you currently are with me," I said.

He groaned. "Alright, Rebel. Let me get you home and then give me what you got. I'll take my punishment."

I squeezed tighter once, not saying a word for the rest of the drive.

TWENTY-NINE
ROOK

She stomped up the steps as I slammed the door behind me.

"I just wanted to go out for one night. One damn night and someone is trying to kill me?"

"I told you I would go with you in case something happened."

"I thought you meant if a guy was hitting on me or something. I didn't think you meant in case you needed to shoot a man."

"I can be more clear next time," I said, stifling a laugh.

"Next time? You think there is a next time? You think me not being able to go out for girls' night without you tagging along so I don't die is okay?"

"It doesn't have to be me if you need a break from all my charm. Zack could go. Or Mason. He likes to get out sometimes. I'd offer Hero to go, but he would start a fight on purpose if nothing happened. Aiden is already one step from Evie's full-time bodyguard, so he'd like to keep a night off."

"You think this is funny? My dress is covered in some random guy's blood. Am I supposed to pay to have that dry cleaned? Or scrub it out myself?"

There was no shortage of money in this room, let alone the house, but I still smiled. "I will pay to have your dress dry cleaned. Or buy you a new one. I would like to add, though, that I was there to save you. Sometimes it gets a little messy."

"*Messy?*" She nearly yelled the word, but her mouth snapped shut as she screamed against her sealed lips. "You are insane."

"You've said that before," I said, sitting back on the bed.

She disappeared into the bathroom. The shower turned on, and I waited.

"Do you need help in there?" I yelled out.

"If you so much as step foot in this bathroom, Rook, I will cut you."

"With what?"

"Oh, some dumb man left a giant knife in my room after he tried to kill me with it, and I was so freaked out that it was a murder weapon that I hid it. I can reach it from here. Don't even try me."

"You put it close enough that you can reach it from the shower? Interesting choice. You're really getting good at this threatening thing, Rebel. Before you know it, you'll be running a damn empire, making men scared of you without them even meeting you."

When she stomped back out, my chest tightened. She was still mad, but now she was wet, wrapped in a towel, and as beautiful as ever.

"Don't be condescending."

I held up my hands. "I'm not."

I liked when she was mad. I liked to see the wild woman she hid away and gave just to me. I didn't think it would be just for me for much longer, though. She was born to be in charge, and I didn't think her temper would last long inside these four walls when she knew she could let it out. She seemed comfortable with me now and had no fear in facing me to tell me exactly why she was mad at me.

I was in her room and she was comfortable to shower and get ready for bed with me here. It was so domesticated and, with her, I loved it. I wanted my woman with me every night, telling me about her day or asking about mine. I wanted someone who was at my side and would help me run our world. I knew it would include getting yelled at by her sometimes.

"I called you to help me tonight. It's not like I took care of it myself," she said, the sadness in her tone making me upset.

"And?" I asked, stepping closer now. I reached up, running a hand down her jaw. "You are a fucking queen. And just like a queen, you don't have to fight battles on your own. You have a damn army behind you. Maybe not a big one, but I promise, we are enough to fix any issues you have with anyone."

"And I'm just supposed to rely on you to always show up?"

"We can teach you how to defend yourself more. Or you can learn how to shoot. Whatever you want, but I will always show up. You can always count on me showing up."

Her face fell, and she looked away. "I'm supposed to count on that? I'm supposed to believe you just truly want to protect me? Or is your solution going to be asking me to not go anywhere or do anything for my safety? Will I have any say in anything? Or will you just say you're more powerful and get the final say?"

"Never. It's not an option for me. Do you know what a rook does in chess?" She shook her head, and I wrapped my arms around her. "He protects the queen. He can't take her down, he can't win against her, he only protects her. If you want to be queen of it all, I will cut down anyone in your way. I won't stop you or lock you up, and yes, I would happily kill anyone who bothers you."

Her lip curled. "You shot that guy."

"I fucking did and loved watching his hands drop from you."
I leaned down, kissing along her neck as I pulled at the towel. I
loved the moment he fell, the second his hands stopped touching
her. I groaned. I liked her being mine, and I was pretty sure I
would do just about anything to keep her to myself. "I would do
it a thousand times over."

"You're serious," she said.

I stepped back, looking at the bed and back at her. "I'm very
serious. You know, there's something I've wanted to do since I
met you. Could we do it now?"

She stepped back, pulling the towel tighter again. "That
sounds like you're about to tell me some weird kink you have."

"What counts as a weird kink?"

Her eyebrows furrowed, like she was thinking about it.
"Maybe anything illegal?"

"Oh, then yeah, I for sure have some weird kinks," I said,
heading to the bed.

"Okay, I'm going to need to know what they are before either
of us gets even a foot closer to that bed," she said, the horrified
tone nearly making me laugh.

"I was just thinking about exhibitionism, but I think your
mind went somewhere really gross."

She shuffled back towards the bed again, grabbing a t-shirt to
throw on before sliding back under the covers. "Okay, well, we
aren't in public, so what is the thing you want to do?"

"I want to lie down in this ridiculously big, comfortable bed
and watch your endless episodes of Dateline."

"That's it?"

"For now? Yeah, that's it."

THIRTY

REGAN

Rook stood next to the bed, pulling off his hoodie with a heavy look in his eyes after he asked me to lie in bed watching my favorite show with him. I didn't know if it was a ploy for anything else, but I didn't think I cared either way.

The shirt came off next, and I took a deep breath. I loved looking at him. He made himself a canvas, each special piece telling a different story about himself. The dark swirls over his skin came together into one beautiful piece of art. The left side always caught my eye. The scarred side of his torso had to be a constant reminder of the fire that took everything. The scars were rough and uneven, a stark contrast to the smoothness of the rest of his skin. But they only made him more interesting, a beautiful imperfection that I could appreciate from any piece of artwork. Each time I saw him like this, I couldn't help but feel in awe of every part of him.

He had said nothing, but he smirked when he realized I was staring at him.

"Come on," he said, kicking off his boots. "Turn it on."

"You really just want to watch TV?" I asked, already clicking it on as I lay back.

"Yes," he said as he undid his belt. His eyes stayed locked on mine as he kicked off his shoes and jeans until he was standing in front of me in nothing but boxers. "All those nights I was here stalking you, this is what you did. Well, up here or in the living room, and I was dying to come inside and lie down."

"I thought you were bored out of your mind watching me?"

"Oh, I was, but it was nice. I run around chasing the worst types of people doing the worst types of things. We don't stop. Most nights, we don't sleep. Even when I do get to bed, I don't sleep much. I have so much on my mind that I can't."

"What type of stuff do you have on your mind?"

"The type of work you don't want to hear about," he said with a smirk. "Then Maverick Moto work, and now we are kicked out of the place we were living. Apparently, enough people complained about our bikes."

"Don't you have enough to get a new place?"

"More than enough. But it's hard to find somewhere that houses seven or more people with loud bikes. A place that's also private and can be discreet as far as our names on it. I guess we have to buy a place, so we are working on it."

"Oh, I'm sorry. I didn't realize."

"Realize that I don't just go around killing people and actually do have a house?" he asked, laughing quietly.

"Yeah, I guess so," I said, laughing along with him. "You just don't go around talking about your home life or anything, so I didn't have any idea about it."

"I do have a home. I mean, usually. And I sleep sometimes. I'm not a vampire. Although, that would make my life easier."

"For the killing part or the not sleeping part?"

"Both." He laughed again, pulling me against him now as he rolled under the covers next to me. "Are you still scared of me?"

"No. I don't know how much I was truly scared of you. Maybe a time or two, but there's no reason to be now. You've had plenty of chances to hurt me."

"I promise you will never be safer than when you are with me."

"I think tonight proved that is a lie. When I am with you, people die." I almost laughed, but stopped myself. It wasn't a joke. That was truly what happened.

He rolled over until I was pinned underneath him.

"No one will ever hurt you if I am with you." He bit at my ear before kissing down my neck. "I will kill them. It doesn't even take a second to think it over. That's why people die when you're with me," he said with a grin, "because I won't be giving them any chance to hurt you."

"Why?"

"Because you are mine, and I will protect what is mine until I die."

"That's gross and almost sweet."

"I'm a monster, Regan, but I can be *your* monster. And in these four walls, with you, I only want to be sweet. I only want you to feel safe because I wouldn't let anything happen to you."

"Then tone down the murder talk."

"Then tell me how the beginning of your day was before you thought going out to party with my sister would not end in a murder," he said, kissing along my neck.

"You really want to hear about my day?"

He nodded against me, running his hands over my hips again and again.

I told him the little I had done before going to the shop to meet with Evie, and he murmured his questions and answers until I could hear the drowsiness in his tone.

How could someone kill a man and then crawl into my bed to talk?

I talked a little more about my drawings and hanging out with Harper, but when I looked back over, his eyes were closed and he was asleep.

His face relaxed, every part of him finally calm and peaceful. Black hair fell over his forehead, and I stared at the tattoos that ran on the side of his neck.

One tattooed hand laid across my stomach. His knuckles were red, with one split open. I didn't know when he had gotten into a fight, but it had obviously been a few days. He hadn't told me about it. It had to hurt, but he gave no sign it bothered him.

I ran a hand down his face, surprised when he nuzzled into it.

"Hey, baby," he murmured.

"I thought you were asleep. You look so much less dangerous when you're sleeping." He smiled, his eyes still closed as he turned and bit at the palm of my hand. "Ouch," I whispered, smiling.

"Still dangerous."

"I'm terrified."

"You keep saying that."

"You keep doing things to make me terrified."

His eyes were heavy as he nuzzled against my hand again. "You're the first person I haven't wanted to be terrified of me, but I still have to be me. Do the things I do."

"But who do I trust you are? The guy who is out there doing those violent things or the guy cuddling up to me in bed?"

"I'm both. It's all me, but I don't think anyone knows this part of me. I'll still get blood on my hands in my life. I can guarantee it, but not yours."

"We're back to gross, but sweet."

"I think that's what you are agreeing to with me."

"What if I'm agreeing to nothing with you?"

He grinned, closing his eyes again. "Then you are going to have one pissed off stalker."

"Not fair."

"Not at all."

"I want a lot with you, Rook. I think I can handle the good with the bad."

"You think so?"

"It's definitely a *think so*," I said, laughing as he pulled me in closer.

"I'll take it," he whispered before drifting back to sleep.

THIRTY-ONE
ROOK

I paced the garage. The pack sat in front of me, sprawled out around the office.

"What the fuck does it all mean?" I asked.

"If something happened at the warehouse that night, we saw no sign of it," Hero said.

"Then who the fuck is Candy?" I asked, shoving a hand through my hair. "We really didn't find anything else about her in the office?"

"Nope. Nothing on his computer, either," Evie said. "Although, with how clean it is, I'm thinking the more important things are on his office computer."

"Which would make sense if he worries about Regan snooping," Aiden added.

"I don't think he worries about that at all now," I said. "Why would he be meeting with Asher and Cross? Cross obviously still wants our help, so it's not like he's taking our business."

"Maybe he's trying to?" Mason asked, getting up to walk around with me. "If he wants an in with them, it's a good route to take. We help them, but they don't rule over us. A win-win. If

Cameron heard about us, maybe he saw how good of a position it is to be in."

I could feel the rage and anxiety climbing. "If Cameron really thinks he's going to take over our business, he's dead before he even has a chance."

Aiden leaned forward, resting his arms on his legs. "What about revenge and those grand plans?"

"Fuck revenge in that case. We kill him before he gets too close."

"Won't your new girl be a little mad about you killing her dad for business purposes?" Hero asked.

My chest ached. Regan would never forgive me if she thought I killed her dad over a simple business deal.

"More importantly," Evie started. "Do you care?"

It was a weighted question. My answer would change not only my life, but all of theirs. If I said I cared, they would all know she was with us now.

The only thing that ran deeper than my loyalty was my need to protect and care for the people I loved. If I added Regan to my list of those people now, everyone here would know nothing was going to happen that could hurt her.

And it would put me right at odds with my revenge and now, possibly keeping our business.

"I do care," I finally said. "Which means this will be handled with more care than we have ever put into taking someone out. Nothing happens to Cameron until I talk to Asher and Regan. We need more information first, and I need to find a way to tell Regan everything without her hating me or running to her dad."

Hero let out a harsh laugh. "Yeah, okay. Good luck with that. You think she's going to be cool with your long-standing hatred for her dad and your bloodthirsty attitude about trying to kill him?"

"Well, asshole, I will obviously word it better than that," I snapped.

Evie headed my way, the determined look on her face making me nervous as the rest of them started talking amongst themselves.

"Listen, I like Regan, and I get from her side it may seem like you are doing something really terrible, but please remember you're not. You aren't terrible, and you go out of your way to do the right thing by all of us."

"I mean, telling her I'm doing the right thing is going to be a hard one to get across."

"I know, but just don't put yourself down or put your wants aside to take care of her. You're still important in all this, and even if she's upset, you're doing the right thing."

It wasn't often that Evie was anything but her psycho, smartass self, but I knew she cared about me, and I appreciated it.

"I will try to keep it in mind as much as I can," I said. "And thanks."

"Anytime."

I checked my phone, looking at the tracker on Regan's car that now showed she was only a few minutes away. It was Syndicate night, and I had invited her to go out with us.

"Come on," I yelled out. "Until tomorrow, let's go, because I need a fucking break from this mess."

Syndicate was packed as we pulled up, Regan holding tight onto me as I leaned to turn in. She had grown more comfortable on the bike now, leaning and moving with me instead of against me.

I parked as the rest of the pack lined up next to me, before I helped Regan off. I kept wondering if I would regret the decision to say I cared about her, but nothing came. Instead, I felt excited.

She was mine, and she could stay that way if I handled things right.

I wasn't sure there was an actual right way to handle it, though. It wasn't something I needed to worry about tonight.

My arms snaked around Regan, pulling her closer. "What do you want to do first?"

"Are there options? I thought this was about it."

"We can go watch people race, walk around and look at bikes, or just sit here and see what comes to us."

"What are all of you doing?" she asked as the rest of them walked up.

"Heading over to watch people attempt to race," Mason said, grinning. "You two coming?"

"Yeah," Regan said, her eyes wide when she glanced up at me. "I want to see what all the racing is about."

"Alright," I said, shocked. "Whatever you want."

My arm wrapped around her shoulders, and hers went around my waist as we headed that way. The chaos of Syndicate went on around us, but she didn't seem bothered.

"Really settling into your rebel ways?" I asked.

"Just feeling more comfortable. You all aren't that bad."

Evie scoffed, catching up to us. "Don't speak too soon. Wait until you spend more time with them and tell me what you think after."

"Oh, come on. We really aren't that bad," Mason said. "Aiden takes you everywhere you want to go. You don't have to worry about being jumped here, and literally no one bothers you because you try to get them killed off if they do."

She shrugged. "It comes in handy, but I think you all need to let me start taking care of some of these creeps on my own. I can handle them."

"What a surprise," Aiden added with an eye roll. "Psycho girl wants to do psycho things."

"Are you really one to talk when you are already doing those psycho things?" Evie asked.

"What about you, Regan?" Kane asked. That shocked me even more. Kane wasn't a big talker, and I didn't think he would be asking Regan anything, let alone talking to her.

"Yeah, what kinda psycho stuff are you into?" Hero asked. Evie knocked against him, rolling her eyes.

"None?"

"Oh," Hero said, and I could hear the disappointment. "Then what kind of normal stuff are you into?"

"Art, I guess."

"Good art. I'm getting one of her drawings tattooed on me," I said.

"No, you aren't," she said.

"Yeah, I am. That one you showed me of the tree of skulls."

Mason pushed through next to Regan. "Does that mean you are taking tattoo design requests?"

Regan looked up at me, and I leaned down. "No need to hide it. Like I said, I wouldn't be walking around talking about art if I didn't think it was good. They will like what you create. Hero might like the girl with horns one you showed me."

"A demon girl?" he asked. "Might be the only kind that would ever love me, so I might as well get it tattooed on me for good luck. Does one of those just rise from the ground or do I have to do some ancient ritual shit?"

"I'm pretty sure it's one of those get naked and dance under the moonlight type of things," I said. Regan laughed, the sound like a burst of light in my life.

"Damn, I was hoping it was more of a ritualistic killing type of thing," Hero mumbled. "I'll still take you up on the tattoo design, though. Can you bring it the next time you come to the shop?"

"Yeah," she said, sounding surprised. "I can do that."

We reached the makeshift race track, the air thick with the scent of burning rubber and gasoline. The roar of engines filled the night, and Regan's eyes widened with excitement as she watched two bikers revving up at the starting line.

"This is insane," she whispered, her voice barely audible over the noise. "You just come here and randomly race?"

"Pretty much. They take bets, and the types of challenges change. Sometimes, it's who can do the longest burnout or fastest time races, or who can hold the bike up in a wheelie the longest. Things like that. A little insane, but fun."

She nodded, her grip on my waist tightening. The races started, bikes shooting forward in a blur of speed. I wanted to care about the races, but I was too worried thinking about her. Regan leaned into me, her hand slipping under the back of my shirt, tracing absent patterns on it, and I felt a rush of contentment. I could feel when she moved over the scars and back onto normal skin, but she didn't seem to care about them.

I leaned down, my lips at her ear as she watched. "Do you like it?"

"The races or you?" she asked, grinning as her hand splayed out on my back.

I couldn't even hide how much I wanted to smile, hoping no one here would notice. "The races."

"I love it," she said, turning to look at me. Her eyes were bright as they searched my face, and I held my breath.

"And me?"

I could see her suck in a hard breath, her eyes widening the slightest amount before she turned her attention back on the races. "That's okay, too," she said with a grin.

My grip on her tightened, and I struggled to release it as I took in her words. The idea that Regan could care about me enough to count it as love one day felt wrong, and perfect in a twisted way.

The races would continue on all night, but I was already growing bored of it after a third fistfight broke out.

"We're heading back to my bike," I said, not asking Regan as I turned her towards the way we came. They all nodded, half of them staying and the other half heading into the crowd of bikes. I assumed the guys would be looking for a girl to hang out with and, for all I cared, Evie could look for a guy. I wanted to sit with Regan and only her.

When we reached my bike, I lifted her up onto it, my lips finding hers immediately as my hands roamed over her hips and sides.

She pulled me close, her hands gripping the front of my jacket to keep me there. "Thank you for bringing me here."

"Of course," I replied, my hands resting on her hips. "I'd take you anywhere you wanted to go."

"Anywhere?"

"Absolutely anywhere," I whispered, kissing her again. Her tongue moved against mine as her hands slipped under my shirt again, sliding up my back.

"How about taking me to my bed?"

I was already lifting her back onto her seat and handing her the helmet. "You barely have to ask for that one, Rebel."

She leaned on my back as I started up the bike and I rubbed at my aching chest.

I knew it when she walked around, laughing at my jokes and getting along with the pack. I knew it when she wrapped her arm around my waist to nestle up against me, and again when she got on my bike to stand on the pegs and kiss me.

I was already falling in love with Regan Fletcher, and true to the Fletcher name, she was bound to ruin my life.

THIRTY-TWO
REGAN

I t was the next night when Rook decided to take me out. He pulled the bike into a parking spot and helped me off, not saying a word as he wrapped his hand in mine, leading me down the street.

"You really have this all planned?"

"Yes. Is that too surprising?"

"Honestly, yeah. You don't exactly come off like the 'plans out a date' type."

"Well, I'm not. This is my first, so don't judge me too harshly."

Soft light spilled out from the shops that were still open, and I could smell the food from nearby restaurants. I leaned into him, enjoying every peaceful second of the night.

He slowed at the next intersection, taking a right down the next street, and I pulled him to a stop.

"What are you doing?" I asked, looking down the creepy road I knew all too well.

"Taking you to where we first met," he said, waving a hand towards the creepy road. "Obviously."

I laughed, pulling him to a stop. "While that is a very good start to a date, normally, we really don't have to go get killed or robbed."

"Nothing would happen to you."

"I guess that's true. No one's bothering me when my robber is with me already."

He grinned, looking back down the street. "I still want to make it clear that I never robbed you, or tried."

"But you are trying to take something from me now?" I asked. The words he told me when he was drunk had still been on my mind, but I hadn't found out what they meant.

He straightened up, looking into my eyes, and I froze. "Yes, I am." He pulled something out of his pocket, making me glance down. "But I have so much I am willing to give in return."

"You think gifts make up for you taking things from me?"

"No, but I thought it might help."

He opened the small box in his hand. A light pink heart shaped pendant hung off a chain that he lifted out.

"You bought that for me?" I asked, surprised at how perfect it was. "I love it."

"Then turn around."

I did, waiting as he slipped the necklace around my neck and clasped it. I spun, wrapping my arms around his neck to pull him in for a kiss.

He groaned, kissing me hard. "I have something else to give you, but we have to go first."

"Oh, so the creepy road we met on isn't the date night?"

"No, it's not. Although, if you want it to be, I'm happy to take a walk. I have my knife."

"No gun?"

"I was trying to be a gentleman tonight."

"Oh, perfect, no blood splatter on me, then, just you."

He grinned, pulling me into his side as he started walking

down the main road again. "You are getting so good at all of this, Rebel."

I smiled at the compliment, knowing it was strange. "I'm glad you think I'm handling you being a killer better. That's what every girl dreams of growing up. Are you going to tell me what we are doing?"

He shook his head, making another turn until we were in front of the art gallery. Rook pulled the door open, waving for me to go in.

"Here?"

"That's why I'm standing here with the door open."

"Yes, but you are also the man that said he would rather be shot than have to walk around a new art exhibit. I believe that's a quote."

"And I still will say that's my preference between the two, but now I have a girl who likes this, so I go."

"I don't need to go with someone who is going to complain the entire time."

"Then I guess you should be happy I'm here. I've dealt with so many worse things and not said a word."

I couldn't help but look down where I knew his skin was ruined. I still wished he would tell me more about it, but past that it happened, he didn't share anything.

"So you really want to go in and watch me look at paintings and that's it? You stay quiet and I enjoy myself?"

"I will be enjoying you. That's enough for me."

He was dressed nicer tonight, at least for him. The dark jeans and black button up were cut perfectly on his body. The one button undone was showing off just enough of his chest tattoos that I wasn't doing well at looking at anything else.

I knew what he could do, what he was capable of, and yet he was standing here all dressed up to take me to an art exhibit.

He pulled me inside, heading to the first line of paintings.

He didn't say a word, just held my hand as I looked over the first painting. Then, he did the same for the second and third, and by the time we made it to the next row of paintings, I was focusing less on the art and more on the man who was quiet next to me.

"Are you enjoying yourself, or are you counting down the minutes until we leave?"

"I'm enjoying myself," he said, his hand sliding lower down my back.

"Really?"

"Yes." He wrapped an arm around my waist from behind, his lips at my ear. "If looking at this art makes you feel an ounce of what I feel when I look at you, then we can both understand why I wouldn't be bored. I could never be bored with you, Regan. I don't have to like anything else in the room. If you are there, I have my own personal form of art to look at."

"But you live for adrenaline, for excitement and danger. How could this be any fun for you?"

"None of it compares to you, Rebel. None of it, and it never will. I like your quiet life, and I am happy to be a part of it. You tell me when we leave, and please stop worrying about me."

I moved to the next row of paintings, liking the way he followed after me without a word. And how he asked about every painting and if I liked it.

We got to the last aisle, but I pulled him towards the door.

"What are you doing, Rebel?" he asked, letting me pull him towards the door. He grabbed our jackets and continued on.

"I can't take looking at you anymore," I said, dragging him outside.

"Ouch, what a way to break up with a man. I appreciate the honesty, though."

We made it another block, and I stopped to wrap my arms around him before jumping into his arms.

"You're ridiculous," I said, laughing. "I meant, I can't stand just looking at you. I want more."

I kissed him hard, and he spun, pressing me up against the brick wall of the building

My hands moved down his back, loving every muscle that flexed underneath my fingers.

"Can we go? I need clothes off," I said before kissing him again.

"Come on." He was already carrying me to the bike. "I have one more thing to give you before we go."

"At your bike? Or preferably on your bike so we can get home?"

"While I'm happy you are so eager, hold on," he said, digging into the bag strapped to his bike.

"The necklace wasn't enough?"

He grabbed the little heart that hung around my neck, pulling it. Metal slid against metal until the chain tightened around my neck. My mouth dropped open, not realizing what the necklace was designed to do. "Did you put me in a collar?" I nearly yelled.

"I did, and it's so beautiful you didn't even know." He grinned. "But there was one more piece of jewelry I thought you would like." He pulled out a small black bag, handing it to me. My eyes narrowed as I took it. It was heavier than any bracelet or necklace. I opened it, pulling out a pink gemstone heart first before I saw what it was attached to.

"Oh my god, this isn't what I think it is. Is it?"

"Oh, it is. I thought you would like a matching set. Bend over, Rebel. You have a new piece of jewelry to wear home."

"Are you serious?"

"Yes. Bend over or I will make you."

"You wouldn't. Here, Rook? People could see us."

"Good. They can see how much you like being mine. Over the bike, Rebel. Spread your legs."

I listened, my heart hammering in my chest as he lifted my skirt. "Good girl, always doing what you're told." His fingers moved through my wetness, making me arch into him. "And already soaked? You're so excited to be fucked. You would let me do it right here, wouldn't you?"

"Yes," I said, moaning as his fingers found my clit.

"Good answer." Cool metal moved through my wetness until the head of the plug pressed against my ass.

"Rook, wait. Is this going to hurt?"

"Not much, baby. It will feel good after a second."

I could feel the metal slide into me. The fullness where I had never had it before made me stay motionless over the bike.

"Breathe, Rebel. Just breathe." I listened, taking one deep breath before pushing myself up more.

"That isn't so bad," I said, my body adjusting. "I can handle this."

"Good, because that's the smallest one," he said, grinning. "We have plenty of others to move up to."

My mouth dropped open as he pushed me over the bike a little further, pressing the small gemstone.

I gasped, the sensation making my body clench as a thrill ran up my spine.

"Ready to go home now?"

I nodded, taking another deep breath. "Are you taking this out, then?"

He leaned down over my back, his lips at my ear as he laughed.

"There's not a chance in hell I am taking this out now," he said, bending me over further as he pushed my skirt up more. The cool night air swept over my bare ass.

I could hear people talking as they headed down the sidewalks and knew they would see me if they looked down the side alley we were parked in.

"Rook, can we go? People are going to see us."

"That's okay. They can see how filthy you are for me." He ran his hands along my exposed skin, sending shivers down my spine.In one swift movement, he spun me, finding my lips in the dark. "Come on, get on. I need to get you home."

I stepped forward and moaned, the sensation of the plug making my legs nearly shake.

"Fuck, filthy looks so fucking good on you," he growled as his arms wrapped around me, dragging me against his body. "Get on the bike, baby. Let's get you soaked, and I promise to take care of it the second we stop."

I swung onto the bike, nearly whimpering as I slid over and sat down behind him. He eased the bike out, pulling out onto the main street and heading towards my house.

I barely made it five minutes. Between the vibration of the bike and the new piece of jewelry, I was already turned on. I could feel myself getting wetter, my core tightening at the thought of him fucking me at the same time as the plug vibrated.

My hands slid off the tank onto his thighs, trailing up them until I reached his hard cock.

The wave of want washed over me, and I ran over his length once. I couldn't wait any longer and I didn't have time to worry about connecting to explain this to him.

I tapped his leg, pointing to a pull-off on the side of the road.

He listened, parking the bike before ripping off his helmet. "What's wrong?" he asked, but I was already sliding off.

I moved fast, undoing his belt and unzipping his jeans before I bunched my skirt up higher and got on the bike right in front of him.

"Oh, fuck, baby, it's that bad?" he asked, adjusting me in front of him.

"Yes," I said, moving until I could feel him pressed against my entrance. "It's that bad, and I need you now."

I pushed back, trying to take all of him, but he stopped me. He pressed the gemstone, pushing it harder into me as I groaned.

"Okay, baby, I'll take care of it."

He grabbed the handlebar, hitting the throttle as he slammed into me. The vibration and sudden fullness made me yell out. He didn't stop thrusting into me over and over.

I was desperate for release, the need building up inside me until I wanted to scream. Every thrust brought me closer. I could feel my body trembling, my heart racing.

The buildup had already had me on edge and one more hit of the throttle pushed me over.

"Rook," I yelled, reaching for anything to hold on to.

"Come for me, baby," he said, as his movements became more frenzied. "Just a little more and you'll be soaked," he growled into my ear, sending shivers down my spine. "Such a perfect little slut, Rebel. Begging me to pull over and be fucked right here. You are so fucking perfect."

As he thrust into me one more time, I lost control. My body shook violently, the release overwhelming. Wave after wave of pleasure washed over me as I clung to Rook, feeling him pulsate inside of me. Finally, as the last shudder subsided, I let out a ragged sigh, my breaths coming out in short gasps.

Rook's grip on me tightened, holding me close as he slowed.

The engine rumbled as I caught my breath. He pulled me up, getting closer to my ear, and kissed along my neck.

"I'm addicted to every part of you, Rebel. You are mine, and I will be spending every day reminding you of that."

I couldn't find words, my body exhausted as I leaned back against him. He kissed my shoulder, a simple reminder of how gentle he liked to be. We stayed like that for a moment, and I savored every second.

"Come on, Rebel," he whispered, his voice low and rough. "Let's get you home."

I nodded, feeling a sense of contentment wash over me. Rook got off, sliding me back onto my seat before getting on in front of me.

The engine roared to life, and I wrapped my arms around his waist, feeling the steady thrum of the bike beneath us. The night air was cool against my skin, but I leaned down, wrapping my arms around him and resting my head on his back as we headed home.

Rook had helped me into bed last night before sliding in next to me. We had talked for a while, but it didn't take long before I had fallen asleep. Now, I woke up alone. I assumed Rook had snuck out until I saw his helmet still on my dresser.

I leaned over the side of the bed. His boots were still sitting there, too.

"Rook?"

He didn't answer, and I couldn't hear anything, which didn't mean much in a house this big.

I crept downstairs, stopping to listen every few steps but still not hearing anything. My heart hammered in my chest, wondering where he was or what he could be doing. None of the options I could come up with were good.

And when I turned the corner into the huge kitchen, I really hadn't been expecting the sight in front of me.

Rook had his back to me, his jeans slung low on his hips as he opened cabinets and pulled out ingredients like he was right at home here. He moved confidently around the kitchen, and then back to the stove to mess with one of the burners. It was all so simple, and surprising. Here was a man whose life was filled with danger and darkness, yet he stood in the kitchen, cooking breakfast for us as if it was the most natural thing in the world.

"What are you doing?" I asked, making him spin back to me. The entire room smelled like coffee and toast, and I took another step inside with a deep breath.

"Making breakfast?"

"But...why?"

He smiled, turning back to the stove. "I was hungry. I thought you would be, too. So breakfast felt like the natural choice."

"And you thought you should come down here to make it?"

"Is there a problem?" he asked.

I moved around the island to him. "Not at all. I'm just surprised."

"That I eat?"

"That you cook," I said with a grin.

"Don't you? Or do rich princesses never have to cook?"

"I have to cook!" I said, knocking his arm. "Do you see a private chef around here?"

"Yeah, why is that? Your dad is one of the richest guys in the city. Why not have a chef?"

I shrugged. "We used to when I was younger. Then he got more paranoid about everything as I got older, until he decided we wouldn't have one at all. I think he has one that brings him meals once a week because I cannot imagine my dad over there in that small kitchen cooking."

"He seriously has his own kitchen?"

"Yeah. There's something about this side of the house that he just seems to hate. Maybe something to do with my mom, I don't know. She passed away when I was younger, so I don't know much about her or them."

Rook's eyebrows furrowed, the frown on his face growing. "I forgot your mom died."

"Yeah, not long after I was born."

"Sorry. It sucks you never got to know her."

"It's kind of strange. I wish I had the chance to, but at the same time, it's hard to miss something you never had. You miss your parents?"

"Yeah," he said, not elaborating more.

He turned, sliding a full plate of food in front of me. Not only was it not burned, it looked amazing.

"You really do know how to cook."

"I took over everything after we got back to town. Cooking included. You experiment enough, you learn the basics of cooking. Poor Evie, though. She won't eat hamburgers anymore because I made them so bad once, she threw up."

I laughed, taking a bite of the pancakes first, moaning at the flavor.

"Rook, these are amazing."

"I'm glad I impressed you with one of the easiest things to make," he said, looking at me over his cup. His blue eyes were bright today, the heavy look of exhaustion not there as much. His dark hair was still a mess, but the soft smile on his face nearly made me melt.

"Well, what else can you cook?" I asked.

"A few things. I'm busy tonight, but want me to make you dinner tomorrow?"

"I can't. I have a dinner party to go to for my dad. Maybe the day after?"

"Wouldn't your dad be home?"

"I thought you could meet him at some point?"

He got up, setting his plate in the sink and heading back over to me. The dark scowl on his face was familiar, the soft, kind part of Rook disappearing at my question. "I don't think so."

"Is it really that big of a problem?"

"It is. What are you doing today?" he asked.

"I have some lunch meeting with my dad, then back here."

His shoulders rolled, the soft smile not coming back. "What type of meeting would you have with your dad?"

"I'm not sure. I have to meet him at Sweet Haven Cafe around noon." His frown deepened, and I laughed. "Is that an issue?" I asked.

"Maybe not if that's where you're going. Can you text me if you have any issues?"

"Issues at a lunch with my dad at Sweet Haven? The cutest coffee shop in town. Do you think something big and bad is going to happen there?" I asked with a smile.

"I don't know, but I have a bad feeling and I don't know about what. So will you just text me today and let me know how it's going?"

"Yeah," I said, more seriously now. "I will do that. You okay?"

"I'm fine. I have to go." He leaned down, kissing me once. "I'm going to grab my stuff and head out."

He disappeared around the corner before I could say anything, but I went after him. "What is wrong, Rook?"

"Nothing. I just need to go. I need out of this house."

"Why?" We made it to my room, and he grabbed his things immediately.

"I told you, I have things to do, Rebel."

"And that's it?"

"That's it. Text me."

He left, and it wasn't long before I heard his bike start up and take off. I stood there for a while listening, but I couldn't ignore the nagging thought that whatever bad feeling he had was about to crash into our lives.

Thirty-Three
Regan

I pulled into a parking spot at Sweet Haven and stepped out, the scent of coffee already hitting me. The cafe's warm, inviting atmosphere was a harsh difference to the chill of the morning. I had chosen black flowing pants and a cute long-sleeve top, opting to skip the jacket for the sake of looking professional —though the cool air made me second-guess that decision.

My phone pinged, and I pulled it out to see two texts from Rook already. I thought he had been mad at me, with how he left today, but he had been quick to text me earlier and was still texting.

ROOK

Are you there yet?

And did you drive yourself?

REGAN

I did. And I just got here. What is going on that you are freaking out?

ROOK

I'm not freaking out.

You are, too.

He didn't respond, and that only made me worry, but I didn't have time to think about it more. Instead, I rolled back my shoulders and headed inside. The scent of freshly baked pastries filled the air with the rich scent of coffee. Sunlight streamed through the large windows, casting a warm glow on the wooden tables and cushioned chairs.

My dad had never asked me for any type of meeting outside of the house or anywhere, honestly. Even when he asked me into his office, it wasn't to talk about anything besides where I needed to go for the week. This had to be it. I had spent a year of my life waiting for the moment he would give me a chance, and as much as I wanted it before, for the first time, I actually felt ready. I didn't want to hide away, and I knew I could handle the people that came along with the business.

My dad had been right before. I thought I was waiting around to take care of him, but I was also waiting around for my life to come to me instead of me going to it.

But I wasn't doing that anymore. I had gone after Rook and handled every single thing he showed me. If I could handle all the terrible things Rook did and the people that went along with it, I could handle my dad's business.

I almost laughed as I pulled the door open. The men my dad worked with were starting to seem like teddy bears compared to the guys Rook was dealing with.

I made it to the host stand, and they pointed to a table in the corner. I saw my dad first, my stomach dropping as I looked at the man across from him.

Elliot sat on the other side, laughing as my dad spoke to a woman next to him.

Bile rose in my throat as my confidence wavered with each

step. I came in here thinking my dad and I would finally get a chance to talk about my future with his company, but I knew that wasn't the case now. There was no reason for Elliot to be here that would be good for me.

Was he trying to get me back, and this was some weird way to force me into it? Or maybe he was here to tell my dad about Rook and me, even though I didn't know if he knew about us. He might. The people at the party we'd thrown at the house were mutual friends, but Elliot hadn't been around much, and I wasn't sure if any of them had even talked to him lately.

I slid into the open seat next to Elliot, not hiding the curl of my lip as he looked over at me.

"Hey, Regan," he said, the cocky smile on his face making me want to punch it off of him. I had almost forgotten what he had done to me.

The entire encounter with Rook had ended up being good for me, but Elliot didn't know that. He left me alone to be killed after walking me down that dangerous road.

My eyebrows furrowed, wondering why I had been so naïve not to ask before. I had been so wrapped up in Rook, I had nearly forgotten about it.

"Morning, Regan," my dad said.

"Yeah, morning," I mumbled. The woman next to him gave me a tight smile, and I looked her over without a word. She was dressed up in business style clothes, the button up jacket not doing much to hide the breasts spilling out. I couldn't figure out if she was here for my dad to work with or something else.

I pulled out my phone. I didn't care if it was rude to text at the table. The bombardment of bringing Elliot and the random woman across from me felt worse.

REGAN

What reason would Elliot have had to walk me down that road?

ROOK

To get you killed? Push you off a bridge? The options are limited.

REGAN

Is there a pretty overlook there?

ROOK

I wish you could hear how hard I'm laughing. No, Rebel. Nothing pretty down there unless you want to see a dead body.

Is he bothering you? I can go find him.

REGAN

Bothering me? Yes. But he's sitting right next to me, so there's no need to go find him.

"Regan, are you here to text or are you here to have a discussion?" my dad asked, his voice booming just enough to scold me.

"To talk, of course. I'm just a little confused why Elliot is here, and who this woman is?"

"*This woman*," he said through gritted teeth, "is named Candy, and she is now my fiancé, so please, call her by her name."

"Candy?" I turned to look at Elliot. "As in your mother, Candy?"

He smirked. "Looks like we are related now."

My mouth had dropped open, and I wasn't sure how to close it. "And your *fiancé*? You didn't think that it was important enough to even let me know you were dating someone, let alone proposing?"

My stomach churned as my eyes jumped to each one of them.

"I didn't tell you because I didn't think you would handle me dating your ex-boyfriend's mother very well, and it seems I was right."

"I thought we were closer than that!" I yelled.

"Really? Because Elliot says you've been dating someone new and you haven't said a word about him. Isn't that the same thing?"

My mouth finally snapped shut. He did have me on that one. I hadn't wanted to talk to him about Rook until I knew more about him at first, and then when I did learn more about him, I worried that my dad would know him and his reputation. I planned on introducing them at some point, but it hadn't felt like the right time yet.

"Well, based on the lack of a smartass response, I think you are understanding of that, at least."

"Couldn't we have talked about this in private first?" I asked, looking from Candy to Elliot. My phone buzzed over and over in my hand, and I knew Rook had to be pissed about my last text.

"I didn't have time for that," he said. "And I needed to talk to you before Elliot and I take off for a few days."

"Take off where?"

"We have a meeting in Chicago with a new...client."

"You and Elliot?" I asked, not sure if I could handle that he would take Elliot to a business meeting. "Am I going, too?"

His eyebrows furrowed. "For what? Did you need something in Chicago?"

"No, but if you are taking Elliot to a business meeting, couldn't I go, too?"

"I don't see why you would need to go to that."

"Because I have been asking for months, *months*, to help you with your company more, and now you immediately take Elliot without hesitation?"

Elliot looked at me and then my dad, his face scrunching before he gave a small laugh. "Why would you need to help with the business?" Elliot asked. "I'll be taking over most things with the business, and I don't see what you being there would help. There's no need to confuse people on who is in charge."

My heart dropped and my stomach flipped, wishing I had heard Elliot wrong. "Did he just say that he is taking over the business?" I asked my dad.

"He is. At least, he is going to show me he can, for now. Nothing is promised until you show me how you handle yourself."

Elliot had known I wanted this business. We talked about it a few times, and he knew why I came back after college. Now this?

My hand tightened around the knife and fork, trying hard not to stab it into the table. "I've wasted a year of my life. I gave up my dreams to come home and be with you. I've asked over and over to help with your company, to take it over one day, and every time you have shut me down. Now this?"

"Quiet down," my dad scolded. "I've been waiting to see you do anything other than lie around the house. Then I meet Elliot, and wouldn't you know it? He has taken all the initiative to help."

"Because you have let him!" I yelled.

"And maybe you could have helped if you would have tried. But no, you break up with Elliot and he tells me you are immediately out looking for a new boyfriend. That you only seem worried about who you are dating and what Harper is doing. I paid attention, and I believe he is right."

"Excuse me?" I asked. "Are you kidding me right now? I broke up with him when he left me stranded while we were being mugged because of him!"

My dad looked at Elliot, who rolled his eyes like I was being absurd. It did sound absurd, and there was no way for me to prove it unless I brought Rook in, and I didn't think that would end up any better than this.

"So, just to be clear, I've done nothing but wait for you to let me help. I put my life on hold because you were sick. I've listened to everything you told me to do, and now I get told I didn't do anything good enough to show you I can handle taking over *our* family business."

"It will be our family business once our parents are married," Elliot said, beaming.

I dropped my voice lower. "If you say one more fucking word, I'm going to kill you," I said, surprised at how much I meant it.

He scowled and sat up straighter.

"He's not wrong, Regan. I'm sure there are plenty of other things we can find for you to do if you want some hobbies, but I'm not giving you an empire just to run it into the ground."

I didn't know if I had just spent too much time around Rook and his friends, who seemed to not mind violence, or if I really was just finding my backbone, but the thought of slamming my knife into Elliot's neck was sounding easier and easier. I should be horrified with myself, but I just wondered how Rook would react if I did it.

Maybe he would help me clean up the mess.

I shoved my chair back, the wooden legs scraping against the floor as I grabbed my bag. "I'll be back in a second."

"Good. Collect yourself so we can talk about the wedding," my dad said, as if he hadn't just ruined my life.

I nearly ran towards the bathroom, and I was already pulling my phone out as I locked the stall door.

"What the fuck is going on?" Rook asked when he connected the call. I could hear the sound of his bike in the background and I wondered where he was going, wanting him here with me, but I had too much going on in my head to worry about asking.

"It's not good."

"What is it?"

"Elliot," I managed to say before tears welled in my eyes. "He wants to give the business to Elliot."

Rook was quiet, and I waited. "Elliot? Why?"

"I don't know. I guess my dad is dating his mom and they have this idea that they are a family now. He wants a man to run it."

"And that's the only reason he gave?"

"Kind of. I guess this has been going on behind my back for a while now."

"While you were dating him?"

"I think so."

"And does Elliot know you have been with me?"

"He knows I'm with someone. He told my dad that I'm more worried about finding a boyfriend than anything else. As if I care. The only reason I met you was because he's a piece of shit. I never told him explicitly it was you, and I doubt anyone is expecting me to actually date the guy who tried to rob us," I said. Rook gave a soft laugh, making me smile, but more tears spilled out. "People he knows were at the party and saw us. I don't know if anyone there has talked to him, though. He's kind of disappeared from the friend group. Which now, I guess that's because he's been too busy taking over my life."

"You should find out if they know who I am."

"What? Why?"

"Because there are going to be bigger issues if they find out you are with me."

"I can ask, but I don't know how much they are going to tell me either way. I'm out. I'm kicked out of my own family. I've done nothing but be there for him. I've done everything he asked. I've been there to take care of him if he needed it."

"Take care of him?"

"I never said anything," I said, more tears coming now. "I never told you because he doesn't like people to know, but he's sick. Terminally sick."

"When did you learn this?"

"Last year, right before I graduated college."

"And you've gone with him to all his appointments, taken care of him, and now this?" he asked.

"I mean, I've done what I could, but he's been so upset about it, he hasn't really let me in on any of that either. And what do I get out of all of it? A year of my life gone? I have no career, no life. A dad who doesn't even want to spend time with me and let me take over *our* family's legacy before he is gone?" The panic rising in my voice was clear, but I was doing everything to stop the tears. "I don't know what to do."

"You handle one thing at a time," he said. "Go talk to them and see if they know it's specifically me. Make sure you get the fiancée's name. Then get whatever answers you can and meet me out front. I'll take you home."

"I drove."

"And I will take you home," he repeated.

"When will you be here?"

"Five minutes. Go do what you need to and wait at your car for me."

"Okay. I feel so stupid."

"Don't," Rook demanded. "He betrayed you, not the other way around."

"Is it betrayal, though? Or am I really just that bad at this?"

"I don't know if this is really any help, but there isn't a way I could date you if you weren't good at this. If it wasn't obvious that you can handle yourself and shitty situations. Elliot is a useless excuse of a human, and I can prove it to you if you need more confirmation of that. Don't for one fucking second think you aren't the better choice for running literally any business. Just go out there, ask what you need and demand answers. If you want secrets to ruin your dad, Regan, I will give them to you."

"For what?"

"In exchange? Nothing."

"You said secrets aren't free."

"For you, they are now. Do you want them?" Rook asked.

I bit at my lip, knowing that anything he told me couldn't be good, and I wasn't sure if I was ready to deal with more heartbreak today.

"Yes, but can it wait?"

"Yes," he said. "Go finish what you need to. I'll be out front in a minute."

I hung up and took a deep breath. I could face my dad and Elliot one more time today, because Rook was right. I would always be a better choice than Elliot.

I kept my shoulders back and my head up as I stepped up to the table. All eyes turned to me, Elliot's and my dad's already looking annoyed.

"Do you know who my boyfriend is?" I asked.

They looked at each other and then back at me. "No. Do you need to tell us?"

"No. And do you know that Elliot is horribly addicted to gambling?"

Elliot only shook his head, denying it immediately.

"He is, so be careful on how he manages your finances. I would like to be left alone, so I would prefer you not call or bother me at home until I'm ready to talk," I said, the words sounding diplomatic enough, but I just wanted to scream.

"Fine, Regan. That won't be an issue, as we will be gone for two days. We can talk when we get back."

"We can talk when I am ready. You've betrayed me when I was doing nothing but be ready to help you. You're the one who asked me to stay home, you're the one who said I wasn't ready, and you're the one who told me to come back after college so I could continue the family legacy. I didn't do any of that. I stayed ready to help, and you didn't let me."

I heard Rook's bike rumble out front and I winced when it

caught my dad's attention. I glanced behind us as Rook swung off the bike and walked towards the front door.

"I need to go. We will talk later."

I ran out before he could respond, reaching the door as Rook started inside. His helmet was still on, but I could already imagine the scowl that was plastered underneath.

"Come on. I'm done."

"Fine. I changed my mind. I want to talk to Elliot and your dad," he said, pushing around me. I grabbed his arm, pulling hard.

"No. You are not. Get me out of here," I said. He stopped, seemingly stuck on what he was going to do. "Now, Rook. I want to leave."

Another second passed before he wrapped an arm around me, heading back to the bike.

"Give me your keys. Mason will be here soon to pick it up."

I handed them over and grabbed my helmet strapped to the back before getting on behind him.

I didn't know what I would do next or about my dad, but I knew that right now, I wanted to go home and hide away until I figured it out. I held on tighter to Rook as he took off, finding some comfort in the fact that he came for me.

Thirty-Four

Rook

There were only so many times you could drive up to your home, or anywhere that feels like home, and see it up in flames before you break. My limit was once, but as I pulled up in front of Maverick Moto after spending the night with Regan, I realized someone came to push my limits.

The entire front of the building was engulfed in flames. Firefighters were already there, making progress on putting it out, but I could see there wasn't much to save.

Thick, black smoke billowed into the sky, the flames burning hot as it took over.

I kicked my stand down, jumping off my bike and running up next to Aiden as he watched the building burn.

"Nobody's inside?" I asked. The panic of history repeating itself made me nauseous.

"No, everyone's out," Aiden said in a daze as Evie walked around the firetruck towards us. Hero wasn't far behind her.

"What the fuck?" My brain struggled to find anything else to say, but with Aiden, I wouldn't have to.

"Evie and I just got here. They were already here getting it out."

Evie came over, wrapping her arms around me as tears welled up. She wasn't one to cry, but I knew she remembered that night. She never talked about it, but it wasn't something you could easily forget, even if she was younger when it happened.

Hero came up, the tightness in his jaw making him look as pissed off as I felt. Evie stepped back, leaning against Aiden.

"They are thinking that accelerant was used on the lineup of new bikes in front."

"All gone?" I asked.

"All those are. The bikes in the back might be okay. They don't think it spread to the back as much yet, but they are struggling to get it under control. The chemicals and gas that we have all over keep popping and reigniting fires. They don't know how much will be saved."

"So we are kicked out of our home, and now can't even stay here," Evie said, turning to me. "What do we do now?"

My fists clenched at my sides, rage simmering just beneath the surface. If accelerant was used, this wasn't just random, this was a targeted attack. I stood there in silence, watching the flames consume more and more of the building. It was like watching someone eat away at your life. Inch by inch, foot by foot, the flames ate away at everything we had built.

"How sure are they that accelerant was used?" I asked Hero.

"If you are asking what I think you are, yeah, it was deliberate."

I nodded, taking a deep breath to steady myself. Did it have to be fire? It wasn't like it was a unique way to attack someone, but it felt so targeted at me. I hadn't told many people outside the group what had happened when we were younger, and even then, I didn't tell new guys like Zack and Kane. Not until I knew them better.

I had told Regan, though.

I didn't think she would set it on fire, but maybe her dad had connected the dots after Sweet Haven. Or maybe he found me through the work we did. I had no proof, but the nagging voice in my head made me wonder if Cameron Fletcher was behind this.

I leaned back on my bike, pulling out my phone.

ROOK

Your dad been around today?

REGAN

No? I think he left already. Why?

It wasn't enough. He could have and probably did, lie to her about everything. Including where he would be. I didn't know why she would tell him anything about my past when she hadn't even told him my name, but I still had to check.

ROOK

Just wondering if you were still home alone.

REGAN

I am. Are you coming over tonight?

I looked back at the fire, the snort of laughter coming from me, making everyone turn their heads.

"This is suddenly funny?" Evie asked.

"Regan asked if I would be coming over tonight. Is it too much to tell her I have no option but to come over?"

Aiden started laughing now. "There are enough rooms for all of us. Can we all come over?"

Hero didn't laugh, but turned to me. "That's not a bad idea. Could we all get in the rooms?"

"He's got a lot of cameras, but we could put up our dummy screens again," I said, actually contemplating it.

"You guys are dumb. Do you really think all of us could move into a house and go unnoticed? Where are you locking up your bikes every night?" Evie asked.

"True," Aiden said. "I'm not risking leaving them all out in the open to be found by Cameron."

"Or that *we* could all be found by Cameron," Evie said with a shake of her head. "Dumbasses."

I shoved a hand through my hair, trying to think of any solution that wouldn't get us kicked out or killed.

ROOK

Miss me already?

REGAN

That would be ridiculous.

ROOK

You can be pretty ridiculous.

REGAN

Look who's talking.

ROOK

I'll be there, Rebel.

I wasn't going to add that six of my friends might be, too.

"We'll see what's left of this place and then find somewhere for the night," I said. "Maybe Regan will let us stay until her dad is back. That way, we aren't sneaking you all in, and at least have time to fucking think."

Mason drove up, pulling off his helmet as his mouth dropped open. "How the fuck did this happen?"

"Someone is after us," Hero said. "Decided to burn the building down."

I nodded to Aiden, urging him away from the rest of them.

"I don't want to say this in front of Evie," I said once we were out of earshot.

"You think it was Cameron," he said, the words a statement, not even a question.

"I'm wondering. Yeah. It seems a little coincidental that this happens right around the time we are catching on to him and I'm fucking around with his daughter."

"We have no way to know if it was."

"But I'm going to have to find out."

"Let's wait until our entire lives aren't burning down in front of us before running off."

My jaw clenched. "I don't need to stand here looking at this."

"Maybe not, but I think the rest of us are going to need you to. Evie included."

He was right. I couldn't run off quite yet, even if I wanted to hunt Cameron down.

"Fine, but I'm going as soon as I can."

"I can go, too."

"Thanks," I said as we headed back. "It looks like they are starting to get some control on the fire. I guess we go see what's left of our lives?"

Aiden groaned, but he headed towards the building with us.

For one more day of my life, I would get to sift through the ashes and see what I had left.

I was going to kill whoever did this. That was pretty easy to decide on, but that nagging voice still made me wonder if it was Cameron.

And if it was, what I did to him was going to be so much worse than death.

A few hours later, the fire department cleared out, leaving us with a smoldering shell of a building. None of the bikes made it. Even my backup bike was ruined. The office we had was gone. Luckily, most of the back of the garage had nothing in it except steel and our toolboxes, which were charred, but everything inside made it.

"My computer is trash," Evie said, looking at her little corner that had her desk. "I'm going to need a new setup immediately."

"And where the fuck are you setting it up?" Hero asked. "Going to set up thousands of dollars of computer equipment in the alley?"

"Shut up, Hero. I don't need your smartass comments," Evie snapped.

"No? I have to deal with your smartass comments all the time. What's the difference?"

"Fuck you," she snapped.

"You wish," Hero said. I knew he meant it as a joke, but I wasn't in the fucking mood for his jokes. Aiden apparently wasn't either.

He stomped over, throwing one punch to Hero's jaw.

Hero stumbled back, already coiling to throw a punch back at Aiden, but I froze, hearing the squeal of tires on pavement before they did.

"Shut the fuck up," I yelled, turning back towards the road. The building was so burned, I could see out the front easy enough. A car peeled out, the back of it disappearing before I even had a chance to look at the plate.

Everyone finally stopped bitching long enough for all of us to head out front. A heap of clothes sat near the road. I kept moving, getting close enough to see part of an arm sticking out from the clothes.

My heart stopped.

It was a body.

Zack, Kane, and Regan weren't here, which meant all three of them were a possibility. I ran now, rolling the body over with a small sigh of relief.

It didn't last long when I realized that I did know who it was.

My informant, the guy I had worked with for years, was now rolled over dead in our driveway.

A bloodied note was stapled to his body.

"You're next," Aiden read over my shoulder. "Is this for you?"

"Me or all of us," I said, looking the guy over. It seemed like he had been beaten to death, but there really wasn't a way to know if he had been shot.

"So someone is burning down our place and threatening us on the same day?" Mason asked.

"Looks that way. I'm guessing it has to be the same person," I said, standing up and pacing. I needed to think. I needed to figure out what was happening, and I needed to do it fast.

But I wasn't even sure where to start.

"What are we doing now?" Hero asked, picking up the bloodied note to inspect it more.

I looked from the burned building to the beaten, wrecked body of the man I had worked with for years. He wasn't an upstanding citizen by any means, but he was a good guy and didn't deserve whatever torture they put him through.

Tortured because of me.

What if any of them were next? Or Evie? Or Regan?

We had nowhere safe to go, no way to stay protected or regroup. Once again, I had to sort out my life without a fucking thing to start with besides ash.

I grabbed my helmet and swung onto my bike.

"We find out what the fuck is going on," I said. "Reach out to anyone you think could know something. Aiden, can you—"

"Not let Evie out of my sight?" he asked with a smirk. "Yeah, no problem."

"Thanks. We're out for blood now," I said. "So let's go spill theirs before they spill ours."

I parked my bike in front of the office building. The ridiculous ways these drug lords didn't even try to hide anymore made me roll my eyes. A sky-high office building right in the middle of downtown Valeport.

Asher, one of the top four drug suppliers in the city, was nearly a friend now. Or at least as much of a friend that you can call a drug lord when you do business together. I pulled open the glass doors, stepping inside to see the receptionist, who smiled at me.

She was younger, but she didn't seem worried or scared. Which made me think she had been working here long enough to know the type of people that walked in here.

"How can I help you?" she asked, still smiling.

"I need to see Asher."

"Don't we all," she said with a shake of her head. "Do you have an appointment?"

"Does he even take appointments?" I asked, leaning on the counter. There were plenty of times I would blow past a front desk, or ignore the receptionist to get to the boss, but not here. I wouldn't fuck with Asher or the security setups he had in place. I would be dead before I made it through the door.

The receptionist was laughing now, clicking at her computer. "Not really, but I still like to ask. Let me see if he's in. Your name?"

"Rook. And it's urgent."

She picked up the phone, whispering into it before hanging up with a smile. "Apparently, he was expecting you to come by at some point. You can go up."

I didn't say a word, pushing past through several doors and

one ridiculously long elevator ride before I stepped into Asher's office.

Asher glanced up from his desk. The suit and tie he was in almost made me laugh.

"Such a proper businessman now. This is nothing like the shit warehouse you used to work out of in jeans and an old t-shirt."

He smirked, leaning back in his chair. "Really moved up in life, didn't I? Business is good and you've helped keep it that way."

"Does this mean you aren't the one threatening to kill me and my guys?"

His eyebrow cocked. "Your guys? I think you mean your girl, too."

My blood ran cold, and I fell back into the chair across from them. "Evie, too?"

Asher knew all of us well enough and I knew he still had a thing for Evie. If someone was out to kill her, he wouldn't be in on it.

"Her, too, but apparently you have a new girl on your bike and people have taken notice. No word on who she is, but there is a price on her head, too. Actually," he said, clicking open his phone, "it looks like someone will get paid pretty nice if they kill you or you and her, but if they manage to just kill her for now, the price is higher."

The words took too long to process. Someone wanted me dead, and not only did they want me dead, but they wanted me to suffer first. They wanted Regan killed, and me left alive, probably just long enough for me to suffer before the price on my head went up.

"You've got to be fucking kidding me," I mumbled.

"Who the fuck did you piss off so bad for this?"

"I piss off a lot of people. And with you all continually getting your shit stolen and having me come clean up your mess, the list of people wanting me dead seems to get longer with each job."

He shrugged. "Yeah, I'm getting pretty fucking sick of whoever keeps messing with my shipments. You figure out anything about it?"

"Considering the guy I had running for information was dropped off dead in front of my garage that was burned down today? And he had a nice note left for me that I'm next. No. I have an idea, but no fucking proof."

"Wow, you're having a great day," Asher said with a smile. "Someone is causing trouble for you. Want to share who?"

"I think it's Cameron Fletcher."

"Why?"

"I have my reasons," I said. I didn't share about my past, leaving nothing clear enough to trace back to who I was whenever I could.

Asher shifted in his chair and leaned back. "He has come around asking if I needed help with my security. Supposedly, he wants another meeting tomorrow."

"Did you take him up on the offer?"

"Not a fucking chance. The man is a rat. He'd weaken my security before he ever helped it. He works for hacks and is a hack himself."

"I heard that a few of your competitors are taking him up on his offer."

"Are you fucking kidding me?" he asked, mouth dropping open. I shook my head. "Those fucking idiots. So they are taking him up on his offer of extra security and now we have rats running through the city stealing shipments?"

"What a coincidence, right?" I asked.

"And how does this tie back to you getting your business burned down and a hit on your head?"

"History. If he knows who I am, he would put a hit out on me immediately. I'm telling you this because I know damn fucking well you wouldn't put Evie in danger."

He didn't say a word, but he gave a sharp nod in agreement.

"That girl on my bike with a bigger price on her head is Cameron Fletcher's daughter."

His mouth dropped open again, before he burst out laughing. "So we are looking at possibly her own father putting a hit out on her and not even knowing? God, that's fucking good. I miss you guys. You're always up to some wild shit."

"I think he fucking hates her. He might even know it's her and still put the hit out."

"Cold. What a piece of shit. How are you going to find out if it's him? If he's turning the rest of the lords against you, you're fucked."

"Has he said anything to you about me, then?"

"Not yet, but like I said, he's coming back tomorrow, and now I'm more curious than ever what it's about."

"You going to turn on us, too?" I asked, not truly thinking he would.

"You can do more for me and my business than Cameron ever could."

"What about the hit on my girl? Because there is no way they will know if it's her or Evie on my bike."

"I hope you know just because I had a thing for your sister years ago doesn't mean I care now."

"I know that."

"But, yeah, already told my guys to stand down and they won't get paid even if they do the job. Can't guarantee anything, though, because we are talking about a life-changing amount for most of these guys."

"I get it, but appreciate it. I have to go sort out... Well, sort out fucking everything. Will you keep me updated? I'll do a few jobs on the house if there's no delay in information."

He smiled, standing up with me. "You know I like keeping my money, don't you? Yeah, I'll keep you updated. I suggest finding somewhere locked up for a few days with your pack. People will be combing the streets for you all. I don't think there will be any concern if they hit the wrong rider."

"Already on it. Hey, since someone burned down my shop, you know any good buildings I can buy?"

Asher smiled. "I might actually know just the place. I'll text you the address, but you're not allowed to go by until after this shit is settled. I don't need to lose my sales because of you."

"No problem. One more thing. If you find out any confirmed information that Cameron's behind this, let me have him. We have plenty of history and I would like to be the one to get rid of him."

"No problem. Easier for me if he's dead and I don't have to clean up. Does this have anything to do with you fucking around with his daughter?"

I headed back towards the elevator, turning back to him.

"I'm not fucking around with his daughter. I don't care who she is to him. She's mine, and he just threatened to take her away."

THIRTY-FIVE

REGAN

The party tonight was one more that I would go to alone. My dad had texted me earlier that he wouldn't be home for a few more days, but for the first time, I didn't care if I had to go alone. I preferred it.

I clipped the diamond necklace around my neck. The pink heart pendant that Rook gave me hung perfectly with the string of diamonds. I pulled my shoulders back, taking a longer look at myself in the mirror.

For the first time in my life, I felt like a grown woman. I felt ready to not shrink back and not hide away. I wanted to be seen and feared.

And I would be.

Rook had made it clear I could handle being on top, and his words repeated in my head. I was capable of this.

So I headed to the dinner alone, but this time I held my head up.

I stepped out of the car onto the sidewalk, looking up at the flickering lights on the front of the sprawling mansion. I didn't know what I was doing anymore, or why I was here. It felt like my brain couldn't piece together what had just happened to me, so I just kept going through the motions.

I had nothing left. There was no other career waiting for me, no other family that would welcome me in. I didn't even know if I had enough talent in art to know if I could make that a career. I forwent pursuing it in exchange for helping my dad, and that wasn't going well for me now.

I might have Rook, but who knew how real all of it was for him?

I kept staring at the building. Another dinner for no reason, another dress no one cared about, diamonds that showed my wealth and hid every terrible, disgusting thing that was underneath. I ran my fingers over the pink heart that Rook had given me.

Everything he did felt special, like I was special to him, but his words still nagged at me. He was going to ruin me, and I think I was starting to realize that he meant he would take my heart and shatter it into a thousand pieces.

And he had been right. It would ruin me, because I was going to let it happen.

I started up the steps again, but I stopped when I heard the rumble of a bike engine. It was funny how I was recognizing them now, since I never cared to listen to them before.

The bike got louder, the rev of the engine making me turn to watch the road. Another few seconds went by before a dark bike rounded the corner, the hue of pink lights making my breath hitch. I didn't know if I would ever get used to Rook riding up to me.

Or kissing me. Or looking at me.

Every time it made my stomach flip, the small burst of excitement made it impossible to stay still.

He pulled up in front of me, cutting me off on the sidewalk. My smile fell when he ripped his helmet off, and I saw the scowl.

"What the fuck are you doing here?" he asked.

"Hello to you, too. I was going to dinner." He swung off the bike and grabbed my arm, dragging me into the shadows.

"But why?"

"I didn't know what else to do," I said, trying to keep my voice steady. I didn't want to shy away from my decision now, and I didn't want him to think he could scold me for anything. "I was sitting around that house and I had nothing else."

"And you are happy with this choice?" he asked, still sounding mad.

"Maybe. I don't know. I have wasted a year of my life for this world. I can't give up all of that because of one thing."

"One thing? You can when he looked at you and said you aren't good enough."

My chest tightened. "I am good enough."

"I fucking know that, Regan. So again, why are you here playing dress-up for a man who said you aren't good enough to run his company, but good enough to parade around for appearances? One who apparently thinks you are pretty but have no brain."

I stepped back, the words hitting me hard. "Did you really need to say that?" I asked. "Do you really think I need to hear it again?"

"Considering you are still here being the obedient girl he wants you to be without getting anything in return, yeah, I think it needed to be said."

"And you're perfect? You never do anything you shouldn't? What *should* I be doing, Rook? I have nothing."

"You can have anything you want, and I've told you that."

"But only if I rely on you to give it to me."

"No, I will help you start and then you will get it all yourself.

I'm not promising you a fake life on a silver platter like he has. I'm promising you a real life. One where some days it fucking sucks, and you don't sleep, and you're covered in blood, but after it all, you're on top. After it all, you run the world around you. It's a real life, Regan, not playing dress-up like a stupid doll."

"And real life isn't going around killing people whenever you're a little annoyed," I nearly yelled, and he glared at me.

"Sometimes it is if you want to stay alive."

A bike pulled up behind him, skidding to a halt. I assumed it was one of the group, but Rook looked from the bike to me, his eyes wide with worry.

"Go inside. Run," he said, nodding towards the door. "Now."

"Why? Who is it?" I didn't recognize the bike, but I didn't know exactly what bike everyone drove yet, and honestly, with helmets on, they all blurred together.

"Go inside, now. Find somewhere to hide out for a while."

"I'm not leaving. Tell me what's wrong."

He moved me back, pushing me behind his bike as he pointed towards the building. "I will tell you, but I need you to go."

The rider parked, lifting his shirt and pulling out a gun. I nearly laughed at the visual of this being the way we met, but none of it felt the same.

Rook moved in front of me, blocking my view, and I wasn't hurrying to look around him.

"I already know why you're here and I will pay you double," Rook said.

"What does that mean?" I whispered, but he didn't respond.

The rider made a noise, but I couldn't see what he was doing.

"Shit," Rook said, making me finally peer over his shoulder. The rider had taken his helmet off, smiling at me. He looked no different from Rook or his friends, but my hands still fisted into Rook's shirt as dread filled me.

"I don't need the cash as much as I need you dead," he said.

"Yeah, that makes sense. Are you killing us both or just me?"

"Excuse me?" I asked, pressing against him.

"Both. I at least get the most amount for the same job."

Rook stepped forward, keeping himself between me and the guy as he continued to move closer.

"Why are you walking towards the gun?" I hissed, hoping this meant he was going to shoot him first.

That hope died fast when I saw his gun strapped in a small holster attached to the bike.

The rider raised the gun, aiming it at Rook's chest, and my heart hammered in mine. I couldn't do this. I couldn't watch this.

It felt like Rook was all I had left. The only person on this planet that might care about me enough to put himself between me and a gun. I couldn't watch him die because of that.

I looked down at the gun again and back at Rook. He hadn't turned to face me even for a second, not taking his eyes off the rider.

"Even if you kill me, you aren't going to get what you want out of it," Rook said. "It's not like you can walk right in and take over what I've created."

"Maybe not immediately, but I can start."

"You're going to kill him?" I asked, feeling like I needed some confirmation before I crossed the line. Before I made a decision that I would never forget.

"You, too, princess," the rider said with an unsettling grin.

I grabbed the gun off the bike and stepped around to the back, closer to them. Rook was off to the side now, the rider diagonal to me and the bike as I raised the gun.

He smiled. The laugh that escaped him made me realize he wasn't scared of me. No one was.

"Already know you can't shoot, princess."

I couldn't, but I knew the logistics of it. I steadied my hand, taking one quick breath before I pulled the trigger.

The shot rang out, the quiet night around us breaking before settling eerily fast. The gun dropped as quickly as I had shot it.

Rook watched the guy fall, blood splattering onto us as my stomach churned, threatening everything I had eaten to come back up.

"What a fucking shot," Rook said, turning back to me. "Did you really just kill a guy for threatening to kill me?"

"I did," I said, dragging in hard, ragged breaths. "Aiden was right."

Rook's eyebrows jumped up. "About?"

"That is surprisingly easy to do when they are threatening something you care about."

He took three large steps in my direction, wrapping his arms around me to drag me against his chest. His lips found mine, the desperate, deep kiss making me forget for one second what had happened. He groaned, his hands sliding around the back of my neck to hold me closer.

"You look so fucking pretty, Rebel," he murmured. "You look so good, dripping in blood and diamonds. I told you, you're a fucking queen."

"You find this attractive?"

"Yes, unfortunately. I find my girl putting a bullet in someone's head to protect me sexy as hell. Sorry, buying me flowers or something doesn't get me off the same way."

"I can assure you now, you can expect more flowers than dead bodies."

"Then I'm going to need to kiss you a few minutes longer to make the most of this."

His hands roamed over my back, pulling me tighter against him as his kiss deepened. I felt the urgency in his movements, the raw desire he had for me, making my heart race. He pulled back slightly, just enough to look into my eyes, his breath hot against my lips.

"Every fucking time you surprise me, Rebel. Every time I think I've seen all you have to give, you do something like that and show me over and over how strong you are. You show me how much of a rebel you want to be."

His lips crashed back onto mine, his kiss demanding and wild. I wrapped my arms around his neck, feeling the heat between us intensify. His hands slid down to my waist, lifting me slightly off the ground as he moved us against the wall for support.

He rested his forehead against mine, his breathing heavy. "We need to get out of here," he said, his voice softening. "There will be more of them."

"Then I would like to go because I don't ever want to do that again."

"I can't promise a situation like that won't happen again, and I would like to request that you do kill anyone who is trying to kill me. Preferably, at least."

"But that was terrifying. What if I can't?"

"If you want to rule the world with me, Rebel, you are going to have to stand on your own. Next to me, but on your own."

"So you lied? You wouldn't protect me?"

"Until my last fucking breath, but that isn't the point. You're strong, smart, and capable. You can't be a weak point in our lives, in mine. No one can think you're a pawn or a bargaining chip. They have to know they will die if they touch you."

"Or die if they touch you?"

He groaned, pulling me back into him. "Fuck, that's the hottest thing in the world. Yeah, they can know my little rebel girl doesn't like people trying to kill me."

"What if I don't want to kill people?"

"Then they at least have to know you're in charge enough to send someone else to kill them."

I shifted on my feet, the clear answer making me feel in control. "I can do that. At least, I think I can."

"I know you can, and it's not like you have to all the time, but I need to know you can when it comes down to it. You just proved you're capable, and I didn't even have to tell you to do anything. You did it yourself."

"If I had to choose who I had to watch get killed, it was him. I wasn't sure I could see something bad happen to you."

"I understand. I don't even want people to look at you wrong without wanting to break their limbs. Thank you, Rebel."

"I would say anytime, but I wouldn't mean it."

He laughed, wiping something away on my cheek, but I wasn't going to ask what it was.

"How about you agree to do it when it's a situation like that and I can't get to my gun in time?"

I frowned. "Depends on how mad I am at you that day."

The smile that broke across his face was heart-shattering. The man so willing to put himself between me and a gun, the one running himself into the ground to keep his friends and sister safe and happy, seemed shocked that I would do anything to protect him.

"Feel like taking me home now?" I asked. I really was covered in a lot of blood and there would be no way I could go to the party now. Not that I truly wanted to.

"Yeah," he said, running a hand down my jaw. "We have to talk."

"That doesn't sound great."

"Technically, it's not, but after what just happened, it's a lot better than I thought." He looked back over his shoulder at the guy slumped on the sidewalk. "I think I might have to take care of this before we go."

I didn't even want to look. Instead, I turned, leaning against the bike as I stared up at the building. "You do that and I'll wait here."

"Do you want to call your car back? I'll have to do what I can and then wait for the guys to get here for the rest of it."

"No, I'm good here. I can wait."

He leaned over the bike, kissing my neck once before his lips came to my ear. "I'll make it worth the wait, Rebel, promise."

"Don't make a promise you can't keep."

"I never make promises that I can't keep."

THIRTY-SIX
ROOK

There had been a few times over the past few weeks that I wondered if I could ever tell Regan what I was doing. If I could ever tell her why I had really gone after her when I learned her name, and what I had been trying to do since.

I had thought it over so many times, and none of the outcomes ended up with Regan happy with me.

What I hadn't been expecting was Regan choosing me.

She went far beyond my wildest dreams and protected me, and now I felt like I had a chance. It felt like there might be a chance that Regan would be loyal to me more than to her dad, and I suddenly had a real way out of this mess.

I could get my revenge, and it would only be sweeter when Cameron found out that his only daughter was so in love, she would kill for me.

She held on tighter as I sped down the road to her house. It would all be so easy. I would take her home, we would stay the night together, and I could tell her everything.

My heart raced as I pulled up and parked the bike.

The blinding anger at Cameron Fletcher that ripped through

me was unexpected. I knew Regan didn't know what her dad was up to at all. I had learned she was naïve to every single thing he did, and he had crafted such a perfect world to keep it that way. Keep her close, naïve, and occupied just enough to not worry about asking about any of it. And when he did, he gave her the perfect excuse as to why she should stay around and not bother him.

Keep your friends close and enemies closer. Regan was his enemy. She was the one flaw in his life, the one person who he knew wouldn't go along with the terrible things he did and would ruin it for him. He saw her as a burden instead of making her an asset. He was too jealous that she would have it all one day, and he couldn't stand to give her an ounce of what he had. He made sure to keep her close and on a tight leash.

Well, now she was mine, and my woman would never be put on a leash. She could rage at the entire world, and I would happily be there to stop anyone who tried to intervene.

She didn't know any of the truth about her own father. Not that I could blame her, a simple Google search wouldn't bring up all the depraved things he had done or played a part in, but she had to know now. She had to understand before I ruined him or she would never listen to what I had to say.

Part of me hummed at the idea she could believe me, and maybe even be on my side. I helped her off the bike, and she gave me a tight smile.

"What did you have to talk to me about?"

"Up to your room first. I have a surprise there for you."

"What were you doing in my room?" she asked, looking from me to the house.

"Delivering presents? I thought you liked that."

"I do, but not after everything that happened, and especially not after you saying, *we need to talk.* Because if you break up with me after I...shot someone for you, I'm going to be so pissed."

"You think I want to break up after you saved my life?"

"I think that you're being weird and I'm already freaked out, so yeah, it's a concern of mine."

She didn't move, but I grabbed for her, sliding my arm over her shoulder and leading her into the house.

"I'm sitting here building our entire lives together in my head, Regan. I have no intentions of being done with you anytime soon."

"Ever the romantic," she grumbled as we headed upstairs. I laughed, pulling her in to kiss her neck once.

Regan had shown me over and over that she would be by my side, loyal to me and my secrets. She knew every side of me and still seemed to love all of them.

At least, I hoped.

I never trusted people. It took years before I really let them in, and even then, so many people were kept at arm's length. But not her.

I spun her, making her face the bed and the piece of canvas I had hung over it.

"What is this?" she asked, looking over the painting. Her eyes were wide, the awe in them settling me.

The painting always reminded me of the starry night one, the swirls of black and blue in the sky circling around a bright moon. The field underneath was filled with blue glowing stars, and a ghost stood at the far end.

Art never made sense to me. People were always looking for deeper meanings in every piece, but to me, it was just art. But this one always got to me. Something about it making me feel too alone. The ghost felt eerie and beautiful all at the same time.

I stepped up next to her as she looked over the painting. "It's the last thing I have from my home, from my parents."

"And you brought it here?"

"Yes," I said, stepping closer to it now. "I have nowhere else that is safe to put it."

"It's beautiful, and you can keep it here. I wouldn't let anything happen to it. Why did your parents have it?"

I walked around, sitting on the chair she had in the corner of the room, her back to me as she stared at the painting still. "They were art brokers. They dealt with high-end paintings mainly. They had hundreds in the house," I said, trying to tone down the anger that was threatening to come out. It wasn't her, it was her father that took it all away. "Sometimes, I would get so annoyed at the amount of shit they would hang on the walls, but the rest all burned up. I found two paintings left, and this was one of them. Evie has the other hidden away somewhere. There was nothing left of our home but ash." My jaw tightened, the angry curl to my lip making her step back. I tried to stop it, but reliving it brought every ache and memory of them back. "There was nothing left of my parents but ashes."

Her eyes went wide, but she didn't look at me. Her focus was still glued to the painting. "Picture it. A pile of dust is all that's left of your life and they have to dig through it to find the burned bones of your family."

That seemed to do it. She turned back to me now, her face falling with sadness as she came over. I didn't even have to ask before she sat on my lap. Blood was still splattered on her and her dress, but I had smeared most of it off her face.

"Rook, I'm sorry. I'm so sorry."

"They aren't your sins to apologize for, are they?"

"No, but I still wish it had never happened to you. There were really only two left?"

"Yes, the fire burned it all. There was nothing else."

"How? The fire department didn't get there fast enough?"

"No," I said, finally meeting her eye. "They did. But fires burn hotter and faster when the person who started them uses accelerant."

"Someone started the fire on purpose?" she asked. Her lips curled now, the disgust in her voice obvious. "The idea that someone could purposefully burn your house down with all of you inside. Of course you are angry. I would be, too. How could someone do that?"

"*Someone* did it, and *someone* was happy about it."

"Do you know who?"

My hands tightened on her thighs, the sudden worry that she would run away making me want to hold her in place.

"Yes," I said.

"And? Are you going to tell me who it is or what happened to him? Or is that some sort of secret, too?"

Her voice was so soft, the sadness in it making my chest tighten. "It has been a secret. One I've kept from you, but I think you should know."

"Okay. That kind of freaks me out, but I'd like you to tell me more about it. You've kind of kept me shut out of a lot and it's made me wonder if this would be over for you soon. Like, you didn't want me intertwined in your life, so it was easier to take me out of it."

"No, Rebel. I've been weaving you into my life, even when I didn't want to be."

"But you want to have me in your life now?"

"Yeah."

"Then tell me."

I took a deep breath, pulling her harder against me. I wasn't sure if I would let her run away, even if she wanted to.

"I know who did it, and I know exactly what he is doing today. He is on top of the world. Nothing bad has ever happened to him. I waited for karma and nothing ever happened. He only got more in life. More money, more power." I shifted her again, holding her so tight my fingers were digging into her thighs now. "It was your dad, Regan."

I could feel her body go rigid, the way she nearly stopped breathing as she took in what I said. I almost felt bad for her until I remembered how much better her life would be without him.

Another beat of my racing heart and she was fighting against my hold.

"Do you think that's funny, Rook? I have enough issues with my dad right now. I don't need you making it a joke."

"It's not a joke. Your dad used my parents, and when they wouldn't help him any longer, he killed them."

"And you know this for a fact? Or are you just trying to find someone to blame?"

"For a fact." She fought against me again, but I held on. "Stop moving, Regan. You're not going anywhere until you understand."

"I'm not going anywhere, but you are. You should leave."

"Do you understand that I've known? I've known since I was dropped off in front of that burned house and investigated more into who would have done it. Your dad killed my parents, and he tried to kill me and Evie."

"My dad wouldn't do that. I know he's been mean to me about a few things, but he wouldn't kill people. He wouldn't try to kill children!" she yelled.

"He would, and he did. My family wasn't the first he ruined, and I know for a fact it wasn't the last."

"That can't be true. He protects people. He runs a security company to protect people and their things, not hurt them."

"Oh, he does, but it's not even close to what you are thinking. He protects disgusting, terrible people who can't find any upstanding company to do it. Do you know what else he did?" I asked, pulling out my phone. "He burned down our business today because he found out who I am and that I'm with you."

Her eyebrows furrowed as she looked at the screen and back at me. For one second, I thought she might be on my side about this.

"You've thought this from the beginning?" she asked, pushing away from me now. I let her go, thinking she might need a little air until she came back to me.

"Yes," I said.

"The night I told you my name, I saw the look on your face and the way you stormed off. I thought you wanted nothing to do with me, but then you came back around stalking me. I never understood what that was about and stupid me, never thought to ask because I was just so damn happy that you cared about me in some twisted way."

"I do care about you, and not just in a twisted way, although that is included." I grinned, wishing she would come back over to me.

"Shut up, Rook!" she yelled, her eyes wide now. "You knew I was his daughter, and that's why you cared about me. Because you have some stupid idea that he killed your family, what, ten years ago? That's the reason you were stalking around here, for him. I thought you wanted me, but you were really looking for him."

"I was looking for a weak point in his life, yes, and I thought it would be you, but it wasn't. Not in the way I was expecting. I want to ruin his life the way he ruined mine, and I thought I could use you to do that." I got up, walking towards her. She stepped back, but I didn't care. I reached for her hands, forcing them onto my chest. "Using you quickly became needing you instead."

"No, no, no," she said, ripping away from me. "You don't get to act like any of this wasn't some fucked up plan to use my dad or hurt him. Were you going to kill me? Is that what all this was about? All those times I wondered if you were going to kill me, and you were, weren't you? You were going to take me away from him, so he had to feel your pain."

"Honestly? No, that wasn't a part of my plan. It might have crossed my mind when I first found out, but I thought you were worth more than a sacrifice to ruin your dad's life. And I was right."

"Your *plan*?" she asked, like the words left a bad taste in her mouth. "You are sick. You have a plan? To what? Kill my dad, ruin him? Use me to ruin him, and then what? Walk away when *my* life is in ashes and never talk to me again. What?"

"All of it."

"That's still your plan, then? You want to kill him?"

"I want him to see his entire life crumble in front of his fucking eyes. I want him to know there is nothing left on this Earth for him before he dies, yes."

Her mouth dropped open. "And how did I unknowingly help with this plan?"

"You gave me access to his schedule, his house, his life. I know that he and Elliot are working behind the scenes to steal shipments of drugs from the top drug lords. He wants to become one himself. I know Candy has been one more pawn in his game to hide what he's doing. He's using her name on buildings and storage units to hide stolen drugs. He probably doesn't even want to marry her, but needed to string her along." I stepped closer, already knowing she wouldn't believe this. I barely did when I pieced it all together. One thing after another, pieced together like a puzzle. "And I know he burned down Maverick Moto because he found out who I was after he saw us at Sweet Haven. Which I knew could happen, but I didn't care because I was worried about you, not him. Not that I expected him to burn my business down. I also know that the man you killed tonight was after us because your dad put word out to kill me. A hit. He is paying to have me killed, and the girl that rides with me. They will be paid more if they kill you first and leave me alive for a while, then kill me. He's paying more for my pain, Regan." The anger inside me swelled and surged until I felt like I would burst, but I held it back.

"You think my dad put a hit out on me? His daughter? And that he will pay more for me to be killed because they think you care about me? Have you lost your mind? I understand you are wrapped up in this dark, twisted world, but that's not where the rest of us live, Rook."

"I am telling you all of this because you showed me you can be on my side. You want the truth?" I asked, angrier now. "You don't want to be left in the dark? Well, then, you are going to need to see that the entire fucking world is dark and twisted. You're the one that's been shielded from it all. A naïve fucking princess who I thought wanted to know what was happening around her. Nothing I have told you is a lie, and every single thing can be proven."

"And you thought now was a good time to let me in on this plan? Not weeks ago? Not when I was crying to you that I don't want to be lied to and left out of things?"

"You also said you could handle the truth. And weeks ago, I didn't realize you were going to fall in love with me. I also didn't realize I was going to fall in love with you. So no, it wasn't an option then."

"I am *not* in love with you. You're sick. You think my dad kills people and put a hit out on his own daughter? And you, because we are dating? Are you insane? Get out and do not come back."

"I already know you love me, Regan. There is no way you would have done what you did if you didn't love me. I liked you the first night we met. I was already chasing you down *before* I knew who you were. Don't forget that I didn't know who you were until after Hallows Night."

"It doesn't matter! You still used me after. And maybe I thought I loved you when I did that, but you just made one thing very clear to me."

"And what is that?"

She squared her shoulders, picking her head up, but I could see the hurt in her eyes. "You never loved me. Never really cared about me, either. Not even close. I was a pawn in your game, and you can't suddenly change that fact. That's not what you do to people you love. Now get out."

I shook my head, already heading towards the door. I wasn't truly leaving, but I needed five minutes to sort out my mind.

"I loved you, do love you, all of it. I did plan to use you as a pawn, and that plan quickly went to fucking hell. Now I have a new plan, and yes, you are a part of it."

I slammed the door, everything piecing together so easily.

Unfortunately for Regan, I was still convinced she loved me, and like it or not, she was still mine.

THIRTY-SEVEN
REGAN

I never heard Rook's bike start after he disappeared. I didn't know why he finally gave in and left, but he seemed more angry than upset when the door slammed behind him.

I walked over to my mirror, the one I had been standing in front of just a few hours ago, intent on proving to myself I was strong enough to hold my head up and go. I had wanted to prove to myself first that I could handle being torn down and still come out the other side.

But all I had shown myself was that I was now a murderer.

I couldn't stand watching something happen to Rook, and I had made my choice. For one moment, I was okay with it. I had ridden back here with him with some silly thought he might care about me and I cared about him.

He proved me wrong so quickly that I couldn't even comprehend what had happened between us.

He thought my dad to be such a monster that he had killed his family, but was somehow still in love with me?

I unzipped my dress, ready to throw it out. I had spent too much time with Rook and had to remind myself that none of this was normal. I should be with a guy who doesn't kill people, or stalk them, or manipulate them. I wanted to call Harper, but I didn't even know where to start.

Instead, I showered fast and got into bed, staring up at the ceiling for what felt like hours. Rook's bike still hadn't made a sound, and I wondered if he would stand outside my window all night or just sitting on his bike. Not that it mattered.

I didn't want to want him here. I didn't *want* to feel safer with him here, especially if someone really was trying to kill me.

I flipped onto my side, the blankets wrapping around me like a straightjacket. Could there really be someone out there willing to pay for me to be killed? Or Rook?

I mean, I guessed someone wanting Rook dead would make sense with the type of people he worked with, but why would they add me to the list?

And how did they know he was with someone now? It isn't like I went everywhere with him enough for people to see me with him enough. And it's not like Rook would be telling anyone outside of his friend group that we were together.

Had been together, I reminded myself.

I flipped again. He said he had proof, but he didn't show it to me, and I hadn't asked. It had been too overwhelming to see any proof of someone wanting me killed, let alone Rook trying to convince me of it being my dad who made the request.

I kicked off the sheets and got up, wrapping one of my throw blankets around me and putting on a pair of boots before stomping downstairs and out the front door, into the cold night air.

Winter here was never terrible, but the night temperatures easily dropped into the thirties, making it feel freezing after being warm in bed.

I shivered, the little blanket not doing enough to protect me from the cold. I knew where Rook would have his bike parked and headed in that direction. The night sky was nearly black, clouds covering any sliver of the moon. I shivered again, this time out of fear of the things in lurking in the dark.

As soon as I made it closer, I yelled out. "Rook, I know you're out here, and you have me all freaked that someone is going to kill me, so please come out of hiding until I get to your bike," I said into the darkness.

It took less than three seconds before Rook stepped out from behind the trees and headed my way. His eyes roamed over me as he shook his head, already pulling off his leather jacket.

"What are you doing out here?" he asked, sliding the jacket over my shoulders. I didn't fight him, the warmth wrapping around me as I pulled it closed.

"I came to see what proof you have."

"About which part?"

"Someone trying to kill me."

He nodded, not even fighting me more as he pulled out his phone, clicking through it before handing it over.

I read through the text messages, the number having no name attached to it. The first one was information, a list of the prices that were being offered for each of us, and the second was the reminder that I was worth more if I was killed first. My stomach churned as I read it. No one really wanted to confirm that there's someone who hated you so badly, they would pay to have you dead.

"That doesn't mean much to me when I don't know who sent it."

"Then call the number."

"No way. I don't know who it is."

"Asher. One of the most powerful men in the city, and a friend of ours." The name sounded familiar, but I couldn't place from where.

"What if it's just Mason, or Aiden, or Hero pretending to be someone else?"

"Call him. You will know it's not any of them."

"Won't he be sleeping?"

"Maybe. I don't know," Rook said. He seemed sad now, the quiet demeanor nothing like the one he had earlier.

"I'm not calling some rich, powerful asshole in the middle of the night to ask."

"Then I'm not sure what else you want me to say to prove it right now. You aren't believing my words."

"Why would I? You've been lying to me the entire time I've known you!" I yelled, my words echoing into the night.

He looked around, but he didn't shush me.

"How am I the bad guy here when you have been mad at your dad already? You know he's an asshole to you. You know that he thinks you aren't worth shit when he's giving his business to an idiot like Elliot before you. When he doesn't even tell you he's getting married? Have you even questioned why he's getting married when he's apparently so fucking sick, he can't even care to help you after you gave up everything for him? He can take on a wife and brand new son, but he's too sick to make sure you are okay?" He stepped closer, glaring down at me. "Stop only questioning me, Regan. Start questioning him and then decide who wants you safe." He reached up, running a hand down my jaw, and I hated that I didn't fight him on it. "I am glad you are questioning me, and I will give you any proof you want that I have, but don't only ask me these questions."

I couldn't take any more. From the way his hair fell over his forehead, to the way he looked at me, even to the smell of his jacket wrapped around me. I couldn't be near him and not want to give in. I shrugged off the jacket, making him take it before I spun, heading back inside without a word.

Maybe I needed to ask my dad questions, and maybe I needed to ask Rook a few more, but for now, I needed to be alone.

Rook hadn't been around all day.

I had paced my room, cried, and tried to get ahold of Harper, but she was apparently busy because I hadn't heard a word from her yet. Night fell, and I tried to not get myself more scared than I already was. I checked the lock on the window first, securing it closed before locking my bedroom door. I didn't know what a flimsy lock on a wooden door would do to keep Rook, or anyone else, out if they truly wanted to get inside, but it at least made me feel like I was attempting to keep people out.

But I shouldn't be surprised it wouldn't stop Rook.

He walked into the room like I didn't even have a door, let alone a locked one.

"What are you doing here?" I asked, already glaring at him.

"Came to see if your dad is home, but his side of the house is pretty quiet."

"Because he isn't here."

"How sad. I was hoping to get this entire thing done tonight so we could move on with our lives."

"What's that supposed to mean?" I asked, barely wanting to know the answer.

"It means I came over to see about killing your dad tonight and forcing him to tell you the truth. Now we have to wait."

"You know, I've said it before, but you are a monster, Rook."

"No, I just don't want to spend another night away from you, and he's in the way of that. And you can't act like you aren't one now, too."

"I did what I had to because I didn't want you dead. It's not like I liked it," I said.

"Then what aren't you understanding? I will do what I have to do to keep you safe," he said, taking a tentative step towards me.

"And that includes killing my father?"

"Maybe. If he is trying to kill you, then yes. You are mine, and I will protect what is mine. That's my job."

"You think your job is protecting me now?"

"No, I know it is. You can hate me, Rebel. I will still give you every fucking thing you want."

"I want you out," I said, my breath hitching as he leaned down, his lips pressing once to my neck.

"Are you sure?"

Every hair on my body stood, the shiver that ran through me making me shudder as his fingers trailed up my hips and sides. The light touch made me want to give in. He brushed up my neck before his hands wrapped into my hair and tightened until he pulled my head back, forcing me to look at his face.

"Yes," I said, my body betraying me as it sank against him a little more.

"I didn't know, Regan. I didn't know that you were smart and strong. I didn't know you were so desperate for more in life. I didn't know you wanted to rule the world, or understand my life, or kill for me." He grinned at the last part. My stomach flipped, and I pushed against him hard. He kept his grip on my hair, but he stepped back. "Come on. I know you are more pissed off than a simple push. You want to claw my eyes out, you want to hurt me, so do it."

"No. I'm not a monster like you are."

He laughed, pulling me back against him. "Yes, you are. There's no fucking halo on your head anymore, Regan. You're a killer. You can punish me how you see fit, but you can't hide what you are now. Not from me, at least."

His words pushed me over the edge, anger making me blind

to what I should do and letting what I wanted to do take over. I had crossed lines I never thought I would, all for him. All to keep him safe, and now he threw it in my face. In a sudden surge of anger and desire, I twisted in his grasp, pushing him hard until he stumbled back and fell into the chair we had been in when he told me that my entire life was a lie.

I stepped in front of him. His eyes dragged up my body until they met mine. The lust and desire in them made my body tighten. I hated his blue eyes, and the way I liked the tattoos running up his neck and down his arms. I hated him for what he would say to me. He kept poking and prodding me, making me want more of his life.

I stepped closer, my hand coming back. I almost surprised myself when my palm connected with his cheek, the stinging sound of skin on skin making me wince.

His eyes went heavy, and he leaned forward as he reached out. His hand fisted in my tank top before he ripped it back. Fabric tore as the straps broke.

My chest heaved as he pulled it more, leaving my breasts exposed.

His eyes locked on mine for one beat of my heart before he stood. His hands slid around my thighs until his arms locked around me, lifting me up as he kept moving. My back slammed against the wall, the sharp pain making me hiss before I leaned down, biting into his neck hard.

He moaned, gripping me hard. The sound made me burn hotter, my thighs clenching at the sudden wave of heat that came over me. He shifted me and I grabbed on, my nails digging hard into his back as he arched.

His mouth found mine, his tongue taking over like he owned it, and I was starting to worry that he did. I wasn't fighting this. I was taking it.

Not only was I taking what he offered, but I was demanding

more. I slid my hand between us, pushing my way into his jeans until I found his cock, already hard and ready for me. My thighs tightened around him. The need to sink onto him was getting overwhelming.

His eyes staring down at me didn't help my resolve. If I actually had any resolve left. It wasn't anger in them, or even a hint of that deadly glint that always made me a little nervous. They were soft.

He was looking at me with that sweet gaze any girl would dream about from a man like him. A man who probably never gave that look to anyone.

My heart stopped, and I pushed back, scrambling to duck under his arm as I realized I once again was giving in.

"Leave, Rook."

He didn't say a word, but he his eyes roamed my face. No anger flashed, no scowl came, he just gave me one sharp nod.

"I won't be far," he said, the deep rumble of his voice making my legs weak.

"Please go home. I don't need you close."

"There is not a fucking chance I'm getting out of sight from this house. Whether you believe it or not, people are trying to kill you, and I won't let them."

"Out, Rook." The door slammed behind him, and I slumped onto my bed. Shadows danced outside the window as I pulled a blanket tight around me. Now I had to sit here all night, worrying that Rook might not be the only one out there.

Thirty-Eight

Rook

I stared at the house, anger burning through me the longer I stayed there. I had nowhere else to go, and nowhere else I wanted to be. There was no home for me, and the rest of the pack would be waiting for word on what we were doing next.

Now Regan hated me, but she didn't understand the truth. Her dad was the actual monster, and mad at me or not, people would still be hunting her down, so leaving her alone here was out of the question.

There was only one option for me now, and I would happily take it.

I pulled out my phone, clicking into our group chat.

ROOK

Pack up. Bring your shit to the Fletcher mansion.

EVIE

Are we moving in or is it temporary?

AIDEN

You think we would move in and what? Share the house with Cameron Fletcher?

HERO

He will love that. Maybe we can start having sit down family dinners.

MASON

So wholesome.

HERO

It will be really wholesome when Rook puts a fork in Cameron's eye.

AIDEN

Fuck you, Hero. Please get over your disgusting eye mutilation fetish. I can't take anymore.

HERO

It's not a fetish. It's a fixation. Don't be disgusting.

AIDEN

When does it end?

HERO

When I find a new fixation?

ROOK

Shut the hell up and get over here. Bring everything.

A round of cursing and salutes came through before the chat went quiet, and I sat back.

The light in Regan's room was still on, and I knew had to be fuming at me. Maybe not even only at me, but at herself, too.

She gave in to her own hatred and love for me so fast, she couldn't help it.

I could understand why she was mad I hadn't told her the

whole truth, but she couldn't be mad at me for who her father turned out to be.

And she couldn't only be mad at me when he was doing something way worse to her.

The group pulled up thirty minutes later and shut their bikes off fast, like I had told them to. I didn't want Regan to know what we were doing until it was too late to stop us.

"What are we doing?" Aiden asked.

"And why did I have to pack all my things?" Evie asked, pointing to the filled car.

"We are moving in."

Mouths dropped open, everyone staring at me like I had lost my mind.

"Just to be clear, we are moving in there...permanently?" Hero asked, pointing to the Fletcher mansion.

"Yes, in there," I said.

"And Cameron is...cool with this?" Aiden asked.

"No, he has no idea."

"And you don't think the police are going to raid this place the second he gets home and sees us?"

"No. He won't have a chance to call the police. Hence, the moving in and setting up before he gets home."

"Does that mean Regan is cool with this?" Evie asked.

I knew the scowl on my face got worse. "No, she's mad at me. I told her everything."

"Fuck," Aiden said. "Everything?"

"Everything," I confirmed.

"And she isn't going to kick us out?" Hero asked.

"Regan is going to be locked in her room until this is all taken care of. After that, she can choose what she wants to do."

"Rook, that is not how you keep a girl," Evie said, rolling her eyes as she grabbed a suitcase out of the car and started dragging it up the stone walkway.

"I got you a damn place to live, Evie. Can't you just give me a break?"

"You are stealing a place to live, big difference, but I'm excited to have such a nice bedroom. I would take the one by Regan, but I'm assuming I will want to be far away from that."

"I second that," Aiden said.

"Trying to get a room next to mine, Aiden?" she asked with a grin.

He groaned, mumbling about her as he grabbed another bag out of the back and headed up the walkway behind her.

Mason came to my side, staring up at the mansion. "You're locking her up in there?"

"For now."

"Is it already done?"

"No, she thinks I'm just sitting out here."

"Surprise." He grinned, following after them.

We made it into the foyer, everyone dropping bags and looking around.

"Honey," Hero screamed, "we're home!"

I smacked his arm. "Seriously? I was hoping to be a little more subtle."

"For what? You're breaking into her house to take it. Might as well make a scene."

I shook my head, but grinned as Regan walked up to the balcony that overlooked the foyer. Her eyes went wide, looking at us with all our bags and suitcases.

"What are you guys doing here?"

I didn't answer, already heading up the steps to her. "We need to talk," I said. "In your room."

I grabbed her arm, but she ripped it away with a frown. "You're not allowed in my room anymore. You need to go."

"I'm not going anywhere. Either get in your room or I'll carry you in there."

"No, you won't," she said, her hands on her hips now.

I didn't wait before leaning down and throwing her over my shoulder, and continued walking to the bedroom. "You're right. I won't carry you to *your* room. I will carry you to *our* room."

She smacked at my back. "What are you doing, Rook? Why is everyone here?" I slammed the door shut behind us and tossed her on the bed. She bounced once before getting up onto her knees and facing me. "What is your problem?"

"We are here because we need a place to live and my girlfriend has one of the biggest fucking houses in town that happens to be empty most of the time. It's private, too. No one to complain about our bikes, and it has a beautiful garage we can lock our stuff up in."

She scoffed, sitting back. "You think you are moving in?"

"No. I *am* moving in. All of us are."

"You are not," she said in disbelief, her mouth dropping open.

"What's the issue? You said you didn't want to be here alone all the time. Now you might never be alone in this big house ever again," I said with a laugh. "We are all busy, but with so many of us, someone is usually home. Which is great because you can't leave until I get rid of the price on your head."

"You think you're locking me up here?"

"I know I am," I said.

"What about my dad?"

"He's out."

Her eyes went wide. "Did you kill him?"

"No, Rebel. He isn't even back in town yet. But he's out of this house. If he's going to burn mine down, he technically owes me one. A garage, too."

She shook her head. "You seriously believe this. So you think my dad burned your house down, killed your family, and now burned your garage, all while putting a hit out on both of us? How do you think you know it was my dad?"

"When I came back and got settled back into life here, I started asking around. Friends, people who worked with my parents, any hint of information I could find, I went after it. Your dad stood to gain the most from their deaths. He took over their company and dissolved it immediately, putting every dollar and asset into his name. He made it seem like they had never even existed."

"Why would your parents sign everything over to him?" she asked, and I was relieved she was asking questions to make sense of it all.

"Their business was doing good, but they had debts. It made it impossible to grow, and they were looking to expand. Cameron promised them everything they needed if he was signed on as a partner. It was supposed to be a silent partnership, from what I understand. We never found the original paperwork, but Evie will be searching his office for it soon."

"So that's it? You are moving in, locking me away, and digging through my father's life to try to prove these ridiculous theories you have? And then what?"

"I'm going to give you undeniable proof. Once you believe me, you'll agree that we can live here. Then, I'll destroy your dad's life, and we'll have our future together."

"I understand I am mad at my dad, but I don't want his life ruined."

"Why? He ruined yours," I said.

"No, he didn't."

"He absolutely did. Are you happy? No. Are you doing what you want to be doing in life? Also no. And why? Because he told you to be here for him." I slid out my phone, already hitting Asher's name. "Asher is a friend, but he really doesn't care if I'm dead or not. At least, not completely. He will tell you the truth about the hit, whether it hurts me or not."

"Hello?" Asher asked.

"Hey, Regan's here. She wants the information on who is trying to kill her." I said.

She was already shaking her head. "How do I know you didn't just pay him off to lie?"

"Because I have more money than Rook. I don't need pennies to lie over something so simple," Asher said.

"I don't know how to trust either one of you. From what little I've heard, you're another criminal, and he's got me locked up in my own house."

Asher scoffed. "So you don't die. You should trust the guy trying to keep you alive a little. Rook already came down to my office to convince me to not go after the cash being offered for you. Luckily, I'm happy to keep Rook's help, and he will make me more money alive. You won't, though. The only reason you don't have another dozen men out looking for you tonight is because Rook offered free services for me to make it clear they couldn't pursue you."

Regan's eyes went wide, and I hoped that meant she was finally realizing that this was actually happening.

"So there really is someone willing to pay to have us killed?"

"There is," Asher said. "You should be flattered, it's a sizable amount. I usually only see that for high-ranking people. They are really needing you gone."

"Who?" Regan asked.

"Who wants you dead? Pretty sure you know him well."

"Who?" she asked again.

"Cameron Fletcher put out the request for Rook and the girl that rides with him. Gave their descriptions, their gear, and the bike."

She dropped back, her face blank as she stared off. "Did he give a name for the girl?"

Asher laughed. "Hoping Daddy isn't trying to kill you?"

"Wouldn't you?" she snapped. Pride swelled again in my chest that she wasn't scared of yelling back at Asher.

"No," he said. "If someone wants me dead, I kill them first."

"Even if it's your parent?"

"*Especially* if it's my parent. You better learn who your dad is before he gets his shot because I know him well enough, and I know for a fucking fact he will take that shot the second he has a clear one. Metaphorically, at least. Your dad is a coward when it comes to killing someone himself."

Her mouth dropped open, as her eyes went wide. "I've had enough."

"Do you believe me now?"

"Yeah. I'm done."

"Keep me updated, Asher."

"I would like to say the same to you, but I think you are going to be busy attempting to keep a girl. Although, let me know if locking one up works because I think I need a wife and can't seem to keep a woman around."

I groaned. "So far, not great, but I'll keep you posted. Talk later." I slipped my phone back in my pocket, facing Regan again. "Do you believe me at all yet?"

"I do."

"You do?" Hope filled my chest, and I forced myself not to reach out to her.

"I do, but it's obvious that my dad didn't know who I was. He just said the girl on the bike. There would be no way he could know it's me. In what world would I be dating some criminal guy that rides a motorcycle?"

I stalked over to her, pulling her hard against me. "In this world," I said, grabbing her chin and lifting it until her lips met mine. "In this world, that's who you are dating. Currently dating, and that won't be changing soon. You deserve to not be locked up anymore, Regan, but to do that, terrible things need to change fast. I will show you everything. Please, I just need you here so you aren't killed."

I pressed my lips against hers, surprised when her lips pressed harder against mine, but it was short-lived. Her hands pushed hard on my chest as she shoved me back.

"Get out. I'm tired and don't want to talk to anyone."

"I can't let you leave."

"And you can't force me to stay. Get out, Rook."

I watched as she crawled into bed, flipping until her back was to me.

"If you want to come down and talk, we will all be here all night."

"Great," she mumbled.

"And I'll cook you dinner."

"I'm not hungry."

"Okay, then come out when you're ready to rip me to pieces."

I slammed the door, stalking back downstairs to the group.

"That sounded like it went great," Evie said with a smart-ass grin.

"Shut up, Evie. You have a fucking house, don't you?"

"If you wanted to move in with your girlfriend, there are better ways to do it," Mason said. "I don't know, maybe find a house first, then ask her politely."

"I prefer storming the house and telling her I live there now, honestly," Hero said. "Less mess of emotion and more common sense."

"Congratulations," Aiden said. "You have lost your mind so bad that Hero agrees with you."

"It's my house now, so unless you all want to be kicked out of it," I said, "I would like to stop hearing all of your opinions. I'll be back in about thirty minutes. If I'm not, find me, preferably. If Regan comes out, call me immediately."

"Wait," Evie said. "Where are you going? You can't leave, either. Someone wants you dead, too, Rook."

"I have an errand. I'll be back. Just keep an eye on anyone coming here."

I grabbed my helmet and keys and headed out to my bike. The uncertainty in my plan was making my chest tighten. I glanced up to Regan's room again, the light off now. I knew she loved me. Or had loved me.

But I loved her, and I would do anything to keep her safe now.

Anything.

I sat downstairs in one of the weird, oversized chairs in Cameron Fletcher's personal living room after I got back from Asher's to check in. I didn't really understand the idea of having two living rooms, and I didn't understand why you would want to fill them with such uncomfortable furniture.

Aiden paced at the window as Hero and Mason tried to stretch out on two of the couches.

Evie stormed in, furious, as she handed me her tablet.

"What's this?"

"I got into Cameron's computer and since I had more time now, I could connect to his phone. I found his texts, Rook. He's sick."

I scrolled through the ones she pointed me to. Mainly conversations with Elliot. "So, he definitely burned our garage down," I said to the rest of them. She leaned over, scrolling into older texts, apparently searching for one in particular.

"They make jokes about him killing our parents, Rook. *Jokes.*"

"In all fairness," Hero said, "we also make murder jokes."

"Hero, I will put a knife in you. Shut up," Evie said.

"See, perfect example of a joke about murder."

Evie turned, her eyes wide as she stalked over to Hero. Aiden jumped between them.

"Easy, psycho. Tell us what else you found before you get into a fight."

She scowled and turned back to me. "He did absolutely take the hit out on you and Regan. It doesn't say if he knew who she was or not, but he ordered it."

My head fell back as I let out a hard breath. I finally had the proof. There would be no way for Regan to not believe me now.

A thump from above made us all freeze and listen. Nothing else came for a few seconds until I could hear the faint scuffle of feet on the roof.

"Someone find us?" Mason asked.

"Or Regan is trying to break free," Evie added. "That's what I would do."

"Shit," I mumbled, already getting up and handing her the tablet back. "You three go check the grounds outside. I'm going to check on Regan."

I nearly ran up the steps to her room, cursing when I didn't see her inside. The window was closed, but I still opened it to check, only to find a shivering Regan standing on the roof.

"What the fuck are you doing, Rebel?" I asked, offering her a hand.

"How do you get up and down onto this roof so easily?" she asked, nearly yelling. When she faced me, I could already see the aggravation all over it.

"I jump."

She glanced over the edge and back at me. "Off of *this* ledge?"

"That one exactly."

Her mouth dropped open. "How are your legs not broken?"

"It's not that high. Do you want to come inside before you freeze to death?"

"No. I want to sneak out of here."

I pressed my lips together, trying to fight my laugh. "You're trying to run away?"

"Yes. You locked me up in here, and I'm pissed."

"I get that, but trying to jump off the roof isn't going to help things. Come on."

"No, you are going to keep me locked up."

"Only for a few days. You will barely notice."

"You're the one who told me I shouldn't be locked up. Of course I'm going to notice."

"Get your ass inside, Rebel. You are not jumping off the roof, and even if you do, I will hunt you down on my bike just to drag you right back into this room."

She scowled, glaring at me as she came back to the window and slipped inside.

"You're the worst," she said.

"I know, but I like your head in one piece, so we are both going to have to live with it. Now come on, I have episodes of Dateline to catch up on and need your expertise to get me through it."

"You think I'm letting you spend any time in here?"

"I think you now need a guard before you try to escape and I am volunteering, so yes, I will be staying in here."

She dropped back in her chair and clicked on the TV, not saying a word as I laid back on the bed and started watching.

Even mad at me, I still enjoyed the company and knowing she couldn't run away now. All I could think about was how much better our lives were about to be.

Thirty-Nine
Regan

I made up my mind the next night when I heard a bike pulling back up to the house and saw Rook stalking up to the front door.

I couldn't be mad at Rook without knowing if he was being honest or not, and sitting in my room pissed wasn't going to help anything. If he really did love me, he would answer more of my questions.

Rook glanced up, seeing me in the window, but he didn't wave or acknowledge me further, and that only fueled my determination more.

I threw my door open, stomping to the railing that looked over the entry just as Rook made it inside.

"So you're allowed to keep leaving, but I'm not?" I yelled, making him look up at me. I could see the dark circles around his eyes again, and noticed the way his shoulders slumped. I wondered if he had slept at all the past two nights or just watched over me. "I thought someone was trying to kill you, too."

Yeah, I can because, first, you don't care if I'm dead. It might actually make you happier. And second, I'm trying like hell to figure out what I can do to make you less pissed off at me, and the only thing I can think of is these damn cookies."

"I literally killed someone because they were going to kill you," I said, the words leaving a bad taste in my mouth. "How could you say I want you dead now?"

Evie stepped out of the dining room, Mason right behind her.

"Are you serious? And you left that out of conversation, Rook? What the hell?" she asked, looking up at me. "There's absolutely no way you're not my best friend now." She glared back at Rook. "If you can get over him being an ass for a while."

"I'm trying to not be an ass," he said. "Hence, the cookies."

I didn't know if it was the way I had already cried all my tears or that part of me was understanding everything going on around me. I knew my dad did apparently know the type of people that would kill people for money, which that alone felt shocking. I knew Rook thought he was behind killing his parents, and I knew my dad had been keeping secrets from me.

I just hadn't realized what type of secrets. Or how many of them.

I also knew that someone could do those types of terrible things and still be a good person.

"Are you bringing those cookies up to me or do they have to be slid under my door so it really feels like a prison here?"

He grinned as he started up the stairs two at a time, the devastating smile on his face there because I was giving him a sliver of a chance. I wanted to give him a chance. I wanted to go back to how everything was going before he told me every terrible thing he had hidden.

The smile fell a little when he made it up the steps, his eyes going heavy with exhaustion as he handed me the box.

"When did you sleep last?" I asked, realizing just how much I cared about him. It didn't matter what had been going on around us, I still cared.

"What day is it?"

I rolled my eyes, already walking back towards the room. "Will you sleep if I let you in the room?"

"Depends," he said. "Do I have to worry about you sneaking out? Or will you be there the entire time?"

"If you sleep, I'll stay," I said, already grabbing my tablet and heading to my chair in the corner of the room.

"Regan, wait," he said, reaching out and pulling me back. His hands cupped my jaw, the soft touch a harsh contrast to the angry furrow of his brow. "I'm sorry."

"Sorry for telling me all these terrible things, or sorry for your kidnapping attempts?"

He gave a forced grin, but still didn't look happy. "Sorry that both of those things hurt you. You said you always wanted the truth and I'm trying to give it to you. And the kidnapping thing is because I want you safe. I mean, it's no heartache for me, exactly, to have you around all the time, but I really don't want anything to happen to you."

"It still isn't your job to protect me."

His chest heaved, his nostrils flaring as his hands tightened on my face. "It is when you're mine. It is when I won't let you get killed in front of me. I will do anything to keep you safe, including this."

Frustration bubbled up in my throat. I wanted everything to make sense. The agonizing feeling that I was so close to putting it all together, but not quite there yet was making me lose my mind. "But why do you think you have to?" I asked.

Like I said the wrong thing, his hands dropped from me and he stepped back.

"Because I love you, Regan. I didn't think it would be possible, but I love you."

"With everything you have said to me, now you think I'm supposed to trust you because you say you love me?" I asked, my heart racing at the clear-cut words. He had said he had fallen in love with me the other day, but after his confession, I didn't think it was the truth. "I don't think you lie to people you love."

"I told you I was taking everything from you. I just couldn't tell you how."

"That doesn't count as telling me the truth. You also said you had a lot to give me in exchange. Where is all that stuff?"

He grabbed me, ripping me closer as he forced my hands onto his chest. "I am giving you more. I am giving you *me*. Every fucking part of me. Is that not enough for you?"

"In exchange for taking everything from me? For locking me up? Would you be okay if the tables were turned?"

His lip curled. "This is temporary. A moment of our lives while I build a better life for us. A safer one. I can't have a price on your head, and I won't let you walk around waiting for a bullet. Once I kill the man who did it, you are free again."

"You can't walk around thinking you're my protector. I didn't ask you to be. You think you need to protect everyone you care about to the point you are locking me in my room?"

"And you can't give up who you are to do everything you're fucking told," he said, nearly yelling. "But you do."

"I haven't!" I yelled, pulling away. "I have stood up for myself. I learned and I am trying to do better now. What about you? Are you trying to not keep everyone locked up and call it safe?"

He turned back to me, rage coating his face as he stomped towards me. "I will *not* lose anyone else I care about, and I sure as fuck won't lose them to Cameron again. I don't know what I would do if I lost you now, Regan."

Every part of me was at odds with loving Rook, and not wanting to believe my dad would really do these things.

My shoulders fell, the angry edge to my voice gone now as I gave up. I was too tired to keep fighting him, to keep running around in this circle of being mad and then hurt, and then back to loving him. I knew he was angry, and he should be for what happened to him. He just didn't need to be angry at my dad.

"Why are you so sweet as you are locking me up like a prisoner?" I huffed, sitting back in my chair with a hard breath.

He grinned, falling back on the bed. "I have to be a little charming to get away with the things I do."

I rolled my eyes, pulling my tablet up and sitting back. He watched me for a while until I looked over, smiling when I noticed he had passed out.

I stayed silent, working for another two hours on my drawing until he rolled over, his eyes flickering open.

"What time is it?" he asked.

I glanced at my phone. "A little past eleven."

"Why are you still up?"

"I'm drawing," I said, not hiding the snip in my tone.

"Drawing what?" he asked. He always asked.

He always complimented each one and acted like I was a real artist. I glanced up at the painting that hung above his head now, my heart aching a little.

"You," I finally said. "All your tattoos are interesting. I'm trying to replicate them on a portrait of you, but it's harder than I thought."

"Show me." His voice was still deep and gravelly from sleep, making me want to crawl right into bed next to him.

I padded over, flipping the tablet around to face him. He was quiet as he looked it over. It always made me feel like he was really looking at it and was interested.

He finally smiled. "You really are talented, Rebel. You're going to have to start drawing us up tattoos we want. They would be amazing."

"I can't do that."

"You can, and should. But for now, come on. Get into bed. I want more sleep."

"I'll stay in my chair for the night," I said. I really didn't trust myself sleeping next to him and not making a move for more.

As if he read my mind, he grinned. "Worried you won't be able to keep your hands off of me?"

"No. I'm just wondering why you can't go sleep in another room."

"Safety and all that," he mumbled. "Come on. I won't bite you this time, promise."

He lifted the blankets, and I slid in next to him. His arm snaked around me, but I pushed away, leaving plenty of space between us.

It barely took a full minute before Rook moved across the bed and wrapped an arm around me.

"What are you doing?"

"I said I won't bite, not that I wouldn't touch you at all."

"Rook," I warned.

"Rebel," he said, pushing harder against me. "You can crawl yourself to the other side of the bed if you need space."

"Or you can be the one to crawl over to your side," I said, not moving.

"How cute that we already have sides of the bed, but I'm not going anywhere." I wiggled back more, and his arm tightened around me. "You know, everything I have to do isn't going to be great or easy. I don't want you upset with me all the time, but I have things that have to be done."

"I understand that, but killing my family can't be on your to-do list."

"It's been on my to-do list long before you showed up."

"If you are going to try and say you love me, you can try to not kill him, no matter what your plans were before. Haven't they all changed now?"

"Yes, they have."

"Then that can change, too."

He groaned. "That plan is ten years in the making, Regan. I can't sit around and not do anything. He took everything from me, everything from us, and he deserves to have some sort of consequence for what he's done."

"Tell me you won't kill him and I will stay right here," I said. "I will spend the night here and plenty more after that."

He laughed, his grip tightening again. "You spend every night next to me forever and I *might* not kill him."

"I spend every night next to you and you guarantee me you won't kill him," I said, negotiating more.

"How about I agree not to kill him without permission?"

"Fine," I said fast. At least that would buy me more time to find proof.

He lifted up and leaned over me, his lips finding mine in the dark. "Welcome to forever, then, Rebel, because I don't think there is anything I wouldn't do to keep you as mine."

FORTY

ROOK

I woke up with Regan wrapped around me. Her leg was thrown over mine, her hand laying over my stomach, and her head tucked between my arm and chest. I had never woken up and loved my life as much as I did now. I was so close to having everything I wanted, but I needed to push a little further.

But I couldn't wait around any longer. I needed her dad taken care of so we could move on with our life. The blankets slid off of me and Regan did, too, as I slipped out of bed and changed before heading down to the kitchen.

It didn't take long for Regan to come down, her hair a mess and my hoodie wrapped around her. My chest tightened as she came over and slipped her arms around me.

"Are you making me breakfast again?" she asked, still sleepy.

"Yeah, Rebel. I'll have it ready for you soon."

She held on, moving with me around the kitchen as I cooked. How could I risk this being taken away now? Would I really have to choose between her and getting my revenge on her dad?

She sat, quietly watching me as I finished and slid a plate to her.

"This is pretty nice. I think I could get used to it," she said, smiling as she took her first bite. "Keep this up, and I might not mind you staying here."

I shook my head, laughing as I walked around to sit next to her. "I'll keep that in mind. I have a serious question for you," I said. I had stayed awake half the morning thinking this over and needed to know what she thought.

"Okay, I'm listening."

"If it wasn't your dad who did all this—the burning of my house, my garage, my parents—why would he put a hit out on me? Why specifically me? Anyone in our world knows we're a group and would put a call out for all of us."

She seemed to think it over, but she wouldn't meet my eye. "Maybe he saw us together at Sweet Haven and didn't like you. It's not like you make a great first impression." She nearly smirked, but thought better of it.

"If that was the situation, then he would know exactly who the girl on the back of my bike was before he set out to have her killed."

Regan didn't say anything, choosing to take another big bite of her pancakes. Finally, she swallowed and met my eye. "I don't know. Maybe he just wanted to get one of you, and not pay for you all."

"Come on, Regan."

"Come on, what? I need more proof, Rook. He's my dad. I mean, I'm pretty pissed about the business and Elliot stuff, but I can't completely think he's this big, scary bad guy without proving it. He is still my dad."

"Fine, hurry and eat, so we can go look through the office."

Her eyes narrowed at me as she finished up before heading out and right into the office.

Evie and Mason had been in here most of the night setting up Evie's little war corner. Her new computers cost a small fortune, but supposedly, they would do better than ever for getting her into any corner of the internet we wanted.

Besides that, the rest of the room had been largely untouched. I didn't want Regan to find any reason to not trust me.

"If we are going through the office, I have a question. Harper and I found something when we went through it. I wanted to ask you about before, but then all this happened, and I didn't have a chance."

"Okay, what is it?"

"In here," she said, walking around the large wooden desk. "There's a locked drawer here that Harper got in. The documents inside... I don't know what they mean. If you want me to believe you, start with opening that up and tell me what the papers mean."

I looked around for anything sharp enough to shove in and pick the lock, happy that it clicked open easy enough.

"At least you being a criminal is beneficial sometimes."

"Just sometimes? I think you've benefited from it plenty of times," I said, clicking open the small drawer and reaching in.

"It's almost got me killed plenty of times, too."

"Fair point."

I threw the stack of papers on the desk as the entire group filed into the office. Luckily, the place was big enough that everyone could spread out. I flipped through the pages, taking in every word before I said anything.

Lists of shipments, amounts of money, large and small, and different names were all there. Page after page of lists until I got to one with four shipment names with very large sums of money listed next to it.

The pack waited. Even Regan was quiet as I read until I handed it out for them all to see.

This would not be anything I kept secret. They passed it around as Aiden turned to me.

"Do you know what it is?" Regan asked.

"Can you tell her?" I asked Aiden. "Because I don't think she's going to believe me."

"They are shipments," Aiden started. "Ones that have gone missing over the past month and we have been trying to help find." He pointed out one of the larger ones. "We got this one after one of their runners snitched to us. The others haven't been found. The money amounts next to them are the values."

"What are they shipping that is worth millions?" she asked.

"Drugs. You know Asher, and you heard the conversation we had with Cross. These shipments have been going missing fast and causing an uproar. None of the top guys are happy and have started blaming each other."

"Why would my dad have the list?" she asked. I understood why she didn't want to understand, but we didn't have any more time for her to stay naïve to it.

"The same reason your dad is also going and offering his services to the same guys he's stealing from. He's weaseling his way in as a trustworthy person to these guys while also stealing from them. I would bet everything I have left that he's also selling these shipments he's stealing to start taking over new territory. Once he has a bit of business, and the trust of all four of them, he will start pinning them against each other and hope they take care of themselves. Then he has a top spot at a table."

She was already shaking her head. "My dad wants to be what you are calling a drug lord? That's ridiculous."

Hero held up the papers, shaking them. "What the fuck do you think he would have these for, then?"

Hero was a little abrasive, but I was glad he was clear with his words. The proof was piling up, and it would be hard for her to keep pushing off the inevitable truth. I reached out, grabbing her hand and holding it tight. Part of me felt scared that she would run off, and the other part of me felt bad that the world she had known was falling apart.

"It might seem ridiculous, but the dad that you know is not the one everyone else knows. He's kept you locked up and pushed away for a reason, Regan," Evie said. "He didn't think you would go along with the things he wanted to do and found someone he thought would. Rook said that he saw you two at Sweet Haven. He knew who the girl riding with Rook was and asked to have you killed."

"Because you are smart, and he knew you were the one person close enough that could ruin his plan, and would," I said.

Regan hadn't cried or said a word, but she hadn't let me go either.

I pulled her closer until she fell into my lap, and I adjusted her there as I flipped through more paperwork.

Evie stepped forward. "I think you should see this, Regan," she said. "We all know about it and I think you deserve to know, too, even if you don't want to. I managed to connect this tablet to your dad's phone, including his texts."

Regan started scrolling through the ones I had already seen. The ones admitting to burning down our building, and burning down our home ten years ago, even the ones detailing him putting the hit out on us.

"He still didn't know it was me," she mumbled. "But he did it all?"

"It looks like it," Evie said, and I was grateful that someone else chimed in. I felt helpless. I didn't want Regan hurt, but she couldn't hide from the truth, either.

The front door to the house opened and slammed shut, and we all froze. I nodded to the pack as footsteps headed our way. They all stepped back, with Hero and Mason by the door and Aiden moving closer to Evie. Regan's free hand fisted into my shirt, and I held my breath, wondering if Cameron would walk in and this would all be over soon.

But it was Elliot's face that filled the door, and I felt Regan stiffen on top of me.

He glanced around, his eyebrows furrowing as he looked at everyone. "What the fuck are you all doing in here? What's going on, Regan?"

She didn't say a word, and he was already pulling out his cell phone. Hero and Mason grabbed him before he could, forcing him further into the room until he was sitting in the chair across from us.

"Hey, Elliot," I said, smiling with Regan on top of me. "Come to check in with dear stepdad and get some cash? I wasn't taking you for someone wanting a sugar daddy, but I really shouldn't have ruled it out."

"Oh, fuck you. He's a business partner, not a sugar daddy."

"No? You sit around and do nothing but chase after him and he pays you. Isn't that a sugar daddy?"

"I believe it is, but usually there's sex involved," Hero said, looking Elliot over. I swear Hero looked at people like they could be his next science experiment, like he was inspecting them to figure out how to best cut them up.

"What are you doing to me?"

"Depends," I said.

"On what?"

"On what Regan wants." She glanced down at me, eyes wide. "You make the call, Rebel. What do you want done to him?"

"Rebel?" Elliot asked. "That's what he calls you? And you like this, Regan? You know what he does and you go along with it?"

"Go along with it?" I asked with a laugh. "I'm having her run it now."

"And yes," she said, sitting up straighter, "I like it."

I reached up, pulling out the necklace she still wore. I grabbed

CHAPTER FORTY

the heart, and flipped it between my fingers before using it to pull her lips down to mine. "I think saying you like it might be an understatement, Rebel." I felt her thighs clench and tried to tame my own thoughts. "I told you, you left a prized possession on the side of the street with me. I took her, and I really have to thank you, Elliot. Without you, I would have never met the woman of my dreams."

"You think she's the woman of your dreams? She's boring and useless."

"You hear that, Rebel? He thinks you're useless. Do you want to tell us what you would like his fate to be? Should we kill him now? Take a few fingers off first? Maybe just cut out his tongue for saying those things to you. Why don't you tell us what you want done to him?"

"And you all are going to listen to her?" he asked, eyes wide.

Evie walked over, falling back into the chair next to him. "Don't like a woman you tried to kill having control of your fate?" she asked, before flipping out a knife and slamming it down into the chair, right between his legs. It didn't hit anything, but he still screamed as though it had sunk into skin.

"Shut up," Regan yelled, moving to the edge of my lap. "Why did you walk me down that road? Were you trying to kill me?"

Elliot's eyes were wild as they jumped from the knife between his legs to Regan. "No!" he yelled, the panic in his voice bubbling up. "Well, no, I wasn't going to kill you, but we thought if you went missing, it would save me and your dad some work!"

"How sweet. Too much of a coward to kill her yourself, and too stupid to know if the person you were leaving her with would kill her or take her. I've never been happier to ruin someone's plans. What do you want with him, Rebel?"

"Can we start by shutting him up now?" she asked. "I don't know if I can hear any more of that."

"The tongue, then?" Hero asked, already pulling the knife out of the chair and leaning over him. Aiden grabbed his head, tipping it back so Hero could force his mouth open.

"Wait!" Regan said, attempting to get up, but I pulled her back. "Leave his tongue for now! Just gag him."

"Why?" Aiden asked. "We don't mind doing it if that's what you want."

"Just not yet. In case we need any more information from him."

"So smart, Rebel. Alright, keep the tongue."

Hero rolled his eyes. "I swear if you don't let me—"

"Oh, knock it off, Hero," she said, almost lovingly. "There will be plenty of time for you to do your freak stuff."

He grinned back, stepping away to lean against a window as Aiden gagged Elliot.

My chest swelled with pride. She wasn't shying away or scared. She was ready to take on the world, and I only hoped nothing was going to stop her from doing it at my side now.

A fucking queen. I smiled up at her as she scowled at Elliot. My lap could be her throne any day of my life.

The front door slammed again, and my heart rate jumped. I think it was finally time to get my revenge.

FORTY-ONE
ROOK

I never knew what my revenge would be for Cameron Fletcher, but I had thought about it endlessly for years. I had thought about burning his house down, ruining his business, wrecking everything he loved.

But none of it compared to him walking into his own office to find his daughter sitting on my lap behind his desk.

His face fell, the world coming to a halt as Aiden and Kane grabbed him.

"What is going on?" he asked, his eyes flicking to everyone else now. "What are you doing here? What are you doing on him, Regan?"

Evie's eyes went wide, the rage and pain there so clear that I wanted to kill him right then and there for it. I knew Regan's face had to mimic hers. I tightened my grip on her, trying to remind myself I had promised Regan I wouldn't just kill him, but fuck I wanted to.

"She is right where she's supposed to be. We are here because we live here now. And what is going on is that your house of cards has fallen. All your secrets are out, Fletcher."

"I don't know who you are or what you think you are doing, but you need to get the fuck out. You know who I am, and I think you can comprehend that this isn't going to work out however you are hoping it will."

I urged Regan up, keeping her standing next to me as I stood up and pulled off my shirt, showing off the scars that marred the side of my stomach.

"And you know exactly who the fuck I am."

There was no reaction from him. He didn't seem shocked, and I knew I had been right.

I could feel Regan at my side, and I sat back down, giving her room if she wanted to sit with me again.

"You do know who he is, don't you?" she asked.

"I do, and I can't for the life of me figure out why the fuck you let him into our house," he snapped, and she flinched.

"I wouldn't yell at her if I were you," I said.

"I'm her father. I can yell at her if she lets criminals into the house."

Regan moved in front of me again, sitting back on my lap. "If we are ruling out criminals," she said, "then I think we all need to leave."

I grinned, looking at her before turning to him. "The first guy to take you up on the hit offer failed. My pretty little rebel girl shot him before he could get me." I reached up, running a hand through her hair until my fingers were dragging down her neck and over her chest. "She really didn't like you threatening my life, and I don't like you threatening hers."

"You didn't answer me," Regan said, watching him. "Do you know who he is?"

Her dad rolled his eyes, leaning back in the chair, apparently no longer thinking his highbrow act was necessary here.

"Of course I know who he is."

"Then I can assume you would remember my father, Michael Emberson. Or maybe my mother, Andrea?"

The flash of fear was brief, the cruel smile taking over so fast I almost missed it.

"Oh, I remember. They are dead, right? Burned to a crisp in a house fire, if I remember correctly."

"That's them," I said, letting the harsh visual hit me, fueling the hatred and satisfaction of what came next. "You can see I was almost burned alive along with my sister, but we got out."

"I do remember the two little orphan children, but I thought they were shipped off to a grandmother. I'm surprised you came back around here."

"Interesting fact, all our grandparents were dead. We were sent to live with strangers, who quickly realized their mistake and shipped us back."

"How sad to come home to nothing but rubble and debts. Daddy didn't leave you a dime, did he?"

I didn't look at Regan, but her hand wrapped in mine. I wanted to see how she felt about loving a poor, orphaned monster of a man, but I couldn't bring myself to look up.

"How could you say those things?" she asked. "You know he lost his parents and you talk about it like that?"

"Because he's the one who burned them up," I said. "And you're proud of your work, aren't you, Cameron?"

He sneered. "I'm proud that I was about to make something of that company. Your father was shit at running the business, and I don't actually know if your mother had a brain past artwork."

Evie got up, her eyes flashing with the burning hatred I knew she had for him. She grabbed the knife that she had stuck between Elliot's legs and reared it back. The blade slammed down, sliding against Cameron's thigh before it stuck in the wood.

"What the fuck?" he yelled. "You cut me!"

"Oops. You know, like mother like daughter. I just don't have a brain past pretty things like shiny knives. I'd say it won't happen again, but I promise, it's going to." Her lip curled, and Aiden stepped closer to her, his arm wrapping around her as he led her back towards the window.

"So that's it?" Regan asked. "It's all true? Killing their parents, burning the house, their garage? What about stealing the drugs?"

I threw the papers we had found over the desk, his eyebrow cocking up when he saw them. He groaned, the annoyed tone making my fingers dig into the arm of the chair. He had the nerve to be mad at her when she sat here learning her entire world was a lie?

"How the fuck did you get this?"

Hero jumped down from the window seat he had been on. "How the fuck do you run a security business and think a dummy drawer compartment is a good place to hide things? Regan and Harper found them in minutes," he said.

"You went through my stuff?" he asked, glaring at Regan.

Aiden's mouth dropped open, the shock of it getting to us all.

"I think we are past scolding her for looking through your things," I said.

"And they are her things now anyway," Evie said, throwing one more paper in front of Cameron.

"What's this?" He read the paper, his face tightening into rage as he finished. "I didn't give Regan the house."

"No?" Evie said, leaning over. "This says you put it in her name a year ago. That was so sweet of you. Was that some sort of graduation gift?"

"I didn't do that. How did this happen?"

"Evie's good with computers, so yes, you did," I said. "You also are returning the drugs you stole. Money, if the drugs have been sold. Asher is helping with that."

"You can't do that. You talked to Asher about this?" His eyes flicked to Regan. "Honey, you have to stop him. We can talk about the business. I swear, we can talk it over. We can get you what you want."

I lifted Regan up, making her stand next to me one more time. I knew she was going to hate this, but I needed one thing. One big thing to show her that he would never do the right thing because the man would say and do anything to get out of a bad situation.

"Instead of begging her, there's another way to get yourself out of this," I said, pulling out the gun I had brought. I slid it across the desk towards him.

"We can come to an agreement. You don't have to do all this, Rook. What do you want? More jobs? More money?" He grinned as though he could give me any of it. "More power?"

"Do I need any of that from you? The irony, Cameron, is that you didn't want to let her into your life because you were worried she would ruin all your hard work and snitch. You were worried she would rat you out and ruin it, but then I let her into mine. I showed her all the despicable things we do, and do you know what she did?"

His face hardened, looking over at her with disgust. "What?"

"She liked it. She wanted more, and then she asked if she could run the entire fucking thing."

"Then, what about another deal?"

"I don't want anything from you. At least, not the things you are offering. I think there is only one way to make it fair. A life for a life. You killed my family. Kill one of your own and I will let you walk out of here without so much as another scratch or loss. An eye for an eye type of deal."

He glanced at Regan, and then quickly back at me. "Why?"

"I've thought about it for ten long years, Cameron, and I think you need to feel what I felt when you stole my family. For ten years, I've been living with the agony of my parents dying in that fire, and I think you need to have an image like that in your mind. Maybe then we will be even. Plus, you already involved her in the hit you took out on my life. I believe the words were, 'Take him out, and if she dies, she dies.' You must have already come to terms with her death. She knows you saw us at Sweet Haven that day, and she knows you put a hit out on both me and her. You knew that if she was dead, no one could touch you or your money. There would be no one left in your way to bother you or reveal your secrets. Is there any problem in making that a reality now? Then I'll leave you alone with your fortune. Maybe I'll even offer my services to you and your business."

"And all you want me to do is kill her?"

"One bullet in her skull and you'll have everything. Your business and fortune all to yourself."

"Why?"

"Aren't we all just climbing to the top, Cameron? Wouldn't a deal with you make me more money, give me more power? You just said it, so you must understand." Every word from my mouth fell out so easily, each one goading him to take the bait.

"And if I don't agree?"

"I expose every single one of your goddamn dirty secrets until your business is ash." I smirked. "Kind of like what you did to my home and parents. I think both options are fair. More than fair, even."

"I could go to jail if you tell everyone those things."

I shrugged. "You didn't mind sending two children to a stranger after burning their parents. Why would I give a fuck about sending you to jail?"

Regan reached for me, her fingers digging into my shoulder. "What are you doing?"

"I'm sorry," I whispered to her. "But I love you, and I hope you can understand exactly how much. I should have never loved you, Rebel, but I did, and I can't let him take you from me, too."

Her dad eyed the gun again, and then her, apparently trying to make his choice. At least he was giving it a second thought, but his decision would make mine.

"Please, Rook," she hissed. "You just said you loved me. Please don't make him do this."

"I'm not making him do anything. He has a choice. A clear one." My voice stayed low, not wanting him to hear.

"His choice is to kill me or lose everything?" she asked, her voice hiccuping as she fought back tears.

"And? There is no fucking choice with you, Regan. I would burn my entire life to the ground all over again if it meant standing with you in the ashes. Shouldn't he have the same opinion?"

"Maybe, but is this really the way I need to find out?"

Her dad picked up the gun, his face hardening at us. "Fine, but I swear, if you don't undo any damage you have done to me or my business, I will come for you with everything I have," Cameron said.

Regan backed up, her eyes going wide as he lifted the gun to face her.

"You aren't serious?" she asked. "You would kill me to save the business?"

"I'm sorry, but I've worked my entire life, and I knew, I fucking knew, you were going to be my downfall. If not today, it would only be a matter of when, not if."

"I wouldn't take anything from you! I came home to help you. I came home because you were sick and needed someone and I was there. Why throw it all away now when we don't even have much time together left?"

"Oh, for fuck's sake, Regan. I made up the illness so you

would stick around without getting your nose in my business. So you would help me by shaking hands when I needed and staying home when I didn't. I couldn't worry about you running around learning anything about my business, and I couldn't risk you being too far and finding anything out. Yet what did you do? You brought the problem right into our home. How could I ever trust you again, anyway? I'm a good shot. It won't hurt."

"You made it up," she yelled, stepping back against the wall. "You made up being deathly ill. Have you lost your mind?"

I breathed in relief as I read the rage on her face. She finally understood. Her chest heaved as her eyes went wide, jumping from him to me.

"Rook, stop this right now. I get it."

"He can't take it back now," Cameron said. "I need my business and he promised that to me." He flicked the safety off and pulled the trigger. I could only smile as the gun clicked repeatedly, but nothing happened.

The realization dawned on him, and I got up, turning to stand in front of Regan as he pulled the gun back, throwing it hard in her direction, but it only hit my back.

"You get it now?"

The guys had grabbed Cameron again, forcing him to sit as he yelled.

I leaned down, pressing a hard kiss to her lips. "I will do anything you want, Rebel. If you want him dead, he's dead. If you want him kept alive, he will be. You're in control now, and whatever you want, I'll make it happen."

Her eyes went wide as her hands laid on my chest. "Really?"

"Really," I said, relief coursing through me as she moved onto her toes, kissing me again.

"What about your revenge you've wanted? I saw the texts. I don't blame you, Rook."

"I realized you next to me every day and night it more important."

She kissed me again, and I pulled her close, hoping we were getting to the end of this mess.

"Wait!" her dad yelled out from behind me. "I have a better deal!"

FORTY-TWO
REGAN

There were so many times in my life where I looked at my dad and forgave him. When he said or did something that hurt and I brushed it off.

I hadn't realized until this second how resilient I had become.

The day at Sweet Haven, he had looked me in the eye, told me I was never going to run his business, that I was useless, and what had I done? Brushed it off and went to go to a party for his benefit. Nothing had been there for me that night, but I had gone so no one would think he didn't care because he couldn't attend.

I had been helping him get on good terms with people so his campaign would run smoothly next year, and he had said nothing but cruel things in return.

Maybe I had gone numb to my feelings or my wants, maybe I was weak and cowardly, or maybe I was just strong enough to handle it. Each time, I pushed it aside and moved on.

But was I strong enough to watch my father put a gun to my head and pull the trigger?

My chest heaved as I pushed Rook aside, facing my dad.

"We don't want any deal you have," I said. "You would kill me? For what? Your business? So Elliot can run it one day and I don't get in the way? Why?"

He fought off Aiden and Hero, who were holding him down. While they let him go, they didn't let him stand up. "Elliot will never have my business. All of you young kids are so stupid, I couldn't trust any of you to run it. Elliot will die the minute the lords find out what we did, and I need somewhere to place blame."

I glanced at Elliot, who was fighting against the ties and gag now, hatred and fear coating his face as he glanced from my dad to me.

"But why? Why not pass your business down to your own child?"

My dad sneered, looking up at me with pure malice in his eyes. "Because, Regan, you were never meant to be more than a puppet. You were supposed to make me look good, nothing more. But you, you had to bring all of this on us. You are trying to ruin everything."

I could barely move, shaking my head as I turned to Rook.

"There is nothing to ruin now," Rook said with a smile. "The house belongs to Regan. Asher knows about your theft and is already working to undo the damage and calm the lords back down. He's also helping to assure you have no business left."

My dad's eyes went wide. "What have you done?"

"Took every single one of your clients and business partners and told them the truth. You are stealing from every single one of them. They no longer want to do business together. Everything else left was donated. Money, assets, buildings. All of it was given away this morning to people whose lives you helped ruin." Rook leaned back in the chair, grinning now. "And best of all, your daughter, your own flesh and blood, is now loyal to me. The only person in this world who might have been able to save you is now sitting on this side of the table with me, ready to determine your fate, and I will carry out any fate she decides for you. I honestly thought killing you would be the only thing in this world to make me feel better about what you did, but this, Cameron—your own daughter telling me how she wants your life ruined and me getting to carry out her wishes—is the best revenge I could ever ask for."

His eyes jumped to me again. "Regan, I'm sorry. Please, I shouldn't have done the things I did, but you know how important a legacy is to me. You know how important this business is to me."

"I think we are way past a simple 'I'm sorry,'" I said. "I don't want you to have any of it back. I'm glad he took it all away from you."

Rook stood up, moving next to my side, but I turned to face him.

"I'm so sorry," I said, not taking my eyes off my dad, "I didn't believe you."

"You shouldn't have. I'm glad you waited for proof, Rebel. I wouldn't want anything less, and I have no issue proving the truth to you."

Before I could respond, a loud crack echoed through the room. Elliot had managed to free one hand and had grabbed the knife Evie had shoved into my dad's chair. His face twisted with rage as he lunged at my dad.

"You think I'm just going to sit here and let you throw me under the bus?" Elliot snarled. "You think I'm going to die after you make a mess of things? You told me I would get it all, but I was just one more puppet for you."

My dad's eyes went wide with shock, but before he could react, Elliot plunged the knife hard into his chest. He yelled before he collapsed to the floor, blood pooling under him.

A stunned silence filled the room. My heart pounded in my

chest as I stared at him on the floor now. I felt like I should do something. Like I should run over and help him, but I couldn't move.

Rook turned to wrap his arms around me, hiding the view of it from me. I didn't want to see it, but part of me felt like I needed to see proof of what had just happened.

Evie yelled out, and Aiden's voice boomed for Hero to grab Elliot. I fought at Rook, forcing him to let me glance around his arm to see what was happening.

Elliot stood in the middle of the room, a bloodied knife held up, swinging wildly if anyone came closer.

"No," he yelled. "No way are you guys stopping me now. He's dead. The company is already set to go to me. I need out of here."

"Rook," I whispered, pushing away more. "Stop him. He's going to kill someone else. Just stop him."

"Stop him, as in..." His voice trailed off, eyes wide as he watched me.

"Yes, as in, *stop him*."

"You know what that means," he said, his hand moving up and down my arm.

"Yes, I know what it means. If we let him go, he's going to blame this on us and go after everything. Do it," I said.

Rook nodded and stepped towards Elliot, who was still waving the knife. "Alright, put it down."

"Stay back!" Elliot yelled, his eyes wild with desperation. I knew he would kill anyone in here and not feel an ounce of guilt over it.

Rook kept moving his hands up in a non-threatening gesture. "Put the knife down and we can negotiate something."

Elliot's gaze darted around the room, sweat dripping down his face. "Negotiate? There's nothing to negotiate! He betrayed me, and now you're all trying to kill me. There's nothing to negotiate because I'm leaving here and telling everyone what happened."

In a sudden move, Elliot lunged at Rook, aiming the knife at his chest. Rook twisted to avoid the blade, but Elliot's fist came up, connecting with the scars on Rook's side. I could see the moment the pain shot through Rook's body. He stepped back, momentarily debilitated.

Elliot grinned, thinking he had the upper hand for a second, but Rook recovered fast. With one swing of his arm, Rook landed his punch.

I knew what came next. There was a knife in Rook's fist, and I knew he was going to shove it into Elliot's neck.

Rook looked over his shoulder at me, and I could see the small wince as he twisted his body.

"Rebel?"

"Go ahead."

I could only stare as Rook slid a blade across Elliot's neck.

The blade curved in, sinking further into his neck before Rook pulled. Blood spurted, coating Rook as the other guys watched. Some part of his neck fell to the ground, and I gagged, clamping my mouth shut as bile rose in my throat.

"That solves that issue, then. He can't come after anything your dad might have promised him or make us out to be the killers," Aiden said.

I looked over at Elliot, thankful that Rook had rolled him over, so nothing seemed wrong with him at this angle.

"Karma really caught up to him for leaving you alone with me," Rook said with a tight smile.

Hero cocked an eyebrow. "Or maybe the trying to kill her, ruining her chances of getting the business, or, I don't know, maybe killing him?"

"Okay, I get it, but that night is how we ended up here," Rook said.

"I'm glad, though. For all of it," I said. "Not only was he a very shitty boyfriend, but he was turning out to be a worse step-brother."

Hero and Mason grinned as Aiden and Evie walked out of the room.

"Come on," Rook said, his voice gentle now as he wrapped an arm around me. "Let me get you out of this room first and we can figure out what to do next."

I nodded, tipping my head back to look at the ceiling as I walked out past my dad's body. Some part of me felt numb to it, but I wondered if that was the shock more so than me being cold or uncaring towards him.

As we stepped into the hallway, the weight of everything that had happened crashed over me. The pain of losing my father, the betrayal, the violence—I could barely breathe. But then Rook's arm tightened around me, and I knew I would at least never have to be alone in it.

Rook walked me out to the hallway and into the main house before he turned to wrap his arms around me.

I leaned in, but I couldn't bring myself to say anything for a few minutes.

"You asked me every step of the way," I said. "You let me have a say."

"I told you I would try not to do anything without asking you first. I mean, I had to do a few things without running it by you, but I thought you would be okay with them."

"You gave up a lot of that hope for revenge on him."

"It's alright. I got what I wanted."

"Him dead?" I asked, the words still not hitting me yet.

"No, Rebel. You. I decided I wanted you and I could live without any of the other stuff."

Tears welled in my eyes again, and I moved up him until he lifted me. "I love you, Rook," I whispered, kissing him hard. "I love you so much and I'm sorry I ever doubted it."

He kissed me back once, smiling as he sat back on the couch with me on top of him. "I told you, I like that you stood up for yourself, even against me. It makes me know you aren't just loving me because I'm forcing it somehow. It lets me know that you are going to love me even when I am difficult to love."

"And you love me even when I am difficult to love," I said. "I didn't know I would find someone who would somehow make me face all of my fears and desires at once. You've dragged me into your dark, dangerous world and shown me how strong I am. I've never felt more like myself. I love you."

His forehead dropped against my chest. "I have spent days wondering how this would all turn out. It's been a long time since I had such little control over my life. This outcome felt like a faraway dream, something I was stupid for hoping for. Thank you, Rebel."

"For what?"

"Trusting and loving me every step of the way, even when it pissed you off."

We stayed like that for a few minutes, enjoying being wrapped up together.

"What do we do now?" I asked, looking back down the hall towards the office.

"We can either work to get it all pinned on Elliot, but it's going to be a huge investigation that could ruin our business and Asher's since he helped me with a lot of the logistics of it," Rook said, his face scrunching as he grimaced. "Plus, if Candy has any care for either of them, she would fight it."

"Or? Because that doesn't sound great."

"We take out the bodies, burn this half of the house down,

make it look like an accident, and shut down the investigation as fast as we can."

"Couldn't we do that if we blamed Elliot?"

"Not quite. A murder investigation is going to go a lot further than a house fire, especially if the next of kin isn't going to push for it to be investigated, and we offer them a bribe to stop looking. The house fire option would raise less suspicion for Candy too, and she would know everything would be left to her since they weren't married."

"Okay. We do that, then."

"Are you sure? I don't want you to make the decision just for us. You need to be okay with it."

"What's done is done anyway. Just get it over with."

He gave a soft smile and leaned down to kiss me. "Whatever I can do to help. Go over to the living room. I'll send Evie in. She already texted Harper."

As I walked to the living room, the weight of the situation began to press down on me. My father was dead, Elliot, too, and our lives had just changed in ways I couldn't fully grasp yet. I sat on the couch, my mind racing with everything that had happened.

Evie filed in, then Harper, who had a million questions, and finally Rook came back.

"Hey," Rook said, filling the doorway. "It's all done. Well, almost. How are you doing in here?"

"Good enough, I guess. Can I come back out there now?"

He nodded, reaching out a hand to me. "Come on." He led me down the hall until we reached the hallway to my dad's side of the house. The add-on had been so unnecessary and I realized now it was to keep me out of his business. A whole separate house so he could hide away and make sure I would never be involved.

Not only that, it was so he could hide away and pretend to be sick in bed when he had really been working away in here to try and run drugs. The anger surged again, taking over until I was nearly shaking.

Rook squeezed my hand once, bringing my attention back on him.

"Want to burn his entire place down, Rebel?"

His eyes met mine when I turned, and I felt a rush of relief. "With you? Yes."

FORTY-THREE
ROOK

<u>Month Later</u>

1   Regan climbed on my bike again, her toes straining to touch the ground. The R6 was the slightest amount slower than my normal bike, but it would have to work for now.

"I think you are forgetting that this thing could crush me if I fall over."

"It won't crush you if you don't fall over, and I'm more concerned with you accidentally hitting the gas and launching yourself across the driveway."

"Can't I just ride with you? Evie said she doesn't drive one."

"No, but she knows how. There's a big difference. I need to know that if everything goes wrong, you know how to not only defend yourself, but how to get away." I held the bike as she adjusted herself on it for the thousandth time. I knew she had to be nervous, but it wouldn't be hard to learn the basics.

"Why would I be leaving if you are still there?"

"How sweet, Rebel. I meant if I was dead."

Her mouth dropped open, and she smacked at my hand. "Why would I leave, then?"

"So you don't die, too. Can you please try to ride it down the driveway? It's a long, straight line, Rebel. You will be fine."

"Maybe we should go back to the bicycle. That felt safer."

"That was so I could make sure you could keep upright on two wheels. You did great. Now go."

She hit the bike into gear like I had shown her a hundred times already. I didn't need it to be perfect, but I needed to know she could get out if I needed her to. As much as I loved her, my life wouldn't be slowing down, and I knew there would be plenty of chances for this to be a possibility.

She pulled in the clutch, hit the bike into gear, and eased forward.

"Perfect, Rebel. You got it." Finally, the clutch let out and she rolled down the road in first gear. I walked alongside her.

"I like this pace," she breathed. "This feels nice."

"This won't get you away any faster than running would."

"Maybe not, but I can't run very far. Slow and steady would be better with this."

"Or fast as hell, so you don't get shot." She huffed, glancing over at me and making the bike wobble. A scream escaped her. "Eyes on the where you are going. And I'm thinking of worst-case scenarios. Then I know no matter what, you will be safe. Now, clutch in again and shift it into second gear. We need you to get to third at the very least."

"Why?"

"Because if you try to outrun anyone or anything in first gear, you are going to lift that front and crash. Get yourself into second at least."

"I would prefer a scooter or something."

"First, I will not be letting you ride a scooter with us. It wouldn't even keep up," I said, scrunching my nose. "And second, how the hell would that work? I tow it behind my bike in the rare case you need to get away without me?"

"I think that's a great idea."

I smacked her ass as she adjusted. "Go. I want you to hit thirty miles an hour at least, get to the end of the driveway and turn around, and then thirty again. You're not getting off the bike until I know you can do it."

"You are mean," she said, picking up her pace.

"Yes I am. And I love you too much to leave you helpless."

It took another hour before she finally managed to do it.

Regan jumped off, hitting the kickstand before jumping onto me. "I did it! I'm done! Never make me do that again," she yelled, but she was smiling now.

"No deal. I need to see that once a year, so you don't forget."

"I think I've hit my breaking point with your criminal lifestyle."

I laughed, lifting her up the rest of the way and heading back towards the house. While Cameron's quarters of the house had burned, they had saved everything else. Everything that Regan claimed as her half didn't have a scratch or burn on it, and now it was all of ours.

She leaned down, her lips finding mine, and I groaned. Watching her straddled on my bike for over an hour had me currently without a thought in my mind besides wrapping her legs around me now.

"*That's* the breaking point?" I asked. "Driving a motorcycle is what's making you reconsider?"

"Yeah, so don't make me do it again. Or maybe get a bike that makes me feel like I won't die if it falls on me."

I opened up the front door just as everyone walked out.

"What are you doing?" Aiden asked. "Asher texted. He has the space for the shop ready."

I groaned, setting Regan down. "Can't it wait?"

"The place we've been waiting to find for a month now? No, it can't wait."

A surge of excitement washed over me at the idea of finally having a shop open again. "Alright, let's go check it out."

Regan's eyes lit up. "A new shop?"

"Asher's had something he thought would work for us, but had to empty it out."

She was already pulling me back towards the bike. "Then let's go. I can't handle another second of you all trying to work out of the garage here."

I smiled, slipping on my helmet as the roar of our bikes filled the air. Regan clung to me, and my excitement built with each mile. This place was closer to our new home at the Fletcher mansion, although we really needed to find something new to call it. Asher thought we would do better with a place in a nicer part of town, which I didn't argue. We did most of our illegal business outside of the garage, so having it in a nicer warehouse area was good. It also made people less concerned about how legitimate our business was.

As we pulled into the lot, the sight of the new garage made my heart race. It was perfect. The old warehouse style building was large enough to hold all our bikes, with plenty of space left over for anything else we needed to do. The main river that ran through the city sat right behind the building, making disposal of anyone we needed a little easier.

Hero and Mason jumped off, bumping fists as they saw the location.

Regan jumped off the bike, her eyes wide. "This is amazing. It's so...cute," she said, scrunching her nose with a smile.

"Is that a problem?"

"Not at all. I don't think anyone will be worried that you're anything but a stand-up motorcycle shop."

"Perfect, then we will take it. Any objections?" I asked as we walked inside one of the roll-up bay doors.

Everyone glanced around, Evie screaming in happiness when

CHAPTER FORTY-THREE 365

she saw the side office. It was half walled with one large window up top. Enough that she could see out if she stood, and would be hidden away when she sat down.

"This is mine!" she yelled.

Aiden grumbled, scowling at her as she ran over. "Asher said he put it in just for her. What an asshole."

"For putting in an office for her?" I asked. "Isn't it better to have her out of our way?"

"Yeah," he said, walking away. "Way better."

Regan patted my chest with a strange look before we walked around the rest of the shop.

"I love it," she finally said. "I think it's perfect."

"A fresh start on everything," I said, leaning down to kiss her.

"Together this time."

I nodded, feeling a sense of contentment I hadn't known before. "Yes, Rebel, together."

I had Regan, the pack, a safe place to live, and now we had a new place for Maverick Moto to open up again.

There was nothing in the world that could make me happier.

FORTY-FOUR
REGAN

<u>Months Later</u>

4 Every moment I thought life couldn't get better, Rook proved me wrong. Now, he walked me in the doors of my favorite art gallery, and my eyebrows jumped up when I saw the rest of the pack standing around, Harper there with them.

"What are they doing here?"

"They wanted to see what I was doing, and Evie had to help me," he said, leading me deeper into the gallery. "I assumed you would want Harper here, too."

"Evie helped you with what?"

"Turn around and see," he said, helping me spin to face the farthest wall.

The back wall was lit up with digital screens, ten of them hanging on the worn brick. My breath hitched as I looked them over. Each screen displayed my artwork—all of them recent paintings I had poured my heart into.

Tears welled up in my eyes as I turned to face him. "Rook, this is... amazing. You did this for me?"

He nodded, a small smile playing on his lips. "I wanted you to see how incredible your work is, and I wanted everyone else to see it, too."

I threw my arms around his neck, pulling him into a tight embrace. "I can't believe you did all this. Thank you."

He held me close, his breath warm against my ear. "Anything for you, Rebel."

Rook turned, leaning down until his lips found mine. The weight of everything we had been through seemed to lift, replaced by overwhelming love and happiness.

There was still darkness, plenty of chaos, and it's not like he had changed the way they handled business, but he never hid it from me, and I was always free to speak my mind about what he was doing.

I'd even been comfortable telling him off once or twice when I really didn't agree with something he did.

It was a mess, but I had control over it. I was no longer a passenger in my own life. I rested my forehead against his. "This is perfect, but there is one more thing I would love to have tonight."

"Anything," he breathed, capturing my lips again.

I pulled him over towards the front, finding the painting that still hung in the same place it had been months ago.

"I want to take this one home," I said, showing him the painting swirled with black and the icy blue center.

"Okay?" he asked, looking it over. "Why?"

"I saw it the first night we met, right before we met, actually. It reminds me of you, all the dark clothes and blue eyes. I want to get it."

"Then get it. Anything you want."

I laughed, leaning into him. "I know this is going to shock to you, but I'm actually broke. Someone made all of my inheritance disappear."

He wrapped an arm around me with a grin. "Sorry. Collateral damage. You have no shortage of money, though. You've done nothing but help us since we moved in and you helped us get moved to the new shop. Our money is also yours, you work for it. And, after tonight, you will be selling your art for a fortune."

I lightly smacked his stomach. "I will not. These aren't for sale."

"No, but this one you want is, so please get it."

The rest of the pack circled around us, everyone talking about different paintings.

"Damn," Mason said, sidling up to us. "These girls really love a guy tattooed with the art hanging in front of them. They won't stop asking to see my arms. I'm going to need a few more of them."

"Count me in, too," Hero added, scowling as Harper grabbed onto his arm, steading herself as she adjusted her heels. "Are you done?" he snapped.

She stumbled, the heel of her shoe landing on the toes of his.

"What the fuck?" he groaned. "Can you watch what you're doing?"

Harper's eyebrows furrowed as she glared at him. "You'll be fine. I barely stomped down. I can do it again to show you the difference."

"Do it and I'll cut off your toes."

"Oh, did you finally get over your eyeball fetish and move onto feet?" Harper snapped.

"Yes, exactly, so let me cut off your toes," he grinned. She smacked his arm, moving to stand between Zack and Mason.

"Come on," Rook whispered. "I want to get you home."

I didn't fight him on it, already too excited to get back to bed with him. He led me out to the bike before helping me on, and speeding towards home.

The door slammed behind us as I raced towards the steps, taking them two at a time. Rook was already running up behind me after I spent the last twenty minutes of our ride feeling him up.

"You know I love chasing you. Run, run, Rebel. I will chase after you for the rest of my life."

I groaned, pushing open the door to our room as he grabbed me, continuing on until we fell back on the bed.

"Caught you."

"Would you stop before you did?"

"Never."

His lips found mine, and like every time before, it didn't take long before I was drowning in him. Loving him was chaos and darkness and warmth, and it was a thrilling mix I wanted for the rest of my life.

"I love you, Rook. Forever."

"Forever, Rebel."

ACKNOWLEDGMENTS

First and foremost, thank you—to *you*. To those who have been with me since day one, to the new readers who've just discovered my stories, and to everyone in between. Your support has changed my life in ways I could have never imagined. I am beyond grateful, and words alone will never be enough to express how much your belief in my work means to me. You've given me the drive to keep writing, dreaming, and pushing forward, and for that, I am eternally thankful.

Karley Brenna — Thank you for being my constant support system throughout this entire process. Your friendship, kindness, and willingness to listen to my endless voice memos (even the ones last minute panic ones) have meant the world to me. I couldn't have made it through without your support and constant encouragement. You're the best and I can't wait to be able to walk to your house to rant instead of yelling into my phone.

Hunter — There are so many things I could say but I'm going to start with a huge thank you for saving my sanity during the process of getting this book into the world. From being the first one to read it to helping me every step of the way with covers, PR boxes, ARCs and being the best with keeping up with the street team. I truly couldn't have made it here without you and I could never tell you how thankful I am!

Bobbi Maclaren — To my amazing friend and editor, this book wouldn't have been finished on time without you! Your sharp eye and skills made this book perfect, and I seriously don't know what I would've done without your help. Thank you for putting up with my chaos and making sure this book turned out better than I could have imagined. I'm beyond grateful for your friendship and all your help.

To Maeghan, Kesi, and Sarah — my early readers who helped shape this book and gave me the feedback I needed (and sometimes didn't want to hear!). Thank you for pointing out all the parts you loved, making me laugh, and encouraging me along the way. I couldn't have done it without your insights, support, and for putting up with me through the process. You three are amazing!

And to Nate — The funny part is you are never going to read this but you're a huge reason this book is here. Not only being there to cheer me on (and bring me cookies) through long days and late nights, but to being the greatest business partner and helping me live out my dreams.